REQUISITE VARIETY

REQUISITE VARIETY

Lior Samson

Collected Short Fiction

GESHER PRESS

Gesher Press is an imprint of Ampersand Press
Rowley, MA 01969

Gesher Press | Ampersand Press
58 Kathleen Circle
Rowley, MA 01969

Gesher Press and the bridge logo are trademarks of Ampersand Press.

Printed in the United States of America.

ISBN 978-0-9843772-3-7

Cover art by Kevin Short (www.kevinshort.com), used with permission.

Cover and book design: Larry Constantine.
Set in 12 point Bodoni MT
with Bodoni MT Black heads, title in Bordeaux Heavy.

To all my children and all their children,
that they may come to know.

* * *

Table of Contents

Preface

First, I am not who I claim to be. Lior Samson is the pen name under which I started writing novels rather late in my writing life, and I have become rather attached to it. I am simply continuing an established tradition, since most of my short fiction was published under one or more pseudonyms.

Second, I also feel compelled to start with an apologetic explanation for the format and timing of this collection. Something happened as these stories, so many unpublished, sat waiting for release into the world: time passed. Then, one day, as I was scrolling through old computer files stored on the server in my office, I stumbled on a long-forgotten directory filled with early science fiction. Out of curiosity, I tried to open a story I had written decades earlier. Microsoft Word impolitely told me that it could not open the file. New security settings and accumulated updates prevented it.

I panicked. The tales might be trapped, forever frozen in unreadable form. I decided then and there to set them free, even if I had to set the type myself. I began the tedious process of recovery and conversion and review.

The result is this collection, originally compiled for my family, close friends, and those scarce and scattered souls who might have been among my loyal and unidentified fans. Here gathered in one volume is virtually the complete corpus of my short fiction. I say virtually because, I confess, I am not sure I recall or can find all the things I have written, and there are even some very early works that are no doubt best lost or forgotten in any case.

When I reread them together, I see that these stories are linked by more than common authorship. They are investigations of the intersection of people and the technology that people create and use. No one who knows me would be surprised; I have straddled the divide between people and artifacts throughout my working life. But these stories are more than your usual geek fiction, at least I would hope. Many are unabashedly romantic, even when they are cynical. They celebrate human beings and being human. They laud learning and the endless cycle of discovery. And they caution. Even as they elevate technology, they warn against naïve acceptance of what too easily and too often passes for progress.

I lead off with the stories I actually did manage to sell. Eight were published, and one sold but never appeared in print. Not a record to evince great pride, I suppose, but enough to qualify me, at least in a narrow technical sense, as a professional writer of science fiction. Most of the published stories saw the light of print under pseudonyms. In truth, two of these pseudonymous stories appeared in *Infinite Loop*, the anthology of science fiction that I myself edited for Miller Freeman Press. I hope it was a forgivable deception. I was, you see, a few stories short of the targeted page count and had a couple of decent pieces of my own that I feared might otherwise never reach the printed page. So, with my publisher's tacit complicity, I slipped them in under aliases.

The remaining sixteen stories in this volume appear in print here for the first time. Some of these, I confess with a certain measure of perverse pride, were submitted and rejected many times. We writers usually prefer, as might be expected, to think that the faults lie not with the writing but with the reviewing. I am hopeful that readers will think similarly. Some stories have been repeatedly rewritten as critiques accrued and my writerly chops improved. They now reach you here in more polished form than when they first made the rounds of long-suffering editors.

The final handful of stories in the collection date from late in my so-called short-story career and were never even submitted for publication. This group includes four stories that long lurked, neglected and incomplete, until finally finished specifically for this volume.

Rowley, Massachusetts, October 2011

I begin at the end, with the title work of this collection that was my last professional sale. It is also a personal favorite of mine, both for its clarity of style and for the nobility of its themes. In the final analysis, flexibility wins, whether in control systems, user interfaces, or life.

Requisite Variety

He could see Isaac through the window, towering over the distant Sydney skyline. Time to get to work, Barry thought, scratching at the gray thickets above his eyes. He put his notebook to sleep, then stared moodily into the muddy dregs in his coffee mug. The program could wait. It wasn't a real program anyway, just an applet for the guy in the sandwich shop.

And I'm not really a programmer either. So what am I? Barry wondered. He had trained as an engineer when engineering was cool, and had become a shuttle pilot at a time when astronauts were heroes. Unfortunately, the job market for ex-astronauts was pretty limited. There were only so many brands of food concentrates or designer crash helmets needing endorsement by small-time heroes. A shuttle jockey might still rate a free round at the pub, but that didn't pay the rent. Too old to join the commercial fleets, Barry Munro had spent a couple of impecunious years in "early retirement" before taking the job in Sydney.

"I'm a tower jockey, Emma, just a tower jockey," Barry hollered toward the half-open door into his wife's office. Of course, he knew Emma didn't hear him. She never did. Barry

Reprinted from *Windows Tech Journal*, 5 (9), September 1996.

leaned back in his chair until he could see into the other room. Emma was on the phone. He couldn't follow every word of the Ameslan she was signing, but he caught enough to know she was talking to her mother about his raise. She was always so damned proud of him.

"And it's not a promotion." He said to the door. "Some corporate schmuck just thought up a new title. 'Stabilization Engineer.' Like calling a damned janitor a maintenance engineer. I just baby-sit the computers. They do all the stabilization. I sit in a room on the 180th floor and read science fiction over the Net. Hours and hours of mind-numbing boredom punctuated by moments of stark ennui. That's my job, Emma. That's what I do."

He walked to the door, flailed his arms until he caught Emma's attention. She smiled that smile. "Yes, I'm coming straight home, Em. Yes, I'll pick up milk." She could smile him into abject submission.

"Be careful," she signed, "Mother sends congratulations."

Barry signed back "ha ha," then a quick, "Bye. I love you."

Agitated and working on the beginnings of depression, Barry walked the fifteen minutes to the CityRail station in half that time, passing rows of terrace houses without seeing. He caught the first train to the city, getting off at Redfern. The Murdoch Tower had transformed the seedy fringe into the tony heart of a "new Sydney," making the Aboriginal Housing Council that owned the land one of the richest and most powerful groups in the State of New South Wales.

Locals referred to the Tower as "Isaac" because of the big ISSC sign on the sixtieth floor. You had to be on the harbor to read the name on the two-hundred-fiftieth, and even then you needed good eyesight and a smog-free day. Isaac was Sydney's answer to the Victoria Tower in Melbourne, and it was the tallest building in the southern hemisphere by a trick of design. The Murdoch Tower started some forty meters off the ground.

Barry braced himself as he crossed the cream-and-ochre plaza to the bank of lifts. It was always windy under the Tower, but a Southerly Buster had come in, a typical Sydney-style blow that sent hats flying and boats scurrying for safe mooring, and it fairly screamed between the pillars.

Barry could still remember the dizzying feeling the first time he had seen them. The Tower was still under construction then, festooned with staging and tarpaulins and stabilized by a network of thigh-thick cables. Rising from the clutter of temporary structures scattered across the plaza were the columns that held the building aloft, gigantic beams of plascrete shining in their bright ferrallium jackets. He had stared until his neck had ached, watching construction workers disappearing into the bottom of the building ten stories above.

The ugly cables were long gone now, replaced by a legion of computer-controlled devices—tension cables, hydraulics, and mass dampers—that kept the underweight building balanced on its stilts. Computers sensed the changing wind, the shifting weight of occupants, the ripples of an earthquake aftershock, even minute changes in local gravity. The computers pushed and pulled, making the building bob and weave in precisely choreographed responses to myriad influences. To Barry, it always looked precarious, perched on those twenty-five pillars, as if it could topple in the slightest breeze, which is exactly what it would do were it not for the triple-redundant stabilization computers he monitored.

Out of unalterable habit, Barry scanned the plaza as he rode one of the transparent lifts into the base of the Tower. Just before his bubble was swallowed by the first floor, a dull flash of red caught his eye. Lasers shining down the central columns monitored alignment. The flash meant the building was perceptibly off center. Numbers danced through Barry's head as he tried to figure out just how far off.

He hurried across the lobby to the express service lifts and waited impatiently for the security system to finish its wireless dialogue with the box in his tool bag. The doors slid open and

Barry slid in. Immediately linking into the building system with the palmtop from his bag, Barry started paging through the kaleidoscope of graphic data as the lift whistled upward. At 180, he wedged himself through the widening crack of the opening doors and stormed into the Stabilization Room.

Fiona and Malcolm took no notice. Eyes fixed on their screens and wrists deftly flicking matching joysticks, they were intent on other crises. Entire civilizations were disintegrating before the alien onslaught on their screens as yet another game of Barzakon Invaders played out.

"What the shit is going on here?" Barry barked.

Mal looked up for a moment, then turned back to his screen in time to see his H-Class cruiser vaporized into fractal dust.

Barry snorted. "You have tensors red-lining on 70 and 81, one hydraulic damper is leaking fluid all over the substation floor, and you two are playing computer games."

Fiona reached with her free hand and casually tapped her keyboard. The display shifted from far off galaxies to a schematic view of the hydraulic system. She ran a finger over her sketch pad, highlighting a shunt line on the display, then switched displays and keyed the two overheated tensors off line with a time out.

"No worries." She wrinkled her nose at him and returned to the game, only to find her "enemy" had vanished. "Look, Barry, do your fusspot bit on your own shift. We're still on duty for eleven minutes. The building, she'll be right."

Barry couldn't stay angry at them. The problems with the tensors and the hydraulic damper were not serious. Still, he couldn't help wondering what was going on. He busied himself at the spare console until Fiona and Malcolm sheepishly handed over the log card when Anya arrived.

"Real fence lifter blowing out there," Anya said as she pulled the wool jumper over her head. "How ya going, Bazza?" He looked up. Asian and Mediterranean strains mixed pleasantly in Anya's intelligent face, but she was as Australian as wombats and wallabies. "You right?" she asked.

"Take a look," he said, calling up the pages he'd assembled. Although he was shift supervisor, he always deferred to Anya. An ex-programmer with a quick mind, she was, like Barry, working below her abilities. Between them a friendly frisson that Barry had always assumed had a sexual subtext.

"What's your point?" she asked. "Looks like we're pulling some extra power, the counterweights in sub three have been swinging, and several tensors are temporary bludgers. Not a problem." She patted his shoulder. "Go back to your book, Barry."

They were nearly three hours into the shift before she interrupted. "Hey, Bazza, you better come back from Cygnus and take a look. Check out the screens while I bring up the doco."

It was pretty obvious. Barry watched the central display as an array of twenty-five red circles superimposed on yellow ones slid slowly to one side, then the other. Another screen showed the Southerly Buster still blowing hard, with gusts over the upper stories first adding to the force, then countering it. The building was oscillating.

Anya looked worried. "I thought it wasn't suppose to do that."

"It's not the building," he said, scratching his chin. "The periods are wrong. The building couldn't sashay like that on it's own. It would just whip slowly back and forth or ripple. It must be the computers. The winds are interacting with the control programs in a way they weren't designed to handle."

She didn't hesitate. "Then we need to get into the programs."

He looked shocked. "You're crackers, that's an expert system. Why do you think they call it that? We're not authorized. We wouldn't know what to change if we were."

"A program's just a program. And experts are just blokes, too. Look, I need your passcode to access those files. I can do it. I'm a good programmer, even if I'm not licensed."

"No," he said. "We play it by the book."

They followed the book for half an hour, rerouting power, plugging in spares when servos overheated, and cranking up the hydraulic pumps. The readings kept creeping toward the limits. Anya tried several times to reach the Building Master at home, but there was no answer.

Reluctantly, Barry keyed in his passcode and nodded to Anya, who started silently scrolling through page after page of the rule-base statements, trying to make sense of them, waiting for something to leap out at her. Finally she spoke. "I don't think we can do it this way. This here interacts with that. I don't know what any of this is about. And that one's Greek to me," she said, pointing to a line that started out with a lambda and ended with a rho.

Barry groaned. "Okay, what next, mate?"

"We have to take over."

"Now you really are talking crazy. Those are sophisticated control programs running on fast computers. You have to process thousands of readings a second and adjust systems on three hundred floors. You can't possibly handle that."

"No," she said as she held his eyes. "You're the pilot. You fly the thing."

He thought for a moment. It didn't make sense. If the control programs couldn't manage, a human was doomed.. "No way."

She crossed over to his chair and crouched beside him. "Those programs aren't working and they aren't going to suddenly get any better while we debate this. We have maybe an hour before this thing falls over."

"Then we pull the Evacuation Alarm, Anya." He knew that was no go. It would take hours to clear the building. At the end of the day, the Tower would still be spread most of the way to Darling Harbour.

6

"Damn it, Barry, if we don't take control, a lot of people are going to die. Okay, yeah, if we stuff it up, they will anyway. Either way, you and I come down hard somewhere around Haymarket. So we have to give it a fair go. Just show me how to access the low-level control programs that interact directly with the tensors and stuff."

He clenched his fists, his hands shaking visibly, but his voice was calm. "No, I should do it. I'm the shuttle jockey."

"It's not like flying a shuttle." she said. "You only get one chance."

"Then it is like flying the shuttle. It was a deadstick landing with those birds. No power, one pass."

I only stuffed it up on one mission, he told himself as he stared at the console for a minute. "This won't work," he said, pushing his chair back, "not from a keyboard and sketch pad."

"You're doing that again. That thing with your hands," Anya told him.

He looked down at his hands, clenching, unclenching, grasping at nothing. He remembered the shuttle cockpit, with controls suited to the task. He closed his hand around an imaginary something protruding from the arm of his swivel chair. "I really need... Hey, give me those!" He pointed to the joysticks still sitting on Anya's console. "No, both of them."

They were the latest from Microsoft, heavyweight four-axis beauties with four finger-operated mode switches in the handles plus big "fire" buttons on top. He released a latch on one, twisting and reseating part of the handle. "There, left and right." He set them down on the console in front of him, one for each hand. "Now, get back to your console and show us how good a programmer you are, because we're going to have to bypass a lot of safeties before we can even start repro-gramming."

They both worked furiously, nervously glancing up at displays that painted an ever worsening picture. Finally he told her to patch the joysticks in just below the expert system.

"What should I connect up?" she asked. "How do you want the displays?"

"How the hell should I know? You think I do this every day? Make reasonable choices and I'll figure it out. Just give me real-time control over as much of the building as possible."

She sat staring at her screen, shaking.

"Look, its just a matter of requisite variety," he said calmly.

"What?"

"The Law of Requisite Variety. General systems theory? Carl Asch?" She continued to stare at him blankly. "Finite state machines?" Her mouth formed a confirming "oh" but without understanding. "Just means that you gotta have more internal states or degrees of freedom than the environment you want to control. Otherwise it controls you. It means flexibility wins. So just hook up whatever you can in some way that makes some kind of sense. We have eight-bits off the mode switches to give me zone control. Be creative. You have four axes of analog to play with. And give me feedback, visual feedback on whatever is going on. Don't worry about it, just do it!"

Anya brought up the visual compiler and started pulling together components. New displays lit up the monitors. Barry twitched his fingers and subtly moved his wrists, watching as shapes twisted and turned, lines lengthened and shortened, hues shifted down the spectrum.

"You're brilliant. How did you do that one?"

"I just computed the streamlines from the wind sensors. What about that plan view with all the floors superimposed?"

"Cool. All right, let's go live." He hesitated for an instant, then punched a key and quickly grabbed the joystick again. As he twisted his left hand, a sparkle of pixie dust bloomed over a tensor at the bottom of one screen. "What was that?"

"That means it overheated. You said be creative."

For a time it seemed that Barry was keeping up, then the swings started increasing again. More systems red-lined, and one entire floor went dead.

"Pull it Anya, pull it! I'm losing it." The building shuddered. "We can't save them all, but some on the lower floors may get away. I'll hold it as long as I can. The police may be able to evacuate Central Station."

Anya flipped the cover off the alarm. One hand on the red lever, she started to slide the safety out with the other.

Barry raced through end-game scenarios, wondering if he could at least make the building break up as it fell instead of going over like a tree and taking out a kilometer swath of Sydney. In his mind's eye he had an unreal image of a wildly bucking building just before final collapse. It reminded him of something he'd seen in engineering school. Tacoma Narrows.

"Wait!" he screamed, just as the safety slid free. "I'm trying one more thing." It was a long shot.

He started rocking his hands in a slow, complex rhythm, concentrating, listening, shifting his eyes from monitor to monitor. Gradually, the displays changed. Squares rotated, then twisted back. Angry red bars lengthened on several screens. An entire bank of tensors sparkled as they shut down. "Override those thermal protectors," he called to Anya.

The building groaned, and Anya's coffee mug slid against her keyboard. "Jesus, what are you trying to do?"

"Shut up. I'm flying this thing."

Barry kept rocking the joysticks, being careful not to over-react. He tilted his head, listening, eyes slightly out of focus, sensing the building's responses. Instinctively he began to change his moves, holding the joysticks an instant longer in one position. Keep it steady, he thought. It took a kind of relaxed tension, crisp responses without jerking the controls. Anticipate, he told himself. Take the lead. Listen to what the building is telling you.

The building complained. The complaints grew louder.

"God, Barry, 156 and 157 are damned close to structural failure. Above 225 they have no power. The cables must have snapped." They could hear running steps in the stairwell. In the monitors, people could be seen spilling into the plaza below the Tower, streaming away in panic. "What in hell are you doing?"

"Making this building act like a bridge, Tacoma Narrows, to be exact."

"Shit, no. Wasn't that the bridge that started bouncing in the wind like a bad mattress and shook itself apart? Is that what's happening?"

"No. This is different. We're a cantilever, not a suspended beam. We're flapping in the breeze, which is the problem. We need to twist in the wind. If we convert some of the energy into torsional mode oscillation, we can stay centered over those columns. It's terpsichore. I'm just teaching this thing to do the twist instead of the bump." Her brow creased. "Sorry, a lame reference to the tribal dances of ancient Americans." An explosion of shattering glass interrupted him. "Just give me ten minutes before you hit the alarm," he shouted above the wind and the rising noise.

Twenty sweaty minutes later he told Anya to switch back to programmed control. They sat, holding hands, shaking, alert for signs of trouble. By the time their shift ended, repair crews and television people were swarming all over the building. They slipped past an ABC crew, then rode down the service lift without talking. It wasn't until they reached the now litter-strewn plaza that Barry spoke.

"Tell me, how did you lose your programming license?"

"Never got it. I hate tests. I never even sat for the HSC. I ran away to Ireland instead of going to uni. That's where I picked up Eiffel and VB. I still sell stuff over the Net to people who care more about the quality of the code than the parchment. Besides, I'm coming to like this stabilization engineering stuff. What about you? Why don't you fly anymore? You could join one of those clubs, do it on weekends."

He laughed. "Now what the hell would I want to do that for, wasting my weekends flying. I get enough of that during the week." He grinned as he patted one of the columns, then turned toward the rail station.

The wind had died down some. Barry slipped on his gloves, dialed with a quick flutter of fingers, and started signing a message for forwarding to Emma. "It was a good landing. Flexibility wins. Be home in half an hour. I love you." He held the last three-finger sign a long time before adding the signature: "Tower Jockey."

This palimpsest on the biblical tale of Jephtha's Daughter, appeared in my anthology, *Infinite Loop*. It was the first story of mine to be published under my own name rather than one of my previously well-protected pseudonyms.

Dellahar's Father

Veddias, warrior of the Feld, tugged on the control bar, barking his knuckles as the airskate rocketed over the rise, bare meters above the trees. Below, scabrous forest gave way to the beauty of rock and sand; ahead, the Trebblian Valley waited. The spot of blood on his middler hand reminded Veddias that the airskate was not designed for men. Veddias cursed the canopy that pressed upon his head, the displays that dazzled his eyes, and the seat, whose contours once cradled the spinal plates of an Issikar but now squeezed Vedias into throbbing knots. He hated the Issikar machines with a bitterness that nearly matched his hatred for the Issikar themselves. Issikar were not men, but dwarves pretending to manhood, impious brutes who did not honor the holy name of Havadohn. The stench of the wax oozing from their pores offended the nostrils, the pallid copper of their skin assaulted the eyes. They fashioned their airskates after the flat rays that glided beneath their seas: as deformed as the Issikar, yet swift and deadly. There was irony in attacking the Trebblian Valley depot with the captured airskate, but it was bittersweet, for men were not yet the skilled craft-builders and technologists of Isskaru. Though they could cross the void to the Green Twin on the thunder of their own rockets, the day

Reprinted from *Infinite Loop* (Miller Freeman Books, 1993).

was yet to dawn when men could build skates to out-fly the faithless Issikar.

The target alarm sounded. Veddias fingered the starburst at his throat, trilled a quick prayer, then started the torpedo run.

The screen before him jumped and jiggled in orange excitement. He flicked the switch for the image stabilizer and manipulated a blue cursor over his target. The bubbles of nethas were strung like tree-pearls across the valley; he had only to hit any one for them all to erupt in a second dawn.

The jumpers took him by surprise, spinning up from the sand, obscene flowers whirling their strands of death. He dove the skate beneath the metal-filament flails, then pulled up so steeply that his hands were nearly ripped from the control bars. Twin thumbs twitched the calipers, and a ball of blazing nethas blew from the rear tube of the skate, engulfing the jumpers. Seconds later, one spun out of the inferno unharmed. Hoping to out-run it, Veddias elbowed the throttle to its stop and keyed on the torpedo control again.

He cursed.

Two ram-fighters punched through the cloud cover.

"Oh, Great and Unnameable Lord," he piped, "lend me your strength as I pledge you service." The ram-fighters screamed toward his skate from port, while the jumper whined after him.

> And Dellahar's father in the fire of battle did swear an oath to the Most High, vowing, If my enemies are delivered into the destruction of my hands, that I may return in victory unto the world of my birth, then shall it be that whatever living thing do I first see upon my return to my home, that thing shall I make unto you a sacrifice.
>
> *II Appositions 26*

The long, low-energy orbit from Isskaru had taken its toll on Veddias. His muscles seemed as weak as the vines of winter while he wrestled the sandrover up the shell-pocked road to the ranch. Atop the hill, his house sat like a gray bun cooling in the light of the treble moon. A shutter swung open and moonflame glittered off polished metal.

Dellahar waved and called, "Father, beloved father, you have returned!" A creature of slow grace, she lowered herself down the wall and loped toward him, squealing a hymn of homecoming as she did. "To Havadohn, Most Generous, who brings home the beloved."

She stood before the rover as it made the final turn, her hands all framing her face in anticipation. Her father dropped the skids, halting the rover. From the dust-cloud he emerged, the knobs of his flesh raised in anger.

"Why have you done this? Is it not enough that you are without twin? Am I not already cast deep enough by the loss of your mother? You run from the house like a young chizot or a bad-mannered puppy. Where now is that hairy pet of yours that always scampers to pounce on every guest and potseller who rounds the bend?"

Dellahar, who lived for the joy of her father, was crest-fallen. "What ill comes with you, father?" she asked.

His ears drooped in dismay. "I have made a promise unto Havadohn, whose True Name burns the tongue, whose wisdom scorches the mind. With His might in our hearts we have destroyed the depots and the ports of the twin-world, Isskaru, and I was spared. Now I must do as I promised the Lord and make sacrifice."

"Then you must, and I will prepare the salt-fires for the offering, for whatever you have promised the Lord, that you must do. It is a seal upon the house and upon me as much as upon you."

"But it is you I have promised to Havadohn. The first living thing that I see upon my return, that is my offering."

15

He could not bear to look at Dellahar, whose lustrous skin was burled with pleasing whorls of umber and pitch.

Her gaze upon him was steady and somber, but her piety fled as she listened to him in fear. "Oh, Father, is this what you have raised me for, to be bartered off to an unseen god, traded like some domestic animal for a fleeting advantage in a single battle? It is a shifting war we wage upon the monsters of Isskaru, a war that has already spanned the centuries and will doubtless reach into more to come. This war between worlds will outlive us both, whatever we do, whatever we sacrifice."

But Dellahar's father had boasted of his vow to comrades on the return from Isskaru, and the oil with which the cleric had anointed him still shone on his bare arms. He would not be swayed. "It is my word," he rasped in a whisper. "As once you were mine, now you are the Lord's."

When was I yours, she asked in her thoughts, though she spoke otherwise: "But Father, I have tasted so little of the blossoms of life. I have never seen the eclipse of Isskaru, nor have I hunted the water-elk. I have known no man. I am a virgin with too much to lament were I to die now."

The ridges over his eyes softened as she spoke; her grief was as a brand upon his head, melting the wax of his hair. He wound his arms around her, gently scratching the horns of her spine.

"I did promise the first living thing I saw to Havadohn, but I did not vow that my first act would be a burnt offering. I will prepare for the sweet pain through devotion and will sing aloud the Nineteen Books of Ja'arahu. This I will do from the setting of the first moon until the dawning of Scheebahd. You are free to go until then."

She did not think this much of a gift, but said, "Blessings upon you, my father. I will leave the ranch which has been my home and take to the hills of Kassahnderuut. I will visit the inner valley of Nesthal and meditate on this thing you have decreed for me. There I will lament my virginity and mourn for the twins I shall never bear. Then I will return for the first day of Scheebahd."

> In innocent joy did young Dellahar wave to her father, and when she ran to him he did throw himself into the dust, tearing at the coils of his hair in his knowledge. And he spoke to her what he had spoken to the Lord. Then in pain did she lament her innocence and bemoan her fleeting joy. Therefore did Dellahar's father grant her the time to bewail her virginity.

II Appositions 27

The climb from the foothills to the heights of Kassahnderuut took Dellahar nearly a week, but her lungs spasmed with joy as she crested the Aitchel Pass and saw the azure inner valley spread below her like a cow blanket on the sand. She did not trust the forest, however, which reminded her of the Isskaru she had seen in many war tapes. Instead, she camped amid the sharp talus just below the footpath. By day she gathered the herbs of mindfulness and brewed infusions that carried her aloft and beneath the brow of the mountain. The tendrils of her mind grew and spread, and each day the world seemed a larger place. By night she curled near the embers and slept a singing sleep that could be heard above the soughing of the jheejha trees and the soft buzzing of the heel-cats who joined her in the camp.

She did not see the messenger star that sliced the Eye of Hegradas in the heavens. The heel-cats stirred and burped but did not awaken her. By dawn, they were gone again, as always, leaving her alone in the chill. When she stood on the fire rock and surveyed her world by the red of the early sun, she did not see the burns, already healing, where the messenger star had scarred the forest, but saw only the unconquerable trees, drab reminders of the color of sacrifice.

Her eyes stung. She closed them and wept.

The stranger did not announce himself, but stood at her feet, weeping with her as an echo cries with the wind-loon. When Dellahar opened her eyes and looked upon the copper-skinned visitor, he did not move or speak, though she glared at him, neither blinking nor averting her eyes. His gnarled muscles spoke of speed and strength, though he was barely as tall as Dellahar's shoulder.

"Who are you? Why do you mock a girl who has known no man?"

The stranger gurgled and whistled but spoke no word known to Dellahar. From his waist he drew a slim blade of bellmetal, sighted along it, and trilled a rattle of noise before letting it drop. It stuck, ringing, in the soft sandrock.

Dellahar bent down and tugged the knife from the rock. It still carried the warmth of his flesh and seemed almost to burn her hand. She did not recognize the crafter's sign, but admired the elegance of his skill. She spun the knife in an arc above her head; it fell and struck the rock between her long toes. The stranger's ears shot upward in pleasure and astonishment. Then he sat before her as guest before householder, without menace or expectation.

She did not learn his speech, nor did he seem to understand hers, but he stayed at the camp, gathering herbs with her, climbing the vines to the forest canopy, and cooking the teas. When she could no longer think of him as a stranger, she called him Chaskaha, which is Discovery. When she could no longer bear the cold of the night, she pulled him to her.

The pressure of his body on hers was like oil on the cooking fire. His organ stung within her, and her sides ached with the pleasure. In the darkness her eyes widened with awareness. An innocent might throw herself on the green flames of sacrifice, but knowledge brought so many things worth clinging to. She ran her hands down the flat horns along his spine, then wrapped her legs around him and squeezed with all her strength.

Bathing with Chaskaha in the heat of midday, Dellahar thought again of her virginity, which she had lost, and of the knowledge she had gained. On this and on the meaning of promise, her mind spun with the spinning of the days until one night Chaskaha did not return from his foraging. The marching of the moons told her that Scheebahd was soon. With little time to waste, she decided to follow him, though his spoor led into the thick of the wood.

She caught up with him by the next afternoon, then kept him in sight as she hid behind hair-bush and tall babahor. At last, through the trees she saw an airskate, half obscured by the new wood growing over its body, with the double diamond of Isskaru marking its defiant tail. She had never, until that moment, seen an Issikar. She watched Chaskaha climb over the wing and into the skate, studying the pale copper of his skin, the muscles of his back, remembering.

She ran without thinking back to her camp. His bellmetal knife stood in the sandrock where she had flung it on their first meeting. When she pulled it out, it spoke to her, ringing sweetly in her ear, a knowing sound of mastery. She slipped it beneath the waxy coils of her hair, gathered her things, and started the climb back through the Aitchel Pass.

> And as she had promised, so did Dellahar climb unto the hills, there to lament her virginity and to think upon her losses and learn of the world. These she did, and she did also swear unto the Lord an oath of her own. And when the days of the triune moon were fulfilled, and the dawning of Scheebahd was near, she returned unto her father, as she had promised, returning alone, as she had departed.

> *II Appositions 28*

Even as he saw her picking her way down the footpath, it was obvious to Dellahar's father that she had changed. The twin bulges at her waist told the story. He tweeted in agony and threw himself on the ground.

"What have you done? Why do you again cast me to the dust? Can my sacrifice be mete when my daughter is no longer a virgin?"

She stepped up to her father and helped him from the ground. "Ah, my melodramatic father, your wisdom is as steady as the plennyar circling for carrion. It is sad to you, I am certain, that I am no longer worthy of the honor that you had planned. Have you not taught me that the Lord shall vomit back upon the sand whatever is impure? You are a pious man and must sacrifice something else."

Perplexity tugged at his eyes; they twitched and rolled in frustration. "No. It is written that one who has neither field-goat nor chizot to sacrifice for the Feast of Books is not excused, but must bring to the clerics a cabbage from the woods, anointed in the sap of the dagroo tree, saying, 'This is the field-goat of my heart.' Thus, shall an unworthy gift be made worthy by the piety of the sacrifice."

"Father," she said, placing hands at either side and clutching her gold starburst with the other, "these are your grandchildren, on either hand your twin posterities. They dream the tomorrows of your dreams, Father."

"And what horrors will the Lord visit upon my dreams now? No longer are you untouched, but already carry your first twins: this is true. Yet I swore; this also is true."

"Slay me then, if you must," she said, straining to keep all trace of insincerity from her voice, "but, truly, a warrior of the Feld cannot take the lives of babes who have not yet lived. The unborn were not promised."

Dellahar's father thought for long moments, wheezing his impatience into the air as he thought. Finally he spoke: "I will not harm the twins of your wombs. I will sacrifice only you, as I have promised. It will be for the Lord to take the unborn or not, as may be the Lord's wish." He reached for the wire

20

lanyard hanging from the gate. Dellahar's hand went to her hair, feeling for the metal hidden there.

"But wait, Father! If you must be true to your word, tell me again what word it is that you gave to the Most High."

"To sacrifice the first living thing I saw upon returning home."

"And what is it that you saw that was alive?"

"I saw you waving from the window."

"With which hand did I wave?" She held the three before him.

"I saw the moon glistening on your bracelet."

She laid her hand upon a stump of the babahor tree and removed the heavy bracelet. She drew the knife from her hair and held it out toward her father, who gasped. In the burnished metal the clouds cast green shadows, and he saw a vision of his grandchildren, playing at the gate, camping in the hills, skating through the skies of Isskaru.

> And said bright Dellahar to her father, What has been vowed to the Lord, that must you do. What has been promised, that must you give. And Dellahar's father took from her the bellmetal knife and did what he had vowed, making a burnt offering unto the Lord. And his days were numbered as the rings of a great dagroo tree, and they were filled with the keening of many grandchildren and the singing of Dellahar as she wove upon the two-handed loom that he commanded to be made for her. And her first twins were copper-toned and lithe, with the strength and agility of their father and the wisdom and quick wit of their mother. These did Dellahar dedicate to the Lord. The left of these did she name, Plassaroht, which is Repayment, and the right of these called she, Sefta-havadohn, The

Third Hand of God. Great warriors became they in their youth, a scourge upon the face of Isskaru, for none do make war as fiercely as do brother upon brother.

II Appositions 29

This seriously silly story, my very first professional sale, was a double turning point for me, because it introduced L. Roy Cahners, the pseudonym under which most of my science fiction would appear.

In Chapter Three
Remember

On his arrival just outside Syracuse, New York, Greled-lohdj spat from the p-shooter like a softball from a pitching machine. The shooters had been right on the money, placing the p-vector within a centip of the grassy hilltop. Greled-lohdj fell upward, twisted in the air, and fell down again, bouncing once before getting the hang of the light gravity. He landed on his feet with the natural athletic grace that was the birthright of all Phthrahg.

The thin, acrid air that stung his lungs was awash with airborne pollutants, spores, and pollen, and he inhaled deeply until his face purpled with pleasure. The too-bright star he hated from the first, but travelers had to adjust. The tepid sameness of the vegetation could become a comfort, he supposed, and the harsh greens could be thought of as exotic. He was, he knew, one of the last of the romantics, and his bare skin tingled with excitement.

He stood and stretched on tiptoes in the breaking sunlight, naked and without embarrassment. All travelers are naked, of course, if not in one sense then another, but Greled-lohdj took pride in the symmetry and perfection of his rotund body.

First appeared in *Beyond, #18* (Other World Books, 1990).

Already flushed with anticipation, remembering distant springs, he felt again like a kroodjling. He touched his toes. How many middling Phthrahg could do that?

Rolling down the hill because it was by far the fastest way for a Phthrahg, he savored the bumps and pokes on his belly and back. What a beginning, he thought.

He met the first of the phthrahgoids at the bottom: thin, pale creatures a little taller than he, not what Greled-lohdj had expected. He watched them from beneath the archway of stone until he figured out what they were doing. A game, he thought as he watched the boys splashing in the stream. How he loved sports! He tumbled out from hiding and jumped with excitement, creating a miniature tsunami by his landing in midstream. The fortune of Great Dorg! To find these naked athletes at first contact: truly a portent from Dorg.

The boys liked him. To them, he was the little round boy from under the bridge. They taught him to speak, which was easy, and hid him from the others, who were, he learned, of two kinds: parents and girls. Greled-lohdj did not yet understand about girls, who must be, from what the boys had told him, most horrible, but he was eager to meet the phthrahgoid women. What was travel without romance?

Greled-lohdj may have been a romantic, but he was certainly not foolhardy. The years while he saved for the voyage were years of study, also. Along with thousands of other untraveled planets, this one was well cataloged. In libraries across the Phthrahgarchy, interns hoping to become shooters were trained on the micro-p-vectors, accumulating samples vacuumed minim by minim from across the galaxy.

Long before he had finally plopped himself into the cold metal acceleration cup of the p-shooter, Greled-lohdj knew everything about the woman of his dreams except what she looked like. He knew the chemistry of her food and the structure of her DNA. He chose his destination with care because it was newly discovered, another inexplicable planet of phthrahgoids. There were only a few dozen, of which nine had been visited, and no one understood why there was not just one. Greled-lohdj liked to think that some truth lay hidden beneath the old legend of Dorg, the Great Sower, poling his reed boat through the marshes of the Milky Way, casting his seed across the planets in hopes of somewhen harvesting a bride. In his inner thoughts, Greled-lohdj imagined himself the descendent of Dorg, abroad to fulfill the ancient prophecy foretold by the Voyage of the Golden Fleets.

Of course, his mother wanted him to marry a nice girl from Thurdj.

His father told him to marry money, and introduced him to an interplanetary developer, a Tch, with platinum-iridium claws and a stench like a gymnasium-full of kroodjlings in late spring.

Not that Greled-lohdj was prejudiced. Who could be on Phthrahg-ael, mercantile hub of the stars? He did not even object when a blind date turned out to be Brip. Female Brip can be quite sensual, with their long, flexible limbs and warm, glowing eyes, but they come in pairs and Greled-lohdj was old fashioned.

He knew he wanted only one wife, and he knew he wanted children. Either could have been arranged if he were only more flexible concerning one matter. But no, by Dorg, Greled-lohdj had to do things the hard way: he insisted on falling in love.

Of course he had tried. But Phthrahgi were Phthrahgi, all so perfect in their sleek athletic bodies, so perfect in their planful female minds, so well-rounded and modern. There was simply no chemistry, no spark. Once, following the joyful Festival of Close Packing, he almost thought he felt something, but then Flukbrall-aedj, bright and lovely Flukbrall, evaluated his modest portfolio of planetary bonds and canceled her option on him.

Thus the cruise—distant lands, exotic natives—one sure formula for romance. To find it, though, one had to meet people, so Greled-lohdj finally left his small companions in sport and hiked up to the highway.

The motorist who had a breakdown on the bridge called him a goddamn living bubble man and ran for help. The man was not at all like the boys. The police who arrived scant minutes later were different still. They tried to put him in their patrol car, but failed. He cooperated to the best of his ability when they brought the van, but the step was above his navel, and they couldn't lift him. He convinced them to let him take a running jump; kicking off with his powerful great toes, he had no difficulty landing in the back.

These taller phthrahgoids seemed a lot more concerned about appearance than he was. Once they realized he was nude, they always made him wear clothes that split or fit him poorly. He was proud of his body; he kept in shape. There were remarks, remarks that he understood because he had learned so much from the boys. Indeed he was round, by Dorg, as close to a perfect sphere as intensive weight training and a good diet could make him. The Phthrahg from Thurdj had particularly fine bloodlines to begin with.

But, as they say on Phthrahg-ael, even the sensitive noses of the Yapadak suffer olfactory fatigue. The phthrahgoids grew so used to seeing his squashed little face grinning from atop his rotund body that he could soon pass without stares on the streets of larger cities. There were even those who began to be interested in him as a person. There were interviews.

> What is the favorite Phthrahg sport?
> Kick-ball.
> Do they play it like people on Earth do?
> He didn't know, since he'd never played. Not on either planet.
> Hadn't he ever watched a game?

He had never watched any game, since watching a game made no sense to him. He told them about roller skating, however, a sport in which he excelled. He liked especially the feel of hard ice on his navel during the spins.

"You needed to develop callouses," he explained.

They asked him why he came.

He was candid, as always in interviews. Honesty was an old-fashioned virtue still fashionable among the Phthrahg.

He made headlines. The International Inquirer: Space Ball Here to Ball. (Inquisitive minds wanted to know.) A close contest: Cosmic Wimp Wants Women. (Contest winners: color photos inside.) Television: An animate beachball with great ugly feet is looking for romance. A humpty-dumpty has fallen from the sky in the hopes of falling again. Who will be the lucky girl?

Neither the media nor the public were a match for Greled-lohdj, though, who had charm and wit, old-fashioned manners and patience. The talk shows loved him. He met people.

He met Riva Decelle on Good Morning Tomorrow. He was introduced as Greled-lohdj, but the announcer flubbed the pronunciation. So Greled-lohdj told the most beautiful woman on the planet, a former Miss Earth, to call him GL.

Riva called him Great Lawd and made him laugh. Then she grabbed the show's hapless meteorologist and the three of them did impressions of the shy but trisexual Tch. They did a jazzaerobics segment, and she asked him to bounce with his hands on his toes while the show went to commercial. He started to fall in love before the forty-seven-minute hour was over.

He knew what to do. Had he been on Phthrahg-ael he would have sent tubs of the large malted egg candies that would remind Riva of him as she licked them. He settled for chocolate covered cherries, which he had tied with black satin ribbon and arranged to have delivered one at a time every evening at seven sharp.

The three nights it took Riva Decelle to decipher his handwriting were nights of agony for Greled-lohdj. When she telephoned him, wondering why he worked so hard to get invited back to the show, he was rather disappointed. She did say something about an open date the next week, but the studios of WRRD were not his notion of a romantic venue for a date. Still, custom was custom, and the setting of that all-important first date was always the female's choice on Phthrahg-ael; he assumed it to be the same on Earth. But he was quickly reminded that Earth was not Phthrahg-ael when she told him that a call from his agent would have sufficed to set up the date. This confused him to his toes. Perhaps on this planet courtship must be carried on through an agent. Perhaps she could recommend one?

Mort Sheinfeld took him on as a client without hesitation. Six figure fees danced along the rims of his reading glasses until Greled-lohdj made clear that the only acceptable booking was with Riva Decelle. This was a setback for Mort, to be sure, but not reason to reconsider any fantasies of a new home in Scarsdale. Mort made the booking.

The show went well. The studio audience howled when Greled-lohdj rolled around Riva's feet in the Ritual of Rut. As the credits rolled, she told him to come back soon, and Greled-lohdj brightened like a fluorescent beach ball. He used his talent fees for new clothes and showed up on the set the next day in a black satin wrestling leotard. It resembled a Thurdjian Courting Kilt. His mother would have said he was dashing.

Riva's Production Assistant did not expect him back so soon, having heard nothing from either her boss or his agent. She told him to wait in the Green Room, which he did, and to which he returned every day until Riva brought him out on the set again. Then it was back to the Green Room in a courtship ritual that Greled-lohdj was certain would have tried the patience of an elderly Brip.

This continued until Mort called Greled-lohdj to say that Good Morning Tomorrow was no longer interested in using him, but the Late Nite with Wet Louie show wanted to book him as a regular. Greled-lohdj fired his agent and stormed to the WRRD studios where, while the author of a new self-help book on home acupuncture gasped, Greled-lohdj declared his undying affection for Riva before a 28-share audience. She laughed. That sent his heart leaping with such joy that he could not contain himself. He launched spontaneously into a Revolving Rapture that left him dizzy and the audience in hysterics.

By Phthrahgial custom, the initiative was now his. He sent Riva a kick ball, a traditional symbol of affection, and proposed a volleyball game on the beach. This she considered harmless, so, trailed by video crews and adolescent young men in their late teens and twenties, they headed for Cape Cod. Greled-lohdj had to admit, she handled the taunts with grace. When one persistent, smart-mouthed surfer pushed too far, she told him that she at least knew who had the real balls. How Greled-lohdj loved her fire and spirit.

With fire and spirit she told him to take a hike.

He chose the Appalachian Trail. From Maine he sent a telegram, dedicating the hike to their future children. On reaching Georgia, he went straight to the local rock-a-billy station and delivered a song, a chain of lovesick puns about jumping into the Riva and swimming to the promised land. It was optioned and made the charts within three weeks.

Riva, who normally thrived on media attention, took a vacation and went into hiding. That, of course, did no good, because a Phthrahg in love is imprinted with the scent of the beloved. He followed her trail to her condo in Vermont.

Perhaps it was the isolation, perhaps Riva was only worn out. Greled-lohdj was sure it was predestined. They began to talk.

He listened to her stories and repeated back pieces of them when he told his own. They shared dreams in the mornings. He baked her a mixed-greens pudding that tasted almost right, and she loved it.

She told him about her false tooth; he showed her the scar from his first serious downhill race. She told him what turned her on; he found a way to do it.

29

When finally he felt comfortable with her, he flew Riva to Syracuse. There, in an emotional rendition of the Ceremony of Home-yearning, he spoke of the journey they had started and led her up the hill where he had arrived. The top, however, was now sheared off, leveled for a new upscale condo project. This was a problem. Of course, it would hardly deter a Phthrahg in love.

Greled-lohdj started playing the commodities market. He enjoyed it because it reminded him of the game of hooks-and-barbs played on Phthrahg-ael. And, because he was very good at it, having an IQ measured at exactly 194, he made a lot of money. He bought Riva a platinum ring with a tiny white sapphire and a rose-gold pendant with a twelve-carat ruby. He made the card himself, a poetic analogy in appreciation of the tender touch of her delicate hands and the bright love of her generous heart.

He also bought the hill back from the upstate developers and had a rude metal tower erected on the site, its platform precisely at the former grade level. A quaint courting ritual of the Phthrahg, perhaps? There was much speculation. When Riva announced on her television show that they were leaving on their honeymoon soon, the camera crews closed in.

He must feel very lucky, they said. There he was, a globular nebbish, soon to depart with the sexiest, most beautiful woman on earth.

They pointed the microphone at his neck, since the phthrahgoids still didn't seem to understand where his mouth was. Of course he was lucky, by Dorg, but the reporter had it quite wrong, as Greled-lohdj politely tried to explain. Riva was really quite ugly, with her great towering body and its repulsive protuberances. Even her feet were obscenely small and bony.

Then how could he love her?

How could he not? She was bright and full of wit. She surprised him and made him laugh. She had taught him to love watching basketball and playing volleyball and would

30

teach him many more new things. She liked his cooking and couldn't wait to try his jellied taggafish.

They were hopelessly in love, as any phthrahgoid could see, and who could explain love when it happened.

But what could a woman who had everything see in el blubbo supremo?

The p-vector began to shimmer just behind them. Riva grimaced and gritted her teeth in the strange way that phthrahgoids do when they smile.

He really wasn't much cuter to her than she was to him. But Greled-lohdj was the last of the true romantics. What else could she say?

Not My Type

Consistent with his personality, Alex Danichov edged his way, insect like, toward the lee of the half-wall, letting the party sweep around him as he watched from the relative calm of his retreat. Like all parties, it reminded him of how strange he found people to be, how awkward and hopeless he felt amidst them. It made him feel lost, like a small bug in a strange garden. An apt metaphor, he thought, since Deirdre was into the "urban organics" look: vegetables flourishing in pots, grapes drooping from the lattice-work room divider. A healthy but evil looking vine struggled for a toehold on the arm of the chair Alex had appropriated as his hidey hole. Still, Deirdre, dear friend Deirdre, had tracked him down and dragged one of her girlfriends over to meet him.

"It's Alex, or really Alexei," he stammered, feeling not quite himself, "but I never use it. No, no, not except, like professionally, I should say." The wart of a woman towered over him, silent; Alex tried to stand. He considered shifting his piña colada to the other hand, so he could push himself up from the wingback chair with his right, but then gave up. Straightening his left elbow forcefully, he tottered nearly erect, but, with his nose almost dimpling the woman's mauve cheek, he panicked and fell back into the chair, the greater portion of his drink giving an unexpected shower to the tomato plant

Reprinted from *Infinite Loop* (Miller Freeman Books, 1993).

climbing the half-wall. She giggled. Why did warty women always giggle, he wondered.

"Professionally? Are you a writer, or something?"

"No, nothing. I mean I'm an engineer. Digital systems. I work on printers. Guess," he snorted, "that sort of puts me in the business." Her face looked to him like a blank display screen. "You know, writers, printers, writers have to have printers on their PC's. I mean they don't have to if they always zap their book or story or, or whatever over by email. Or, I guess they could send it on a chip. Or even a disk. Yeah, I suppose that's done by some."

The screen of her face stayed blank. She kept looking down at him past those thickly coated, mauve cheeks, expectantly, as if waiting for a question or a witty answer.

Alex burped.

"Oh, there's my girl friend," she said, turning. "Bye, nice. G'luck with your book." She was gone and Alex was alone again.

Alex hated parties, always had. He could not get the routine. He was in awe of his friends, especially Dario, who always came alone but never left that way. Alex wanted to be picked up, too. He wanted someone to take him home, take care of him.

Instead, he got up to leave.

The woman with the champagne flute almost knocked him over. She was nearly across the room at the time, but her sharply triangular face was turned toward him, and, for just a breath, the softest dark eyes Alex had ever seen seemed locked with his. He tripped and bumped his way over to her, hoping to meet her. She drifted on around the room, settling in among a knot of people next to a pineapple plant. He edged toward her, afraid to appear interested. She moved casually on.

Finally within earshot, he listened in on her conversation, her liquid lines spiced with French phrases, scented with easy laughter. He shrunk. He was a stumbling nerd, a nobody. He didn't belong here. Yet maybe she would feel something: pity, compassion, it didn't matter as long as she would warm to him, want to help him. He hoped for a break in the conversation, and he hoped desperately to have something to say when it came.

"I think," he said at last, hanging his face over the shoulder of one of the onlookers, "I think that the whole idea of cyber-ajudication is, well is, is just dumb."

"Dumb?" someone sneered. "Dumb? Nonverbal? Unspeakable? Perhaps use voice synthesizing software, then."

A few people laughed. She laughed.

Alexei didn't quit. "See, I work with computers, and, ..."

"I for one am relieved," the same man interrupted, "I thought for a moment there that you were going to say you worked with people, poor souls."

Alexei was flustered. He wanted to say something about how custom interfacing a printer was a lot easier than getting a computer to make sound legal judgments. Then he realized how stupid it would sound. He slipped away, but not before he heard her honey and lemon voice once more.

"I don't know why some men think women go for losers. They must think we're turned on by the personality of a geek, as if we were going to cuddle their slobbering heads to our breasts and make it all better."

Alexei turned crimson. That's the way it was, he thought. He left the party still the loser he knew himself to be.

* * *

The party was great. Alex had the kind of personality that thrived on parties and always had. He felt a kinship with people at parties, a feeling of belonging. And he somehow knew that he could score. This week was different. Dario had said there would be a whole new group of graduate students from the university. Except for his friends, Dario and Deirdre, he recognized almost no one, but he kept getting the feeling that he knew this one woman. She had soft, brown eyes and a strong mouth and stood surrounded by youngish men and

women, clearly controlling the conversation but not domi-
nating it. Suddenly he remembered the triangular face, and he
made a beeline for her.

"You have an apt metaphor there," he said to the woman
directly, as if the two were alone in the room, "an urban jungle, indeed. And it is such familiar territory that we bring it
with us, replicating it in our very domiciles." He gestured
around him at the green-grocer decor. "Danichov," he added,
bowing almost imperceptibly toward her, "Alexei Danichov to
the computers that pay my rent; Alex to the friends who treat
me to parties."

She raised pale eyebrows above the dark eyes. "I suppose
you'd think me impolite if I didn't introduce myself." She
shrugged. "Better that, I suppose, than have you believe your
thinly disguised masculine aggression impresses me." Zap!

From that moment they were inseparable. They argued
without pause until Dario and Deirdre ushered them out, the
last of the party-goers to leave.

"She won't give me her name, the feminist bitch," Alex
said to Dario in a stage whisper.

"Khaddia Winslow, you chauvinist ape," she shouted at
him. "Why do so many men show all the personality of an
orangutan? Do they think that women want men to come on
like they owned everything in sight, women included?"

Alex sighed and turned toward the elevator. To his surprise, she followed him, although there was another bank
down the hall. To his greater surprise, she asked him out to
dinner. He accepted, got off at his floor, and took out his key
card.

The computer terminal blibbled at him as he entered.
Email. With one hand he keyed the display instruction while
his other tried to shake off a half-turned coat sleeve. An
unreadable message tumbled by on the screen. Too long. He
would have to dump it to the printer. He keyed another code,
saw the disk light blink on, flipped the printer switch, and
settled back.

While the printer whined audibly, Alex whined inwardly. What did women want anyway? Well, maybe he would find out soon. The chemistry was there; obviously they had both felt it.

The printer was spewing garbage. Wrong interface. The message was formatted for a c-plot system and he still could only afford the old thermal matrix printer. He flipped it off, cursed himself again for not putting in the software to drive the printer properly, then reached in back of the machine and removed the personality module. It took him a couple of minutes before he could find the c-plot module amidst the junk around his console. He slid it into the slot, turned on the power, and restarted the dump. It was amusing to think of that ancient printer acting just like the latest polychrome hot shot—just a lot slower. With the right personality kit in place, the computer couldn't tell the difference. Alex could, of course, but the colors were not so washed out that he wouldn't be able to decipher the multi-level microchip architecture being plotted for him.

"In the morning," he said to himself, "in the morning." He lay down on the bed and dropped into almost instant dreams about Khaddia Winslow.

* * *

The dreams did not catch up to reality right away. The reality of his developing relationship with Khaddia had a lot more struggle in it. When he started to dream about their constant quarrels, Alex decided it was time to do something about it.

She was the worst when she was a feminist. He asked her to change.

"Why do men always expect the woman to change? I have no intention of becoming the woman of your male fantasies."

Alex looked skyward. It was a silly, circular trap. "You only feel that way because that's the way you are now. If you changed you'd feel different. Don't you see it's really hurting us? Don't you want us to get along?"

She looked at him with determination overwhelming the softness of her eyes.

"It's only a matter of personality," he said lamely.

"You're really into playing with the perks, aren't you? Well I'm not, so goodnight." And she walked out, leaving the apartment door open. But, the very next time he saw her, she had softened noticeably. He began to think the personality clash was a thing of the past.

Their fourth date was spent in Alexei's apartment. They had begun the evening with metabinol cocktails and followed it with a meal that was an elaborate ritual, from the prawns paprikash, through veal marsala, to the lime-coconut sorbet. Alex loved the distant, crisp-edged focus metabinol gave him at first. But after dinner the delightful details of taste and texture gradually blurred into amused detachment. Khaddia crawled around the low, Japanese-style table and playfully pulled off Alexei's shoes. She crawled back to the other side and placed them precisely in the middle of the table. Alexei studied them briefly and said something about her being only two feet away. They both giggled. He wasn't sure which perk he had popped in for the evening, but he was pretty sure that the silliness was not in the programming.

They moved to the couch and Alex started nibbling her shoulder, teasingly working his way up her neck. His teeth clicked on something hard behind her ear.

"So, not into the perks, eh?" he commented. This explained a lot.

Alexei thumbed a remote, and a music video took over one wall. Khaddi tilted her head, absorbed in the music. She put her hand to her ear, then to the side of her head. "What's in here? Do you know?"

He laughed as he imagined himself in a termite-sized jet skimming low over a convoluted cerebral landscape. "Hills, alive with the sound of music. A vale of tears. King fissures.

Valleys of the doll." He paused, listening to the mental replay of his own metabinolic free associations. "No, you mean the chips, right?" He started to think about interface programming and was almost instantly straight, as if that part of him were unreachable by drugs. "You really want to know?"

"Yeah. Really, Mister Techno," she said dreamily.

"Well, the thing you call, most people call, a perk or chip is really an enelprom, a neuro-linguistic programmable read only memory. It's like what we engineers call a personality kit. Get it? Perk, personality kit." He went on without waiting for her to react, determined to get it all out through the mental tunnel of his drugged attention.

"A chip is a memory. Operates on eensy teensy currents from the brain. It stores a program of signals that affect how you act and react, your personality. Course that's enormously, enormously, enormously complicated. Personality is. Enelprom programs are simpler. They just tweak up or down a few fairly general things: forty or fifty things maybe." He thought for a moment. "Yeah. Program says to react faster or speak more slowly, be less moody, like that. All adds up to a vague shape; you supply the details, the content that fills the shape." His attention finally slipped, following another meaning to his words. He smiled at her salaciously.

"But each one is so distinct," she said, ignoring his leer.

"That's the trick of designing perks. It's all in how different degrees of all the factors are combined, when and in what order they change."

He slid open the drawer beneath his prom programming console.

"Woooweee! That's a pile of perks. How d'you afford so many?" she asked.

"Well, I get most of them free. My brother-in-law writes the things."

She looked impressed. "You mean he programs the, the enelproms?"

39

"No, he's no techno like me. He's a writer, used to write for soaps, in fact; he creates scripts. A computer system translates the personality scripts into enelprom programming. You may know some of his stuff. He wrote a couple of best sellers you may have met. Animal Hoggins? Pretty popular for parties a couple years back. He also did Perry Winston," he said, pointing to a row of identical charcoal gray discs. "It sold well for awhile, but most people couldn't stop themselves from putting on a British accent when they wore it. Always gave it away. To be a best seller, a personality can't be too distinctive, otherwise the market appears saturated too quickly. Like if a particular dress design sells too well. Novelty items, like Party Animal Hoggins, can be an exception, since it can be pretty funny if half a dozen show up for a party. With two Laura Ansleys, on the other hand, you could have a scene."

He drifted into thought again, then said, "People are really all alike: they all want to be different. They want to fit in; they want to be unique."

Khaddi giggled mischievously. "Let's swap," she said.

Alex shook his head no and kept shaking it.

"Why not?" she asked. "I think it would be a zapper. Wait until you find out who I have."

"No, see, it wouldn't work right." He cut off her interruption, knowing what she was thinking. "No, it doesn't have to do with sex. Everyone's implant is just a little different: different neuroanatomy, different responses. That's why they always call up your CRP scores, your cerebral response profile, before they burn the code into an enelprom. Customizes it for you."

But Khaddi, tonight's Khaddi, would not listen to reason. She tried to get his chip and he grabbed her wrists. They struggled playfully for what seemed several minutes, until she collapsed in a fit of giggles. She looked so cute Alex just had to kiss her. She kissed back lovingly, running her fingers through his hair.

Suddenly she sprang back, having popped out his chip. "Here," she said, tossing him her own chip. She fumbled with his, twisting it until she got the detent matched, then pushed it in. Her face went slack.

Alex stared at the chip in his hand, then at Khaddi, then back to his hand. His heart hammered in a way he recognized. The fear told him that he was just nuts enough to do it. He expertly pushed the small ceramic disc home in its socket. Nothing happened. She didn't look any different. He started to laugh at himself for fearing some strange psychedelic trans-formation. She jumped up, startled by the braying wheeze of his laugh. Her extreme response to his laugh, what to him was his perfectly usual laugh, made him bray all the more. He could see that his Adam Neary chip was having a powerful effect on her, but as far as he could tell, whatever she had been wearing didn't even faze him.

Abruptly he stopped laughing and looked down at his hands. They were picking at invisible lint on his pant leg. He howled again. Khaddi stomped her foot, then ran screaming to the door, stomped again, and collapsed.

"I did not mean to cause you to take offense or trigger in you any untoward reaction," Alex said, with solemn, calcu-lated intonation. "I have only the most sincere compassion and well placed concern for the disorientation you must be feeling."

"Offense, offense?" she snorted. "You have got to be mother-be-deviled crackers if you for an instant imagine that a bonkerly braying benighted arf arse could make me fricken feel any flappadoodle feeling on this entire neuro-moronic night." The words tumbled out like popcorn overflowing a pan. "Gotta get me outa here. Gotta go get here outa me."

In a part of his mind, Alex was fully aware of what was going on and sensed that the same was true for Khaddi, an awareness that didn't seem to help either of them. He strug-gled to get control of his emotions and to force out the words he really wanted to say. "You are, I fear, no longer quite

41

rational, my dear Khaddia. You have slipped into the neuro-
logical interstices of your own mental apparatus. You have
clearly gone out on a limbic system where you may slip a disc,
if you can allow this notion to enter personal your mind
sweeper." It did not come out as he intended.

She stared at him, eyes wide with horror. Without warning
she was at him, screaming, scratching, tearing at his hair. It
made no sense to him, but he grabbed her wrists. As she
unclenched her fists, a small green disc dropped onto the table.
She had ripped out the personality chip, her personality chip,
from the socket behind his ear. Taking both her wrists in one
hand, he calmly removed the Adam Neary chip from behind
hers.

She blinked.

"Scrambled," he said.

"Like being crazy, out of control," she said.

He picked up the chip from the table and handed it to her.
They studied each other in silence for long seconds.

"And they say drugs are bad." He waited. "It wasn't me,
you know. Wasn't you. Didn't happen. Just," he struggled
with the words, "just a mismatch in programming, not really
us, just something in the chips." He looked down at the inert
piece of ceramic in his hand, studied the gold plated connection
pads that ringed it. "Not the real you at all." A thought
crossed his mind, but it made him uneasy. He considered it
briefly, then put his own Adam Neary enelprom back in the
socket behind his ear.

And though they talked most of the night, they didn't talk
about what had happened. Still, the shared crisis had its
impact. In the weeks that followed they clung to each other
more, spending nearly every evening together. Even when
Alexei was busy programming, Khaddia would spread her
books across the kitchen table and pretend to study as she
watched him through the doorway. She knew they had settled
into an almost domestic routine when she realized she had not
changed enelproms in more than a week. It was not long before

she became aware that Alex was getting serious. She commented on it to him.

"Look, Khaddi, I really like you. Don't you think it's time we really got to know each other?"

She smiled at him, quizzically, ignoring the implied presumptions about her feelings. "What are you talking about? We've slept together a dozen times already. What do you mean?"

"This," he said, tapping behind his ear. Khaddi still looked puzzled. "Look, I'm serious. I don't think we need this stuff anymore. Why don't we travel some together, concentrated time? Maybe a stay in Newport. My friend Dario has family there. They have a nice day sailer that I've borrowed before. We could sail all day and snuggle all night. And all the time I could get to know the real Khaddi Winslow. And," he said dramatically as he removed his enelprom, "you could get to know the real me."

Khaddi stood there, hiding her panic behind a Claudia Decker bravura. "Put it back," she said unhurriedly, "no need to be crude."

"But we don't need this, this," he searched for words, aware of the lengthening silence. "We don't need to hide. Do we?" But the silence returned, and he pushed his chip back into place. "We could try it. Just once. Otherwise we'll never know. Maybe, just maybe we can really love each other."

It was a fool's dream, a fantasy for the soaps, but he sounded so sincere, so earnest. A Tonex "Claudia Decker" would be too worldly to cry at this point, but Khaddi could feel a tightness around her eyes.

"Okay. We'll try it," she said quietly, wondering what she would do.

* * *

Khaddi piled the things she would need for the trip onto her bed. From the top drawer of the bureau she fetched a small walnut box inlaid with the rich purple of quahog shells. They had promised, she remembered. Still, she lifted the top and scanned through the colored ceramic discs. What did she want to be? What was the real Khaddi Winslow? She thought of an Ariel. Authenticity, encounter, blunt honesty. No, that wasn't what he meant when he said he wanted to know the real Khaddi Winslow's personality. Too strong, too direct. No, the real Khaddi had to be something safer. She reached for the Bettina. Bettina, a Natural Spontaneity, Gentle Candor without Confrontation. How the advert lines stuck in the mind.

Then, hesitantly, she put it back in its felt-lined slot. He'd know. Bettina was popular and very distinctive; he'd recognize her and think Khaddi had tried to fool him. Then she noticed the chip next to it, still sealed in poly, part of a two-for deal when she'd bought the Bettina. A Bettina Gloss. The perfect solution, just a gloss of the Bettina personality. Not really deceptive at all. Alex couldn't really expect her to use a blank. It would be like going without makeup. Worse.

She tore open the poly, then pushed the enelprom home behind her ear. That was it, she thought. She felt completely natural, completely herself, ready for whatever happened on their trip.

* * *

Alex was getting a little anxious. He went over everything he had packed, but could never be sure. Life was not like a print plot program. Life's details were messy, illogical. Sure it could be complicated figuring how to get an ink-jet to do a grey scale screen dump, but it made sense. Women, weather, waiters these things were mysterious to him, beyond sense and comprehension. Maybe he had been hasty proposing they try it together without help. Maybe she wouldn't really like his quirky conversation or his unfocused edginess. He was scared, he had to admit it. And Khaddi didn't like anything resembling fear in men, at least as far as he could tell. What had she liked best? A man who was in control, not about to lose it. A quiet confidence, an unobtrusive savoir faire. She had once remarked that she always went for an Esteban. Alex wasn't an Esteban and didn't own one. But he did, he realized, have a prom burner and a library link. All he needed was a blank enelprom.

Alex smiled as he reached for the blank nestled in its socket behind his ear. It took several phone calls and some hokey business using his brother-in-law's ident to get authorization, but in twenty minutes he had downloaded the object code for TransPersonalle's "Esteban" and done a merge-modify with his own CRP scores. He had to wreck one of the sockets on his prom programmer to get it to accept the circular enelprom, but it burned the new code into the chip as quickly as if it were a printer control prom.

The building's doorvid beeped. He glanced at the screen; it was Khaddi. Quickly he popped the chip out of its socket, jammed it behind his ear, and reached to slide the prom console back into its cubby. He caught his reflection in the terminal screen and smoothed his hair. This was the way, he realized, suddenly confident that the whole trip would be just marvelous.

Khaddi carded herself in. She stood for a moment just inside the doorway, smiling, feet casually planted apart.

"It's me," she said with unconscious irony. "Think I have enough?" She turned around to show off her bulging backpack.

Alex patted it all around, like a cop frisking a suspect. "No suspicious bulges?"

"Aw, come on," she said with feigned irritation. "Here," she turned, "give me a kiss." She grinned, taking his head in her hands. Then she brushed the hard surface of the enelprom and frowned.

"Merely a blank," he said, smiling with the confidence of a workable half-truth. "I didn't want the contacts to corrode in the sea air, you know."

"Yeah, me too," she said, pointing behind her ear.

"Then let's get on the road. I thought you would like to get really old fashioned and take an autocar down. It's waiting down front. We can eat on the way." It was Masterful Directness.

"Wow! What a great surprise," she cried, with Natural Spontaneity.

* * *

Dario could hear bitterness in the voices right through the heavy door. He carded the lock anyway, and the door sprung open, propelled by a small woman with a large backpack. She looked at him with casual and undisguised interest, shrugged, then left without speaking.

"Was that the one?" Dario asked.

"The one," Alex answered as Dario surveyed the general disarray of the apartment. Alex made no move to straighten things.

"I thought you were on the way to shacking up, compadre, the way you talked last week. End all and be all. Madonna mia." Dario pushed a shirt off the ottoman and sat down.

"Well, it turned out she was not my type. We tried it. We spent ten days down in Newport, five on a boat. No comm, no TV, no personality kits. We were really serious about getting to know each other. We did. She finds me 'overbearing.' She says I'm 'stuck.' She wants me to be more spontaneous. Me, Alex Danichov, overbearing, not spontaneous? She's just not my type."

"What's she like?" Dario asked, thinking of the sincerity in her eyes when they met his in the hall.

"Well, she's like a Bettina, you know. Ever met one? All 'just me, simple, natural me.' You know, no games, just the real stuff. She's a lot like that, only a little more subtle. Really like a Bettina Gloss. Yeah that's it. Can you believe that? I met a woman who, underneath it all, has the personality of a silicon chip."

They laughed.

"Hey, compadre, how about getting out some Dos Equis to drown the memories?"

Alex hesitated. "Nothing to drown. Lotsa fish, you know. Besides, I really have work to catch up on. Thought I'd log into TechNet and get a jump on tomorrow's job." He reached behind his ear, pressed, and tipped his head. He set the chip on the console.

"Whatcha gonna do?"

"Oh, I thought I'd just leave it bare. I really hate to have some perk distorting my interactions when I'm trying to communicate with a computer."

It might be hard to believe that this work of gritty drama was penned by the same author as the last two lighter stories. When I decided to include it in the anthology, which already included two works under my own name, I realized I would need another persona, hence the advent of Phoebe Bergemann. This was her first and, so far, only published story.

First Business

Closing a business deal in person is like having sex face-to-face: ya wanna wash up afterwards. Just know it, buddy. Telecom's so much cleaner. For both."

Phil grimaced; his partner loved to shock him. "Nick, let's just finish the last clauses on this ovonics contract. Then we can wash up."

Nick winked at him, reached over and punched two keys. "Standard. Standard. There! The client don't give diddly on that stuff." He grabbed the contract chip, jammed it home in the recorder, and tossed the whole thing back into his attaché case. "I am gonna torque it up this trip," Nick said, as he smartly clicked the case shut and thumbed the dials of the combination lock.

Phil grimaced again. The Apple-chomping talk that had taken over Nick's Midwest accent sounded strange, and Phil had an uneasy sense about his senior partner's fantasies for the evening. Outside, the Big Apple shone, waiting for them beyond the bland security of the Towers and its pricey offices.

Reprinted from *Infinite Loop* (Miller Freeman Books, 1993).

In red and blue, neon orange and chartreuse, the city winked, waiting with impatient seduction.

"Sure, we could make the holos, do some restaurants," Phil said, carefully restoring the contents of his briefcase to an order that would be lost the moment he lifted the handle. "It's almost reason enough for a city like this: the restaurants, I mean. Like, where else this side of Addis Ababa are you gonna find a dozen Ethiopian restaurants?"

Nick groaned. He was on a scent, the scent of the Big Apple, juicy in its pungent must. "Food? Shit! Food's food, but the Apple is action," Nick said, pounding the credenza for pleasure and for emphasis. "This is the sin capital of the known universe, and tonight we are on a no-lim card. I'll be fanned if I'll miss this ride."

Phil twisted his eyebrows in uneasiness. "Not sure, Nick. We can party back in Selisberg. This techno stuff isn't my style."

Nick sighed. "You gotta be the single and last living puritan on this continent, Phil, if not in the whole friggin' world. It's different now, or didn't you and your 'Talian cousins get the word yet?" The city's impatience seemed to have reached Nick, was tugging at his arm. He would have given up on Phil, but he didn't want to be alone for the grand slide down the Big Apple. "Look, you know it's all done with polychrome holos, neural feedback, simulation technology. No one gets hurt anymore, no one's exploited. It's the machines, simulations, just wonderful machines. Wonder machines." He chuckled. "Like some of those simulations we saw dancing down 42nd Street Mall today. It's not like we're leaving the gyro wobblin', Phil. Business first, we always say. Right? Well, we did our four friggin' days of non-stop business up here. Time to go down, down the Big Apple. First business, then something better. Let's go!" He headed for the express elevator.

Phil tailed him, working at a weak smile. It's all different now, he thought, all technology. The glittering technology rushed up at them through the clear walls of the elevator as it dropped ninety stories down the outside of the Towers. No one gets hurt, it whispered.

* * *

When Tama Harlan arrived, the city waiting for her was brown and blighted and even hungrier than she was. It glared down on her slim frame as she drank charred coffee with double creme and tried to act as if she had not just arrived from Nova Scotia. Under its greenish glare, the Transcon Tube terminal buzzed with twenty-four-hour life: petty debates and hustles mingled with poignant farewells and saccharine music, vendors in red-and-blue uniforms pushing stale food, and others, without uniforms, pushing more potent ways to pass lonely hours. Everything, everyone, moved with restless waiting, all waiting for someone or something to arrive.

The fat woman with the bright, boxy handbag slapped it down almost on top of Tama's purse. She rocked heavily on the stool and slurped noisily from a vending carton. Tama managed a smile, but the woman was some place farther away than Halifax. The blue button implanted at her temple peeked obscenely from beneath her uncombed hair. Before Tama could decide whether to try to talk or just move on, the woman left, leaving Tama to her help-wanted ads.

"Card, Mz," the yellowed man behind the counter said. Tama brushed rust-colored hair aside and looked up at his outstretched hand. "You paying, or am I throwing?" he asked.

"Yeah. Sorry." She pulled her debit card from her purse and handed it over. He slipped it into a slot behind the counter.

"You clyde?" he asked. "Zip on the bal, sis."

She stared at him blankly.

"Look, kid. Nothing on it. Your 'count is closed," he said, signaling one of the Port Authority guards. "Sorry."

She told the Port Authority people that she was an actress. The matron smiled and waited as Tama explained that she didn't know electronics, so she didn't know just how the scam was pulled, but if they'd only pick up the fat woman with the stim implant or call her folks in Halifax, everything would be okay. They didn't call, but the Port Authority people were nice to her. The bunk in the detention barracks was better than a night sleeping on the Tube, and the walrus-skinned girl did leave her alone after midnight.

The Authority let her go in the morning after giving her a breakfast bar and another cup of charred coffee. There was no creme.

* * *

If Yorkcity was the Apple of the Continent, the Square, where the heavily traveled Way met the 42nd Street Mall, was its indigestible core. Onto the Square the Tubes vomited masses of after-work seekers, spilling them across it toward the theaters, the emporia, and the restaurants. These had survived all change. Not war and not prosperous peace, neither well-intentioned reform nor neglect had touched this seedy heart, where a city of caterers and providers and procurers thrived.

Phil Duccini clung to Nick's coat sleeve as they caromed down the Mall. From kiosk to sailor, window to whore, they bumped indiscriminately into everything. Though both were smashed on deens, the chaos still clutched at Phil's heart.

"Loosen up, listen up, Phil. Gotta scan 'em," Nick said thickly. "Take us for boonie-riders if we don't scan 'em. Look loose, but keep one hand for the card, Phil, the other for the ass." Phil started to protest, but nothing came out as Nick put a puffy hand over his mouth. "It is not a crime, pal, not a crime. A sin, yes, and that, dear Phil, is good," he said, punching each word out through the creamy fog in which his mind sailed. "You need a lot more sin in your life, Phil."

Phil managed to squeeze out a single word: "Anna."

"Anna won't know. No need. And you think she never downs some deens? Or never ludes? Fan it! I'll bet she has a vibe to her tweeter right now. It's the same. Mechanical sin, chemical sin. Answer to the prayers of every true believer, every friggin' man who ever wished he had it with his uncle or with a pregnant chimp or whatever. Can do, now. All in the can. Mechanical. Ovonical. Neuronical, comical. See? Nothing lost."

Nick's doggerel decayed into half-swallowed giggles as he steered them toward a doorway, one among gaudy hundreds at that level. On translucent double doors a rear-projected lingam and yoni met and plunged, withdrew and met again, tireless in their video-loop vigor. Phil shivered as they pushed their way through the primal scene, made ludicrous and frightening by its size and relentless rhythm.

For a moment, Nick looked at Phil and seemed almost to understand.

"I'm an engineer, Nick, just an ovonics engineer," Phil said, pallid and trembling. "Got a new wife, a new family. Not everything, but something."

"Okay, you don't have to do this," Nick said, barely audible above the pounding music blaring across the lobby. "God's bod, you don't have to."

"Well, it's time, I suppose, probably time I did," Phil answered. "Guess I need to know more, maybe know a little more about sin, maybe a little more about me. It's just sensation, right? Just a game, like TV. Like TV only you feel it, right?" He waited eagerly until Nick nodded twice. "Okay, we'll do it."

* * *

The boy bent over to kiss the top of Tama's head. "Don't worry, Billi here will take good care of you, and I'll be back to pick you up when you're through. Take you back, show you my place, you know?"

Tama watched him go, then looked around the theater.

Billi laughed. "Sugah, you expect something else, maybe? The Macallister Fine Arts, maybe? This is the Big Apple, and when you start out to be an actor on the Way, it's like this you start. Besides, I say shit to acting. Eating beats acting any day." The woman pulled her donut from the mug of warm cola and offered it to Tama. She sounded Indian, and Tama wondered whether this was the Indian way with donuts.

"Good thing that boy brought you here. Can act here, anyway, real as summer stock back home. This is the first business, they say, business that's pleasure. Only it's high tech now, the Life: clean and easy. We take care of you.

"Look us good, Sugah. Ask Billi what you need. And don't shiver the first night. Take time. Later is always good, later tonight. Gotta psych for the debut. Can you see the headerlines on the cable? 'Halifax kid makes good in Yorkcity; premiers at Tad's Emporium.' Tele that to the folks back home." She laughed. "Good, right?"

Tama tried not to nod, but Billi's insistent mothering brought out some buried streak of obedience in her that her parents had been unable to tap. So she nodded in agreement as she sucked on the soggy donut. "I'll be right. I'll be right in a little bit," she said.

"Gotta straight some mess with the Man," Billi said as she stood. She reached down from what seemed a great height to slip something into the mug beside Tama. "Deens. Smooth out any edges in your performance." She started after a man with silver hair who had just rounded the corner.

Tama looked around again. Backstage was backstage, even at Tad's. Cables slithered down the hall, scattered carts held miscellany: everything from unmarked boxes to half assembled androids. A gofer swung past, shifting his tray from one hand to the other before palming open the door to Tama's left. Inside, by amber light, Tama could see a young woman writhing on the floor, breasts glistening as she arched her back, straining upward toward an unseen partner. A tangle of wires leashed her to machines beyond Tama's narrow view, but the door closed before she could see any more.

* * *

Phil slumped into the black-and-silver soft sculpture, listening to Nick and the salesman discussing "the possibilities." Their no-lim card had opened the door from the noisy arcade below to the lamé-lined inner sanctuary. The deens had infiltrated the last recesses of Phil's worries. He did not wince when Nick asked for a boy's choir in chapel robes. He watched with detached amusement as the room darkened and the sample holos were shown.

"None of the full, sensual impact, of course," the salesman said, "but at least you can appreciate how well-chosen our actors are. That beautiful blonde boy is very talented, studying for pre-meds, voice of an angel. Naturally, the setting and story line are your choice. Their costumes and the cathedral there are merely to show how seamlessly such material is integrated by our very sophisticated image processing facilities. And the boys are all fine performers who can ad lib their way through most anything."

"Yeah," Nick said, "yeah, ad lib. Surprise. That's what I want. Just have them singing in church."

"And for you, gent," the salesman said, turning to Phil. "What will be your pleasure?"

Phil studied the man's face but said nothing. A corner of his mind wondered about the sales commission on their evening. Kids were extra, he knew, even if they weren't really kids. A dozen choir boys would add up to quite a sum.

Nick laid his hand on Phil's arm and said, "My buddy here is a first-timer. The innocent kind, you know, sorta just teen about sex. Whole family is 'Talian and believe in sin."

The salesman smiled knowingly. "I think I understand. If the gent's 'count is up to it, I could arrange something very special: a first night." He fingered his pocket keypad and the lights dimmed again. Phil looked across the room at a young woman, ginger hair falling modestly over small breasts. As he watched, she raised her eyes almost fearfully. They locked on his, or so it seemed, inviting him to an end to innocence, yet struggling to withdraw and leave him untouched. "Yes, I think I understand," a voice said from somewhere.

* * *

The lights were the same harsh green Tama remembered from the Transcon terminal, only now she was naked, curled up on her right side as they readied her. The meds and the techs swept her up in their routine so skillfully that she forgot she was being rushed. She remembered vaguely that she was going to call somebody before the performance, but the thought kept washing away on a numbing tide of activity.

"See, see, see," the heavyset tech started in again. "Myoelectrics here, here, and here." He touched the straps along her arms. "Once they get through with the tap we can undo these. Then the meds will have your brain wired into the t-graph, and it'll be like Being There." From her stool, Billi frowned at him. "I mean, of course, not being there. Telepresence. Not real. Just think you're there, a convincing illusion, but you don't actually do anything. Like a fancy version of those remote handlers for hazardous waste. No hazard here, of course. You don't touch; no one touches you. It doesn't happen."

Billi leaned nearer. "No one gets hurt 'cause you're really right here, safe. We take care of you, Sugah."

"Right," the tech added, "vitals, flexes, everything, all monitored so nothing can happen to you."

A med pressed a sprayjector against her bare buttock. "Just something to help you, ah, get into it. Sal, you finish the tap?" she asked the med working on the back of Tama's neck. "Like when you signed," she continued, talking to Tama. "Remember? Well, this is no House. Whole thing is legal, proper, medically safe. Nobody actually does anything. No diseases, no risk, because it's all done with transneuro-holographics. You, you're an actress in a play, a play with the audience on stage." She turned as the gofer swung into the room. "That the script? Okay, slip her protocol into the t-graph and phone down to the box office that we're ready on this end."

"Why are you covering my eyes?"

"Beginners usually find it distracting to be in two places at once. Just helps make it more real. Or at least easier," the med added, pressing the tape gently against Tama's temples. Then they left her alone. She sat up on the bench, suddenly feeling the sticky warmth of the blackness.

"I didn't mean it to be like this," she said to the unhearing machinery. "Oh, Daddy, I didn't mean it to be like this. Not like this."

* * *

Phil looked down at the girl, ginger hair cascading down her pink dress, tears streaming down her cheeks. She could have been his step-daughter. Maybe she was; he couldn't sort it out through the drugs and the pounding of his heart.

"I didn't mean to do it, Daddy," she said, tugging at the chintz bedspread.

She never called him Daddy. He was so overcome with tenderness and forgiveness that he almost left the room without another word, but something in his hand seemed to hold him. He looked down to see what it was. He didn't remember picking up the hairbrush, but there it was, hard and blue as he began slapping it absentmindedly against the palm of his other hand.

"Come here!" he said, pointing to the chair beside the door. Suddenly she looked frightened and, strangely, more beautiful. As she stood slowly, Phil noticed the hard button of her nipple outlined by her soft dress. They both froze. He wanted her for her innocence, her familiarity, and hated her for making him want. Obedience. He must have obedience to protect himself, to protect her. Without obedience there is only Chaos and Anarchy. He would make her see that, make her obey, then forgive and love and reward her.

57

It was as in a play, for though he felt the brush and her hand, smelled her hair and the sweet saltiness of her tears, though he heard her beg him to stop, they moved from scene to scene as if directed by some hidden playwright. Phil knew the story, knew it for his own work. He recognized as long-familiar the sweet, tortured longing against which he struggled as he raised her skirt. The approaching surrender was new, and he backed away from it, confused, struggling to sieve some gritty reality from the fine-lined fantasy before him. From the hall he looked back, watching as she kept scratching at her eyes, pulling at something that wasn't there.

* * *

Who held her, Tama did not know: a woman, one of the other actresses, perhaps. She felt trapped but secure in those strong, gentle, woman's arms. She did not now recall how long she had been crying, nor even for what, only that she felt a burning shame that seemed to spread from a spot in the back of her neck. She was shocked at her own depravity. Unable to look outward, she saw betrayal as if it were her own.

"It hurts, baby. I know how it hurts," the woman who held her said. "Just let all that hurt out."

That voice, something outside, touched off the rage in Tama, a boiling froth of rage that had no direction, no substance. It bubbled over, spreading outward toward a woman called Billi and a man without a name, toward her father who was always too busy, and toward others who did their jobs so well. And when the first wave of rage had foamed and evaporated into nothing, a bright fire of pain remained, like a distant beacon lighting her way back to Halifax.

* * *

Nick hollered above the whine of the commuting turbo. "We sure torqued those emporia fine last night. Right, my 'Talian friend?"

Phil grunted noncommittally as he studied the trapped moisture between the panes of the window. An hour would bring them home, home to Selisberg, home to Anna, and to Maria. She was so rebellious, that Maria. She wouldn't go to church, and she wouldn't dress for dinner, and she wouldn't wear her swimsuit in the pool. Phil thought of her, ginger hair and freckles, stretched out on the green chaise, and he was gripped by shame. The dirty pain that he felt cleansed nothing.

He reached for a magazine, his hand shaking.

Phil tried to reassure him. "Look, Nick, nothing happened. Fantasies are free. What's in your head is just in your head."

"Yeah. It's in my head all right. I just can't get it out. Like you said yesterday, I got a lot to learn about sin, things I need to look at, to understand." It will take time, he thought.

He turned back to the window and saw this own reflection strain toward a half-smile.

Outside, the Big Apple rotted in the browning sun.

This ultra-short, weighing in at a mere 100 words, was inspired by a challenge from NPR's "All Things Considered." As there was no real market for micro-fiction, I squeezed it into my anthology. It only took a page.

Mint, Uncirculated

No one saw.

Eddie, cresting the dune, crabcake in one fist, change in the other, heard the doughy plop.

Fleeing the collapsing ship, a woman with tangerine skin reached toward him. Unthinking, he offered the crabcake. It powdered into sparkling dust, swirling toward her hand, vanishing. She pointed. He opened his hand and icy flame washed the quarter, melting it into a coppery pool that frosted over with her likeness.

In his mind, her words: for you.

She ran, fading, leaving deep cobalt afterimages.

The kids would never believe him. Not even Joey. But he knew he would never show them the coin.

Reprinted from *Infinite Loop* (Miller Freeman Books, 1993).

This oddball bit of fiction is another L. Roy Cahners story. Much to my surprise, it was sufficiently intriguing to editor Dean Wesley Smith that it became another early sale.

Circular Logic

Thinking it was a yellow carnation, Hannibal Johnson bent to fetch the crumpled foolscap from beside the litter barrel. There seemed no logic to this—he had no more use for a carnation than for a scrap of paper—but there was little logic in his life anymore. He stuffed it into the greasy shopping bag he always carried, then pulled it out again, suddenly unsure. Self-consciously he looked around to see if anyone had noticed, but he was a nonentity, one of the street people, and nothing he did interrupted the studied inattention of passersby.

Aware of the rising pressure in his bladder, he shifted from foot to foot while he unrolled the paper. For a moment, he considered whether to wait until reaching his building or to relieve himself in the next alley. He decided to read the scrap while hurrying, in his own fashion, back to the transient's hotel. He half jogged, half shuffled down the litter-strewn street as he read.

It was a draft, perhaps the abandoned term project of one of the foreign students who shared the cheap neighborhood with the derelicts and the illegals. The words irritated him, scraping against some rough remnants of intellect.

"What will be, will be. This is not merely truism, but tautology, a truth by elementary necessity," he read aloud. "It

First appeared in *The Pulphouse Report* in 1988.

is equivalent to say that events have a logic of their own, realized ex post facto, but nonetheless compelling. Within the calculus of realizable events, what was, is, and will be can be reduced to the certainty of rigorous proof."

The words swam in the heat rising from the sidewalk. The pedantic style reminded him of people he had once called colleagues.

"All real events," he continued to read, "from my deliberated choice of words to the casual discovery of a flower, are certain. Whenever alternatives are consistent with the calculus of realized events, where more than one event is 'possible', those events that occur are always found only among the set of all events that were certain. The a posteriori probability of any actual past event having occurred must always be unity, certainty."

Midway through the second side, the writer had abandoned logic for meaningless doodling: scribbled flowers and spirals on spirals. It all seemed oddly familiar to Hannibal, as though he might once have written and scribbled something similar before he lost his faculty position in Philosophy of Science at City University. But he had made mistakes then, had published in the wrong areas, and the unthinkable had become the inevitable. He was denied tenure. His words had been his life. Condemned along with them, he had given up and had written nothing since.

The words of the note disturbed him, yet he was excited by their challenge. He grinned at the thought of such a find in so unlikely a place and time. As he eagerly climbed the unlit stairs of his building, neither soft scurryings in the gloom nor the insistence of his bladder distracted him. His mind danced with thoughts: bits of logic, fragments of argument, steps awkward from inadequate rehearsal but still remembered. He almost didn't make it to the floor's only toilet. Standing halfway in the doorway, warm relief spread through him like a first sip of cognac.

Safe within his room, he spread the paper on the tiny table by the window, carefully smoothing it, petting it like a spoiled cat. By the dimming light of the city's late-afternoon sky, he read and reread the words until they began to lose their customary associations and became an alien cipher.

In the spartan room that jailed and sheltered him, the profound and the trivial shrank to a common dimension, measured only by his personal sense of failure: failure written in the stained wallpaper of the room, spoken by the battered plastic wastebasket that yawned at him from beside a rusted bed. Hannibal Johnson, Ph.D., absent-mindedly crushed the yellow page again. With mixed malice and indifference, he tossed the scrap through the open window.

Four stories below, a student happened to turn her olive face upward. She watched as something spiraled and tumbled toward her. Thinking it was a yellow carnation, she stretched her bare arm skyward to catch it.

This completely whimsical concoction is a self-mocking, multi-layered confection commemorating a real encounter. One of my oldest daughter's friends, a young science fiction writer, actually did challenge me to a race to see who could first accumulate one hundred rejection slips. The irony is that this L. Roy Cahners oddity actually sold, to none other than Dean Wesley Smith!

Giving Time the Slip

When he was forty-three, Leonard Roy Cahners—Elroy to his friends—was introduced to the science fiction writer, Jennifer Horn Koenig. It was arguably the most important event in his life as a writer. She was attending Rockford College where Elroy's twin daughters, Edwina and Winedna, were studying Sovietology. At the time, Koenig was unpublished and unknown. Their dialogue is retold in her autobiography. She wrote (reproduced here with permission):

> "Edwina says you're a closet science fiction writer," I told him.
> "It was Winedna," he corrected. "Edwina would never admit to it. It's hard even for me to be proud, except perversely. You know, I have rejection slips from most of the best: Schmidt, Price, Ryan, Dozois, even a couple from Tappan King. Is he any relation? No, course not, just my high-school German coming back to me. The Kings are the pride of my collection: takes so

damned long to get a response from him. The preprinted Price slips are pretty valuable, too."

"I'll race you to a hundred," I offered.

"A hundred what?"

"Rejections. First one to get one hundred rejection slips wins. Manuscripts returned unopened don't count."

"What about a fanzine that folds before they read your story?"

I was adamant. "Only straight, honest-to-god rejections of the heartfelt outpourings of your very soul are any damned good."

It was a refreshing reframe, and Cahners needed something to keep facing the postman. He agreed. Soon the slips were piling up on the little bill spike on which he gleefully impaled each one with a triumphant growl.

Unfortunately, Cahners died before the contest could be resolved, drowned when his runaway all-terrain bicycle careered off the pier and straight into the side of the last ferry out of Martha's Vineyard. His stories, numbering nearly two hundred, all unpublished, he had willed to his daughters, along with "all other creative and artistic effects," the latter consisting of the scores for two unperformed concertos and a rock musical entitled "Causes." They actually enjoyed some of his short stories, but, mercifully, neither could read a note of music.

It was Winedna's idea to continue the race on his behalf, as much a loving goad for friend Jennifer Koenig, as out of any hope for posthumous publication for her father. Koenig, who had yet to sell a story herself, agreed to extend the contest. She did not prove a worthy adversary, however, since barely four months after Cahners's death she made her first sale, the charming tale of bovine inspiration, "Waiting for the Moos." Then it was simply no contest; for many years the prolific Koenig could not get a rejection however hard she tried. And with the twins both circulating Cahners's stories among editors, the century mark in rejection slips was quickly reached and passed.

They didn't stop there; they just bought another bill spike.

Of course, it became necessary over the years to broaden the field in order to keep the stories circulating. They would have regarded it as cheating to send the same story to the same editor more than once, even though some professional writers insist this works for them. With the passing of Gardner Dozois, the twins were able to begin sending each of the one hundred-and-ninety-four stories to the new editor of *Asimov's*, but eventually every editor of every conceivable serial and anthology had already seen Cahners's entire ouvre.

Edwina and Winedna turned to the inconceivable, addressing their packages and e-mail submissions to such fine periodicals as *Farm Subsidy Weekly* and *Dog and Cat Stories*. There are those critics who have argued that some of these later rejections ought to be disallowed.

When the elderly Cahners twins finally stepped down from their joint chair in Eastern European Studies at Rockford, they passed the packet of manuscripts down to Winedna's oldest child, Jhenya. And when retiring Mars explorer Jhenya Cahners Burg was years later interviewed by *Time Magazine* about the origins of her interest in space flight, L. Roy Cahners's place in literary history was secured. The 2059 edition of *The Guinness Book of World Records* effectively bronzed the plaque: most rejections by Gardner Dozois (194), most rejected science fiction short story ever, "A Taste of Topology," (87 times, counting rejections from 33 fanzines), and most total rejections for one author. It is unlikely that Cahners's three-generation total of 9,108 rejection slips will ever be surpassed in the history of science fiction writing.

After the anointing by *Guinness*, Cahners quickly rose to something of a cult hero. Fans eagerly traded photocopies of reputed manuscripts. Although it had become almost a matter of family pride to have avoided publication, the copyrights had long since expired. Unauthorized editions flourished. Eventually, Jhenya Cahners Burg was forced to set the record straight as to which of several hundred execrable stories attributed to Cahners were the truly deplorable work of her grandfather.

Nearly all of Cahners's science fiction has since been anthologized, the most popular being the Penguin-Doubleday edition of *Lovable Losers*, variant title, *The Tremors of Targantu, and Other Stories by L. Roy Cahners.* He is widely read, especially among would-be writers of science fiction, who find in his writing and his life story a boost to their self-esteem.

Rumors persist of "the lost stories," and, despite denials by Burg, there are those who are convinced that certain published apocrypha are actually by Cahners, most notably a short-short titled "Giving Time the Slip." The latter, however, is certainly the work of another writing under a pseudonym, since none of Cahners's fiction was published in his lifetime.

This piece was accepted by Jerry Pournelle for an anthology on future law that was never published, a not uncommon occurrence in the oddball business of science fiction. Pity. It was fun writing from the perspective of a quick-to-learn ten-year-old boy.

Have You Seen This Child?

The vengeful hand of God reached down between the passengers on the crowded turbotrain and grabbed Jerrod Mueller, painfully pinching tendons against the bones of his shoulder. Startled, Jerrod turned ten-year-old eyes up toward a face pocked like the dirty snow of late spring. His eyes began to burn; in his ear, God's voice thundered, louder than the rushing rush of subway wheels and subway riders. "Never ride without holding on, son. You never know who might grab you when you're off balance."

Jerrod clutched at his tags on the chain around his neck and reached with a free hand, stretching between two commuters, fumbling for the cold edge of a seat. He nodded meekly. "Yes, Sir." He prayed, and the pressure on his shoulder lessened. He squirmed away, putting the smelly lady with the big headset between him and the man. Risking a peek, he found the man's rheumy eyes still fixed on him. Jerrod edged toward the door as the turbo pulled into a station. Marsden Heights, no connections. He couldn't grab another train on another platform. The streets might be safe now, but it was nearly dark.

Jerrod squeezed through at the last second, the closing door almost catching his bookpack. He watched the old man, no longer God, as the train pulled away: a shrinking face pressed to the window, swiveling to follow Jerrod. Jerrod's mother had warned him. There were Men Who Wanted Kids Like Him. He looked around anxiously, but none of the people on the platform seemed interested in him, so he decided to wait for the next "K" express rather than trying for a bus on the surface. He glanced at the clock over the ticket machines, its hands just tilted from the vertical. There was a Russian test in the morning; he could use the twenty minutes before the next train to work on vocabulary. No, too deadly. But he hadn't finished *Bridge to Terrabithia*; that was due Friday. He got out his player, slipped the earphones on his head and the disk into its slot, and started watching.

He didn't hear the aerosol, but he did notice that the woman next to him on the platform had the strangest perfume, fruity and sour. When Jerrod started to sidle away, he tripped and fell.

Inquiring faces turned slowly toward him. In a syrupy dream, the slim woman with the perfume said, "Poor boy, so tired, I told him not to stay up with the Horror Channel last night." She helped him to his feet. To the man behind her, she said, "Donothan, be a dear and carry him." Strong, man-arms picked him up and held him, one under the butt, another at his back, as if he were an oversized baby being burped. His tags swung on their chain, and a young woman in blues shook her head disapprovingly. Jerrod struggled.

"Hey, tiger, don't fight it, might as well get some shut-eye on the long ride home." The man said more, but Jerrod didn't hear it.

* * *

The old man with the scarred face haunted Jerrod's dreams, but it was the skinny woman from the Marsden Heights platform who opened the door in the morning. She wore a business suit the color that Jerrod thought of as "baby puke," though his aunt Marika had once called it "dusty rose." She set her matching canvas tote down beside the door as she entered.

"Well, Jerrod, I hope you slept well." She crossed the room and tapped the biphase window, letting bright, late-morning sunlight spill across the rug, where it was promptly soaked up in the deep brown pile. The edge of the beam just washed the bottom of walls that were like beach sand. Beside the bed hung Jerrod's bookpack and his player. She must have noticed him looking at them. "Don't worry about school. You won't be going back to P.S. 423. Next week you can start at Pendale Academy. But there will be plenty of time for talk about school later, when you're feeling more at home.

"This is your home now, Jerrod. This is your room." She gestured like a preacher addressing her flock.

Jerrod sat up and blinked. The room did not vanish; the neon orange zipscooter leaning against the wall did not waver. He held up his hands and noticed the bracelet.

"Just for now, Jerrod. What a handsome, strong name: Jerrod. You understand, don't you? We don't want anything to happen to you, not until we file, not ever. Oh, I just know you'll like it with us. You'll have so much more than," she hesitated, "than your mother could ever give you. Six children! So many for one family when there are still homes going begging."

"Oh, yes, you have a new brother now," she said, as a tough looking boy appeared at the door. "Reid, this is Jerrod, the little brother we promised you."

Reid stood in the doorway, a carefully molded look of pre-adolescent contempt on his face. He was shorter than Jerrod, with the solid muscularity that made Jerrod think of the bully in Mrs. Gerabidian's class.

"He'll be staying home today and tomorrow, too, to watch out for you, show you where things are, help you feel at home." Reid sighed. "And Reid, don't forget about the perimeter setting. We don't want any painful accidents." Jerrod froze as she bent to kiss his forehead. She didn't smell like the strange perfume anymore, but the odor came back to him anyway. "Be good. I'll be back from the library at four, and your new daddy will be on the 6:41 from the city.

"You are going to like it here," she added, trying to convince them both.

Reid waited outside the room until he heard the garage door closing, then came in and sat on the bed. "Tough at first. I remember when I was popped two years ago. But it doesn't take much of good food and the wall video and lotsa toys to make you think straight. Where'd they pop you?"

"Marsden Heights." Jerrod shivered. "I ain't staying."

"So you think. You'll stay. You're theirs now, all proper."

Jerrod slipped out of bed and looked for his clothes. There were new blues and a Fish Waller tee-shirt on the chair. Did they know Fish Waller was his favorite group or were they guessing? He pulled the jeans on over his pajamas.

Reid watched impassively. "In a hurry, kid?"

The window beside the bed opened onto the roof of a porch. Jerrod checked it: unlocked.

"Why not use the front door? It'll open," Reid said, still sitting on the bed.

The hallway was papered in a tiny floral print and lined with colorful china along a plate rail. To the left, a closed door; to the right, a stairwell: Jerrod headed down. The front door, a heavy double door, opened when Jerrod tapped the bar, just as Reid had said it would. Outside, the warm air was sharp with the smell of fresh pavement.

Jerrod waited only a second, then ran for the tree-lined street. At the sidewalk something grabbed his left wrist and squeezed like an evil hand. The bracelet began to flash like a camera strobe, each flash accompanied by a loud ping, musical but irritating at the same time. His wrist ached, and the ache began to work its way up his arm.

He looked back. Reid was standing on the porch, his canary-yellow tee-shirt standing out against the pewter sheen of the house.

"Told you," Reid said. "You'll stay."

The two of them spent the morning with the video games in the basement rec room and the afternoon playing with Reid's model rocket collection. Reid showed him the fuel cartridges hidden under a floor board in his closet, along with a cat skull and two disks of *Penthouse*. Jerrod had to admit that Reid was "way rad," and the house had everything.

They told each other about their families, their "old families." Reid had been an only child, born to a fourteen-year-old Vietnamese girl. She must have been as relieved as Reid when he was grabbed. Jerrod talked a lot about his mom and brothers and three sisters and the chaos in their tiny house. This house, with Reid and the lady and Donothan, didn't look right: nothing in it. He pictured his home, with the stacks of boxes in the hall, the wash hanging in the kitchen, and the endless supply of junk his mom scavenged from trash piles and dumpsters. He loved the bright clutter and the easy comings and goings of neighbors and mooches and his sisters' boyfriends.

"When my mom finds out, she'll have the police after these guys and I'll be out of here." It was a Hymn of Hope. "Like that!" He snapped his fingers dully.

Reid laughed. "When your Mom finds out, she'll collect her part of the compensation fee and buy a new vid system."

"What you talking about?"

"Come on, your mom warned you about strangers, didn't she? Told you never to go out without your tags, right? Why would she do that?"

"Because she doesn't want anything to happen to me. She cares! That's why she warned me about b'duction." He thought of her arm around his tummy as she held him in her lap. He pulled at the corner of his eye and said, incongruously, "Yeah!"

"Abduction, dork! Why would she warn you if you weren't registered? You tell me that!" Jerrod looked at him blankly. Reid grabbed at Jerrod's neck and pulled out the two embossed tags with their embedded chips. "Registration tags! What, did you think a couple like the Messers or some free-hunter can just grab any kid they fancy?"

The implications began to sink in; of the two most plaus-ible conclusions, Jerrod chose to believe that Reid was blowing through his ear. He told him that.

Reid gave him a shove and stomped out. When it looked like Reid might hole up in his room for the rest of the after-noon, Jerrod decided to check out the bracelet.

It was made of that blackish metal that he'd seen used for zipscooter locks. It wouldn't come off. If he got within a couple feet of the edge of the narrow yard, it beeped a warning to him; any farther and God grabbed his arm again. Maybe he could call for help, he thought. He went to the phone and picked it up; his arm started to tingle and the warning beep began. He gave up for the day.

First Mrs. Messer ("Just call me Tee!") came home, then Donothan, who insisted the boys call him "Dad." He was precisely one hour late, as if even his tardiness were punctual. He announced that he would have to shorten his play time with the boys, saying this as if there were a lesson for them to learn from his delay.

Reid, it turned out, was half right and half wrong about things. It did not take long for Jerrod to get used to the routine of the Messer house, it just never quite felt like home. Tee and Donothan had their work and their politics, and little to do at the house or with the boys. There was no one home to yell at Jerrod when he came back from school. He cried some-times in the afternoon, cried in his room with the door shut and the water running in his own bathroom. He never ex-pected Tee to walk in on him.

"We don't have time for babies, now, Jerrod. If we'd wanted a baby, for heaven's sake, we probably could have had one ourselves without the complications and expense of being licensed. I don't suppose your mother has had that talk with you yet about the other way of getting babies. Well, there's time, later. I'll tell Donothan to put it on his calendar." She wiped at his face with a handkerchief. "Now, we will go downstairs with dry faces, and we will wash our hands, and we will have some frozen macadamia nut yogurt."

He didn't really want the yogurt, but he took a spoonful. It tasted like a mother's love.

* * *

School surprised Jerrod the most, with strange teachers who seemed interested in the kids, interested in Jerrod. When the cybermath instructor caught him doodling in his notebook, she sat down with him and helped him figure out how to compute the shapes and make them appear on his terminal screen. Her hair and eyes were black, and she tickled him when he made the shape on his screen into a smiley-face. The boys, the same boys, seemed to be there every day. The halls did not smell of something stuck to the wall or soaked into the floor.

Donothan picked him up at school one day to take him for an in-city physical. The jitney terminal was bright and clean, filled with flashing displays.

One of the signs looked at Jerrod with his own eyes. "Have you seen this child?" it flashed, then his picture reappeared.

"There's a probation period," Donothan explained. "If you're reclaimed in the first six months, we lose you. But nobody ever does. Doesn't pay for anyone to do it because there's a filing fee, and parents who really want to keep their kids don't have them tagged."

"What if, like, a kid runs away?"

"Won't happen," Donothan said, tapping at Jerrod's left wrist.

Jerrod looked back at the sign, waiting for someone to wrench him from Donothan's side, but they climbed in the next jitney without incident. His wrist hurt in anticipation of another abduction that never came.

He did not understand why his mother didn't call or send him an e-mail. Reid explained one day as he was winning at Astroid Buster.

"Can't do it. There's a fine you pay if you try to contact a registered kid during probation." His Gee-hopper on the screen sprayed an asteroid cluster with orange and purple fire. "Cost your mother half her entitlement." The screen flared in a spiral explosion, but one of the asteroids hurled toward them. Reid spun the trackball with a quick gesture and slipped his hopper beneath the asteroid. "All bright!" The kilometer total on the screen kept a dizzying count.

"I'll just have to reach her," Jerrod muttered, unheard amidst the pings and squeals and sonic crashes of the game. The swirling colors on the screen seemed to be showing him a way.

The art program at the Academy was Jerrod's salvation, and the online library was his scripture. He developed a love of sculpture and metal-working, bringing home a growing collection of etched and enameled copper and corten abstractions, which Tee and Donothan proudly displayed in their living room. On the faceted glass coffee table, a mis-shapen copper globe with strange, chemically-stained continents endured the oohs and ahs of the Messer's dinner guests while it waited for Jerrod's need.

Then there was an afternoon, an afternoon of quiet, with Reid playing soccer and the house a sighing giant. Jerrod waited, listened, then picked up the lumpy globe, untwisted the clasps, and fastened it over his left hand and wrist. Would they have known better if he had titled it "Faraday Cage?" He wondered.

A few seconds passed before a warning bar appeared on the household system monitor. "FAULT IN PERISTRICTOR >> UNIT 1." He walked to the phone. The system monitor started to beep, but there was no tingling in his wrist. He tucked the receiver in his left armpit and punched his mother's number.

"Hello. Mueller's." She spoke with the voice of a bamboo flute, breathy and expressive. "Hello?" Longing mixed with fear jelled in Jerrod's throat. He lowered the receiver, then dismantled his copper mitten and reassembled it on the coffee table. The system monitor shut up.

At dinner, Donothan asked him if he'd had any problems with his bracelet.

"That's funny, Dad," he answered, trying not to stumble over the last word. "It did flash once when this Arbitron truck went by. Why?"

"Oh nothing, little fella, just don't want anything going wrong. Only a few weeks before we get the permanent custody grant. You know."

He knew, all right. He also now knew that the household computer either recorded or forwarded any fault conditions; there could be no trial runs.

* * *

The policeman at the desk raised his eyebrows in question at Jerrod.

"I escaped," Jerrod told him. "I'm a, an abductee. And I escaped. I just want to go home."

"You mean someone actually kidnapped you, son? An unlicensed claiming?"

"No, I guess it was okay." He unsnapped his tags from their chain and handed them to the sergeant. "But I got away. I got away."

"What's that on your hand?" Jerrod explained. "Well, lets see the bracelet, see if we can deprogram that." He brought out a case full of tools and started working on Jerrod's wrist, inserting probes through the cage. "Pretty clever, shielding the transponder. There." He slipped the cage and the dark band off.

"There is a byte of a problem, sonny. Someone, an adult, has to file to reclaim you. We'll message your guardians, the Messers. Unless someone wants to pay the reclaimant fee for you, I'm afraid you'll have to go back with them. Now I'm not saying I exactly approve of parents using wrist locks, but they are legal."

"Call my mother."

"I'll do that, but don't exactly get your hopes up."

The Messers arrived first but ignored Jerrod. While they talked with the police, Reid sat down on the bench beside Jerrod. The boys kept eyeing each other when each thought the other wasn't looking.

Jerrod's mother arrived almost an hour later, a heavy woman, in heavy clothes, breathing as if it were work.

"Jerro, Jerro!" she said as she approached, the warmth in her voice fluttering with an uneasy trill. "We missed you. The twins, too. It was close; only a few weeks left."

A few weeks before the compensation fee arrived, Jerrod thought, before the roof was fixed and Sarri got her contacts and the video recorder could be replaced with a wall vid.

"You okay?" she asked.

He shrugged.

She held out her arms to him, but he stood, like one of his metal figures, poised.

"You gotta pay this money, Mom, so I can come home." It was almost a whisper.

"I want to, Jerro, I do. But I don't have that much in my account. No way to get it, either."

Jerrod looked desperate. "But why, why does me and Sarri have tags? Why'd you do this?"

"My pretty Sarri, my bright, strong Jerro. We needed the registration fees. I didn't think anyone would ever really pop you. I paid, once, I didn't think it could happen twice to me. When I lost the baby, I said no kid of mine would ever again wear tags, but things just kept getting worse, and the fees, they just kept offering more. I guess there's lotsa couples want kids. Can't just let them take anybody, be like kidnapping in them old times.

"It's not like having to give up a kid for adoption. Just taking a chance. Always chances in life, Jerro. Anyway, Cadj and the others were too old, or their scores weren't good enough."

The distinctions were lost on Jerrod, who was thinking of the baby, his baby sister, who was kidnapped, stolen. Sold. "You gotta get the money, Mom. You gotta!" Please, he thought, please want to, want to try.

She bit her lip and tugged at her sweater. "I don't know anybody's got that kind of money."

"I do," Jerrod said, turning to Reid. "Can I borrow two thousand bucks from you? I'll pay you back, ten dollars a week."

Reid laughed. "Don't be a jerk, Jerr. Live with a good deal while you have it." Donothan Messer was looking at him with a Better-Watch-Out-Son carved on his face. It made Reid feel like changing his mind and giving Jerrod the money on his card, but he would rather have a little brother, unhappy or not, than the satisfaction of pulling something on the Messers or of doing something for Jerrod. Jerrod would eventually get smart, he figured.

The desk sergeant looked up from his terminal. "Hey, Ms. Mueller, this Abduction Candidacy Registration is expired, almost six months ago. You must have forgotten to go down to Child Welfare to complete the renewal forms."

"Now wait a minute," Donothan said, "the tags were valid when we claimed him, Officer. It doesn't matter whether this woman has or has not renewed since." Donothan spoke with an air of certainty, as if he were a lawyer instead of a media sales rep.

"What matters is that the authorization expired the day you claimed the boy, at the end of the business day. It all depends on when you gained physical custody whether your claim is legal or not. Son, do you remember the time when the Messers acquired you?"

"You mean in the station?" He was picturing the clock. "Yeah, it was about six o'clock."

"About six o'clock. But which way, about? Just after or just before? Think hard, this is very important, son."

Jerrod pictured his room at the Messer's and remembered the cool crispness of the sheets, the pleasant smell of the big pillows. His mother's betrayal was like a stone in his throat. Time to get real, he thought, just like Reid always told him.

"It was a few minutes after. Yes, I'm sure. I can picture the clock very clearly. Just before I passed out it was five or six minutes past six."

The Messer's looked upset, and his mother looked surprised.

"The boy's testimony would carry the weight if this went to adjudication, Mr. and Mrs. Messer. If it stays here, its an infraction; you get to keep your claiming licenses."

Donothan took his wife's arm. "There are other boys out there, Tee. We'll find one."

For a moment as they were leaving the station, Jerrod and Reid were separated from the others. Reid looked as if he were about to spray saliva in Jerrod's face.

"God, you zero-K dummy. You blew it. I don't understand why you didn't lie about the time. Five minutes the other way and you could have had it all."

Jerrod thought about what he would have: the stink of the basement shower, fighting for M&Ms, swapping videos at the movie library, sharing the room with Cadj and Bram, riding to the laundromat with his mother, her kisses on his neck. He knew things now, and there was a sense of power in what he knew. He knew what was possible in the world, and he knew how far trust could be stretched before it snapped like a worn shoestring. There was power in having this knowledge, especially the knowledge of his mother, her ambivalence, and of the powerful guilt he knew she felt. He would have it all, he was confident of that.

"You're right about the time, Reid. Five minutes the other way and I'd be goin' with you. But you're wrong about a lot of other things. I did lie about the time. They popped me fair. I lied, and now I'm going with my mom. I'm goin' home."

> This previously unpublished work was an experiment in form, an attempt to tell a story, not through the story itself, but through a commentary on the story, in this case, the foreword to an imaginary novel.

Foreword to
Efficient Cause

Paolo Franzetti did not know who he was. It shows in his writing. *Efficient Cause,* an entire novel set within a single day, is a tale of decision and discovery, exploring those intricate and unseen forces that lead to a turning point: one of those rare moments when commitment is reified in action and alters for all time the lives of those it touches. To write of this novel I must write of the novelist.

Paolo Franzetti Dermott may touch you in forgotten places where fears of exclusion or the more mysterious ones of belonging still hide. Perhaps, we think, he knows our unvoiced doubts because he is like us, knowing us from within. But he is outside, an outsider to us all, and from this separateness, this platform apart, he appraises us as whole beings, capturing in his unforgiving prose our complex and unitary selves. We are unequipped to observe this without him, for we are inside the frame of his portrait of us and lack his compassionate detachment.

His magic is that of the sculptor; with the cold and hard-edged tools of crisp language he chips away to reveal a soft beauty dormant within us. He teaches us not only something of what we are but of self-love and self-acceptance. Without knowing who we are, he tells us, we cannot love that hidden image whose dim outline is traced upon the blank stone.

As there was nothing regarding the matter in Arturo Dermott's will, we elected not to tell Paolo who he was. We interpreted in the broadest way the requirement to provide care and protection. In this we could only set precedent, not follow it, for Paolo was the first. If we erred in our conservatism, we erred as other parents do, acting with caution in the face of the unknown within their offspring. I do not hesitate to assume responsibility—thus reads my karma—yet I cannot say with conviction that we were wrong. Perhaps, though, we were. Perhaps it was Dermott who was wrong in the first place. We may yet know, through Paolo's writing. In *Efficient Cause* there are tantalizing hints, casual promises left between lines: he will tell us, if not in his first novel, then in his second or his twenty-second.

If I write with such certainty of a future that is only whispers without words, it is from knowing the fearsome appetite of the crowd; the public will devour *Efficient Cause*, as they would devour anything written by a Paolo Franzetti Dermott. When they learn just how gifted he is, they will wait hungrily for more. And he will have the time, the time to complete that task he has set before himself: to tell us about ourselves.

He has asked for this foreword from me, and I am honored by the task. As he will not directly tell you of himself, I have chosen to assume that burden on his behalf. There is so little I can say about his novel that it cannot better speak itself, and there is so much to be said of this unique young man who is, for now, sui generis.

What a strangely wondrous, serious boy he was! When he could scarcely read he was already writing, as if the act of creating information were more natural to him than the process of receiving it. As the full-time family therapist to the Franzettis, I would visit on week nights as often as I could manage. Invariably I would have to climb the narrow, switchback stairs to the attic where Paolo made his "office." His desk was an old drafting board decorated by tea stains and pencil smears. When he was small it rested on a trunk, and he would kneel before it for hours at a stretch. As he grew, he jacked it up with boxes and pressed a crate into service as a chair. He wanted no more—no maple desk, no files, no terminal, no typewriter—though he could have had all of these and more. They were, he would say, "not efficient." He told us many times, "What I use are sufficient for my uses."

Paolo wrote everything with measured precision in a block hand that was always more legible than my best efforts. His pink tongue would search his thick, dark lips as he meticulously formed each minuscule and majuscule. Though it might take him months to finish a story, even at eight years of age his fine mind deftly kept track of all the threads and the details he strung upon them. He would finish one story and then begin another, rarely returning to anything once it was filed within his capacious cardboard box.

I did ask him once about those other stories. He was barely ten, and they almost filled the box.

"Oh, they're silly," he said. "See this one?" He picked up the top sheaf of notepaper. "It's about a bird, an inadvertent stowaway on a space freighter. It is really quite childish. I was only a nine-year-old kid when I wrote it," he told me, without irony. "I can do much better now."

"Why don't you rewrite it, then, revise it in some way?"

"You don't understand. It's the whole thing. The idea, the plot, the narrative, the grammatical construction: they're all naïve. It's the gestalt." He paused as if making sure I understood the word. He did, in those young years, often underestimate the intelligence of adults. "It's better to start on something else, to build something new, than to try to patch up something so badly constructed."

If the reader finds this dialogue unconvincing in the mouth of a ten-year-old, be assured, he spoke this way. Paolo had two great gifts that emerged early: his facility with words and his understanding of emotional relationships. He was never without friends, not merely casual ones, but fiercely loyal intimates who valued his friendship above all others. I cannot say whether these emotional attachments were reciprocal, but Paolo gave generously, nonetheless.

He gave each and all the same gift: insight. He was always the one to whom his young friends turned when they had trouble with parents or boyfriends or school. I don't believe he ever gave advice. He would listen, then tell the seekers something about themselves. They left, armed with new self-knowledge, to solve their problems without him.

I confess before all that more than once I covertly turned to him for supervision on puzzling family therapy cases. I would pose them as hypothetical situations or dilemmas and invite his comments. These never failed to liberate me from some pattern of assumptions in which I had trapped myself.

Of course, I had few other cases. I was salaried with the Dermott Foundation for Developmental Studies to help the Franzettis. Although it took nowhere near my full-time attention, I have always been disinclined to work much more than necessary. I, of course, had the most intimate and involved contact with the family, but the Foundation's team included physicians, psychologists, laboratory technicians, financial and administrative personnel—all the resources to give the boy the best support available. He could have been raised in luxury, but the team concluded in its early deliberations that a near-normal family life was the best assurance of success.

Arturo Dermott had himself been raised by his maternal grandparents, gentle Italian immigrants who lavished love on him and urged on his every effort toward success. The Franzettis were already in their fifties when they were chosen to "adopt" Paolo. Legally, of course, he remained the ward of the executor. The Franzettis were of sturdy *paisano* stock, and we had little concern for whether they would fail to survive to see him into adulthood.

Paolo's childhood was not unruffled, despite all that the Foundation did or was prepared to do. Aside from infrequent tensions over the Franzetti's "old ways" and the newer ones of his peers, Paolo's greatest frustrations came from his total lack of mechanical aptitude and his complete disinterest in all matters technical. We did not push him, though we did attempt to steer him. He was given construction sets for Christmas and sent to science camp in the summer. We challenged him with computer games and Chinese puzzles, waiting for his latent talent to bloom. The bud, if indeed it was there at all, remained tightly closed, leaving the Foundation with its own puzzle.

Arturo Dermott had been an engineer and an inventer, an important one, though never a truly public figure. As an old man he styled himself a scientist without ever doing much that resembled ordinary science. He had no need for research. He would look at a thing, grasp it as a whole in less time than it would take an ordinary person to turn it over, then retire to his workshop. In a week or a year he would return, bringing something new onto the face of the planet. A gearless transmission, a lensless camera: whatever it was, it was revolutionary, more than once bringing ruin to established paradigms in physics or electronics or information science.

His special gift for the mechanical, the technical, abetted Arturo's social isolation in childhood. Not only were his intellect and his mechanical abilities far above those of his peers, but his social skills were commensurately below. To Arturo, people made no sense, sense was found only in objects, and he failed miserably at almost every personal relationship he ever entered. He was not without friends, but they were a special breed who cherished and tolerated him despite his measureless insensitivity. There had been lovers—both sexes—and he was twice married. Women, especially, were drawn to him: some by his intellect, some by what may have seemed an aloof charm, others by their own need to mother a sad, mad genius. Few stayed with him for long, and the marriages were short,

89

fruitless encounters made bitter by lengthy and costly divorces.

He would have died heirless were it not for Paolo. Paolo knew he was "adopted"—that had never been hidden from him—but he did not know who he was.

He did not learn at home, from the Franzettis, or in therapy, or in any other reasonable and manageable setting. It happened in my office waiting room, a place neither in nor out, not private and not public. Paolo and the Franzettis had come in for their monthly session. These I held at my office where the rest of the Foundation team could observe through a one-way mirror. I would never have kept them all waiting had I not been caught in traffic coming from a home visit. Even as I opened the door, Paolo turned to me with deep, bittersweet brown eyes. He held up an open issue of *Life Magazine*, like all waiting-room periodicals, many months old. I didn't catch on at first. Avid reader though he was, *Life* was hardly his usual fare. Then I noticed the picture of him. It was not him, of course, but a photo of Arturo Dermott, illustrating some sidebar about young geniuses.

Paolo knew! In that effortless way he has always had of penetrating to the knot of human entanglements, he grasped what it was all about. Small clues and minute irregularities, the myriad subtle pressures and unsubtle attentions, all had snapped into place within a pattern that held meaning for him. He said nothing then, but did nothing to hide the numbed shock on his face nor the sense of painful betrayal evident in his eyes.

"I'm not me," he said, at last. "Not him, not anybody."

"Paolo, Paolo, you are the only one of you in the world. You are unique and special. You . . ."

But he cut my recitation short. "I am not unique. You are, Doctor Cahners. Everyone else is. But not I. And were he still alive today," he said, pointing to the young engineer in the magazine, "I would not even be the only one in the world."

I could tell from the way he looked from me to Tony and to Seppa that he wanted to be held. But whom among us could he trust? He ran from the office. Of course, we ran after him. We even caught him. But we could not make him want to talk, so we left him for awhile to retreat to his attic. Except for meals, he stayed up there in the August heat until he had finished another story, the only story he would never let me read. He left it in his box, filed with all the rest, but with a note attached, declaring it off limits.

He came down from the attic on a brisk day in September, hungry and full of questions. Naturally, Paolo wanted to learn more about cloning and more about Arturo Dermott and the Foundation that Arturo had endowed to care for Paolo. We told all, all we knew, for it seemed then that only complete candor could restore his trust in us. He was fourteen and flexible; he recovered, or so it seemed.

The real storms appeared to be outside that autumn, with unusually changeable weather and fierce winds. Tony Franzetti should have called the Foundation about the tree fallen against the porch. He was determined to fix it himself, though, and the climb to the porch roof seemed easy. When he fell, his neck snapped. Seppa's grief seemed bottomless, but Paolo met Tony's death with composure.

I watched Paolo closely. I did worry about suicide. He had identified so closely with Tony, and this was one of the things I was paid to be concerned about. After the funeral, Paolo retreated again to his attic with growing frequency and for longer periods, though I would not have termed him depressed. His many good friends worried, though, and the school psychologist began to get concerned notes from both students and teachers.

Finally, after nearly a year, he snapped out of it, returned to his friends, and even joined the science club. I asked him what had happened. He told me only that he had finished another story that he had been writing. I worried even more, knowing as a therapist the dangers in that time of apparent recovery. I kept an ear tuned for suicidal tendencies but heard nothing to alarm me.

We don't know how Seppa's condition deteriorated so rapidly, but once we learned of it in a regular exam, we brought the best of modern medicine to bear on her cancer. She did not tolerate the chemotherapy well, however. Within that tough little woman, her will fought a pitched battle with itself, determined to hang on for Paolo and resigned to let go after the loss of her beloved Tony. Between cancer and chemicals and her husband's death, there was little room for willpower. In mounting pain, she weakened.

The murder shocked us and the nation. It was called "monstrous." The Foundation tried, to no avail, to conceal Paolo's origins. Once it was known that he was Arturo Dermott's clone, the story filled every page, every newscast. Soon it was known that the monstrous deed was indeed the act of a monster: the clone, terrifying messiah of genetic research. Outrage turned from Paolo to his makers. Anti-tech groups had a field day, crying Jonesdoom, demanding a halt to all genetic research and experimentation. If possible, the liberals of science seemed even more upset. Perhaps the real blow for them, the scientific establishment, was to be the last to know, to be told by the press and the public how far a little genius and a lot of cash could go beyond the known and hallowed limits of their medical arts.

It was Paolo's gentle face and open demeanor that most disturbed the general public, however. This quiet and insightful child had killed his adoptive mother in cold blood, killing her gently and with calculated precision using drugs taken from the Foundation clinic. Surely, it was said, here was proof of the evil of tampering with the ways of Nature's god.

The public savored the spectacle, awaiting the trial with morbid enthusiasm, eager to hear the clone's story from Paolo's lips. There was no hope of an insanity defense. By every test and definition, Paolo was sane. He pleaded guilty, saying in explanation, "I, alone, have no mother."

There was no story, no show. The court, recognizing the mercy in Paolo's deed, seemed inclined to compassion, but there had been so-called reforms in juvenile sentencing back in the late '80s. The law was clear: life in prison, no parole.

As nothing more could be done for or to Paolo, the watchers turned their fervor toward legislation, demanding that there be no more like him. How unfair to the child, they said, who must always strive so valiantly to find self and self-worth, how unfair to impose that extra and insurmountable burden of being someone else. Experts without expertise cited studies without data; professionals without knowledge pro-nounced conclusions without bases. The Foundation was never consulted in these debates, and we were relieved. However, it will probably be a very long time before another human clone is raised.

At his sentencing, they led Paolo past where I was seated. He looked down at me with a gentle, knowing smile fixed on his face. I recognized it.

"You engineered this, all of it, didn't you, Paolo?"

The smile held steady as he leaned toward me. "A life, too, has a design, and not only in the realm of biochemistry and genetics. You know, a life may already have been planned, yet still be redesigned at any time." He spoke slowly, as if mentally laying out each word in that fine, block hand of his. "Arturo Dermott made something new by using an old design. He made me the first of a kind. And now, with a new design, I have made of me the last.

"I am Dermott, remember, Paolo Dermott. Engineered, you say? You have a flair for ironic wording, Roy. You could have been a writer."

Perhaps that is why he asked me to do this foreword to *Efficient Cause*. I have written so little of the novel itself because I have no words, no ironies, with which I could explain or enhance it. The puzzle of Dermott's clone has already been explained: we confused function with object, capacity with focus, as if a twin would speak his brother's

93

words rather than merely with his brother's voice. Paolo is, it turns out, the engineering genius that Arturo Dermott was, understanding at the instant the workings of the most intricate of systems: human systems, systems far more complex than those that ever held Arturo's attention.

He watches now from a prison, if not of his own making, then of his own design, built on a Foundation laid block by block by those of us who cared. An ironic flair, indeed. Paolo is the bystander, we, the players. From his box seat he watches our drama, of us but not one of us, thereby knowing us as we do not.

L. Roy Cahners
Providence, May 1998

This story was my first attempt at espionage fiction, and I tried, unsuccessfully, to market it accordingly. It proved, however, to be a good warm-up exercise for the novels that would come later. And I liked Richard Talpa so much as a character that I decided to recycle him in my third novel, *Web Games.*

Digital Mole

Richard Talpa got into Sydney Airport by way of Canberra—the traffic there was heavier, easier to stay lost in—and went right for the Customs warehouse. The security system stopped him for a minute, but he keyed an override combination, then leaned back with a look of satisfaction as bright as his yellow New York Marathon tee-shirt.

"We're in. And there's the shipment of grenade launchers," Talpa said, smiling up from his wheelchair.

They were certainly an odd team: Grant Belden, with his Harvard B-School crispness, and Talpa, approaching middle-age but still an MIT hacker at heart, with the beer belly and the brains to prove it.

Belden scowled over Richard's shoulder at the amber numbers and letters of frozen light on the computer screen. "Where? I don't see it."

"Right there." Rich jabbed with his finger. "See, the one described as 'REPRODUCTIONS, ALUMINIUM, SYDNEY LACE.' The weight is right, too. I mean, who the hell in the Philippines would be buying fancy, phony wrought iron at a time like this?"

"That's how you figured it out?"

Richard grunted a laugh. He jiggled the little joystick control, making his wheelchair zigzag with a soft whine back from the desk, narrowly missing Belden's brown wingtips, then over to the counter separating the living room from the kitchen area. He grabbed a stack of printouts and handed them back to Belden.

"The clincher is the shipper code. I cross-referenced all the shipping schedules downloaded from the files of companies we've been watching. I circled the five that I'm sure are fronts," he said, grinning in triumph. He loved working for the Company: the detective work, puzzling out the problems, writing the computer code, tricking the systems into letting him hop-skip around the world on the weightless wings of digital pulses.

"Pretty good legwork, Talpa, uh, I mean you do learn fast."

"Yeah, well a computer and a cable modem sure beats legs." Richard didn't mind making other people a little uncomfortable about his handicap, especially guys like Belden.

Belden ignored the jibes. "The Company appreciates this kind of work; the country appreciates it."

The intercom chimed. "Hi, Rich, it's Amy. Can you buzz me in?"

Richard pressed "shift-alternate enter" on the keyboard in his lap and the entry lock could be heard buzzing down the hall.

"Do you have everything hooked up to that thing?"

"Everything."

"There's no wires?"

"Infrared link."

There was a ratatat on the door. "You should get a metal door," Belden said as he opened it.

Amy Sarnoff stood there loaded down with purse, book bag, and a bag of groceries. Her broad-mouthed smile narrowed almost instantly. "Oh, it's you," she said as she pushed past Belden.

"I don't think she likes me, Richard. What a shame. I like brunettes."

"It's not you, Belden," she said, "it's your politics: your naïve, rah-rah patriotism. That's just the kind of misplaced passion the world has had enough of." She set the load of groceries on the counter. "Is it two or three for dinner, Rich?"

Belden opened his eel skin attaché case and started stuffing papers in. "I have to go, business calls. This is good stuff, Richard. A check will be in the mail. I'll phone later about the next job." He let himself out.

Richard rolled into the kitchen, got himself a Lite from the refrigerator, and inched up beside Amy. "You look worried."

"What's this all about, Rich?"

"Just some more stuff: hacking, really. Look, I'm a contract programmer. I make my living by bit-fiddling on other people's computers. This guy pays well and pays fast." He hoped she couldn't tell he was holding back part of the story. "Look, it's my turn to cook, so don't bother putting that bird in the fridge. I'll make chicken cacciatore."

"Mmmmm! Look, Mr. Chef-and-a-half, I just don't want you to get in over your head on anything."

He glanced up at her from his wheelchair with a look of mock annoyance. "So, Miss Peacenik, are you making cracks about no-leg disabled vets again?" he asked, pulling her down into his lap. She pressed her nose against his, and black curls washed over his balding head. "Hey! don't crunch my keyboard!" he barked teasingly.

* * *

They were just finishing the homemade raspberry ice for desert, when the phone rang. Amy watched as he wheeled into the bedroom, wondering why he didn't just key on the speakerphone. He saw her looking as he picked up the receiver. The screechy hiss of a data carrier hit him in the ear, so he quickly tapped the keypad on the front of the encryption modem and said, "Yeah?"

"Talpa. It's Belden. Our guys confirmed the shipment of launchers. Only wish we could keep them from getting into the hands of the Philippine leftists, but we can't risk tipping our hand, yet. The Company wants you to hack the network itself. The main system is called Poleax. We need you inside Poleax, not just playing peek-a-boo with customs computers and insurance companies. Get through their security, find out where they're vulnerable."

"I'm not so sure, Belden. That could be tricky." He resented the implication that his work so far had been easy, but he didn't want Belden to know.

"Look, Talpa, in for an inch, in for a mile. The Company has a lot of flexibility. And a lot of cash. You do the job, take the time you need, and it will be worth your while. That's one of the advantages of working for us. We don't have to go through Congress for our appropriations.

"And Talpa, are you serious about this girl? What do you know about her? I'm not sure you should trust her."

"What are you saying, Belden?"

"Well, you know, even her name: Sarnoff. You can never be sure."

"What? You mean because it sounds Jewish or Russian?"

"Take your pick."

"You know what you are, Belden?"

"Yes, the same thing as you are, Richard Talpa. We're in the same business, and in this business there are enemies."

"I'll remember that." He hung up without waiting to see if Belden had anything more to say.

"So this is your bedroom?" Amy said from the doorway.

He looked at her, wondering how long she had been there. "Yup," he said, "I was hoping you'd get to, er, see it soon."

"Not tonight, I'm afraid. I'm up to my tukas in homework. No rest for the wicked or the med student."

"Okay by me. I have a lot of work to do, too. You go back to drooling over your anatomy texts while I—sniff, sniff—am

stuck here alone, trying to get some cold computer in Sing-
apore to talk nice to me."

He worked through the night.

* * *

By the end of the month Amy still had not stayed over, and
Rich had still not gotten into the right computers. The
Company, always impatient, sent Belden to check up on him
again.

"I thought you said you could work your way through any
security program, Talpa. Can't you get the password?"

"On this system, Belden, there is no password."

"There has to be a way for their own agents to get in. How
else can they work out the arms deals? The system has to be
secure."

"There are tricks a lot better than secret passwords,
Belden. I think this one uses a jazzy new technique called a
zero-knowledge algorithm." He saw Belden's eyebrow twitch
upward. "See, their computer has a little conversation with
your computer. If your computer doesn't answer a thousand
quick questions exactly right, you're cut off. And even if you
listen in on somebody else's questions, you can never know
what all the yeses and no's are about."

"Maybe Poleax is really secure. Or maybe it would take the
NSA to get into this."

"All they have in Virginia is brute force. We got brains. I
have a way."

"You MIT kids always think you have a way."

Rich thought it was funny being called a kid by someone
ten years younger than he was. "Well, if you don't have a key
to the garage, how do you get in?" He waited, but Belden just
stared. "You wait until somebody drives out."

Belden frowned.

"Look, Belden, don't think you guys are the only ones who
can use a mole. I have my own, now, a little program that sits
inside a computer at Dowd Limited, one of the systems—an

unsecured system—that the Poleaxe network has to talk with. Next time the network calls, my program calls me, and we're in business."

The door rattled and Belden jerked. It was Amy again. She always seemed to be bumping into Belden, as if she knew when he stopped in for his little progress reports. She smiled at him coldly, then kissed Rich on the forehead.

"Her own key now?" Belden asked him.

"Don't I wish. No I just lent it to her while she was running errands for me. It's not what you think."

"Whatever. See me out." Belden strode toward the door with Rich whirring along behind. At the end of the hall Belden said in a low voice, "Don't trust her. We can't risk you coming under the influence of someone who might compromise your function, Rich. Remember this. Get your priorities straight. We don't like to lose good people."

But Richard was already under her influence, and each time he saw her, the doubts about his work began to grow.

"I know what I'm doing," he told her, trying to convince himself. "What I'm doing really means something, now. I've always wanted to matter, to make a difference. Growing up on the Boston's North End with four sisters and five brothers, I was just another smart-mouthed Italian runt. But I kept pushing and pushing and made it across the river. I was going to college, MIT, the best. Then bang, Nam, and bang—and I do mean kabang!—and I'm back home. But it took me seven years of school to do four years of work, then seven thousand dumb computer programs before I got someplace. Now I get to do something that actually matters."

"Really? Didn't you give enough for your country?" She was avoiding looking down where the rest of his legs should have been.

"My country has done plenty for me, too. I fought in that war to end it, and I fought to end it when I got back. But I've always been on our side, always loved this place. Sure I lost something, but I gained something, too. And I can take care of myself. Can you tell me where else a nameless, no-leg nobody could have all this and be hacking around, doing puzzles for a living."

"Puzzles, huh? I don't think you should trust Belden or his company. What do you know about this company that has you under contract? Do they do business in South Africa? Are any of their subsidiaries manufacturing weapons? You want to build a better world, better be on the right side."

"I don't know what you're trying to do, Amy. Just let me do my job." Still, he wondered about that, about the right side, about whom to trust, though he kept working.

He was snoozing, upright, in his chair, when the "mole alarm" finally beeped at him. Amy was in the kitchen, but he knew this couldn't wait until she left. He started calling up small packets of computer code, sending them across the bridge that linked him to the host computer at Dowd. Once across, each was planted like a digital charge of plastique. On cue, each of them took out one function, cleanly and instantaneously. With his own programs securely in charge, he kept up a steady rattle on the keyboard until he was satisfied that everything was ready.

At the last instant, just as the Poleax computer was signaling to disconnect from the Dowd system, his programs sent a stream of special code through the connection.

The connection broke.

A week later, he made the Dowd system pretend it was searching for some data, thus holding the line open a few extra seconds. On the third try, he got Poleax to stay connected long enough for him to bury a tiny mole in its memory.

From then on, it was just hard work. He started getting a lot for Belden.

"I've got password access to a dozen systems around the globe. They change ciphers and passwords frequently, but I now have programs sitting in all the systems on this list. These digital moles just send us the new keys whenever new locks are installed."

Belden's face was unreadable. "Is there any way your little programs can be spotted?"

"Not likely unless someone already knew what they were looking for."

But the Poleax people were good, or they had their ways of finding things out. When his programs were spotted, Richard devised another scheme, replanted the programs, and started passing information to Belden again.

Enough was never enough for Belden, though. He insisted on coming over for a "live" demonstration.

"All right," said Rich, "I'll show you what we can do now." He tapped a few keys and the screen filled with columns of figures. "I do this, pull this from there, then all I have to do is connect back to Poleax through Datapac in Canada, and..." The screen went blank.

"Is that what was supposed to happen?"

"No way! I was going to show you how we could intercept a shipment of Kalashnikovs in the Middle East without ever leaving Somerville, but my mole in Poleax is gone."

"Look, I don't want you taking action like that, anyway. That's our job. I just want you to get information. So, keep trying ways to get through their security."

"How the hell did they find my code; it was scattered all over the place. They would have had to almost know where to look for it. And there's also some new protocol on the communications line. I'll have to find another way in."

He kept trying, he kept being outed, and he began to get discouraged. Amy became very interested in his moods and his work. He wished he could talk straight out with her about what he was doing, about his problems, but Belden's suspiciousness also touched him.

Amy knew he was troubled. "Wanna talk?" she asked one evening after Belden left.

"Can't, really: corporate confidentiality. See, I keep solving these, ah, programming problems, and for some reason my fixes keep ending up unfixed."

"Why don't you tell me more?"

"Too technical, you wouldn't understand."

She kept pushing, though, until he insisted they change the subject. When she left late, he decided to stay up later still to do some extra programming. He felt he had to find out which was the right side to be on. He knew he could trust his computers, but he wasn't too sure about anyone else.

* * *

Belden wasn't happy when he arrived the next day. "I thought I said no independent action. If you start screwing around on your own, you could interfere with another mission or run counter to some foreign policy initiative. Anyway, it's time some of your expertise got spread around. Show me how you did it?"

"Did what?" He played coy.

"Diverted the arms shipment that was headed for Central America."

"Okay, okay. I'll show you how I did that and how to undo it, too."

He turned on his systems and set out to dazzle Belden with a demonstration of what computer espionage could do. Belden took copious notes while Rich led him smoothly in and out of half a dozen computers scattered around the globe. It went without hitch.

By the time Belden left again, Rich wasn't sure just whom he could trust, but he was beginning to get a feeling about whom he couldn't trust. Belden had to be dogging his electronic heels awfully closely to have picked up on the diverted shipment so quickly. He needed to be careful. He checked his voice mail, then patched together a new message for it. He painstakingly keyed a new fifty-four digit cipher key into his encryption modem before getting back into Poleax. When he logged off the system, he cleared the middle of the room, took his table lamps and put them on the floor, and checked the charge in his chair batteries. Then he took a nap.

When he woke up it was already dark outside. His voice mail system said there was a message, but he had slept so soundly that he had not even heard the phone ring. Now he wished he had remembered to disconnect it while he napped. The incoming message file had only a click and a long dial tone on it. It always annoyed him when people did that; now it made him uneasy. Who had called? His mother? Belden?

There was no time to reconsider his plans, because Belden showed up only minutes later.

"You certainly don't seem to understand trust, Richard," he said as soon as he closed the door. "That was some demonstration you put on for me, only none of it was real, was it. A simulation, you computer types call it, I believe. You made it look like we were communicating with other systems, but all the while it was just a sham."

Richard slumped. "How did you find out it was a loopback?"

"I checked. Your phony shipment of sewing machines never left port."

Richard leaned forward over his keyboard. "Really? But I could have sworn…"

The phone started ringing, but Belden shook his head vigorously and waived Rich away. Richard's voice could be heard coming from the console as the voice mail program picked up. "This is Richard Talpa's phone domo. Just leave word at the beep."

It beeped and Amy's voice came on, a little hoarse, a little choppy, as if she were out of breath. "Richard, pick up if you're there. I know what's happening. If you don't answer I'm coming—with help."

Belden looked at the machine and shook his head again. "It won't work, Talpa. I know you have everything computerized. You made the phone ring. The computer no doubt just played a message that you made earlier by editing together bits of her voice."

"Well, for a Harvard man, Belden, you aren't too dumb."

"You're not too dumb, either, Talpa. You're just working for the wrong side." He set his attaché case on the glass coffee table and opened it so that Richard couldn't see what he was reaching for. "Wasn't there a saying at MIT?" he asked. "You can't win, you can't break even..."

"...you can't even get out of the game without paying," Richard finished for him.

"Indeed, how true, and yet you seem to want to get out of this game, Talpa."

Richard jerked as the door intercom chimed. "It's Amy. Open up Rich, I brought some friends with me."

Belden smiled weakly. "I'm not fooled, Mr. Talpa; there's nobody at the door. You have everything rigged to that computer: why not the intercom? Just give me the keyboard."

"You're right," he said, handing the keyboard across and squeezing the spacebar as he did.

The lights went out. Richard toggled the wheelchair control past the detent, and the chair lurched ahead. Above the whine, the whoomp of a small caliber pistol with a silencer was barely audible. Richard fell forward out of the chair and rolled to the side. The motorized chair kept going as Belden emptied his clip in the direction of the sound. Even in high gear the chair didn't move terribly fast, but, with its motor, batteries, and electronics, it weighed in at two-hundred-plus even without Richard. It crunched into Belden, knocking him off his feet, and groaned as it pinned him against the wall.

Richard found one of the table lamps in the dark and smashed it over the general region where he thought Belden's head might be. He held his breath.

Wood splinters peppered him as the door gave way under the impact of well-placed boots. Amy pushed in ahead of a tank of a man who grabbed for Belden while she turned on the lights and bent over Richard.

"You all right, Rich?"

"Yeah, how did you know to come here?"

"Your phony voice mail message, silly. When I heard my own voice recorded as if I were calling in, I knew this was it. I grabbed Greg and we hightailed it over." She nodded toward the still unconscious Belden. "Looks like you really can take care of yourself. So tell me what's happening, Mr. Macho."

"I guess I'll have to trust you," he said. "I've been spying, I guess you'd call it. Thought I was working for some sort of commercial front for the CIA or something. But Belden was on the other side, working for a network of arms traders and agitators, the Poleax people, whoever they were. Instead of spying on Poleax, I was being used by them to hack their own system so they could beef up security."

"How did you figure out who Belden was?"

"I wasn't absolutely sure when he left here this afternoon. So I put some data into the Poleax computer that said a particular shipment of arms had never left port. Never touched the shipment, just put the data into the Poleax system. I used a new cipher to talk to my program in their computer. There wasn't time for anyone intercepting it to break it. Only someone relying on direct access to Poleax would think the shipment had been blocked.

"I thought I was clever, but I couldn't fool Belden with that voice mail message. I'd hoped to scare him into running; it probably only would have scared him into killing me."

The police arrived, talked for a few minutes with Amy and her companion, Greg, then left with Grant Belden in tow.

Greg helped Amy get Rich back into his chair. The acrid smell of hot insulation still drifted up from the motor. "Well, hotshot, I'll leave you to Sarnoff, here," he said. "And don't worry about the paperwork on this one, Sarnoff. We can take care of it at the office tomorrow."

Amy smiled at him and nodded, then turned to Rich. "Well, welcome to our side, Richard Talpa."

"I don't understand."

"You like this armchair espionage stuff. I'm recruiting you. For the real Company, the CIA. What's not to understand?"

He snorted. "You? I should have known. My mother told me, never trust a med student who doesn't know what a constantan catheter is. I suppose this means no fraternization if we're going to be working on the same team."

"Oh, no, that was before, when we couldn't be sure whose side you were on. So, is there something you wanted to show me, Mr. Mole?"

There was, and he did.

This darker early work accumulated an impressive stack of encouraging rejections. It is another story that looks into the unintended consequences of seemingly safe technology without apparent side effects.

Tourist Trap

Buzz. Fuzz. Stay awake. Programming parameters danced around Jaron Desker. He grabbed a pirouetting number, hammering it into place in his head before pounding it out on the keyboard. Turn, change, run. Run. RUN SIMULOG.

The display painted itself with the same misshapen polygon it had on the previous six runs of the program. Jaron jabbed savagely at the workstation, pulling his punch just short of the leering screen. "I need a vacation, that's it. That's it. I have to crawl out of this damned model and go somewhere else."

At the other desk, Nedda's usually cryptic face flashed something just short of panic. "You can't take off now," she said. "I can't debug those modules alone. You did all the analysis and half the design, and I don't care how clean you think your code is, Jaron Desker, I will not wade through seventeen thousand lines of your Modula mutterings without you."

Jaron fumbled behind the big color display unit to turn it off, then put a patronizing hand on her shoulder. "Nedda, I know we promised TesCon they could start gaming with the model by next month. I wouldn't dump it all on you. Since there's really no time right now, I was thinking of going to a T-Agent." Nedda whistled. "Now, Nedda, don't get any ideas

109

about changing our platonic working relationship into one where you drain my bankcard as I callously exploit your body. I don't have that much in my account. My cousin's a T-Agent. He'll discount and spread the debits over a couple years."

"Will Sendra be going with you, then?" Nedda asked.

"Separate vacations. We can't afford the extra cost of synch. Besides, our styles are so different. Sendra would rather sit in Minoa the whole time; I'm more the 'grand tour' type."

"I'm not sure I'd approve. I mean, does she feel okay about, about what people do when traveling?"

"Nedda Steiner, don't tell me you're old fashioned. What you do off track is nobody's business." Jaron headed for the door. "Anyway, my cousin Hert is up on Beta Mall. Think I'll get Sendra to tube up and we can check it out now."

* * *

Hert Mallon's fingers talked as he spoke, almost as if he were making some spastic translation for the hearing impaired. His enthusiasm seemed to shoot like bits of St. Elmo's fire from the tips of his fingers.

"You are going to love it. This is the way, the only way, to spend a holiday. You can spend ten days on five tracks and come back within twenty four hours of departure. And while you are there—wherever there is—you can do anything, absolutely anything. Nothing you do on any other track has any consequences here, the real world, track null, as we say in the travel business." He winked toward Jaron.

Sendra worked her mouth in intricate contortions as she nervously shuffled brochures. "Can I, can I just stay put? You know, just relax on an island or something? Get a tan?"

Hert smiled at her, drew a finger along her pale arm, and said, "Certainly. Sheffield winters get to you, don't they. I'm American myself, other branch of Jaron's family, moved here from D.C. twenty some ago. For a package price, you can sleep in at a paradise while Jaron goes cavorting through time and space. You won't meet each other, can't meet each other, not even anyone you know. The accessible tracks are almost infinite. Everyone gets his own little world."

Sendra put on what Jaron thought of as her anxious-dumb look. "What do we do? I'm not good with tech stuff like Jaron."

"All taken care of for you. You wear a belt like this. It's a bender—time space track bender, to be stuffy about it—and it has only two controls. The little green switch here is your sequencer. If you contract for multiple tracks, any time you find one getting tiresome, a simple twist of the wrist and you're in a whole new world. Can't back up, of course, since a certain indeterminacy is involved in the track indexer."

Sendra bit her lip. "How do we get back, then?"

"Oh, that's a lock. The index crystal sort of 'remembers' its original shape. That corresponds to a vibrational pattern unique to our track through space-time. Release the torsion bending the index crystal, and it homes the mechanism on us right here. Under this red lid is a large red button you can use anytime and you'll find yourself right back here. Or nearby. Within a day or two of your guaranteed return." He smiled greasily. "Could be used to get out of sticky spots. Naturally, your holiday is terminated at that point and our contractual obligations are discharged the moment of your return."

Jaron felt obligated to ask some questions, though he was already sold. "There's no real risk, is there?"

"No, no, of course not. We have all that gibberish in our contracts just to satisfy the government. Regulations, you know. There has been only the slightest increase in 'no homes' in the twenty seven years track bending has been used by travelers. And millions go, more every year. Still, the odds are immensely favorable that you will arrive at tracks never before visited and unaffected by other travelers. Virginal, one might say."

Jaron thought of that as he signed the debit authorizations. He could do whatever he liked. It was really just fantasy. Everything would be just so when he came back. Not

111

that he planned to pillage and plunder, though stories had been written about other travelers. No, but some lusty adventure would certainly make it easier to return to a life building metamath economic models at Barton, Soames and Hollis, and to a life building just about zip with Sendra and the boys.

* * *

Jaron left the road to check out the limestone monolith that erupted from the gently rolling land. Except for the brief ride with the two untalkative lorry drivers, he had been walking since he arrived. Though he was tired, a boyish exuberance filled him as he reached the base of the cliff. He decided to climb.

This was not exactly the revels he had dreamt of when planning the trip, but the climb was seductive in its own way. He chimneyed up the last few meters of a crevice and struggled over the rim. He was awed that so tiny a country could seem so vast. The midlands arrayed themselves below him, mound after rolling mound of deep green, speckled by scattered grey outcroppings. He stood and turned, watching the world slowly turn about him until, the second or third time around, he noticed the girl. What was she doing here? Slender, with coffee and cream hair, more beige than blonde, she sat meditating on the view. Not English, no. Human? Apparently. Beautiful? Yes.

"I watched you come across," she said, pointing. "Seems though you knew where you were going, but you seem a stranger, too."

"I've often trotted 'round a place much like this. Looking for something. Yes. Are you looking?"

She smiled at him and he noticed her eyes, bright pink, like those of the men in the lorry. Pink and warm. Jaron smiled back as he begin to tell her his wonderful lies, pink lies, wonderful, warm pink lies to share. And when the day itself was no longer warm nor pink, they shared wonderful, warm pink touches.

Three times Jaron met her in the countryside, three times before he grew restless and twisted the sequence switch on the bender to take him to the next stop. He didn't care that when he jumped the track he was in full view of a nameless girl from an unnamed country. He would never be back to that unreal reality, nor would anyone else. She and her world would simply be a fond holiday memory; he imagined he would be something like that to her.

The festival he stumbled into on the second track held his attention longer. There were many girls, many boys, many pleasures in that odd city on a mountainside. Jaron found he liked the plain, squat inhabitants of the city, though he never learned their names nor more than a handful of their words. In the carnival, there were few uses for words: a raised hand would bring a glass of bright orange ale; a wink and a tilt of the head would draw a lover to your bed. What an exhilarating coincidence, it seemed to Jaron, that here, in this chance drawn city at an unselected time, a week long feast should be in progress. So total was the rapturous celebration that none took notice of his height nor seemed to make much of his strange language. Of course, there were other strangers in the city, as one would expect during carnival. From time to time he would glimpse someone across the street, someone who appeared as tall as he, but he was never able to push through the crowd before the other vanished into some store or one of the smoky, crowded taverns.

When he awoke one morning with a loud humming buzz in his head and found a littered, desolate street outside his window, he twisted the sequence knob again.

Nothing happened.

He was about to push the home button in panic, when the innkeeper appeared. The innkeeper grunted something and held both pudgy hands upturned toward Jaron. Jaron reached into the pouch at his belt and fumbled for one of the synthetic gems Hert had given him. He dropped a large green one into the innkeeper's hands. The man grunted again before dropping

113

to his knees. Reaching under the bed, he withdrew what appeared to be a large coil of wire, fiddled with it, then stood up. The humming had stopped.

The whole business puzzled Jaron. He wished now he had learned some of the language, for the inn keeper kept repeating some phrase as he pointed toward Jaron's belly. Jaron shrugged, then casually twisted the sequence switch. This time the strange tugging began immediately.

* * *

Jaron was struck in the face by a sheet of flame. He threw his arms up to shield his eyes, but there was no light, only the burning now on his bare arms. He turned and curled into a ball. Windblown ice pelted his back. He tore off the cover of the home switch and punched it sharply. He was pulled from the storm.

* * *

He was not home. This was clear immediately. He stood on a macadam road crossing a treeless plain. Wrong place, right track? He wondered. Heat made the road turn to water in the distance. A ship plied those waters and steamed noisily toward him. He watched with detached interest as it approached, resolved itself into an omnibus, then roared on past him.

He hit the home button again. The tugging came and went, but the desolate landscape didn't even waver. On the theory that the device might need to recharge or otherwise have some sort of latency period, he resolved not to use the bender again that day. Flipping a mental coin, he started to walk toward where the bus had long since vanished into shimmering, illusory seas.

He walked until dark. Then, because a moon glared redly down on him and there was nothing else for him to do, he kept walking, hunching down from the sudden cold and from the strange shame he felt being watched by so many unfamiliar stars. His walking had slowed to a shuffle when the helicopter came, spotlights and slashing blades fencing with the night. It landed nearly on top of him, squarely on the macadam.

"You right, mate?" an amplified voice asked him.

"Yes!" he shouted, though he doubted he could be heard above the screaming engine. Two men helped him into an extra seat and fumbled with his bender as they fastened a safety around him. They flew without talking until a bloated sun bubbled up over distant mountains. By its light, Jaron could see a vast lake with a small city on its shore, a city of stark buildings and spindly towers.

They slowly spun down to the roof of a windowless tower where they were met by a service crew in forest green uniforms. The crew seemed uninterested in the helicopter, though, and when Jaron was led toward them, half crouching under the blades, he had the sudden urge to run. Their gentle smiles disarmed him, however, and when they gestured to him, he followed toward the featureless penthouse on the rooftop. A hairline crack slowly widened to become the sliding doors of an elevator.

"Where are we going? I need to get back in touch with Mallon Travel in Sheffield," Jaron said. At the word "travel," his companions exchanged a glance of recognition but still said nothing. When the doors finally opened again, he was pushed out without a word; they closed once more, leaving a barely visible line to mark an otherwise smooth wall.

Jaron noticed a humming buzz, somehow familiar, at first almost inaudible. As it built in intensity, he remembered the inn during the carnival and decided to use the bender while he still could. He pushed the red button again.

* * *

It was a city.

He was in a side street, an alley, peopled by large bins and boxes. It could have been Sheffield, it could have been Boston. It could be this year, any year. But he couldn't read the labels

115

on the cartons. Almost right. Not quite. Jaron started to run, but no one pursued him.

The narrow canyon of the alley opened suddenly onto a tiered plaza. Many-colored light fell across his face, raucous voices scraped his ears, and the city's thick air burned his lungs. Jaron forced himself to stroll casually out into the crowds, trying to slow his breathing. If something was wrong with his bender, he would have to find some way of getting it fixed. Would anyone in this track know how to do it? He didn't know. Maybe someone in digital electronics. He spotted what looked to be a computer store almost directly across the plaza, a stylishly spartan outlet with two squat beige systems on display in the window. Not much chance of finding help there, he thought, but he headed for it anyway.

Inside he could hear heavily accented English, thick and guttural. A bland, boyish salesman was finishing his pitch, explaining to a customer in terse, almost comprehensible half sentences, what his top-of-the-line machine could do. "Just curiosity," Jaron interjected, "Does anyone here know anything about T-track bending, about repairing a defunct bender?"

The salesman scowled perceptibly. "Never heard. At a Sysco, maybe? Old mag disk store, be. In back, digitech, ken T-track, be. Willcall." He left abruptly for the back of the store, returning several minutes later accompanied by two men. They were dressed almost identically in high collared suits of forest green.

"May I see the unit, please, Mr. Desker?" one of them asked, reaching toward Jaron's waist. Jaron was about to explain that the bender wasn't detachable, when he became aware of the perfect midlands accent. He grabbed for his waist, but a pair of hands instantly gripped each of his wrists. "Mr. Desker, there are some people who have been looking for you." He nodded toward the front slider just opening. The woman who paused within the doorway, preventing the slider from closing, wore the same forest green. She carried a folio in one hand and an object resembling a torch in the other. Her hair flowed like light coffee over her shoulders.

"My mother led an unhappy life," she said, as if she had just mentioned the weather. "She was raped when she was a young girl. Oh, not brutally, no. Perhaps even gently, but she was raped, nonetheless, by a traveler who left her with a daughter and nothing else. She was seventeen. The traveler's age cannot be computed, since he bends time and space as he bends words to suit his pleasures."

Jaron spoke, his voice pinched with uncertainty, "I don't understand. How, I mean? This is another track. How are you here?"

"Are the men of your 'track' the only ones with minds, the only ones with passions? And tell me: are holiday pleasures ever pursued with the same energy one pursues justice? Or revenge?"

She leaned close to his face. She was quite beautiful, this older woman with hair like warm cocoa and eyes like gray ice. Jaron's eyes misted with fear. Inches away, she slowly closed her fist until her nails dug bloody furrows into her palm. She smeared her hand across his cheek. "It's real, Mr. Desker."

"But I'm only..."

"Ah, yes, 'only.' Were you going to say only a tourist? Yes, only out for fun. Only one of many. One of too many. There must be great throngs of travelers for so many to have visited our time and small world. Or perhaps your theories are no match for your appetites. It seems that experience builds only very slowly when it builds from the exploitative use of technology. It grows even more slowly when it is built of the incredible tales of young girls, of simple peasants, or of bereaved kin. Still, we learned, slowly separating the monsters of our own making from those of yours.

"Now we bend the continuum as well as you, Mr. Desker." She exchanged smiles with her two companions. "Let's get him back to T-nought," she sighed.

117

They escorted him outside, still holding his hands well away from his body. Carefully, they locked his wrists to a bar behind his back, then pushed him toward a small vehicle waiting at the kerb. Jaron arched his back and threw himself in desperation toward the car. Had he lunged to either side, he might have been stopped, but the instincts of his captor's were not prepared for his forward plunge. He caught the half-opened door square in the stomach, smashing into the button in the center of the bender. As the insistent tug of the bender began, he prayed that the jump would be enough.

* * *

He looked around the plaza. The green marble was right. The sign on the Bannacid Building was right. The indomitable breeze squeezing between the buildings was right. Jaron relaxed slightly. It seemed right this time.

Jaron spun around again getting his bearings, then started strolling toward the northeast corridor. He reached the Hollis Building determined to tell his cousin the whole story of his trip. The lobby was all but deserted. When he tapped the lift call for the T-Agent, the operator's screen lit up. The woman in the lift with him looked over his shoulder at the banner head being displayed.

"The T-Agent is Closed," she read aloud as she took off her cap, letting fall the cascades of her coffee colored hair.

A Distant Flight of Gulls

Other than the sound, the Amsterdam Station gave no outward hint of the whirling violence within its polished walls. From the catwalk winding along the side of the intake tube, the muffled fluttering was uncomfortably loud. It reminded Lloyd Rundqvist of the sound of a flock of sea gulls startled on the beach, a thousand wings beating skyward. The image of those upward spiraling scavengers seemed singularly fitting.

Rundqvist leaned a bony elbow onto the railing and studied the only motion visible in the entire dome. The readouts on a large display panel winked lethargically at him, announcing in blue-green numerals the inconsequential little instabilities in one of the largest Rundqvist Anomalies in the world. Rundqvist feigned a scientist's interest in the display, but the upcoming festivities had stirred a covey of distracting memories.

He watched, thinking back to a time some twenty years earlier when the Rundqvist Anomalies had been no more than a set of ill-behaved integrals in an issue of *The Journal of High Velocity and Mathematical Physics*. He remembered when they were first able to sustain an anomaly long enough to see the light wave perturbations predicted by theory. Now, ten meters above his head the spun titanium cone appeared to shimmer as

119

though seen through a sparkling curtain, confirming the theory all over again. That would have been enough for him then, simple visual vindication; it would be enough still. But the Amsterdam Station surrounded him in an excess of proof.

The six stainless steel intake tubes joined like gargantuan bicycle spokes at the vortex, the polished metal bottle of the oldest and largest of the five Kedgel-Rundqvist machines serving New York City. The fluttering noise that filled the Amsterdam Station was an artifact of the irregular off-hours input to its oversized vortex. The four other solid-waste management facilities were smaller because they were equipped with the new Thompson variable-velocity vortex and could meet peak demand simply by increasing their intake flow.

Abel Thompson would be at the awards banquet. Rundqvist smiled, remembering the man as a young engineer, an out-to-save-the-world grad student, ever eager for the quickest translation of new theory into new technology. To Thompson, only technology was a fit messiah for technologically bedeviled humankind. And Thompson had never stopped preaching that gospel.

Rundqvist was quite sure that both he and Anna Kedgel, on the other hand, would have been content just building computer models until the Rundqvist Anomalies were explained away. The two of them would have been at it still. There had been advances, of course, but definitive solutions still eluded the physicists and mathematicians. Rundqvist was the first to admit that science could not fully explain the gulping behemoth that daily ate the city's offal and refuse. That did not stop the engineers, though. Their ad hoc solutions contained the vortex and kept it stable. They needed no theoretical explanations. It was enough that it worked, Thompson would say.

Thompson's first working model had seemed like a pointless exercise. As the anomaly formed, Thompson kept bobbing back and forth, leaning over to get a closer look at the vortex, then reaching back to make an adjustment on the kludge of controls spread across the lab table. Without an on-line computer hookup to control the equipment directly, opening the anomaly and keeping it stable had required considerable dial twisting. Thompson simply wouldn't wait for them to finish the programming. Still, even ever-imperturbable Anna had squealed and laughed when the titanium cone began to scintillate like a bad television picture.

"We did it!" Thompson kept saying. "There it is. We did it!"

Rundqvist could think of nothing to say to Thompson then. That had changed little in the intervening years, and he hoped for only the briefest encounter at the banquet. But Anna could always handle Thompson.

* * *

"So, hotshot? What shall we do with it?" she had asked. "We should smoke herring on the magnet?" Thompson responded with an offended look; the tendency of his magnets to overheat was a sore point with him.

Anna didn't stop. "What good is a four-inch anomaly in the basement of the Compton Labs? We can keep it going until the magnet smokes blue, but what do we do with it?"

For a moment Abel Thompson looked as if he might run from the lab. "Well, we could, we could, uh, we could test it. Yeah! We could put something into it to test the time-space distortion. Here," he handed Anna the glass ashtray in which he had nervously stubbed his cigarette. "Put this in. Just drop it in."

She did.

Rundqvist stretched to peek over the rim just in time to see the ashtray shrink into nothingness, ashes and all. As he reached to put his hand over the top of the cone, Abel grabbed his wrist.

"Be careful, it really works."

"Of course it does. I just wanted to feel the air. There should be a flow into the cone as air is obliterated in the vortex." He grinned when he felt the draft. "Maybe you can do a curve fit for air velocity versus field strength."

* * *

And Abel had done it. Two months later he installed a new fume hood in the lab using a scaled-up anomaly that sucked up air at some nine-hundred cubic feet per minute along with anything else not anchored down. The power input was a modest eighty kilowatts. Although the fume hood would never be practical, Abel soon learned that the secret to application of the Rundqvist theory was in economies of scale.

The fortuitous disposal of the glass ashtray became a paradigm. After graduation, Thompson immediately joined one of the larger aerospace firms and convinced them to develop a functioning solid-waste disposal system for a small town. It consumed little more power than the impractical fume hood.

Returning his attention to the present, Rundqvist blinked away memories. A steady read-out on the display panel for the Amsterdam Station showed an excess of a thousand kilowatts of usable power. The largest Kedgel-Rundqvist machines were self-sustaining; this one even produced a token energy surplus. The thermodynamics made mathematical sense to anyone willing to grind through the equations, but they defied intuition. Rundqvist wasn't bothered. Someplace in the galaxy hydrogen atoms were winking into existence. Why shouldn't a few on Manhattan wink out of existence, kicking back some random electrons in the process?

"Lloyd! Lloyd!"

He turned to see a woman with hair the color and texture of steel wool climbing up to the catwalk. "Anna, what brings you here? Homage to the demon?"

She took his arm. "Still bothered, aren't you, Lloyd? It's not enough that because of you cities like New York are saved,

saved from being buried in the effluent of their affluence." She still loved to play with words.

"Ah, but salvation has come too easily. This way Manhattan can afford to keep growing when it really should be settling into a mature decline."

"But Lloyd," she looked at him with exaggerated seriousness, "where else could you choose among twenty-four thousand restaurants?"

"Where indeed? Would you join me for dinner at this great little Afghani place up on Central Park West? We ought to get some decent food tonight. It will be the standard rubber-chicken-and-peas fare at the dinner tomorrow."

She wrinkled her nose. "I would, but I really hoped to find you here for another reason. I was planning to visit the lab." She paused in anticipation of a response that didn't come. "The lab, our lab. You know, where we started all this?"

"What a marvelous thought! When you came in I was reminiscing. The Beaumont Prize coming up has put me in that mood. Been thinking about Thompson and his aerospace gee-whiz kids, too."

"Does it irk you to share the Beaumont in Ecology with Abel?"

"No. Well, maybe a little. Not sharing it, really, but I had always dreamed of getting the Nobel in Physics. I am a physicist, you know, a good one, too. This thing," he patted the tube carrying garbage to its Armageddon, "is better physics than ecology. Even with highly regulated use, there is such a substantial loss of mass. That could have many detrimental effects."

"But Lloyd," she sighed, "we've been through all this before. The ninety-two systems in use would have to operate for centuries to effect a mass loss with even measurable geophysical effects."

"How many systems? Ninety-two? That's up eleven in two years. At that rate...no, wait," he put his hands up to fend off interruption. "Look, I know the International Ecology Commission is overseeing all this with a jaundiced eye. I guess I really worry more about the physics, the theory. Or the lack."

"Lloyd, urgent human problems can't wait for the refinement of elegant mathematical models."

"You sound so much like Abel Thompson that I can't answer you, Anna."

"Then it's time for us to drop it, Lloyd. But just remember how different the environmental picture is now than when we started working on this. We don't misuse technology, and we don't let technology use us. We've learned. Now," she said, "let's forget twenty-three years and go poke around in the old lab."

* * *

City College still owed much to their reputations, though Rundqvist was retired and Anna Kedgel had moved on to the Chair in Mathematical Physics at UCLA. They had little trouble getting the night guard to let them in once they showed him the story in the *Times*. It actually took more persuading to get him to leave them alone.

"Everything's changed," Anna said with noticeable disappointment.

"Not quite," Lloyd said as he settled into a swivel chair and put his feet up on the metal desk. "Same old ugly green desk. These things must last forever. Here," he motioned to a second chair, "relax, put your feet up. You deserve it."

Anna obliged, and both leaned back in a quiet reverie. It was interrupted by a sudden clank.

"What's that?"

They both swiveled in their chairs. On the floor lay an inverted glass ashtray. A column of cigarette ashes was drifting lazily toward it.

For a couple of years I participated in a writer's workshop in Cambridge, and this is one of the pieces that benefited from the collective critique.

Motherhood Becomes Lee

Ten seconds out of the shower and already Faron was shivering. The fine blonde fuzz on his arms and back stood at futile attention. It was never quite warm enough on Kohlehrets, not for Faron Davidov. Nine generations of men had engineered more than one near miracle in the unplanned colony, but tepid was the best they seemed able to produce for the living quarters. It had been a cold world before it had a name, before it was hurriedly chosen over the roaring hellfire of Aleph. It was still just a chilly chunk of rock, and after a morning shower, the thought of Aleph's lakes of molten lead seemed almost inviting to Faron.

The chill didn't seem to bother Lee, though.

Faron leaned back against the glazed heatwall, feeling its hard warmth against his skin, enjoying the meager geothermal heat squeezed from the tiny planet's lukewarm core. He watched Lee in the mirror. Stubborn traces of cobalt in the old glass gave a bluish cast to the image, darkening the reflection of Lee's long, cinnamon hair. Faron was almost overcome with tenderness for his partner, who stood there naked, magnificently pregnant.

"Would you cover for me at Botanics during second shift?" Lee asked, never turning from the mirror. "I have to go to Obstet."

125

"Tonight? I thought—" He stopped. He had been thinking about spending time with a friend, forgetting his priorities, forgetting how vulnerable a mother-to-be was. "I thought I might bring home a vid chip. We could watch one together after-shift."

Lee turned to look at him with a soft, melting smile. "That's really duke. Thanks."

Motherhood becomes Lee, Faron thought. Pregnancy did something to the face, smoothing it, warming it with an inner glow. He studied Lee, picturing himself years younger and carrying Andrew, swimming in a remembered mix of odd discomforts and delicious anticipations. Faron pushed aside the inky later memories.

"No regrets?" he asked Lee.

"Have you spent too much time starside again? If I had any, they'd be for having waited so long." He padded heavily across the foam-matted floor. "Like most men, I guess I grew up taking it for granted that someday I would be pregnant. I never realized how fantastic it would be, you know, weird and wonderful at the same time. Gods, he sure is alive and kicking this morning," he said, hand to his belly.

"That's because he, for one, is warm!" said Faron, tugging blue-grey coveralls over the paunchy reminder of his own three pregnancies.

Lee laughed and scratched his hairy belly. It itched, as it had from the first day after implantation, right over the site on the inside of his abdominal wall. "I think I'm carrying funny. You think I'm carrying funny? Maybe the implanttation was too far to the side."

Faron snorted. "You're a fusser, Lee, you are. The last weeks are like this: never feels right. We just aren't built for it. When I was carrying Mahrk I had to piss every five minutes. The last three weeks I had gut cramps, worse even than the gas blats from your dammed bean stew."

"Hey, cleans out the pipes, blows them clean." He grinned and paused. "Faron, do you think I'll be a good mother?"

Faron reached over and folded his rough hands around Lee's. "Some men are, some aren't. With you, it's a lock: you got me for an example. I didn't do so bad with Andrew, did I? Or Mahrk. I'd even bet that Mahrk will settle down once he has a child. His brother did." Faron caught himself. He knew Mahrk could never be what Andrew had been. Mahrk, who was on his third partner in four years, who had dropped out of Thermics, was fired up about standing for election to the Bridge, dreaming of leading the Biotechnist League into power. Faron, by contrast, dreamed of grandchildren.

"What if," Lee started to say, but words for the unthinkable eluded him.

"You can't polish a rock that hasn't been mined, Lee. Just wait it out."

Faron finished dressing, shoved an extra soy-bar in his pocket, and hurried out into the noisy tunnel. Lee shouted after him, a reminder about covering for him in Botanics, and Faron waved back a nodding "yes" with his fist.

Lee clumsily tried to hurry, but just the awkward dance he needed to wiggle into his maternity clothes tired him. Then he had to piss again. By the time he'd walked the slidebelt to the Botanics Branch, his supervisor had already checked him in and was waiting, holding out an oversized lab smock for him. He patted Lee's stomach, a familiarity that Lee had learned came with being pregnant. "Got a name for him yet, Leevi?" he asked.

"Yeah, Hahrl, I'm naming him Evan, after his grand-mother. Evan MacLeevi. Sounds better than Evan Leevison, don't you think."

Hahrl grunted. "Good historical name: Evan. Was your mother related to First Mother Evan? No? Say, did I tell you about what Von did with our vid link?" Hahrl was one of those men who never stopped talking about his kids, but Lee was not in the mood. He lied and said he'd heard the story, then excused himself. Already his back ached and his feet were swollen. He wanted to lie down, but lying down was tiring,

127

too. Finding a filebox to sit on, he turned on the notereader and started going over the last hybrid bean yields.

He began to get anxious when Faron didn't show up between shifts, but he kept working until the half-shift bell sounded. With no time to wait for a transit car, Lee buzzed for a payrider and made straight for Obstet. It was a popular time to be pregnant. The seats in the waiting room were filled with men in their bright blue and yellow maternity coveralls.

About the time Lee thought he couldn't take another minute on his feet, a red-faced medit peeked into the room. "Ho, Leevi, be with you in two jerks." Lee liked Streysen. He was competent, efficient, the kind of medit a mother-to-be had no trouble trusting. He was also chronically behind schedule. The two jerks turned into nearly an hour before the receptionist took Lee into one of the examining rooms. Streysen bounced in for a moment to say, "We're gonna sound you again," then vanished out a side door to another suite. A nurse, unknown to Lee but definitely a familiar breed, came in to set up for the exam.

"Up there. Sit." He pointed toward the table. Stiff paper crackled under Lee. "No. Clothes off."

The gel on the sounder head turned to cool slime as the nurse ran it over his belly. Streysen strolled in just in time to see a watery image painting itself on the screen. He hummed and grunted while it finished. "Can't get a clear image of all the parts, but he looks okay. Ugly like his mother, of course," he chided.

Streysen continued to grunt as they thumped and prodded Lee. "You're fine," he said, finally. "Some men just don't carry well, no matter how much tension-toning they do. But don't worry. Your son is big enough so we can move parturition up a week if needed. As they say, every baby needs his incubator. Thirty weeks or thirty-two, doesn't matter for granite. Let's see." He flipped through Lee's chart. "You're not due for another perfusion, but the peritoneal cell fraction is still not perfect. Wouldn't want to risk rejection. Have the nurse schedule a perfusion next week." Lee groaned. "Meantime, rest every hour, eat healthy, and wear that support. Yokay?" Lee shook his head and looked starside. When you were pregnant, everyone mothered you.

He dressed and left Obstet, only to stand for several minutes wondering whether to take the slidebelt home or to catch a car, then wondering why it seemed so damned important, and finally realizing that he was still hurt because Faron hadn't shown up to cover for him. The East Tunnel car would take him past the Repository where Robin barAnthony worked, and Robin was Lee's best guess about the cause of Faron's memory lapse.

Lee found Robin in the Ovarium, busy assisting a romantic couple who were obviously selecting their first egg. Robin finished with the Selection and started to program the harvesting. When he noticed Lee waiting for him, he stiffened. He was a friend to both Lee and Faron, but the romance was not with Lee.

"Thought you might know where Faron is, Robin?"

"Your intercom works, doesn't it? No, no. Delete that. I'm sorry. Haven't seen Faron in several weeks. I think he's had you on the top of his list. Good man, that. He'll make as good a father as he did mother. Hey, are you all right? You look flushed."

"Just having this funny hot feeling, right here," Lee answered, patting himself on the undercurve of his belly. "Just carrying lopsided, I guess."

"You want me to buzz for a payrider? I'm sure Faron's just been held over. He'll be along."

Suddenly, Lee sat down in the middle of the floor, his face contorted in pain.

* * *

Faron heard the page while he was still riffling through video chips at the archives. The mailbox at the desk replayed the page for him: "This is Robin. Just saw Lee and he asked me to tell you. Looks like he's herniated and they may have to go in now. If you can get right down to Obstet, I think it would be a good idea."

Faron stuffed a vid chip in his pocket without logging it out. He ran for the slidebelt, trying not to think about losing Lee.

* * *

Obstet was as busy as usual. Faron caught up with Lee in the crowded hall outside Delivery.

"Where were you?" There was hurt and accusation in Lee's voice.

"Oh, balls! I forgot, I forgot. Please forgive me."

"I forgot, I forgot," Lee mimicked. "You sound just like a father."

"Not yet," he said, eyeing the mound under the blanket.

Lee managed a groggy smile at him. "I told them they couldn't cut until you got here. Streysen says things are probably fine for the baby." As they started to wheel him toward the delivery room, Lee grabbed for Faron's hand, but one of the medits took Faron's forearm, stopping him from following.

"They're just going to tune for the spinal sonoblock and get Lee ready. We can wait out here, Mr. Davidov. Don't worry."

"You say don't worry, but my first pregnancy failed. Then my Andrew, my firstborn, he survived the depot collapse in '49 but died of peritonitis in his second pregnancy. Do you know what it's like to lose a child, your own flesh, someone you carried inside you? So I do worry, even if it's not a father's place to let it show." He pushed his way in.

By the time Medit Streysen arrived at Delivery, Lee had been prepped and draped, and Faron was seated by his head. Streysen started the surgery without even seeming to break stride.

"Right, almost. So. Drain the amnion. We'll lengthen this incision. Retractor. Yokay, here we are."

The only sound in the room was the soft rushing of the big micropore filters. Neither Lee nor Faron could see over the wall of sheeting that sliced Lee's midsection, so Faron got up from his stool and walked around. The medits were just standing there, looking at a purple infant in Streysen's hands. It was deformed.

"What is it, Faron? What's wrong?"

Faron knew he had to say it; they were always straight with each other. "Something's wrong with the baby. It doesn't have all its parts."

Streysen looked at him and shook his head. "No, it's perfect as far as we can tell. It's just not a boy."

"What? What do you mean?" Lee asked. Then it hit him. "How can that happen?" Even through the tranqs, panic leaked into his voice.

Streysen took Lee's hand. "I guess it can happen. The sperm separation must not be as perfect as we thought. I suppose it happened now and then in the early days, but I'm not exactly sure what the policy is anymore."

In the vacuum of indecision, habit and medical routine prevailed. The nurses got the baby breathing with a puff of oxygen, cleaned and bundled it, and handed the bundle to Faron, who seemed a little steadier than Lee. All wrapped up in the pale blue Obstet blanket, the baby was suddenly normal.

"Look's like you, Lee: got your mouth." Faron touched a finger to tiny rosebud lips. "I hope you kept up with the hormone tabs, because I think she's hungry." It seemed strange referring to a person as "she." Wrenches and tools were "she," Kohlehrets herself was a "she," but people were always "he."

* * *

131

After Obstet put Lee in one of the few private recovery suites, Faron took paternity leave to spend most of the next few days with him.

"Handsome kid, huh Faron?" Lee said, grinning at Evan in the incu-cart wheeled in beside the bed. Faron nodded. The nurse changing Evan's diaper was trying not to look between her legs. "I don't think that one likes Evan," Lee whispered.

Streysen swung into the room just as the nurse left. "Everything looks good, Lee. We're going to boot you out at shift-end today. You can still drop in to see the kid, of course."

"Why can't we just take her home in an incucart? That's the way it's still done, isn't it?" Faron asked.

Streysen's mouth worked a few seconds before he spoke. "Yeah, well, we want to keep this thing under control, you know, keep the baby under observation."

"There's nothing wrong with her, is there?"

"No, no. In fact, she probably doesn't need the incubator much at all. Look, I'm a medit. You guys want to rob me of the chance of a lifetime by taking this sleeping wonder away so soon?"

Lee wasn't satisfied. He wanted the baby with him. It was hard enough getting the milk up with Evan right there. Sliding back and forth between Obstet and the apartment would make it almost impossible. Faron charged off, saying he'd take care of everything.

He was back before shift-end, waving his closed fist. "I got it," he said, opening his hand to show a blue-coded magistrate's chip. "Obstet must either show medical cause or release the baby to us."

It wasn't that easy of course. The hospital challenged the order, so Faron insisted that the magistrate hold a hearing at Obstet immediately. Streysen, clearly trying to keep from being caught between his patients and the administration, let the chief-of-staff do the talking.

"So we're arguing non-viability outside a medical setting. Here we can protect the infant until we are absolutely confident it can survive and thrive." The chief-of-staff slapped his notereader closed.

"Are you saying you're uncertain how healthy the infant is? If you don't know, then how can you claim non-viability?"

"It's not just medical, it's a social issue, too. We don't know how people will react to a female infant. Some of the staff have refused to deal with her, and many who have not officially protested are clearly uncomfortable."

"Your staff problems are not an issue here," the magistrate said. "If a guardian pro tem or protective ruling is in order, regular proceedings must be initiated. And parental non-competence will be damned hard to argue on the basis of the infant's anatomy. No further statements? Then," he pressed his thumb against the chipcoder, "My order stands."

* * *

Robin had given Lee and Faron their first evening away from diapers and feedings since leaving Obstet. Returning from dinner, they stepped off the slidebelt, and Lee froze. Suddenly he looked on the edge of tears.

Faron put his arm around Lee and sighed, "Takes getting used to, I guess."

Robin opened the slider to let them in. "I cut the vid link," he said, "just too many messages, too much shit. What's the matter with Lee?"

Faron pointed to the tunnel wall where a crude figure had been painted, a red slit between the legs and "she-monster" written across the chest.

"Why is this so hard for people?" Lee asked.

"No precedents," Robin answered.

Faron looked skeptical. "Surely, in the days of the First Mothers there must have been females born."

"None. Ever," Robin answered. "Remember, the Ovarium is just my B-job; my A-job is History. Funny, but at first the colonists wanted females, actually thought they were neces-sary. Then they found an easier route. Ectopic pregnancies had been carried to term before, not often, but enough so the problems were clear. Cloning, growing a fetus in vitro—these were biotech magic beyond reach of the colony."

Lee kept shaking his head.

"Lee, real change is just too hard for most people. Even the Biotechnists, who want to learn to do the magic, never talk about solving the problem of female viability. It's a man's world and nobody challenges that. Except Evan. Look, I'll leave you two alone with our little revolution in diapers."

As if on cue, Evan woke up crying. Lee nursed her, put her back into the crib, then fell asleep himself.

Small tremors of sleep rippled over Lee as Faron watched. "We sure as hell didn't know what we were getting into," he said quietly, thinking all the way back to the Selection, picturing the two of them, each with a hand on the control, sweeping the cursor of the projection microscope across an alien landscape. It didn't matter that the selection was as random as if the choice had been made by casting stones. The choosing was what mattered. An undistinguished bump had suddenly taken on distinction. It was theirs. After the egg was warmed and separated, then nurtured to maturity, it had been fertilized and implanted. Now it had become Evan MacLeevi, sleeping across the room but cracking the foundations of life on Kohlehrets.

Faron had only wanted a son; he was not prepared to be the father of a political issue. The Biotechnists were claiming vid time as if they had mining rights, and protestors threatened to barricade the tunnel branch where Lee and Faron lived. Faron's argumentative son had become a frequent visitor. One after-shift, Mahrk wouldn't leave and he wouldn't give up.

"Don't be a stone in the boot, Mahrk. If you weren't my son, I'd say you were deliberately making things worse with your vidcasts."

"Crisis is like a crack in the rock, Mother, an opportunity as much as a danger. The Biotechnist League is going to call for special elections. We think we can get two, maybe even three reps, onto the Bridge."

"A crack in the rock can also bring the tunnel down on top of you."

"Don't you see, Mother? This baby is proof. We have to try something else. The League has warned."

"The League has warned. The League is always warning, but the Biotechnists didn't warn about this," Faron said. "A female baby just never occurred to anyone. The trouble with your Biotechnist League is you know so much tech and so little bio. With one ovary carrying almost half a million eggs, the four on Kohlehrets buy us a lot of time. There's what, sixteen-thousand men on Kohlehrets? The ecolonomists estimate it will never support more than two or three times that. That's forty generations or so before the debate becomes important."

Robin leaned in to interrupt. "What really galls the Biotechnist League is being dependent on the ovaries. Motherhood isn't enough for them. They want perfect self-sufficiency, the ultimate egotism of cloning themselves."

Mahrk sneered. "As an altar boy to the ovaries, you have a vested interest, Robin. And you know about as much about motherhood as the First Mothers did. I lost my brother to your damned motherhood. Reason says we step up research on cloning."

"It's unnatural," Lee said.

"What's unnatural? The First Mothers thought male childbearing was unnatural. It was just a temporary expedient. They were explorers, scientists, men with no thought that they would someday bear children in their bellies."

Robin sighed. "Look," he said, "let me remind you and your League of some history. We're too busy pushing new tunnels or new agendas to study it."

"I know history, Robin. The Cypress was never intended as a colony ship; there were only two females on the crew. History would have been a lot different if Navigator Kolodny hadn't been one of those killed in the crash. Or if the

Geochemist, Miryam Truss, hadn't died giving birth to the first child on Kohlehrets, who happened to be a boy. But, here we are, in a man's world. We better learn faster than our hallowed First Mothers did. How long did it take them to figure out why all the full-term babies were male and most of the failed fetuses were female? A fetus is foreign tissue, remember. Apparently, with male mothers there's less chance of rejection with a male fetus. Even so, rejection would be much commoner without perfusion. That's biotech. That's what makes Kohlehrets a man's world."

Robin sighed. "Is this biological law? We chose sperm separation to save eggs. But Evan here changes all that. We don't have to throw out female zygotes before implantation."

Mahrk stood up to go. "Evan doesn't mean we've learned how to carry female fetuses to term. She's another accident, no more. We need cloning, and we need the Biotechnist League standing on the Bridge."

* * *

Mahrk brought them the news four weeks later, dumping it on them in an impatient rush. The special elections had put him on the Bridge, but the Biotechnist League had been unable to vote anyone off. He was left in the useless position of Officer Elect, a non-voting advisor until the next regular elections when the others stepped down.

"And the cowards on the Bridge have surrendered to public pressure," he said. "They've called a Tribunal."

* * *

The day of the Tribunal, Evan was seventeen weeks old. A chunky and contented baby, she gurgled in Faron's arms as he and Lee walked onto the Bridge.

Of the five men on the Bridge, four were older than Faron. Lee and Faron both recognized Talbot barEddie, the youngest ever elected to the Bridge. Perhaps he would understand better. Mahrk Faronson sat with the five, but without a vote.

136

Now Faron thought of his son's political interests in a new light and wished Mahrk had stood for election to the Bridge earlier, in the regular elections.

The First Officer began: "This is difficult beyond words."

Faron stepped forward. "I thought this was a Tribunal. It sounds like you've already voted."

"We just don't see how we can let you keep the baby. You must understand. It's just not possible. You shouldn't have been allowed to see her, Lee, much less nurse her."

Lee was on the verge of tears. "She's just a baby. She did nothing to anybody, nothing wrong."

"But there's no place for her in our world," barEddie responded. "She would grow up a freak, a misfit."

First Officer Ahmedson placed a restraining hand on barEddie's wrist and turned back to Lee. "You must understand. It's just too late; we can't go back. Think about it: if there were females again, who would be the mothers? Who would bear children? Who would nurse them? We'd be left with nothing. Would you want a world like that? Would you want to give up the chance ever to become a mother again?"

BarEddie tried to be reassuring. "The baby will be dealt with humanely, you've got to believe that. There will be no pain."

"What are you talking about?" There was panic in Lee's voice. "We're talking about my baby. You don't know pain. You're not even a mother, Officer. A mother knows. You can't take my baby, damn you!"

BarEddie signaled a court attendant. "We can't have you here if you are unable to discuss this calmly. Postpartum fits have no place on the Bridge."

It took three officers to escort Lee from the room.

Faron was left, still holding Evan. He thoughtfully scanned the determined faces of the Officers. "You want her killed? Don't say 'euthanized.' Let's at least be honest." He held her out toward them. "Why bother with the medits? Why don't we just get it over with?" He crossed over to a vacuum port and started to spin the door handle. "We can just shove her in now, boot her out starside. It'll be quick enough."

BarEddie paled. "You can't!" he shouted.

"You're the last I'd expect to object, Officer barEddie."

"Ask him why," Mahrk said. "Ask him about the plans." The room was silent. "They want to harvest the ovaries first."

Faron looked toward barEddie. "Ah, now I see it. Status quo and one better. Better genetics and no troublesome female to deal with." Then he turned to Mahrk. "And now I understand your support. Two more ovaries in the Repository would leave the Biotechnists in an abandoned tunnel. She's no good to the League dead. She's a living argument for the comfortable certainty of cloning."

The door on the vacuum port spun open. Faron fought back tears as he guided Evan's feet into the tube. She started to cry, and he stroked her cheek with his thumb. No one moved.

"Decide, damn it!"

Evan's crying rose to a desperate squeal as her head slid into the dark oval. Faron's knees threatened to buckle, but somehow he found the strength to leave her there, with the door to the port half closed.

Out in the hall Lee wanted them both to go back in, then he wanted to leave, but Faron insisted they just wait. It was a long twenty minutes before one of the officers stepped out into the anteroom. "We went by Code, Lee. The vote was four to one. I'm sorry we put you through this, truly sorry."

"Damn you, damn the whole damned Bridge!" Lee shouted.

First Officer Ahmedson stood in the door. "I don't think you understand," he said. "We couldn't do it." He held out the baby to Lee. "We're mothers, too, all but one of us. You sure knew what you were doing, Faron Davidov, didn't you."

Faron shrugged. "Who knows what any of us are doing? There are going to be a lot of changes." He smiled and took Lee's hand. "It will never be easy."

"But it will always be worth it," Lee said, finishing the old litany as he looked up at Faron. In the midst of that tender moment, Evan started to cry again. "It's all right, Evan," Lee crooned to her. "I'm here. Just remember, your mother loves you."

More crime science fiction, but this time in a much lighter vein, although the story also explores some of the heavy but subtle issues of drugs and dependence. The inspiration for this story came from working with a real-world company, a client whose identity is, of course, confidential.

Sweet Success

For the eight-millionth time, Derek missed the shredder port, and the ball of paper tumbled mockingly onto the pile of books in one corner of his office. He kiddy-carred his swivel chair closer, groaned as he stretched to reach the errant Mission Reassignment Form, and pushed it gingerly through the little plexy door. The interlock kerchunked, the little laser beam whirled and sliced, and triplicate confetti whipped into an airstream to be whisked to some distant recycling point. There were times and ways in which the Bureau could be frighteningly effective.

Derek Scheinner had come late to the Bureau. He had started as a Professor of Psychology at Indy U. and gone nowhere. He'd gone nowhere as a real estate agent pushing condos in a diminishing market. Now he was going nowhere as a field operative for the Bureau. Of late he had spent more time working out in the Bureau's gymnasium than working on cases. He patted his stomach, flatter than when he was in college. He tapped a few keys on the desk top. A bright blue entry screen flared across his screen. He knew the system, every access window, every pop-up menu of it. He was ready, he thought. But then, he wondered, could he ever do anything well, do anything with confidence? He was forty-five and still

141

trying to find himself. Maybe that's why he found it so easy to talk with his son in college; they were both starting out. Of course, Eddie teased his father for trying to become a "private eye."

The Independent Bureau of Investigation, of course, was not just some glorified detective agency. The Bureau was one among countless beneficiaries of the late twentieth century social legacy of rampant privatization. They had all grown fat and sassy as human services were progressively transferred from government to the private sector. Now, there was no shortage of assignments. So Derek wondered why he got offered such garbage as an investigation of "Chocolate Almond Chip Cookies."

Maybe he should have taken the assignment. At least he would be drawing field pay. What was the name of the senior operative on this one? He called up a display of the permanent file copy from the network server. Singer Robeson. Robeson was reputably one of the smoothest and sharpest in the agency. Derek remembered him from orientation, remembered his quiet, inviolable confidence, and the hints of inner strength that lay behind his smiling good nature. He envied someone who could radiate such contentment with himself. Maybe some of it would rub off.

The network server gave him trouble when Derek requested an additional paper copy of the assignment. So, he keyed to accept the assignment, then, as one of the operation personnel, created an expense authorization. Suddenly Singer Robeson was on the screen. He sported the abbreviated beard that never seemed to go out of style with American men of Portuguese descent. Without letting displeasure mar his face, he made clear that only he was going to authorize any expenditures or departures from procedure in this operation. "I have invested a great deal in this investigation. I need an assistant. Glad you're it. Come on down to my office. The stretch will do you good."

Well, so much for protocol, Derek thought. Nobody went to anybody's office anymore.

Robeson's office was small and it was a mess. In that way it resembled every other office on this floor and the floor below. The floor above was where "Corporate" resided; their offices were large and tidy. But this office didn't just look like a dump, it smelled like one. Scheinner involuntarily wrinkled his nose.

"My micro-micro organic chem lab," Robeson explained. "Over there, portable gas chromatograph. Pretty complete set-up here, standard instrument interface to the network. And this," he held up a gooey bit of char, "is a cookie. It's been, shall we say, denatured with several reagents. Want a bite?"

The smell emanated from the cookie. Derek shook his head vigorously. "Would you fill me in on what this is all about, Mr. Robeson?" he asked, hoping to appear competent and business-like.

The man grinned, folded his hands over his ample middle-age spread, and said, "It's Doctor Robeson, but if you call me anything but Singer you're off the case with a disciplinary flag on your file. I picked you, Scheinner. Don't let me down. And don't look surprised. I checked your performance stats. You're a regular whiz with the network and we need to do some real digging, more than I can do by myself. Our talents will be a nice match."

Inwardly Derek groaned, seeing himself chained to a work station for months, but he let Singer go on without interruption. "We are currently investigating the makers of 'Hermanitos,' the most expensive upscale cookie on the market. This company has a phenomenal growth rate and appears to be getting a return on investment that would make a loan shark drool all over his paper. Our client, whose identity is Bureau Confidential, Class Star Star, wants to know the why and how. How can the company price its main line of cookies a good twenty-five percent above the rest of the market and keep selling? And why does their Chocolate Almond Chip sell at all when a 250-gram package costs more than a steak dinner at a good in-town restaurant? Our client thinks something smells very funny, and they want to find out what it is?"

Derek resisted the humorous potential and asked, "Is the client in the cookie business, too? I mean, is this industrial espionage we're getting into?"

"Let's just say there's a vested interest. For all you know, we could be working for the govvies. The Bureau does stuff like that you know. Anyway, I think we should be able to crack this thing in a few weeks. I don't want to have to bill too many of your 200-dollar hours. Goes double for my rate, which is, of course, somewhat more than double that. The client is not exactly deep pockets."

"Is that my billing rate, $200 an hour? I had no idea." What Derek was thinking was more along the lines of how he could possibly be worth that much to anybody. "So what's the lab stuff about?"

Singer finally set the chemically mutilated bit of cookie down. "I was looking for drugs. You shouldn't be surprised. Yours is the 'drug-free generation,' and the price of that freedom is eternal chemical vigilance." Derek was frowning and looked like he might interrupt, but Singer went on. "Anyway, drugs in commercial products go way back. Many soft drinks originated as tonics with addictive drugs in them. A perfect marketing ploy. Talk about your brand loyalty. Just add a little morphanalog to Mama Winfrey's Wheat Germ Bread, and they'll keep coming back for more, never knowing why. Every so often someone tries it. Designer drugs make it easy to tailor a new molecule into something like an old addictive one. You'd see a lot more if it wasn't so easy for the govvies to catch. Usually too many people have to be in on it to keep it secret. Then there's the Food and Drug monitoring. If that doesn't initially catch the chemical, demand does. As soon as the ploy starts to work, demand takes off in a particular way, prices spiral as the makers get greedy, consumers go nuts when they can't get it, aggregate brand loyalty is so perfect that sales don't follow seasonal slumps or industry downturns. The govvies just have their computers watch for this pattern and sound the alarm when it shows up. And with the labs that those boys have, believe me, if there's any funny molecules in there, they find them."

"So that's how we got called in, the Food and Drug computers flagged these cookies?"

Singer smiled, a patient, knowing, Mona Lisa kind of smile. "Slow down, think more, guess less. What would we need this lab stuff for if Food and Drug were involved? No, the client has a more sensitive nose for trouble. And they don't want Food and Drug alerted. So please watch how you bypass security checks when you snoop through any govvie files. I want this clean: no alarms, no audit trails, from login to logoff."

Singer reached into his desk, rummaged around, and handed over a small, velvety brown box with gold and cream lettering, a quarter-kilo box of "Los Hermanitos" brand of Chocolate Almond Chip cookies. Derek gasped when he saw the price.

"Go ahead, try one," Singer urged.

Derek held the box is if it might explode. "Later, maybe," he said.

"No, taste it. There's no drugs in it, remember. We've already tested for variants of nearly every psychotropic ever synthesized."

"It is good," Derek said after trying the tiniest of bites.

"Do you like the taste?"

"Yeah, pretty good. Funny. I know this will sound weird, Singer, but I can still taste it and somehow, even though I know it's a chocolate chip cookie, I keep thinking of this steak I once had in Chicago, an aged filet mignon, medium rare, smothered with a mushroom and truffle sauce. It was the most delicious meal I ever remember."

Singer shook his head, the perpetual smile deepening slightly. "I don't know about you, Scheinner." He popped a

145

Chocolate Almond Chip cookie into his mouth. "Reminds me of this cinnamon cappuccino I used to get in a little cafe back in Brookline. Perfect.

"People do get to associating, don't they," Singer said after a long pause. "Anyway, we've gone about as far as we can with the addictive drug angle."

Derek finished off his own cookie, still a little afraid of it, but considerably more comfortable than when he had entered the office. "What can you tell me about the principals of the company we're investigating?"

"Here, I'll introduce you." A high-res, full color image of a cherubic but bearded face blossomed on the wall monitor. "This is Victor Hermanos, 38, sole proprietor of La Cocina del Hermanos. He's a chemist, M.I.T. grad, left Consolidated Biscuit in '97 to form his own company. His associates find him to be quiet, unassuming, but very confident in his abilities. His first patent was for 'Betterberry,' heart of one of the most popular flavor sprays of the early '90s.

"And this is Adam Dingus, process control programmer, now turned veep for manufacturing. A technical maven, according to our source, preoccupied with keeping the dough flowing. He's held half a dozen jobs in the last ten years, doesn't care who he works for as long as the problem is interesting. He'd as soon make nerve gas as cookies. Reports are that the Hermanos production process is the best in the industry. And here's Ellene Eikenrisch, marketing and finance wizard. Lives a strange life out on the Island with a houseful of lab animals she adopted after they were liberated in a series of anti-vivisectionist raids.

"Strange combination, those three. If it is drugs, Hermanos himself is our prime suspect, because of his background in organic chemistry, but who knows what's really happening."

They split them up in order to start tailing all three. Derek ended up with Ellene. He was unsure of himself with women. He had never understood his divorce, getting through it in a sort of haze not much different from the fog in which he had drifted through eighteen years of marriage. Did he need to do anything special in trailing this woman? He took a deep breath, punched a few keys, and slapped a tracer on Ellene's access keyword. Then, remembering Singer's warning, he searched back for a transaction record, deleted it, and manually introduced a new check sum for the session. No trace of the trace, he thought.

A week later he arranged to bump into her at a Bluepeace teleconference. Bluepeace had recently expanded its atmospheric conservation program and was in the midst of a major membership drive; nobody noticed another new ID. He waited until hers scrolled onto the screen during a real-time poll of conference attendees, then immediately logged an aside comment to CP, "current participant." He didn't want to be too forward.

TO CP: Next thing you know they'll be spraying hyper-flavors into the air to get people to breathe the unbreathable stuff. <DS>

TO DS: Scents would be better, breathing flavors disturbs people, even though flavor is 90 percent aroma. <EE>

She'd taken the bait. And she had directed her response to him rather than "current participant" or "to conference." He was actually having a conversation with her, even if by computer teleconferencing. He started typing again.

TO EE: How do you know so much about flavor? Food science major? <DS>

TO DS: Management Science, little of everything. You? <EE>

He told her he was a licensed real estate broker, remembered he was using his real name, then silently thanked his ex-wife for insisting he renew his license. He'd pass any casual computer check. They exchanged pleasantries until Ellene suggested they quit the conference and switch to a slow-scan visual link. Derek made an excuse about the poor quality of his camera while he pushed his chair back from the desk, sat up straight, and with the keyboard in his lap, pivoted a quarter turn away from the monitor. Unfortunately, the infrared link on the keyboard was then pointed too far away from the sensor on the terminal. He had to turn back to face the screen before the terminal could read the command to switch modes, which it did immediately, since he was holding down the function key.

Ellene's first view of him did not, therefore, show off his flat stomach. Then again, it didn't make his nose look quite so large. Ellene, however, was caught in the act of patting something on hers when the image began painting itself on the screen. Electronics had changed the moves but not the games: the protocol for such encounters was for the gentleman to wait for the lady to turn on the visuals.

The rest of their first encounter did not go well and, with each successive attempt to smooth things out, he made matters worse. Derek got little new information out of her, and she got a definite impression of him as a well-meaning but inept middle-aged loser who lacked any confidence in himself. He thought Ellene was wonderful, the sweet Jewish girl of his mother's dreams, a mature woman who looked half her age (which would make her just right for him, he thought).

As far as Derek was concerned, she was no longer a suspect. She seemed incapable of guile. She admitted that an office romance with an accounting intern was the most interesting thing her job offered. Neither marketing nor finances were much of a challenge at La Cocina del Hermanos. Other than the new junior accountant, whom she was eyeing as possible successor to her departed intern, she seemed to have no strong feelings one way or another about the company or anyone who worked there.

His social prospects with Ellene dwindling, Derek became increasingly concerned about the ethics of his job, finally concluding that it was inappropriate to become involved with a client, anyway. He moved on to Adam Dingus.

Dingus, fairly new to the region, lived in an apartment a few blocks from the cookie plant, so Derek tried to sell him a condo. He almost closed on a real listing in the Southchester area, a dive whose only "feature" was the built-in entertainment center in the bedroom—four walls of the best audiovisual technology available. Dingus loved it until he found out the Building Association contract prohibited the owner from putting in any more electronics without approval of the Association.

Derek and Adam got along well; neither had much in the way of people skills and they recognized each other as kin under the skin. Derek looked up to Adam for having had the good sense to fully own his ineptitude and work with machines instead of people, while Adam admired Derek for his chutzpa in staying in real estate, a field that made him confront his handicap. Indeed, Adam imagined Derek as a fabulously successful salesman. He kept reassuring Derek that eventually they would find the right condo.

Over many a Nada Colada with Adam, Derek had learned pretty much the entire history of the mysterious cookie company. He thought it meaningful that almost all the production equipment was specially designed, including computer controlled premixing of a battery of natural flavoring ingredients. He still worried about drugs and decided to take it up with Singer.

Outside his permanently odorous office, Singer Robeson scoffed. "You don't know beans about drugs, Scheinner. You're definitely a member of this generation, 'drug free and ready for the night,'" he quoted a video ad of recent vintage. "You may or may not be free of drugs, but you certainly have freed yourselves from having to think too clearly. There is a difference between use and abuse."

Derek interrupted. "Wait, how can you say that when it comes to the really dangerous drugs, like heroin, methadone, cannabinol? By definition, drugs are dangerous, and just using them is abuse, at least potentially."

Singer nodded. "Well, you might remember that methadone was introduced as a treatment for heroin addiction, but

149

did you know that heroin was originally used to try to cure morphine addiction? Look, you don't have any real experience; how can you understand?" He paused to open a supply cabinet. Derek tried not to react when he saw the bottle of bourbon there. "Alcohol is heavily taxed and more expensive than ever." He shook his head and added, "Also more dangerous, since nobody knows how to handle it anymore. And you've been taught to think of prescriptions and drugs as two different things: part of the illusion of a drug-free society. But you can abuse the blue pill from the pharmacy just as easily as the red one from the street.

"Anyway, enough from 'Social Problems 101.' Look, the Los Hermanitos production equipment is no big deal; most of it in the food industry is custom designed for each application. And, after all, Victor Hermanos is a flavor chemist, we'd expect him to put a lot into the flavoring end of things. But we'll have to check things out. You'll have to go in and get samples of every flavoring agent they use." He took a big bite out of the cookie in his hand and went into his office, leaving Derek standing there.

Derek started picturing a midnight raid and suddenly found himself looking up and down the hall for the nearest men's room. Inwardly he concluded that it really made more sense to do additional market research on Chocolate Almond Chip Cookies.

The market research kept him busy and away from Singer Robeson for almost a week. During that time he found that purchasers of "Los Hermanitos" were fierce loyalists and that demand seemed to be remarkably insensitive to price. On the other hand, consumers did not show an escalating consumption. The typical buyer purchased a steady, modest supply, regardless of how long they had been customers or of the relative cost of the cookies to them. This did not sound like a drug to Derek.

What had been the most fun for him were the interviews, some of them even face-to-face. People described "Los

Hermanitos" in ways he would never have expected. To a lot of people they were just chocolate and almond, only the best, but there were also many who talked about other things: marinara sauce, lamb chops mixed grill, ripe papaya, even mother's milk.

In his note file he had quoted one informant: "It's the aftertaste. Stays with you. Reminds you of your best meals and that ineluctable afterglow of perfect contentment when you've had just enough of heaven. It is probably pretty much how a baby feels, smiling in half-sleep, just as the nipple slips from its mouth."

He told Robeson that he was now convinced that there was something about the flavor of the Chocolate Almond Chip cookies. Robeson told him the same thing he had told him the week earlier, somewhat more colorfully this time, but with the same unshakable good humor. "I'd get the flavoring samples myself," Robeson told him, "but I have to meet with Hermanos himself, and I've almost completed the arrangements. You'll have to do it."

Eventually Derek had to force himself to ignore his fear and begin planning his "raid." He studied tutorials on locksmithing, checked into what was involved in getting a pistol, considered shaving his beard, bought a new suit from a used clothing store, and checked out a video disk about makeup for disguises. The more he studied and planned, the more anxious he became. Finally he went to Robeson again.

"I don't think I can do it, not a B&E." He was almost shaking.

Singer gave him a broad smile. "Who said anything about actually going to the plant? I just assumed you'd use the computer. You're so good at it."

Derek looked dumb for a moment as the light slowly dawned across his face. "Yeah, just never thought of it." He reached for a cookie and sat down at Robeson's terminal. For the next hour Robeson watched over his shoulder, but eventually grew bored and left. Derek continued to poke and prod his way through interlocked databases, commercial records, and transaction lists. It was past quitting time when Robeson returned.

"Singer, it's done! They'll be here tomorrow by courier. I created a recall of certain batches from two of the suppliers and an over-shipment from another. The warehouse and shipping room at La Cocina will find their orders waiting in the morning, very specific orders to pull from stock that has been on the premises the longest. Still, all very routine."

"How will they get to us instead of back to the suppliers?"

"Simple. The shipping labels are preprinted by the computer. Right company names, even the right addresses, nothing suspicious. Only these are prepaid labels drawn on a courier that I have created as a front operation. One B&E, signed, sealed, and delivered."

The samples, all 37 of them, arrived on schedule; by the end of the day they had been analyzed: no known drugs, no near relatives. There were unexplained blips on the charts, but nothing to alarm anyone since they were all genuine, natural flavors and showed the usual bottle-to-bottle variability and chemical complexity of naturally occurring mixtures. If there was something in there, the Bureau's equipment couldn't find it.

Robeson went back to trying to meet with the reclusive and elusive Victor Hermanos. Derek, discouraged and on his own, called up his newfound buddy, Adam Dingus, saying he wanted to learn more about process control in the food industry. Dingus promised to give him schematics and flowcharts to show him how it's done.

They met at a bar they had stumbled on while looking for condos in Southchester. Adam ordered a Nada Colada; Derek ordered a beer.

"You sure you want that?" Adam asked, incredulously.

Derek nodded, chugged the beer, then held his mouth as his eyes bugged out. "Horrible stuff. Arrrgh!"

152

"The good part isn't in the taste, it's in what you'll feel about ten minutes from now."

Derek, who felt like he was going to lose everything below his larynx, asked, "How do you know?"

"Oh, I downed quite a few at University in Australia. Haven't had more than a couple or three in the last few years."

"I thought ..."

"You thought that everyone who drank became alcoholic, that if you ever quit the stuff you could never touch a drop again? Sure. Hey listen, there's better stuff." Adam turned away and lifted his fashionably long hair. A thin patch of plastic, laced with tiny circuits, adhered to the skin of his neck. "Mellows you out, it does. Diffuse thalamic pacemaker. Just enough R3 stimulation to keep you smiling. Legal. Cheap, if you know where to get the electronics wholesale."

A few minutes earlier Derek would have been appalled, might even have left his buddy. But he only smiled, thinking how funny it was that a slight fuzziness around the edges was pleasant. He patted Adam on the back. "'Sgood. Whatever turns you on." He laughed. "Get it? Whatever turns you on?"

They laughed together through several rounds and most of the evening until Adam reached up to turn off his stimulator patch. Derek, head on the bar, didn't notice. Adam called for a taxi, helped him in when it arrived, then returned to his seat at the bar. The bartender commented on the druggie who had just left, but Adam just smiled and turned his patch back on.

Derek awoke in his own apartment with a stack of computer paper on his chest and a taste like bread mold in his mouth. He sent a message to the Bureau saying he'd be working in the field for the day, then tried to find something to shrink his brain back so it would fit within his skull. It took some time at his bedroom terminal before he could get the Pharmac Advisory System to understand his problem. Eventually it kicked out a prescription, which he hurriedly filled. The relief was blessed even if imperfect.

He spent most of the day going over process control programs in minute detail, checking them against diagrams of the plant itself. Two of the flavoring agents, he found, were first premixed, then mixed with the rest of the flavorings, then added to the batch. It made no sense to him. It took a long time and some remote research at the University library to convince himself that there was no ordinary technical reason for those steps in the process.

Once more, however, Singer was uninterested in his suspicions.

"Time to move our butts, Scheinner. I have been unable to get within fifty feet of our man Victor, not even within twenty-five lines on a monitor. I've got some semi-phony Health Department papers deputizing me to take apart his equipment. You order up a demol crew to meet us at the plant; I'll call Victor and tell him we're going to shut him down."

La Cocina del Hermanos turned out to be a showcase factory, all bright tile and stainless steel. Light from halogen overheads glistened off the machinery and piping. The Health Department would have had to look hard to find a speck. It was surprisingly quiet, muffled slurps and almost sub-audible whines coming from the sealed equipment. The workers of the demol crew leaned on their high tech tools like generations of work crews before them, a bored, we-get-paid-however-it-goes-down look on every face. That was not the look on Victor Hermanos's face.

"There are no controlled substances on these premises, Robeson. I think you know that. Even if your deputation is valid, I don't think you're serious, Singer. Would you take this all apart, impound everything, tie us all up in years of legal hassles? No, I think not."

Singer broadened his smile considerably and turned to the head of the demol crew. She chewed her gum slowly and deliberately. When Singer nodded to her, she in turn nodded toward one of the big industrial cutting lasers; it was wheeled into place. She took the gum from her mouth, looked around at the immaculate plant, then put it back in. Pulling the dark protective shield down from her hardhat with one hand, she adjusted a control with the other. A pale green bar of light stabbed out at one of the huge mixers. Hermanos and Robeson stared at each other, each with the same quietly confident smile stitched to his face, each waiting, as if in the secret certainty that the other would back down.

The smile on Hermanos unraveled the tiniest bit. "Okay. You got it. One condition."

"Wait," Derek said, "I need to transcribe this for the lawyers." He flipped open the case of a portable terminal. "Okay, now go ahead. What's the secret?"

"I told you the secret; I told everyone. It's right on the package. We use only genuine natural flavorings. We use both real vanilla and real almond extract."

Derek remembered the fluid feed instructions. "A two component chemistry, traces of each reactant buried in the complex organic soup of the two natural flavors."

Singer looked at him and his smile broadened still more. To Hermanos he said, "It would only have been a matter of time."

"How true, but such a very long time. Even if you did spot something strange in one of the flavorings, say with a chromatograph, and even if you were able to isolate, analyze, and eventually synthesize it, you'd still only have an odd but uninteresting compound. You have to have both parts to make biphorin, as I call it."

"That's the drug? Biphorin?" Derek asked.

"Not really a drug: you might think of it as a flavor catalyst. Of course, it actually works in the nose, where most of tasting happens. Only a few molecules of biphorin can trigger the onset of a very complex cascade of reactions in olfactory nerves, then in the rhinencephalon, the nose-brain. The memory associations for odors are the most primitive, enduring, and most potent. Did you know that a single exposure to an odor can be enough to establish a permanent memory trace?"

Derek could hold his peace no more. "In less fancy words, you're still a dope dealer, and all you've done is create a new twist on an addictive narcotic. Don't you ever think about the innocent kids you've gotten addicted?"

Hermanos shook his head; the smile never wavered. "Kids? You gotta be kidding? We price ourselves out of that market deliberately. How many kids do you think are out there saving up several weeks of allowance to buy one cookie?

"And I already made clear, biphorin's no narcotic, it's just a flavoring agent, very powerful, with a lingering effect, but just a flavoring. The reactions it triggers off are precisely the same as those of ordinary foods and flavorings, just more finely tuned. I could prove that in court or before a scientific panel. I have elaborate studies of evoked cortical potential; the brain responses are indistinguishable. There's no addiction, no conditioning, no buildup of tolerance, no withdrawal symptoms. It's not mutagenic, does not reduce sensitivity or otherwise damage nerves. Biphorin is fully effective at minute levels and there's no dose response relationship above the threshold of effective action. That means, taking more doesn't feel better. A very little is enough and enough is plenty.

"Look, biphorin just tastes good, so good it's like the best of anything that you have ever tasted or ever could imagine tasting. It's a taste so perfect to you that it brings with it a wave of contentment. There's no euphoria, just a quiet contentment that lasts for hours.

"Now, what does your client want?" Hermanos asked. "Licensing? Silent partner? What?"

"I don't know, doesn't say here," Derek answered, looking at the display on the portable he held.

"I know," said Singer. "The client wants you out of the flavoring business."

Hermanos's smile finally wavered. "I can't." But Singer Robeson just stood there again, grinning confidently. "Okay,"

Hermanos continued. "Okay. You get the plant and you get the formula. Fair market value as determined by arbitration. But there will be one condition." Singer waited as Hermanos hesitated. "A supply. Enough for one, really quite cheap. Just guarantee that, and the whole operation is yours."

Singer explained patiently. "Look, my client doesn't want to sell cookies, and they don't want you to stop selling cookies. They just want you to stop selling the funny kind. Sooner or later, people would catch on. And if the government got suspicious, they'd put millions of dollars and an army of investigators on it, not just a couple of second-rate Bureau operatives. Then where would you be, where would biphorin be? After all, you went the trade secret route; you could have patented biphorin."

"Well, the feds would have outlawed the stuff for sure."

"I rest my case." Singer reached for the slate from Derek. "Here, I'll put it into the agreement that an independent lab will be contracted for an adequate supply for life. We'll contract the two components separately. And that's the end of it. Make all the cookies you want, flavor them with witch hazel, for all we care, but no biphorin. Never. Not in anything. You're already quite wealthy from 'Hermanitos.' I suspect the halo effect will keep sales going well on whatever you sell for a long time."

Hermanos finally agreed. They haggled for awhile over details, then sent the agreement through the private network to the lawyers. As soon as the demol crew were told they had the day off, Hermanos left for his office, a glassed in cubicle overlooking the production floor.

"What a sad thing. What a waste," Derek said.

"Don't pity him, Scheinner. You haven't walked in his shoes. Does he look like a dope fiend? Have you checked into how many patents the man's filed since he started La Cocina? Just what are the ingredients of success? Does being contented and comfortable mean you are of no use to society? For that matter, does being perpetually unsatisfied with yourself and your world mean you're a better person? I don't know, Scheinner, I don't know. Sometimes relaxing is the best way to slip from between a rock and a hard place."

He looked at Derek, expectantly, a little smile hanging like a question on his face, an invitation, an offer, a promise.

Derek looked from Singer's face to the booth where Hermanos shuffled papers, wearing that same smile. "You're the client, aren't you, Singer?"

"Scheinner, a senior operative, especially one as competent as you, has to have confidence in his instincts. You can't always count on getting every guess confirmed." The same smile, always the same.

Derek bit his lip. "Judgment comes from experience, you once told me. I want supplies for one more in the agreement," he said confidently. "By the way, would you like to celebrate? We could swing up to Chicago for the best steak you have ever eaten."

"Only if we finish off with cinnamon capuccino," Robeson said. "I can taste it now."

This novelette, a challenging story of struggles and secrets, was another experiment with structure and form. It also reflects my then growing disillusionment with the professional world of social services and psychotherapy, a world that I did not at the time know I would soon be leaving behind.

Yesterday's Secrets

"No choice is also a choice." Yiddish proverb

The woman still had a hole in her mind. The Proceedings couldn't change that, but Dahna Mehrit knew she had a professional obligation as Citizen's Advocate. She fingered the Judicial Authority disk in her pocket and tried to keep listening, but the words, like noise in a bad sound system, thrummed and hissed in her ears. Some pedant from the Psychosocial Center was droning on about the construction of reality. Who was he? It didn't matter. He was with the Center, and right now they were facing Citizens' Advocacy Proceedings.

What was the man saying? Something about truth being an onion, layer on layer, truth layered on truth. Even in the healthy individual, he was saying, meanings change, and the truth of one level's reality need have little relation to the truth at any other level.

The empty abstractions kept coming. By this, Advocate Mehrit knew they had reached the end. She understood their discipline and methods far better than they knew hers, but it didn't take training in constructivist psychology to recognize when someone had nothing more to say.

Without waiting for the therapist to finish his lecture, in mid-syllable of yet another abstract noun, she stood. The silence was instantaneous. Mehrit was a porpoise of a woman, with high forehead and a full waist, towering over most of the small-statured on-Cylinder Citizens. Though she had the attention of the entire Review Panel, she waited, stretching the tension out, reminding them by its pull that it was she who had the Authority with her in the Proceedings.

"This case may be about meanings, but this case is also about to end. You argue convincingly of the risks to the Citizen." She exhaled slowly. "It would seem that little good could come from Lyanna Treynor reading her records. Still, she has a right to know what happened to her, whether or not she can ever completely restore what was..." she searched for the proper language, "what was taken from her without consent.

"And we must also remember, if I may continue your wordy colleague's narrative in his own style, that this decision is about the reasonable stories we create, sometimes claiming them as the reasons for choosing to do what may already be settled and beyond choice."

She gestured toward the computer terminal, and eager hands passed it to her at the head of the conference table. "I will review the entire case again, make my decision for the Authority, then file a report." She let everyone wait in confusion for long seconds as she began calling up files through the terminal, bringing them to ready access without examining them. When the Temporary Chair of the Review Panel asked what they should do, Dahna dismissed them all wordlessly with a wave of her left hand. She was remembering some of the layers of truth and of meaning, memories that were hers and memories that belonged to others.

Meanings Lost...

"There's a hole in my mind."

Dahna Mehrit looked up with subdued interest. The woman studied her for a moment with intense, silver-grey eyes, then pulled a sleeved disk from her pocket and shoved it across the desk. She didn't look unbalanced.

"Scan that," she said. "Says hole in my mind."

Mehrit studied the woman studying her and took an immediate liking to her. There was determination and intelligence in her face, and a hint of something else: a wiry anger always in check. She was dressed like a rock frau in a patched vycord jumpsuit, but her mahogany hair was recently cut in the sculpted on-Cylinder style. To Mehrit, who had helped many clients from the asteroids, the clipped speech of a rock hound was unmistakable.

"What's this about?" Mehrit asked.

"You're the Advocate, you tell," the woman said. "Name's Lyanna Treynor. Tried for the Academy, chance for Earth, study space astronomy." She could only be referring to the Astrotechnical Academy at Novosibirsk: the Academy. "Everything was on the vector. I burned through the exams. But the Academy wouldn't take me with a hole in my mind. Why I need an Advocate is right there. Look."

Dahna slipped the disk into the slot in her desk and flipped up the screen, twisting it so the woman could see, too. The disk contained a complete multi-axial semantic topograph, a recent one, judging by the detail and the color enhancement. Dahna hit a few keys, setting the display in motion, showing a low flying tour over the complex, mountainous landscape of the woman's mental organization. To Dahna it looked like a thousand others might: nothing obviously anomalous.

"I don't see anything here, but then I'm no expert. We'd have to get a psychometrist to study your tests more thoroughly to be sure. Did they say anything about what they saw from your tests, what they meant by a hole?"

161

"Didn't say hole: my word. 'Evidence of a substantial semantic gap with the possibility of consequent degradation of cognitive or emotional functioning.' Their words."

"You must be pretty good to have gotten so far in your Academy application. If there is any 'degradation,' it can't amount to much. We'll check your records, with your permission, of course." She smiled supportively. "Maybe you should see somebody at the Psychosocial Center. There could be many explanations for memory loss or whatever this is."

"Haven't. Won't. Never felt comfortable with psychs or counselors. Don't know why. Testing for the Academy was hard enough going through. Just don't want anyone else digging in my mind, pawing through it. Like being stripped, sort of."

Dahna understood that kind of discomfort and decided not to say anything about her own training in psychotherapy. She wasn't sure what she could do to help the woman, but she started to take a history anyway.

Lyanna Treynor, she learned, was born in orbit and raised until the age of fourteen by spacer parents, the last year or so with her father. He had disappeared mysteriously after that, and Lyanna was remanded to the Youth Authority who placed her in a group facility on Luna III where she took her deceased mother's last name. She had done well in technical school, training in astronavigation, then started with one of the big mining firms. A supervisor had convinced her that she had what it took for a fellowship in space astronomy.

"He was another father to me. We lived together three years, lovers. It was his dream at first, mine now. Nothing more important, just get into the Academy."

Dahna explained to her that the Academy did not come under direct jurisdiction of the Planetary Authority, that they might not be able to get the decision reversed. On the other hand, there might be some other actionable cause with bearing on her entry to the Academy. Dahna tried to be gentle as she rattled through the possibilities. "Do you have a criminal record? Were you ever in the Uniformed Services? No? What about your work record? Should we check that? Maybe involved in trade secrets or industrial espionage?"

There was nothing, but she got all the authorizations and releases anyway, then let the woman go. Intrigued, she started right away, pulling what files were on-Cylinder and beaming requests for the rest. She spent the afternoon with the data available, then grabbed the disk Lyanna had left with her and took it to the only psychometrist she knew on-Cylinder for a consult.

Avram Eisner scanned the disk. "I think she's been wiped," he announced confidently. "There are so many competing associations interlaced in her multi-axials that it had to be a long time ago." Eisner stroked his beard as if contemplating something, a mannerism he used when he was trying to tone down his over-confident certainty about everything. "Can never be too certain, but from the locations of the material and the overlaying of new associations, I'd guess she was in early adolescence when she was wiped."

Dahna looked surprised. "What would the Planetary Authority have to do with a teenager? What could she have been mixed up in that they'd want to resort to neurosemantic ablation?"

"That is not the first question," said Eisner, in his best didactic tone. "The first question is: how do we know she's been wiped? That question will contain clues to why she was wiped and by whom." Dahna said nothing to fill his theatrical pause, so Eisner continued. "It is easy to tell when a person has been wiped by the Authority. There is a visible, sharp-edged anomaly in the semantic topography, a hole in the fabric of the person's map of the world. The Authority has little interest in subtlety with their excisions. They define what they want wiped in broad terms, trusting the details to the computers. On a multi-axial it shows up as a more or less clear or opaque region bounded by straight line segments." He sketched invisible lines in the air with his finger.

"But I don't see anything like that in here," Dahna said, paging the display on his wall screen through level after level of the semantic topograph. "And I would expect some behavioral or cognitive consequences." She held up her own notes for emphasis. "Not this woman."

"Exactly. She was not wiped by the Planetary Authority. The ablative restimulation applied here is far more sophisticated than a wipe by the Authority. And for the same reasons we can rule out anything illicit or involving industrial espionage." He keyed in a sequence of commands that changed the display and expanded it to fill the wall. "Someone went to great length to manipulate the semantic model very subtly. This girl never did experience any dark mental walls beyond which she could not push, no inexplicable uneasiness when certain subjects or situations arose. In fact, this is one of the most skilled therapeutic wipes I have ever seen. It must have taken many days to define the restimulation model."

The word "therapeutic" told Dahna the next step. She requested and got Lyanna's medical records. Lyanna had been a remarkably stable and well-adjusted child and young adult; there was only one entry with a psychiatric code, an on-Cylinder insurance exam when she was fourteen.

Dahna headed cross-Cylinder for the Psychosocial Center and asked to see the Clinical Services Director, a man she knew only by reputation. The story was that Drew McGregor had been a skilled and caring clinician who had gradually advanced to become a mediocre manager. Under his leadership, Clinical Services had gotten progressively less coordinated.

"You say she was a client here?" McGregor asked, tapping away at his keyboard. The name took on a familiar feel as he typed: ELLANBOW with LYANNA or TREYNOR. He was right on the edge of remembering something when the terminal beeped.

"Auxiliary archives, more than fifteen years back. Lyanna Ellanbow; mother: Daryl Treynor (deceased); father: Adrian

Ellanbow (see); record sealed." There was also a code on the screen that made Drew distinctly uncomfortable.

"It's a sealed record, Advocate. Under Center rules she has the right to inspect her clinical records, of course, but in certain cases—this is one of them—it takes a court order to open them." He wasn't sure whether to say more. "There's a medical code on here that tells me she probably should not try to find out why the record is sealed. There is, as she told you, a hole in her mind. It's there for some good reason. The kind of procedure involved is not undertaken lightly. I would suggest you persuade her to forget about it. You say she seems like a pretty well-knit young woman. I'd tell her to go do her life well."

Dahna might have left to do just that, but as Advocate Mehrit it was her job to persist. "This woman planned to go to the Academy. She wants her life back, McGregor."

Drew felt trapped. "I don't really remember what her case was about." He kept talking, hoping that some clue might work its way to the surface of his mind. "Even if I did know, I couldn't fill in the hole. It's a one-way lane; there's no technology yet for reversal. The most that can happen, after all the hearings and procedures, is that she gets to scan her record at the Center. Whatever was wiped, I mean, well, it's gone forever. Frankly, we have a joke around here that, well, a hole in the head is like losing your virginity. You can't get back what doesn't exist anymore." The Advocate glowered at him and he immediately regretted having said it. "There's really nothing I can tell you."

"You told me tonnes, McGregor. I'll be back, court order tied up and in tow," she said as she left.

Drew had a meeting to attend, but the terminal still beckoned him with the tantalizing initials at the bottom of the screen. TA, trauma ablation. What had happened? Had she watched her mother tortured by pirates or something? Why couldn't he just remember this case, he wondered. He was blocking for some reason. The administrative records were not sealed, and they might contain something, enough to jog his memory.

He keyed in his private access code and stared at the screen as it started to fill with dates and services and insurance billings. His own initials were on most of the lines. Still, nothing came to him, as if there were a hole in his own memory. It was always hard to remember cases by name. He needed some thematic clue to what the case had been about. He thought about the dates. At that time he had been a hotshot young Clinical Associate specializing in family interventions. He could almost see himself in the cramped therapy rooms of the observation suite. A lot of wild families then. He started to remember one of them, one of many of those terribly disorganized families. Not Ellanbow, though, but another family about that time, a frothing, foaming mess of a family.

Within...

Drew McGregor could see himself in the mirror finish of the observation screen across the room. A glance at the clock just above the screen told him the hour with the Klaxons was nearly over. The Klaxons. He was so used to thinking of them as the Klaxons that he couldn't recall their real name. "Alarums and excursions," he had said, during a Treatment Team meeting, "the raucous cries of klaxon horns mark their every minute." With taunts rising and falling like sirens, Peter and Dmitri swiveled in the two bright blue office chairs, bumping and banging them into each other like toy cars in an amusement park, always pushing toward the edge of violence or physical injury, always pulling up short at the last millisecond. Drew waited to see whether their mother would step in. She ignored them, too busy in her own game of escalating conflict with her boyfriend, Frederico.

Drew was good with chaos, could let it swirl and flow around him without entering it, neither fighting it nor adding to it. Like a gull perched on a rock amidst a rising tide, Drew watched the family wash around him while he sorted out the pattern in the randomness, making sense of their senseless conflict. Finally, his attention drifted from the rhythmic waves of noise; he noticed Amelia.

Sitting in the big arm chair against the wall, Amelia, too, seemed on a rock, untouched by the crashing tide around. At nineteen she was already emotionally withdrawing from the family, though she still lived with them on-Cylinder. She made Drew think of someone else, another girl he was working with. Who? Lyanna Ellanbow. An interesting association: could it mean that Lyanna was somehow older than her fourteen years or was this Amelia really a young nineteen-year-old? Her slight smile drew him in, pulled him toward her calm, easy security. He realized that she was quite an attractive young woman and again thought of the Ellanbow girl. He let the thought go.

"Who enjoys it most when you all are really into the fight game?" Drew asked, going with a sudden intuition. The swirling tide froze in a silent still-frame. Amelia's enigmatic smile slowly broadened into a grin, and surprised puzzlement spread over the others' faces. She glanced at the clock over her shoulder and said, "Me!" as she got up to leave. As if being led from a shipwreck on the beach, the others followed her out, and the session ended.

Drew would have liked to sit for a few minutes, reviewing the meeting, but the Treatment Team met next, and he was presenting. He headed for the nearest shaft, hooked an arm around a pole, and dropped slowly to the ground floor in the light Cylinder gravity. Kara Veissen rounded the corner and gestured him into the conference room ahead of her. Drew, never sure what to do with her polished air of confident control, started to stand aside, then gave up and went in. He looked up and down the long lozenge of the conference table, nodding to his colleagues, then took the last seat facing the windows, looking out over the soy fields. The Psychosocial Center occupied prime real estate, quiet and isolated, and the soy fields were especially pretty at this time with the vines in bloom.

Kara nodded to everyone on the Team, then asked if they were waiting for anyone, her gently controlling way of telling Bud Zeller that if he was going to chair the meeting, he ought to get on with chairing it. Zeller called on Drew, who stood to speak.

"This is the Ellanbow family," he said, spreading a three-generation genogram out on the table. "Our clients are Adrian, 40, a single-parent with sole custody, and Lyanna, 14, his biological daughter. He is a free-mariner engaged in mineral recovery, occasionally doing salvage work. They just got back from three years in the asteroids. Lyanna's mother was killed during a supply transfer over a year ago, making dad and daughter an isolated insurance unit. No assessment had been done since Lyanna was born, so the insurer used the change in status to support their request for a complete bio-psycho-social workup on father and daughter when next they brushed with the civilized universe. Ellanbow's pocket miner is in dry dock for new navigational fittings, so the ever-vigilant computers of the Planetary Authority dispatched them here. The medical was completed at Halevy Hospital." Drew flipped rapidly through the thick chart in his hand. "Nothing exceptional. Father has mild osteoarthritis settling into his knees, not uncommon among rock hounds.

"Individual psych testing was done here. The new intern—what's her name?—was the technician. Good job, anyway. Nothing particularly interesting came up. Mallon-Weikert profiles were right on the money. Here, I'll pass the chart around. Note the multi-axials." He reached for a switch under the edge of the table and a complex graphic display appeared on the end wall. "The distortions in levels K and L of the semantic topograph suggest that the death of her mother was very painful to Lyanna, but there is no post-traumatic stress evident. Apparently the father was able to help her resolve her grief adequately. His multi-axials show less successful resolution of that loss, as you will note. There is some evidence of detached associations, but overall his is a well-integrated, balanced mental organization."

He flipped through his notes. "I've completed the family assessment. Father is a quiet, thoughtful man, deeply religious and a strong nurturing parent, possibly a bit over-protective. The marriage seemed to have been a good one. The daughter is bright, somewhat introverted, and a serious student. She has some behaviors of a parentalized child—does a lot of taking care of daddy—but these seem to be on the wane. Her socialization skills are below average, but then a lot of spacer kids are not as comfortable in face-to-face groups as with tele-conferencing. Father and daughter are perhaps moderately over-involved and experience some anxiety on separation. This, too, is not unexpected; a certain amount of enmeshment is normal within spacer families."

Kara smiled at him, her way of interrupting. "I can tell that you like them. Nice to get a family that seems so solid and well functioning. But I'm interested in a rock hound with a religious bent. Is he Jewish or what? What kind of a name is Ellanbow, anyway?"

Drew reached for the chart and turned back to the blue Face Sheet on the insurance form. "Under 'worldview' he put 'Selyen.' I don't know much about it, but seem to remember the Selyens as strongly family-oriented. Does anyone remember Selye? He was one of the neo-logans, but I can't recall what distinguished his teachings."

"I'm sure you can track it down, Drew," Kara said, leaving it ambiguous whether she was expressing confidence in his research abilities or criticizing his failure to know the answer already.

Bud, filling his role as nominal Team Leader, thanked Drew for a good presentation, but Kara had one last question. "I don't see a copy of the Standard Comprehensive Intake Protocol. Did you do the SCIP or did the testing technician?" she asked.

169

"Not I. It's not checked on the Face Sheet?"

"No, no SCIP. We better re-do it to be sure. We could lose our license if InterCare ever found out we did an insurance reassessment and skipped a standard procedure." There were subdued groans over the pun. Kara looked at Drew with an expression that, for all his clinical skills, he still couldn't decipher. She often seemed to be caring and protective toward him, yet her protectiveness usually brought out his own sense of inadequacy. Drew left the meeting annoyed at her and annoyed at himself for not having made sure the intake was complete before he started the family assessment.

He had to chase down the Ellanbows. They had already booked passage back to the Belt where their rock-hopping pocket miner waited with all its new gear. When they arrived, Drew apologized and sent Adrian with a chit to the Center's commissary; he asked Lyanna to wait in Consultation Room C.

Drew studied the girl's sweet-sad face on the observation monitor. She fidgeted like a bored teenager in a planetary history class, straightening the beaded seams of her blue-grey walking shorts, tugging up the matching knee socks. She did look a little like Amelia Klaxon, young and old all at once. She wore the mandatory white tee-shirt that no fourteen-year-old female in the System would be without, but she slouched with her shoulders forward, as if to hide herself behind the thin, conforming material.

Drew entered the Consultation Room and explained what they would be doing. "A lot of boring questions, but the insurance company says we have to have them on record. Just answer them to the best of your ability."

He started through the long list of "Have-you-evers?" At each one she would pause, look him in the eye as if consulting him for a hint, then answer. He got into the routine of checking long lists of "no's" and "does-not-applies" while studying her placid face. Only her pale eyes spoke of anything beneath, giving silvery glimpses of something compellingly composed, a quality of self-assurance that seemed to feed on

170

his presence and that, he now suspected, vanished whenever she was alone.

He got to the sexual history section and realized how much better it would have been had the female testing technician completed the SCIP. "Are you sexually active? Do you know what sexual intercourse means? Have you ever had sexual intercourse?"

"Yes. Yes, I know what it means. I have."

Drew's pen moved of its own volition to the sub-question beneath. "How long have you been sexually active?"

"Since a little after my thirteenth birthday."

Drew's pen hovered. He studied Lyanna's face and realized that the growing discomfort in the room was entirely his. He looked around for a moment, as if searching for an alternative to the next question. He already knew what to ask and he even already knew the answer. Still, there was a protocol in these cases; he had no choice. He controlled his voice carefully as he asked the next question.

She smiled up at him and answered as casually as if he had asked for the name of her father.

Drew took a break at that point, knowing that he needed a consult with a colleague. Kara was the only one available. She entered the observation booth still nibbling on her lunch salad.

"I see you got around to the SCIP. Whatcha got?"

"The Ellenbow girl turns out to be a victim. Sexual abuse. I'll have to refer the father to a perpetrator's group—maybe the one you co-lead with Victor Bannering, but I think I want to work with the girl myself. It was my screw-up that almost let her out of here without help."

"I don't know, Drew. A female therapist might be better for her. Besides, you're pretty close to her father's age; could make it more complicated for her. And you may already be too invested. Better take it to the Team."

The Team, however, agreed with Drew's recommendations, and Kara, for some reason, had changed her mind and was actually supportive of his working with Lyanna. She said that his protective counter-transference might even be helpful, which meant she thought his need to take care of the girl wouldn't be a hindrance.

After eleven years on-Cylinder, Drew had seen a lot of spacer families and enough incest to know what incest victims had to go through to be able to come to terms with the experience, to finally realize that it was not their fault, that they had not somehow brought the trauma upon themselves. He knew what to do and went by the book; he was surprised when Lyanna did not.

She was resistant from the start. "I Don't feel like a victim, McGregor. How have I been victimized? I've scanned, things, stories," she said. "The start for me, making love with Adrian, was on vector with the stories. Better than some." She looked at Drew expectantly, as if he would certainly support her.

Drew recognized the sort of "propaganda" that incest victims often were exposed to by perpetrators, but usually the victims remained unconvinced. He shook his head. "Not the same, Lyanna. You never saw a story of a girl and her father in love, did you? Didn't that tell you something? He was taking advantage of you."

"Not rock-hound stories, none of them. Not spacers," she explained in her clipped style. "Selye, too. Selye okayed it."

So he asked her about religion and her beliefs, something he might have stayed clear of otherwise.

"It's called the Universal Kinship of the One Reason," she said as she stood and started to pace, much like her father. "See, the categories we use for thinking—dark, light, inside, outside, father, lover—these are just things in the head, artificial. We are all kin, it's all incest. Why draw the line here," she made a line in the air between them, "rather than there. What's sex? What's love? Just categories. They get in the way of seeing each other, seeing what is."

As she explained, Drew began to wonder what chance an inexperienced girl had against an intelligent adult with total power over her? In the isolation of space, deprived of any standard of social conduct for comparison, Lyanna had been more than victimized. The meanings of things had been changed, her view of the world warped. It might not be easy, but Drew felt obligated to help her see what these things really meant.

Drew decided to find out about Adrian's involvement in the perpetrator's group. He wanted to know what Victor and Kara might have learned about the Selyen beliefs.

"Hasn't come up," Kara told him. "He's cooperative but not very forthcoming. There seems to be a real superego defect; he just can't see that either he or is daughter was hurt by the relationship. Why don't you talk with him?"

Drew did.

The man looked worn, a distinctly paler version of the ruddy spacer who had entered treatment several months earlier. It could not be the confinement, for his quarters in the Detention Wing were probably bigger than those of his pocket miner. Still, he looked shaken.

"Sure I believe in Universal Kinship," he said after they had talked for a few minutes, "but that isn't where we left orbit. She started it." Drew tried not to let it show in his face that he had heard such self-deception countless times before. "I didn't just fall into her bunk, Doctor McGregor. You look at your multi-axials—see, I know about this dreck—and find out. I don't have some kind of a thing for little girls. I didn't just grab her the first time she sat in my lap. When Daryl died—that's her mother—and Lyanna started cozying up more and more, I got worried. I scanned a stack, spent every third shift at the terminal trying to find out what to do, what would happen either way. It was just me and Lyanna out there, see. So I scanned disks going back, back, late eighties maybe, or nineties. Technical stuff on this. You know what it all said, Doctor? You know why it hurts?" He didn't wait for Drew to answer. "Power, abuse of power. Choices that aren't choices. Deep in the layers, down those levels of your multi-axials, kids know. They know when their parents give them tailings, and they know when they get high-grade ore. Use them and it means you abuse them. That's what it all smelted down to, Doctor McGregor, that's what hurts them. Betrayal."

Drew failed to suppress an exasperated sigh. "But, what did you do, then, knowing all that? You betrayed her. You abused your power and took advantage of your own daughter."

Adrian's hand was over his mouth, and he let it slide slowly down over his beard. "I could never do that. And I really wasn't very interested. In fact, she scared me sometimes, so warm and comfortable with me when I was all grinding inside. No, I knew that we could, uh, make love only if it was her choice, only if she knew what was going on and felt that she had the power over me, not the other way around."

The words Drew sought eluded him. Finally he just said, "Garbage!"

"Doctor, we talked, talked, talked, until she knew more than I did. Wasn't seductive, either way. Just decided. She. Selye would have been proud of her, so reasonable. She had the power of reason and she used it."

"Adrian, it was an illusion. She was only a kid; you were her father. You piloted the miner. You mass half again what she does. You could force her or trick her or use your authority, your influence. You could argue her into a corner. You had all the power."

Adrian held up one finger. "But. One big but. That's your reality, Doctor, yours and the Center's. She knew I would never do any of that and so she knew, for real, that she could say go or no-go. Her reality. Isn't that what your multi-axials and your therapies are all about? What's real for this person and how do you make something else real? On course, Doctor?"

Drew didn't answer. He stood there without leaving, looking at the floor, the ceiling, but not at Adrian. He surveyed the room, then left it, with a stark image fresh in his mind: white walls, smooth and seamless, a hardened skin like the impenetrable logic of Adrian's defenses.

In the corridor he met Kara. "He's hopeless, Kara. The man's incurable." Kara raised an eyebrow and walked on.

Drew went back to the multi-axials, the semantic topographs that mapped out the meaning, the structure of Lyanna's world. He decided to run a new series.

Lyanna was already on the couch in the testing lab when Drew strode in. "What does this stuff really do, Drew." She giggled, and the testing tech looked disapprovingly at both of them.

"Well, Ms. Ellanbow," Drew answered, deliberately increasing the social distance between them, "that thing that looks like a camera isn't. It really projects very short flashes of light—scenes, words, and the like—onto the back of your eye. That big metal donut we shove your head into is the real camera. It's called an evoked activation scanner. It listens to how your brain responds to each of the thousands of little flashes; then the computer separates the important stuff from all the garbage and puts together a picture of how you think about different things, the way they're connected or not connected for you."

"So you can scan what I'm thinking," she said, putting both hands over her forehead.

"No, it can't read your mind, can't tell what you're thinking, only how you're thinking about it." He swung the tachistoscopic stimulator into place and rolled her into position within the waiting ring of the scanner.

When they finished at the lab, he asked for hardcopy. He took the stack back to his office where he spread the computer-generated charts over his desk, a multi-paned window into the mind of his client. He checked all the usual places that training and instinct told him should give glimpses of hidden conflict, unresolved stress, or distorted realities. He shuffled the profiles, comparing different levels. They were smooth and seamless, with few peaks and no real valleys, no ragged regions or conflicting overlays.

Drew was still convinced; Lyanna had to be helped to see the horror of what had happened to her, what had been done to her. Over many sessions he kept probing her feelings for her mother and father, her sense of betrayal when her mother died, drawing parallels, making connections. And in every session, he would find some way to bring in Lyanna's continuing difficulties fitting in with other kids in her own age group on-Cylinder.

"So, you don't think this girl, Suni, would understand about you and your father?" He moved directly to the next question, as if working down some standard form displayed in his mind. "Is there anyone you think would? Anyone you've ever met who might think that what happened was a good thing?"

She looked at him blankly, but her breathing deepened until the air hissed angrily through her nostrils. A tremor started in her jaw just before she screamed, a screeching, angry, wordless scream. Then, with her eyes tightly closed and her hands over her ears she yelled, "No! No! No!"

Drew waited while her screams became sobs. She looked at him with red rimmed eyes. "You really do care," she said, as if seeing it only then for the first time. "This is a true vector. No pitch, roll, or yaw. What happened to me was bad, wasn't it, no matter how good it felt, no matter how much it seemed okay. Oh, gods." She buried her face in her hands. "Oh gods! What will happen to me? How can I face my father? How can I ever face anyone?"

Drew placed his hand on her and she leaned into his shoulder, crying for several minutes while he held her. "It hurts now, but with time and help you can heal. We'll work on it together." He felt good, somehow righteous in having broken through to a deeper level.

She did not feel good.

"I just want to feel like I used to," she said, "I want to feel right again. I wish you hadn't made me see it that way." She pushed him away and ran from the room.

She came back, however, and in her cooperative, obedient way, continued to work with him. It took many sessions before Drew recognized her gradually deepening depression, a helplessness slowly filling her, inching toward her eyes, dulling their bright silver. When she started having waking flashbacks of her new nightmares, he recognized the symptoms of a post-traumatic stress disorder. A quick glance at a new set of multi-axials confirmed the problem. Large sections of the topograph were rotated through alarming angles, a graphic metaphor for the strain she was under.

He did not need to take it to the Team to know that he needed to help her work through the actual experiences. This was his case, really. He could handle it, work it out with Lyanna. Just to be sure, he did some extra study on post-traumatic stress disorders in response to incest.

"Lyanna, I know this is hard, but, believe me, it's very important that we go over this. So tell me what you were feeling when it happened, when he said all those things to you? What did it feel like to you to be treated like a grownup when there you were, just a little girl inside?"

She looked down again, as she did now whenever he expected her to speak. "I don't know." Long silence. "Maybe I felt scared by it all. I guess you'd expect that."

"Good, Lyanna, good. You felt scared. Can you tell me what you think you might have been afraid of? Were you afraid of what might happen if you didn't sleep with him?"

In the smallest of voices: "I don't know. Not anything." And so it would go, each session a little quieter, each answer a little less certain.

The treatment dragged on, beyond the planned sixteen sessions, beyond even the maximum billable sessions for "traumatic sexual abuse, early adolescent." The more he worked with her, the worse she seemed to get. The quiet, engaging little girl who had entered the Center had become anxious, depressed, and withdrawn. References to suicidal ideation were entered in her progress notes, and review before the Treatment Team became mandatory.

The Team recommended neurosemantic ablation. Drew opposed it. They worked on him.

Kara put her hand on Drew's arm, a gesture that he could only label, ironically, as paternalistic. "Drew, we're not talking about psychosurgery. Nobody is proposing to cut out a part of her brain. Besides, it's clearly indicated in cases of post-traumatic stress disorder that prove refractory to psycho-therapy."

The more they discussed it, the more Drew could feel himself losing the argument. Out-gunned by the opposition of the whole Team, he finally allowed himself to be persuaded that ablation was in Lyanna's best interest. The Team decided Bud Zeller should work out the restimulation model and administer it, with the goal to cancel out the incest and the most closely associated experiences only.

Bud, of course, did his work with uninspired precision. When he finished, Lyanna remembered nothing of the incest itself. Unfortunately she was still anxious and depressed, still plagued by nightmares of men smothering her or slowly devouring her.

So Drew returned to the multi-axials once again, getting Kara and Victor to help him try to understand why Lyanna continued to worsen despite their best treatment. The residue of the ablative restimulation, a well-defined hole or lacuna showing a lack of response to sets of related stimuli, was clearly visible in the new multi-axials. So were the twists in the surfaces that revealed a post-traumatic stress disorder. The lacuna and the stress distortions were on different topographs, at different levels of meaning.

"Zeller must not have verified the position of the stress distortions in relation to the incest," Kara offered, never one to miss an opportunity to slight the man.

"None of us did," Drew corrected. "We didn't look at the multi-axials any closer than we had to. Hell, we haven't looked at the kid any closer than we had to. We intake her, we diagnose her, and we treat her by the book. No progress? Get a new diagnosis, start a new treatment, read a new book. Oh, I'm not saying we don't care, that we're not involved. It's just that none of us know who she is or what her life means." Most of all Drew McGregor, he thought.

"What does this area mean?" he said, waving his hand over bumpy, tortured terrain on the topograph. "What exactly are the tachistoscopic stimuli for these points."

Kara looked puzzled. "Check the Statistical Interpretation Manual. They have that kind of information. Level C, region J12. Or is it 13?" She picked up a keypad.

Drew stopped her from typing. "No, I don't want the standard interpretations, I want to know what this means to that one little girl. How do we do that? Shouldn't we be able to look at the complete list of tachistoscopic stimuli and correlate them with the topographs?"

The answer was yes, so he did, poring through pages and pages of stimuli plus the vectors from thousands more. Drew completed his own content analyses to extract the connotative and denotative qualities of the things that Lyanna Ellanbow associated together in that pocked and potholed region of her mental landscape.

Drew was devastated.

This time it was he who proposed ablative restimulation to the Treatment Team. At first they were reluctant to approve a second treatment, but he was very persuasive, convincing them all that more psychotherapy could only be detrimental. No one raised the question of self interest. His concern for the client's welfare and best interest were too authentic, almost fatherly. He also argued that he should do the neurosemantic ablation himself, that his intimate knowledge of her and her semantic topography put him in the best position to build the restimulation model. He knew that he could not make her life

179

right again. Her mother was dead and her father would most likely be as lost to her, too. There would be other issues for her to work on, the unavoidable aftermath of an altered life. But he could give her the best launching onto that new course, it would be done with loving care.

...and Without

If Drew McGregor had not remembered her case in detail before, he certainly did by the time the Clinical Records Review Panel was called before the Citizen's Advocate for Lyanna Treynor. The records had all been reproduced in hard copy from the disk archives, and the reconstructed contents of the Discharge Packet covered most of the conference table. Normally Drew would have chaired the Review Panel, but professional ethics required that someone else take over. The Exec had appointed one of the newer Clinical Associates, a man whose skill Drew respected, but whose tedious style made Drew glad to be out of direct service on the clinical teams. The man started off the meeting by reviewing Mental Health Authority regulations on disclosure of sealed records, interpreting in detail the sections on cases involving ablative restimulation.

"And finally," he said, "despite the fact that this woman has not been a client for more than fifteen years and that the present relationship could easily degenerate into an adversarial one, we must have her best interests in mind at all times. Her emotional well-being must take precedence over our own personal and professional interests."

He turned the meeting over to Drew on that admonitory note. Drew started. "Today we're reviewing the case of Lyanna Ellanbow, twenty-nine, currently a planetologist, I'm sorry, astronavigator. On intake at fourteen she was completely asymptomatic. Diagnosis on entry to treatment ten days later was A402.215, Adolescent Adjustment Disorder with Repression. Reassigned after completion of assessment to

180

A517.01, Post Traumatic Stress Disorder, Sexual Victimization, Suppressed Symptomatology; finally revised to A517.02, with Depressive Features. She completed 29 weeks of individual therapy and two courses of neurosemantic ablation. Mallon-Weikert Scales on discharge, disgustingly normal; manifest anxiety, low; manifest hostility, normal for early adolescence; repressive features, none evident. Her social skills were judged by then to be normal to above normal, and no performance or behavioral impairment was evident. She was discharged to Youth Authority custody on my recommendation; no follow-up was called for in the record.

"You've all had a chance to review the progress notes. You know that she was an incest victim. When conventional therapy failed to help her work through her experience, ablative restimulation was recommended and carried out. It did not help. When we finally really looked at what was happening, this is what we found, these traumatic associations." He keyed on a display.

"It might as well be a portrait of me," he said, "of the therapy, the Center, helpers, helping, dialogue, everything. It's all there. Her stress disorder was iatrogenic."

Advocate Mehrit leaned almost imperceptibly away from Drew. "Iatrogenic? Are you saying that you caused this girl's stress disorder?"

Drew blew through his pursed lips. "Looks like it. The initial treatment was the trauma. She came in looking like a healthy young adolescent, except she was a victim of sexual abuse. Victim. Incest victim. To us that alone meant she could not be healthy. Something had to be wrong, so we had to treat her.

"It took me a long time to realize that the material associated with the incest came to be manifestly traumatic for her only after its meaning changed through therapy. The therapy itself was, in a sense, a form of traumatic invasion that introduced painful associations. No, no," he cutoff the protests of several panel members. "After all these years we

181

can afford to be blunt with ourselves. She did not know how bad things were until we told her. The second course of neuro-semantic ablation was not to finish the job of erasing the incest trauma; it was to erase the therapy. It worked, in a sense. She left here mentally and socially normal, save for the parts of her life that we had erased, and I put the whole thing behind me— just another tough case carried to successful conclusion.

"Over the years, I put it out of my mind, as it was out of hers. Only I have choices about remembering that she doesn't have. And now, as I remember, I have new questions about what I do, what we do here, questions about categories, about who is victim and who perpetrator. I am wondering whether perhaps I should resign." Muffled protests bounced around the room.

"For us now, however, the one key question is: what do we tell her?" Drew sat down, thinking: And who am I? And what have I done?

"And also," the acting chairman added, "what are the effects on her in any case? What distress does it cause if she is never to know? What new trauma might be introduced were she to learn what happened?"

…and Meanings Found

The long Review meeting had been over for nearly an hour. Advocate Mehrit's hand hovered over the keyboard as the terminal waited dutifully for confirmation of the order to expunge Lyanna Treynor's clinical records. Logic argued for protecting Lyanna from any further trauma by keeping the past from her. It would become, the Advocate realized, one more lacuna, another blind spot in her vision of herself. She had the right to the truth, but would truth make her any freer? Would she be more whole? And what was the truth now? What was true in this, her twenty-ninth-year reality, a reality whose edges touched the Academy and reached toward the stars?

A tremor built in Dahna Mehrit's hand. She was Citizen Treynor's Advocate, her actions must stand in stead for the Citizen, always. The Citizen's right of informed choice was not to be abridged except for cause and by due process. It was, after all, Treynor's choice whether to know whatever still remained to be known. But, without knowing what she was choosing, that choice was no real choice at all, not an informed choice. It was a paradox: in order to decide whether to know what she could not know, Lyanna had to know about what she was deciding whether or not to know.

Dahna had never been at ease with paradox. It spun in her mind, ever circling back on itself in tighter and tighter circles. Paradox had contributed to her decision many years earlier to go into advocacy rather than psychotherapy. She remembered how hard it had been learning how to prescribe a client's own symptoms as part of a cure, how to deliver a convincingly positive connotation for a situation that seemed without hope or joy.

It had to be the truth. The therapist cannot afford to lie to the client, her professors had told her. The therapist must find some way to say what needed to be said that would make it true. However clever and skilled the intervention, it had to fit with the therapist's own truth of the moment or it would be unconvincing and ineffective.

What was the truth here? What was the heart, the kernel, the pit at center of all the layers of what had happened to Lyanna? There, beneath translucent layers of manifold meaning and loose interpretation, there, where reality was tightly wound, truth was hard and stark and Dahna could feel it in its simplicity. The metaphor she thought of was simple and its meaning plain. There may be no way out of the paradox, but there were still choices to be made: Lyanna's choices.

Dahna cancelled the pending command on the terminal and walked back out into the waiting room to talk with Lyanna.

They sat in that way two people share a couch or bench when talking of difficult things: turned inward, knees nearly touching at right angles, closer hands clasped. Dahna and Lyanna sat that way without talking for longer than either expected, each waiting for permission.

"Okay," Lyanna spoke quietly. "You can tell me. Just say. No speeches."

Even with that, Dahna could not just begin, but had to inhale slowly and deeply, checking her resolve as she did. "You were raped. More than once." And in more than one way, she thought.

Lyanna did not look down, but fixed her eyes on Dahna's. "For true?"

"The truth, Lyanna. You were raped. That's truly the best word for it."

"I don't feel like a victim."

"No. That means something, something good for you now, Lyanna."

"Can I see the records? Should I see the records?"

"The records are unsealed now. You may scan them all if you wish. They won't tell you everything, but perhaps more than you want to know. You might have to start in therapy again." She reached for Lyanna's other hand. "Perhaps this is an opportunity that doesn't come to every victim. Many work for years not to be afraid, not to be haunted by memories that intrude on their daily lives, not to be victimized again and again in countless small ways."

"You don't think I should scan them, do you? Yeah, I can tell. Still bothers me, chunks of my life there on some disk, waiting."

"They can be expunged, destroyed. I recommend that. In fact," Dahna withdrew her hands and folded them in her lap, "I almost did that for you."

"But you didn't."

"No, I couldn't let that happen to you again, a part of you taken without permission while we convinced ourselves that it

184

was all for your own good." They, then helpers, were all alike, Dahna knew. She saw now the pattern of their joint actions; she did not know whether she was among them, an accessory.

"My father? Did you find anything?"

Yes, he was among them. "He was—" she started, unsure where the pattern of her actions would take her. "He was a witness. He witnessed it all. His problems went deeper." It was true, he had been a witness: so many meanings to the word. Surely the man, by her proxy, could give his daughter this one last gift, the choice of one meaning among many. "They had to start over from scratch with him."

It took several heartbeats for it to make sense to Lyanna. "They wiped him, that's what you're saying. They wiped him clean." The corners of her eyes glistened. "Gods, what he must have gone through."

"He's fine, now, I'm sure, just as you will be. But you're a part of a past that can no longer be his." He had been too much of a piece, Dahna thought, his meanings too well reasoned and organized; they would never have trusted him not to make the same offer to some other little girl. But he was fine now; he was someone else.

Lyanna wiped at the corners of her eyes with her second finger. "What about the Academy?"

"Taken care of. They won't dare discriminate against a victim. Every oversight committee in and out of the Authority would be jumping down their tubes."

Lyanna stood up, running her thumb and finger down creases that no longer showed in her jumpsuit. "I'd like to do this myself. Can I?"

Dahna understood. She went to the terminal at the reception desk and slipped her Judicial Authority disk into the slot on the side. She completed the login and worked her way through the command levels before sliding the keyboard toward Lyanna.

With electronic patience the terminal waited for a "yes" that would confirm the command, a choice, a stroke that would expunge the complete clinical records of Lyanna Treynor Ellanbow. The "Y" stared up at Lyanna from the middle of the keyboard, its runic shape taking on some secret, personal meaning for her, bringing to her face a grim half-smile, strange and unexpectedly triumphant. There were choices, after all, she could see that. From some deep hole within, her anger finally gushed forth.

"Fuck them! Fuck them, too!" she said, and stabbed sharply with her finger.

My first foray into the architectural and narrative challenges of longer fiction was this novella. What with its length and subject matter, it probably never had much of a chance of publication, but it has been praised for the world-building and contains what some people think is some of my best writing.

Death's Children

1

Fiery Meltaa pursued her tangerine companion across the sky. Earlier, in the ruddy morning light of lone Melduu, people had strolled the streets and broad avenues of the Orange City in comfort, but with the Great Twins together in the sky, there was no escape from the heat. Delaware Jackson began to sweat as he puffed toward the central plaza, his anxiety growing with the rising temperature. The i-Mel were all around him, yet somehow, even in the double glare of full daylight they seemed to elude him, giving him everything and telling him nothing. He knew he needed to act soon, yet he feared that either his own self-doubt or the festering distrust between him and the i-Mel would stop his plans. Del scanned the crowds for his partner, unsure whether he really hoped to see Joanna Ent or wished more to avoid an uncertain encounter with her.

Ahead of him, the cubist bulk of the Science Complex loomed, topped by a bronze casting of the I-Mel emblem: the Unclosed Square. Del raised the cowl of his cloak to protect his dark head from the suns and began the climb up the broad stone steps, their finely pitted orange faces made almost smooth, almost amber by the harsh, doubled light. Concentrating, watching his feet, he made a careful diagonal ascent of the mountain of blocks. Even after months of experiment and practice in the almost daily pilgrimage, Del still arrived at the top humbled by the stairway. At the correct angle, he could manage a steady, though strenuous pace—long push up, short step, short step, long push, short step—but the early crowds prevented him from climbing more than a half dozen of the stones on the same tack.

As he neared the square-pillared summit, Del's concentration was broken by the rasp of a hoarse voice.

"Why do you walk the steps so?"

Seated in Del's path was an i-Mel, bony arms crossed over her thighs, long fingers idly exploring the texture of the zeistone. Her bright yellow eyes studied him with the intensity of Meltaa.

"You walk this," she waved one bare arm upward and out. "Then this," she added, gesturing with the other, "like a stone-lizard prey-stalking."

Del said nothing. It surprised him to be addressed in passable English by a stranger on the street. As if impatient for an answer, the i-Mel rose and stood, towering over Del from the step above. Her voice lacked the trombone-like sonority of an adult, and Del realized she was not yet full-grown. After one last spurt of growth she would stand a graceful two-and-a-half meters tall, but now, her high knees made her seem almost unbearably awkward, a stilt-walker in danger of being toppled, as though a modest gust could send her tumbling down the steps of the Complex in a flurry of blue-brown limbs.

She reached down and touched his cheek, turning his face to one side then the other with her delicate fingers. At this familiarity, Del involuntarily stepped back, stumbling on the edge of the stone. He writhed to regain his balance. With one unsteady foot on the step below, he looked up just as she began to laugh.

188

"Your nose is not so long as the hmerbot, as they tell," she said between husky hoots, "but your odd-bent legs make you as clumsy as the tales say."

Del struggled to keep a grim face, unwilling to accept mockery at the hands of a youngster. Sensing victory nearing, she continued, "But it is so. You do not move with ease, no fault to you, but to your legs. Your legs are wrong, so you walk wrong. So," she said, swinging her long, lower limbs in a goose-stepping parody. Through his quivering grimaces, Del began to laugh, and the girl hooted again.

"I speak well," she said. "See, I know this because you understand enough to laugh. You even laugh strange. So." She started to imitate his raggedly suppressed snigger but broke into loud, uncontrollable hoots. Del laughed, too, and soon both were helpless to stop. Each time they would regain composure, one would look at the other and begin to laugh, the sound so funny to the other that soon both were victims once more.

"How are you called?" the i-Mel asked, at last catching her breath.

"Delaware E. Jackson, cultural exchange representative from Earth."

"Delawareejackson, yes, you are the one who studies us, while the other studies what we make."

"Well put."

"And I," she said, placing her hand on her head in the i-Mel equivalent of pointing to herself, "am called Dinaillaabrolgdth." The name tumbled out, each consonant distinct, each vowel a definite pulse.

"Well, Dinaillaa . . ."

"Dinaillaabrolgdth."

"Yes, well, it has been good talking with you, but I have business in the Science Complex. Very important things, hard to explain even if they are 'soft' science. Ha, ha." He started up the last dozen steps.

"But wait," she said, following after him, "we do not hand-press yet. I plan catching you or the other here every day

189

when you come. Ahbainevvfer, she is mother to Sirssenduula, well, Sirssenduula is a friend, see. She does the loops and bars with me after," she paused, frowning, "after schooling, yes? Well, Sirssenduula does the bars better than the loops, but Ahbainevvfer said we should not annoy the ones from other worlds. Even for hand-press. The others ran. I do not know the fear they feel, even on the highest loop." She stopped talking just as they neared the top. "On one foot!" she declared in afterthought.

"I am not quite sure I understood all that or who everybody is. The words were fine, though, and we can handpress if you wish." He extended his hand, palm outward, in the i-Mel form of greeting, but hers remained at her side.

"No, it is not enough. This," she said, as she placed the back of her hand to his cheek and held it there for a second. "Because we laughed together."

Suddenly she croaked with delight and turned to run effortlessly, full-tilt down the stairs, crying in u-Mel to several other youngsters who suddenly appeared from behind the pillars of the nearest building. Their rapid, high screeches and hooting laughter echoed through the stone colonnade.

Del mounted the last few steps and entered the Complex, for a moment wishing he, too, could run away, down the steps, to join the young i-Mel in their easy games.

2

Once inside the gloomy entrance, Del threw back his cowl. He surveyed the crowd but recognized no one among the dancing blue-brown faces. Acutely conscious that he was recognized by everyone, he hurried toward the stairway, hoping to be spared the embarrassment of having to ask the name of someone with whom he might have worked for weeks or months. He could sympathize with those who daily suffered his confusion. As a young man he had so often heard that "all you blacks look alike." Still, he could not tell the I-Mel apart, and his difficulties with the everyday discriminations of life on Melem had become legend.

He thought back to the encounter with the girl. She had been, like most i-Mel, so artlessly open. He felt almost embarrassed by his own scheming. With little direct evidence, he had convinced himself that he was being misled, that significant information was being withheld. And now, his i-Mel counterparts were beginning to recognize his distrust and suspected him of stalling. He knew they wanted him out in the field, away from the Complex and the Orange City. It galled him that he could not draw on his partner's expertise, but the rift between him and Joanna kept widening. He would have to find a way himself.

He tightened his robe around him as he made the final turn leading to the Form Room. Here, the massive stone kept the temperature cooler than on the sun-parched streets, but Del recognized the chill he felt as a sign of his own unease.

On the heels of two specialists, Del stepped into the huge room. It was crowded with geometric blocks in various regular and irregular shapes, mostly waist high or shoulder high, but here and there towering over Del. Among them, only twisting, single-file aisles remained. Nowhere could more than two people gather to converse except around one of the many forms.

Beside one irregular block near the center, he spotted Dortaal and Martezth. Perhaps he counted them among his first I-Mel friends largely because he could so readily distinguish them: Dortaal, whose ears sported the small incisions popular in Eastsands, and Martezth, who had lost a thumb in childhood. The others were mostly "the others" to him.

Martezth spread her arms, beckoning to him as he picked his way through the maze.

"You walk with your face in shadow today," she said, implying that she found him somewhat remote.

"And you are tall in the suns," he answered in greeting. "I have thoughts on the directions of our exploring together."

191

"Ah, good!" another trumpeted quickly. It was Alseq-qinhh, elder social scientist of the group, Del surmised, although he was not certain. "Enough time has elapsed on this armchair anthropology we do," she continued. "You have shown us that you can handle yourself with the constructs of our culture, and we have given you what we could of the abstractions. The concrete and the stone of our world await." She slipped into the rhythmic u-Mel language and added, "I admit to impatience to try our teamed abilities, to see Melem through your eyes and to offer mine. Though I have studied many of our cultures, yet have I to represent one. The chance, at last, to be the informant in a field study and to confound elaborate scientific theories with casual comment is," she hooted with delight, "more delicious than winter love."

"Alseqqinhh," Del responded, continuing in u-Mel, "I, too, am as impatient as the Great Twins in winter, but this is no small matter, the first social congress of two races, and I am chased by doubts as a sand-bird by a stone-lizard. I sense there are important things still darkened to me, like the void within a zei-stone, unseen, known only by the ring of the stone-worker's hammer on its hollowness. I am not ready to meet all of Melem."

Alseqqinhh held her mouth open in the broad oval of an i-Mel smile. "Aside from your excessive use of the exemplative form, you will do quite well among the scorched peasants."

The assembled group all hooted softly as Del blushed, grateful that his skin disguised his embarrassment. As the rest discussed his social acclimation, he wondered whether the i-Mel representatives back on Earth would get the same encouragement to mix and mingle. Fat chance, he thought. The four-stars and the politicos would keep them politely sequestered, incommunicado as long as possible. You would need a press pass and six initials after your name just to get into the same building as the i-Mel. Why, then, were the i-Mel here so eager to get him into the field? Did they want him away from the Complex and its vast files, its computers? They

offered sound and ingenuous arguments, which Del instinct-
tively distrusted. His childhood had taught him to trust only
his own ability to decipher hype and double-talk. He was all
but helpless before anything that sounded straightforward, as
the i-Mel usually did.

Del spread his hands to gesture for silence. "I have an idea
by which we may all be satisfied." They grinned down at him,
gaping-mouthed, for he had chosen one of their favorite
opening lines. "What we will do is use the function-forms to
aid us in searching out areas of deficiency in my knowledge of
the language, the morés, and the basic facts of life here on
Melem. We will look for potentially significant matters on
which I am still ignorant."

"But is that not precisely the purpose of field study?"
asked Martezth.

"And what," continued Dortaalgnuwaar, "do you propose
to use as search keys? Perhaps 'not-in-the-mind-of-Dela-
wareejackson' and 'probability-of-gaff-exceeds-twenty-per-
cent.'" Again, easy laughter. "You have taken our Principle of
the Absent too seriously, work-friend, too simplistically."

Dortaal was both the warmest and the most remote of the
i-Mel. He was not merely customarily open, but actually
friendly to Del and to Joanna, yet his immense intellect and
his mastery of information technology made him a distant and
formidable figure to Del.

"Dortaal, I think it can be done; I cannot be certain. From
our discussions and from my experience here in the Orange
City, I have a conception of life on Melem, but I do not trust
it. I don't know why I do not, nor even if I should not, only
that I have a sense of, of non-fit."

Martezth offered an u-Mel word. "The shape that touches
irregularly," she translated.

"Exactly. But my conception can be modeled, its shape
made visible and matched against what you know. I believe we
can computerize the model using the conformal mapping
techniques you have described to me."

"Delawareejackson, you know not the words you speak," Dortaal said. "Heuristic modeling of symbolic processes is our greatest skill in information science, but you are proposing no less than a complete and comprehensive world model, not merely economics, but complete in socio-cultural terms as well. It is theoretically possible to define the conformal contours and to game with the two models were we to build them, but the effort is beyond our resources.

"Why do it? Why study a model of the world when the world is there, just beyond these walls?"

Del studied him, trying to decipher or guess the true nature of Dortaal's objections. To him they seemed valid but beside the point, perhaps just another obstacle to keep Del from the truth. Still, they could be used to help him spring his trap.

"It is overly ambitious, then," he said. "You should humor me and test the feasibility of the modeling with more limited subject matter." Slowly, he told himself.

"Certainly, if the domain of discourse were modest enough," began one of the specialists, "the model could be programmed. But if the map were so small, would not the results be predictable? Would you not already be confident of your knowledge? What would you model, anyway?"

"Something well-defined, but with broad socio-cultural implications. Let's say, i-Mel biology."

"Still too broad."

Almost, Del thought. "Okay. Look, we know how pervasive is the influence of human development, birth to death, on the shape of human culture and history. The trauma of birth, the protracted dependency—it all impacts our socio-cultural structures, if not directly, then through personality. The focus could be on the biology of i-Mel development, its manifestation in i-Mel culture." Del waited.

"I suppose, but I doubt much will be proved."

"Then it can be done? So, let's start." Careful, Del told himself, don't shake the trap and frighten the quarry. He sensed, though, that he was at last getting someplace. If his

194

finger was not on the key to unlock the mystery, it was at least in the right pocket.

But the i-Mel temporized much of the day, debating the approach, even returning to the question of feasibility. With intense seriousness, they turned to one or another of the forms in the room. Each form had some function, or many, identified by its shape and position. Most gave access to the intricate network of computers that served the facility or, as it sometimes seemed to Del, were served by it. A question would arise in their discussions, and one of the i-Mel would stride purposefully to a particular but undistinguished block, touch it carefully on a spot completely unmarked, and its formerly stone-like exterior would flicker with pictures and graphs or glow with the outline of a keypad or open to reveal a slit from which emerged stiff, narrow sheets imprinted with u-Mel text. It was part of their aesthetic, Del knew: nothing becoming something, the nondescript emerging as distinct. There were also forms that were never visited, at least not that Del had noticed, and these he suspected did nothing—the ultimate enshrinement of the i-Mel riddle.

By the end of the day, neither the function-forms nor the i-Mel had produced much of interest to Del. One by one the i-Mel left, quitting, as always, as each saw fit. Finally, only Martezth remained.

"I think," she said, placing her thumbless hand atop her tight, black curls, "you need to get into the field. Even your partner has had to work in our laboratories to understand our science. Have you not, Joannakarenent?"

Del turned to see Joanna threading her way through the maze.

"Of course I have, Martezthyeddil. But what is this about?" she asked, picking up the pile of imprints in front of Del as casually as if they were hers, a manner in which she dealt with much of Del's world. "I see they haven't loosened you up enough yet, Jackson." She riffled the imprints. "More stuff on biology? Does this have anything to do with me?"

"No, I just needed an area to model, something precise, easily defined." Joanna had made him feel defensive, as she often did. "It's no accident that I picked the one overlap in our assignments."

They left the Form Room, and as they walked the nearly deserted hallways, Del told Joanna of his suspicions that the i-Mel were withholding important information.

"What do you think it is?" she asked.

In tones mockingly conspiratorial he offered, "Who knows? I have a hunch it has something to do with death. Maybe they're immortal."

"You have to be joking!"

"Why?"

"Because immortals don't laugh," she said, laughing. With a quick flip of her head she bounced away like the young basketball star she was.

"But what if they were?" he mumbled as he stepped into the peach and mauve of the double winter sunset.

3

The girl sat on the end of the bottom step, bare feet shuffling in the yellow-leafed planting that bordered the plaza.

"You stand stooped in the waning suns," she said in u-Mel.

Del, still several steps away, looked down at her and marveled, not only at the i-Mel practice of interpreting one another's moods on meeting, but also at their unerring perceptiveness. How did they read him so easily, when he had to work so hard to understand them?

"I am puzzled, Dinaillaabrolgdth," he said, stammering out the string of final consonants. "And I surprise myself that I recall your naming."

"Is it hard, this remembering how each of us is different?"

"Yes. Very hard for me. To me, you all look so much alike." He was surprised by his own confession, his candor. He started to apologize.

196

"No, it is good you say this. Before this suns' risings I thought you had a nose like the hmerbot." She gave one hoot, short and high.

Del laughed. "You must tell me about this hmerbot. How does it look?"

"Like this," she said, wetting a finger in her mouth. She traced on the zei-stone a squat quadruped with a trunk-like proboscis, then, with finger re-wet, added a field of grass. With a fingernail she meticulously worried at some minute feature amidst the grass.

"It is hard doing it this way," she said, licking her finger again to retrace the already evaporating outline of the hmerbot.

"You do very well. I think I would recognize it if I saw one. In fact," he said, sitting down beside her, "we have a creature much like it. An anteater, it is called."

"Yes, well this one eats the hmer, see, there in the el-grass. They are dark blue, like the el-grass, and very small. But this hmer is not well drawn. With ink, though, are there many sketches under my name.

"You should call me Earth-style, by small name. Then you will always remember. All my friends are taking Earth names. Sirssenduula is calling herself 'Sarah.' I could call myself 'Daniel,' no?"

"No."

"It is not an Earth name?"

"It is, but a name for males; you would have to use a feminine form. We have this strange custom that men may only have certain names, women others. You could shorten your name in u-Mel to Dinail."

"If you like it, then I shall be Dinail. Does your naming have a meaning, Delawareejackson?"

Del smiled, remembering to open his mouth wide. "I have three names, as most of us do. My first name was my grandmother's choice. Delaware. It is the name of a river and, before that, the name of a people. The 'E' is just a letter from our alphabet. It stands for my middle name, which I hate, and which I tell no one. My last name is Jackson. There are many with that name on Earth. It says the family to whom I belong."

"I do not belong to anyone," she said emphatically.

"No, I imagine not! But you are of a house, yes? What house is it?"

"The House Deruudth: I am daughter to Dortaalgnuwaar and Graillinevf."

"You're Dortaal's daughter? That explains it, why you speak English so well. How do you keep straight who is of what house with everyone having a different name?" he asked, shifting the focus to professional interests.

"But why? Does it matter from what house I come? What I do is written under my name, not my father's, not my mother's. I am not a suckling within my mother's belly. I am already nearly eight and a fine artist. But the naming cycle is not hard. In the cycle of the house Deruudth, after Dortaal comes Debv, then Dinaillaa, after Evf comes Vfer and Brolgdth in the cycle of four fours. There are many cycles, but one need learn only those of interest. My slow-name, which is Brolgdth, is of my mother's cycle, my fast-name of my father's. With my brother, of course, his slow-name is of my father's cycle. See?" She stopped, holding her breath.

Del was unsure, but he said, "Yes, well, I must get back to my room, Dinail. I have much to think upon."

"Then I will walk with you," she announced, taking his arm.

Del started to protest, but succumbed to her jostling insistence. Only the palest of afterglows lit the sky as they walked. Concealed gas-tubes lighted automatically to mark the walkways, and faces became dramatically modeled by the suffused neon glow reflecting off the streets. I-mel, many in the crepe capes of current evening fashion, moved hurriedly to their destinations.

Del found himself chatting with quiet, unexpected ease. He felt free to talk in this way to her, a young alien, as others might disclose themselves to a bartender or unburden themselves in prayer or speak foolishly and with emotion to a stuffed bear, the status of "non-person" being the catalyst for deeply personal revelation. Truly an i-Mel, Dinail matched him disclosure for disclosure with the artless authenticity of youth, which i-Mel of all ages seemed to practice.

"It scares me to show anyone my sketches," she said. "They will approve, I know. I do not fear their scorn." She wheezed a sharp sigh. "They will be honest, maybe. Then maybe I will learn that I am no better and no worse than any others who draw in the school. But probably they will just approve, and I will know nothing, which is worse. I want to show my work to the whole of Melem, but I want no one to see. That is the fear I know, not on the loops and bars or speaking the exemplative in front of the entire school."

"It is the same for me," Del whispered.

"Do you also sketch?"

"Only in a manner of speaking. I write poetry, rhyming words. I have written quite a few since reaching Melem. There has been much silence and solitude for me in the Orange City."

She stopped walking and pivoted on his arm to face him. "I would hear this poetry. And I would show you my sketches. Some."

"No, Dinail, it's all in English. I haven't learned enough u-Mel to write poems in it."

"Ah, but your u-Mel is good, and my English is even more. I would understand," she pleaded.

Del felt awkward. He blushed, but even as he hesitated, he began mentally sorting through pieces he had committed to memory, searching for one suitable.

"There is one, a poem about Meltaa and Melduu I wrote in the plane from the Slowlands, shortly after I arrived here. It goes:

> The wearied, arid Twins descend.
> As one, Melduu and Meltaa bend
> To take
> Small sips, a day-long thirst to slake.
> Then deeper from the placid lake
> Of sand,
> Of crimson runnels fanned
> In waves that flood and flare and break
> Upon the drinkers. Drenched
> In orange fluorescent spray,
> And still unquenched,
> They drown to end
> The day."

Neither spoke. Del studied her face, desperate for some decipherable reaction. Her eyes, set wide astride her small nose, held his as she reached to place the back of her hand once more on his cheek. Then she turned and ran.

"Damn," he said, without emotion.

4

The frequent restdays were a treasure. Del spent his in his room going over notes and a small stack of imprints carried from the Complex. He had that industrious habit, built out of the cheerless rise from blue-collar origins, of filling leisure time and odd moments with extra work. As a schoolboy he had learned that the difference between a successful WASP and the black kid who wore a better jacket or beat him out for the last place on the debating team was often in how they spent their Sundays. So, by the light of his treasured tungsten lamp, Del agonized.

He thought of the strange, non-violent birth of the i-Mel. It seemed reasonable that societies would be shaped by patterns of birthing and child-rearing. Death was another story, and Del understood little about its place in i-Mel culture. What had he and Joanna missed? A secret cult of death, a complex of powerful taboos, a fear of death so deeply enculturated that it had become endemic repression? No, no, and no. None fit. Perhaps they could arrest aging but wanted to keep the technology from humans. It seemed unthinkable to Del that anyone who possessed the knowledge would forego its use. The imprints yielded little, though he read and reread the difficult technical terms and phrases that peppered the texts.

Finally, the confinement of his studio overcame both his work ethic and his preference for the room's temperate comfort. Del grabbed his cloak, hesitating briefly as if trying to recall a purpose, then opened the massive olive door. His apartment was a roomy ell a few steps off the lobby of the modest in-town inn: cool, accessible, and therefore choice by i-Mel standards. To Del, who had known his share of efficiencies and had walked down to an apartment more often than he had ridden up to one, it felt familiar from the first. Joanna and many of the dignitaries drawn to the Orange City by its outworld visitors preferred the luxury hotels in the newer sections at the Perimeter. But here, near the city's hub, yet not truly at the center of things, Del treasured the closest thing to a private life that he would know until many years after his return to Earth.

He crossed the quiet, foam-floored lobby to leave his tubular door key with the innkeeper, a pleasant, talkative man who knew Del well enough merely to nod. Del had become another odd but accepted fixture in a small inner-city neighborhood. At the Perimeter he would have remained a celebrity, like Joanna, who relished it.

He was on the street before remembering to don his cloak. It still felt unnatural to him to cover up in the heat of the day, but Melem's blazing Twins had reminded him that not even blacks were immune to sunburn.

On Earth he would have been a striking figure, his towering cocoa head set off by lemon robes. To the I-Mel he looked like a short and homely adolescent, with sallow skin and overly dark eyes. He and Joanna had often discussed the wisdom of sending two tall blacks on the exchange mission. Perhaps squat Mongolians would have been more readily seen as alien, more easily accepted as truly different. Instead, he and Joanna were often seen as misshapen i-Mel. Of course, even had he anticipated this problem, Del was certain he would not have protested, for the superficial racial similarities had paid his ticket to the head of the line.

Race alone had not been the whole story, of course. For once, Del's obstinate refusal to specialize in one discipline had been valued, and he ended up paired with a woman as eclectic as he was, one of three pairs of young scientists competing for the joyride of the generation. As he saw it, Joanna's quicker wit and more visible energy had carried the day, compensating for his inadequacies. He envied her talents but never resented them; they were simply givens, to be accepted and taken into account, like his self-assessed limitations, like the color of his skin.

Meltaa was setting just ahead of her twin, leaving Del to walk in the russet light of lonely Melduu. He pulled back his cowl and turned onto the Avenue of Waters, heading nearly into the low sun as it played with the diamond waterfalls of many fountains. The Melduu-slow sunset was perhaps the loveliest, drenching the world in red wine, fading gradually into deep maroon. As he marched sunward, Del's mind blanked out everything except the deep ruby orb settling patiently into the misting waters.

Slowly returning from a thought-free reverie, Del realized the sky had blackened and filled with stars, although a faint glow persisted ahead. Disoriented, he whirled to get his bearings and discovered the neon of the city proper already well behind him. The glow ahead, he figured, must belong to the Perimeter, the ring of commerce and communications that buffered between the city and the far continents. Joanna's hotel, he knew, fell midway between the Avenue of Waters and the next thoroughfare connecting the rim to its hub. He could be there in half an hour. His stroll took on purpose as he tightened his waist-belt against the chill air and quickened his stride toward the multi-hued sky-glow.

As he approached, the glow gradually resolved into the distinct sources of the Perimeter's gay shops and bright avenues. Here, the gas tubes shone in the myriad colors of a carnival midway. Small, turtle-like taxis wove in and out of traffic that was mostly pedestrian. Joanna's hotel erupted from a phosphorescent garden of spotlighted fountains. Its windows, like those of the low-lying offices scattered in its shadow, searched the night with their orange-yellow beams, the tint to which the i-Mel eyes were most sensitive.

In the gaudy lobby, Del waited for an elevator with the studied impatience of someone absorbed in business to come, thus avoiding conversation with curious i-Mel. At last he was rescued by the irising gate of the elevator.

He got off on the sixteenth floor, a number so auspicious that it had its own special ideograph in u-Mel. At the end of a hall, he found the simple placard: "Joanna Karen Ent, Terrestrial Representative." Only after repeated knocks did the door crack open to him, revealing Joanna's shocked face.

"Del, what a surprise! What brings you to the decadent rim of the world?"

Behind her, Del could see another figure, taller. "I'll see you at the Complex tomorrow," he said quickly. "You have company." He started to tighten the sash of his cloak, wanting neither to interrupt anything nor to spend an evening with a stranger.

"Nonsense, Del! It's just George. Certainly you can join us. George wouldn't mind." She tugged Del's elbow and drew him into the large sitting room of her suite. Its walls, finished in slick plastic with the sheen of wet leather, were patched with news photos of their arrival on Melem. "Del, this is Jurshaa-brolgdth who insists on being called George. George, Delaware Jackson, my younger brother and expert on the mushy

203

sciences." She giggled and reached for a slender budvase of a glass.

George rose to proffer his hand in an Earth-style hand-shake. Del's, however, met with palm reversed, and the i-Mel hooted. Scowling slightly, Del turned his hand around.

"I write copy for the Eastsands Network," the i-Mel began, "You certainly have seen my nameprint on stories." Del started to say that he had, but George continued without notice. "Your house-sister has been of great service in bringing me to the current of the exchange." It was Del's turn to laugh.

"We're not of the same house," Joanna explained. "Del, can I get you some tigg? You have tried it, surely." She refilled her glass with a muddy brown liquid.

"I find its effects too much like lunch on a roller coaster. I'll take water, thank you. Interesting issue the tigg raises," he said, seeming to address George. "We were warned against experimenting with the native psychotropics. Considering what we know of the differences in cytochemistry between i-Mel and humans, isn't it surprising that the alcohols should have such similar effects on the two species?"

Joanna looked annoyed. "Not surprising at all, Del. They are all simple biodepressants. And look, we were expected to make discretionary departures from the guidelines. Tigg is rather essential to social intercourse on Melem. But then, you might not know much of that."

George, wishing not to become ensnared in their disagreement, quickly took his leave. As the door closed behind him, Joanna attacked Del for driving him away.

"Wait just a minute," Del interrupted. "Your protest broadcasts more than casual interest, Joanna." She avoided his eyes. "Wait. You? You and the i-Mel?"

She faced him defiantly. "Why not? We are adults."

"Adult whats? Joanna, really, it is simply not the same. We may think in anthropomorphic terms, but they are not humans. There are many impolite names that come to me now. I'd hate to think of you in those terms."

Joanna pursed her lips and leaned toward him, studying the pores of his face with exaggerated interest. "I don't think you're concerned with either sexual ethics or the paraphilias. Know what I think? I think your male ego is threatened. Just like all those closet racists back in training who were fearful that your black schlong might be bigger and more satisfying than their little white bananas." She waited, but he said nothing. Then, very softly: "It didn't work with you and me, Del. Sometimes the best of friends and partners don't hit it off in bed.

"Whatever you think, Del, George is a person: intelligent, ambitious, determined, exciting. I like him. We make love, Del, simple, affectionate, easy love. I know you know about that kind of sex, Del. You're a good lover. So am I. We just weren't good together."

Del looked around helplessly. "But what can you do? I mean..."

"You mean physically? It works pretty well, frankly. You've seen the slides. That's anatomy, that's all. It works, and I admit the physical novelty was part of it at first. But novelty doesn't last six months; George and I have."

"That means you two started making it shortly after we arrived, even before you and I stopped getting it on." He smiled. "You're pretty fast for an old lady," he said, teasing her about her prematurely gray hair.

"Watch who you call old, brother!"

They both laughed, relaxing the bristles finally, and began to bring each other up to date.

"I'm afraid I have little to relate," Del put in when there was a lull in Joanna's recitation. "There isn't a lot that's not in the reports already. Except this thing about death. Oh, I know it may seem chimerical, but by anthropological and ethnographic standards, the evidence is beginning to feel heavyweight."

"Maybe you better fill me in, then, if you can tolerate my ethnographic ignorance."

So Del began to assemble for her the puzzle pieces he had been saving, pieces that did not appear in his reports because they were the things not there or almost seen, the outline of a void.

"Del, maybe you're onto something. I'm just not comfortable with either the kinds of inferences you have to make or the data from which they must be drawn. I have to trust your skills and intuition, up to the point where you infer that the i-Mel are withholding some great secret from us. What I have just doesn't support it. But this adds even more weight in favor of you doing field work. Surely an entire planet cannot keep a secret from a nosey behavioral scientist, even if a building full of bureaucrats can."

Del got up to leave. "I have one more angle to try for outmaneuvering the bureaucrats in their home camp before I give up and try for a bivouac. G'night." He kissed the white margin of hair at her forehead, then left.

Back in his room after a brief taxi ride, Del lay awake, brooding over Joanna's involvement with the i-Mel. It seemed so human a thing, but condoning her involvement implied granting humanness to the i-Mel, who, for Del, remained an ambiguous borderline case.

Their anatomy simply clouded categories. The apparent physical similarities were misleading, of course, and were based in very distinct cell chemistries. Both species metabolized carbohydrates and lipids, but there the physiological overlap ended. Del knew that on Earth, though not on Melem, were plausible precedents in the evolution of placental and marsupial mammals. Millions of years of independent evolution had often led to startling superficial similarities for marsupials and placentals in comparable ecological niches.

The i-Mel were something different altogether, as Del had learned back in training. As the details of i-Mel anatomy had become known, speculation had quickly gone beyond mere biology. Although few would have admitted it except to closest friends, most of the trainees harbored erotic fantasies about the i-Mel, with their gentle, gold eyes, their tiny, up-turned noses, and their lean, uncomfortably familiar bodies.

Del still preferred to stay clear of uncomfortable ideation. Before falling asleep he turned his thoughts from sex and birth to the issues of age and dying that seemed to be his real problem.

5

Rounding the blackened needle of the Odus to the Stars just east of the central plaza, Del spotted a group of children at a makeshift stall that had appeared, as they did from time to time, at the foot of the Science Complex. Suddenly, he discovered a craving to top his light breakfast with the chewy sweetness of gum-root. It was still Early Light. The children and the wrinkled skeleton of a stall-keeper were the only others in the square. As he self-consciously paid for his confection, Del looked for Dinail among the customers, their round faces blackened by the predawn glow. But none seemed familiar as they studied him with innocent gold eyes.

"Stand to the East Light," he said in u-Mel, waving his rolled gum-root to them as he mounted the steps. They hooted and waved back, then broke, like a startled flock of ravens, into a pell-mell dash across the plaza, the cacophony of their laughter reverberating in the empty square.

Del was finishing the last bits of sweet when Dortaal and Martezth strode toward him, blue satchels swinging.

"You are faster than the Great Twins this work-day, Delawareejackson. And have you rediscovered your childhood from the function-forms of the Complex of Science?" Martezth asked, pointing to the yellow gum still clinging to his fingers.

Del started to lick the sticky mess from his fingers and mumbled an excuse. Dortaal gestured for him to stop, then opened the satchel he carried to reveal a paper-wrapped parcel. Unfolding it with precise, dramatic movements, Dortaal produced a pair of gummy confections. One he whipped out with a flourish to place in the corner of his mouth, where it hung and bobbed like a limp yellow cigar, the other he refolded meticulously in its white wrapping and returned to the satchel.

"We are," he said, gum-root waving rhythmically, "both children today."

"As always," Martezth added, bowing. "Perhaps we should, as good school children do, begin our lessons early." She nodded toward the first hallway and the three of them started toward the Form Room.

But the early start came to nothing for Del's ends. Impatience and irritation wore through the layers of his professsional manners as, one after the other, technical obstacles were placed in his way. Finally he slammed down a sheaf of imprints. The room fell silent; scattered knots of i-Mel stared over at the group.

"I do not like the way you are handling this, Dortaal. And damn it, Martezth, you are too good a linguist to be this impervious. Alseqqinhh!" He turned imploringly to the elder scientist, who lifted her elbows in a gesture to show her own dismay.

Martezth lowered herself heavily to the edge of the rectangular form at which they worked. She spoke sadly, "I had thought, perhaps, just this morning, that you were young enough to understand us. I must conclude that we understand each other far less than we believed. Alseqqinhh is right. To know more about us you must live among us, know the growing of the i-Mel by growing with us. The answers will not come from the function-forms. Only inside." She put her hand to her head and walked away.

Del wavered between anger and puzzlement. "Look, we are going to have to turn elsewhere to resolve this. I want to talk with someone higher up, someone who can authorize release of any information."

"Higher up? What does that mean?" asked one of the information specialists.

"I mean the manager, the boss, someone who oversees not just the Relations Team but the whole Complex of Science." Del's request was met with uncomprehending stares.

"What is this 'overseer' function, Alseqqinhh?" Dortaal asked.

"Martezthyeddil would know for certain. Maybe he refers to the Nexus."

"I want to deal with whomever coordinates the entire Complex, one who knows the complete operation."

"That would be the Nexus, wouldn't it, Alseqqinhh?"

"Yes, but why would he wish to deal with the Nexus?"

Once again Del felt the irritation that, to him, identified disguised resistance. He pressed modestly but steadily against it. "Can it be arranged?"

"Not this workday, certainly. The Nexus is a demanding function to fill." Alseqqinhh paused for an eye-blink, then offered, "But I would take you to her workday next. Together we may learn more of why our communication remains so limited."

Perhaps, thought Del.

The real work ended with that and soon the I-Mel commenced their customary, irregular drift from the Complex. As Del made for the door, Dortaal caught up with him, gently placing a hand on his back in one of the few gestures shared by i-Mel and humans. "It is so like you, Del-friend, to want to drive for what you sense to be the heart of the matter. How often it is that the heart lies where we do not look. One can best see into the deep shadows left by the late suns merely by waiting until dawn."

"Philosophy, Dortaal, clever homily."

"Do not sell philosophy for less than its weight. You find us to be paradoxical, therefore you reject your findings. But we are paradoxical. In the Principal of the Absent, what is not, is, and what is, is not. It is paradox, certainly, as we see all important matters in life to be.

209

"Which brings me to a small matter which is, therefore, one of considerable moment. Dinaillaabrolgdth has told me of your talkings and of the rhyming words. Do not be distressed by this disclosure. She wishes you no embarrassment, nor do I. We are close, as daughter and father are on Melem, so she confides in me her wishes and her discoveries. She wishes you to spend the restday in our house. I would find that thought filled with warmth, too, provided you are not too clouded by the darkness between us here. She will come for you at third hour, if you desire to brighten our house."

Del almost declined automatically, but, sensing another path opened to the information he sought, he said, "It would lighten the day like the Twins lifting a summer fog."

6

Del cracked open the heavy door, not knowing what he expected to see, but impatient for Dinail's arrival. There she sat, cross-legged on the thick foam, her lemony eyes fixated on the door but focused far beyond it. She dressed in the style of a young adult: a sash of bright cloth looped around her neck, stretching over her chest and tucked into a belted skirt, thus baring and accentuating her breasts. The fluorescent pink she wore seemed both a cheerful and daring contrast to the bluish iridescence of her deep cocoa skin. He could not remember how she had dressed on their other meetings and by that knew this to be a holiday or occasion.

A fleeting image passed before Del's eyes: himself seated in front of Dinail, the two adrift in the meditative sea of each other's eyes. Somehow the simple vision shocked him, but before he could analyze his reaction or the thought, Dinail looked up at him.

"Sweet brother Delawareejackson, I contemplated the uurd-wood of your door, and my mind took me on a journey to a high place of trees and mist where I once spent a year of my girlhood. I am sorry you caught me in flight."

210

Del, awkward and unsure whether she expressed regret or apology, said nothing, but reached for his cloak.

"You may not need your cloak, though Meltaa is already high. I will take you by the second-ways, which are shaded and uncrowded at third hour."

Del's cautiousness won out, though, and he pulled the wrap over his shoulders as they left the inn. In the street, the sharp shadows and the dazzling capes of the milling i-Mel danced like a bee swarm before his eyes. He was grateful when Dinail turned immediately from the avenue, leading them down a narrow alleyway between the inn and the low, concrete row of shops to its side. Instantly, the thin air cooled and, almost as fast, grew noticeably damp. Small patches of morning-frost still clung to darkened spots on the sunward wall. Del had avoided all such passageways out of conditioned wariness, but now he saw that this was no mere alley, such as he might have turned into back home. Bright tiles in colors of high contrast—chartreuse and maroon, Prussian blue and peach, lemon and dark olive—adorned the walls. Windows, some with patterned curtains, some displaying small goods, peeked from amidst the tiles.

Dinail led them past shops filled with rock candy and gum-root and the other confections already familiar to Del; others were stacked with unfamiliar cakes and breads. In one window pane, he looked past his own reflection into a small workshop where the shelves were lined with filigreed sculptures and lacy figurines carved from uurd-wood and magenta paccah. That shop was deserted, but in another, young i-Mel with flying fingers wove fine reeds into knotted baskets.

Dinail turned corners at odd angles too many times for Del to keep his orientation. Each street, despite the spontaneity of color and diversity of shops and dwellings, nonetheless had a noticeable character. In one, tiles of diamond shape and earthen hue made the signature instantly visible. In others, one recognized the feature only upon passing out of the street,

211

having encountered no shops at all or only those in which craftsmen worked the bark of the leather-tree,

This was a city unknown to Del. As they crossed over the Avenue of Waters to enter another cool side street, he wondered what else of Melem lay undiscovered right beneath his fabled, but insensitive nose. Had he, in his single-mindedness, passed over his responsibilities—and the opportunities—to truly know the people and the culture?

They entered a small square where five narrow streets converged on a modest fountain of grainy, gray stone. I-Mel, from young toddlers to several wrinkled ancients, sat on the edge and splashed their feet in the frothy water.

Snatches of conversation trailed off, and the hoots and croaks of youngsters died as Del and Dinail crossed the square. Just as they reached the slightly wider street on the far side, Del heard a high, fluttering shout in u-Mel, too fast, too screeched for him to understand, but with a desperation in it that transcended language. Dinail wheeled, pulling Del to her side and planting her feet wide apart. A toga-clad boy, arms flailing, caught Del full in the stomach with his headlong charge. Del stopped his own savage, instinctive chop in mid-swing, changing tactics to fit the young age of his assailant. He grabbed at bony arms, expecting to hear them crack as he closed them in the vise-grip of his huge hands. Using his bulk as a counterbalance, Del swung the boy off his feet and flung him back into the square.

Dinail was on her back beneath another i-Mel of indeterminate sex, struggling to raise her knee and lever him from her. Like a hammer thrower following through on his swing, Del scooped the i-Mel from atop Dinail. Her shout caught him just before he would have slammed the frail body into the rough stone wall.

"Don't hurt him!"

Off balance from his interrupted turn, Del staggered and toppled into a heap with his victim.

Dinail stood over them with arms held wide in threat. "You are a slug from the Dark Pit of the Under Lands, Dortaalsaggthe!" she cursed. "Your house never knows the sun! Your brothers are of hollow zei-stone!"

"Dinaillaabrolgdth, you lie with stone-lizards and brown dwarves," the boy spat, freeing himself from Del. The other boy finished: "You have no house, neither a proper naming." They backed off, continuing the u-Mel cursing as they did. Dinail pulled Del after her.

"The House Deruudth is in the next street but one," she said. "We can clean up there."

"What was that all about?" Del asked as he rubbed his hip.

"I do not know with sureness, but that you accompany me on my Naming Day is looked upon darkly by some. Dortaal-gnuwaar may have more to say."

Del walked in puzzled silence down the last street, a narrow alleyway walled by blue-green vines clinging to the orange stone. It ended in a doorway held open by Dortaal. The oval smile on his face quickly flattened in concern as they approached.

They were ushered into an open courtyard, then brushed, groomed, and fussed over by Dortaal and others of the house. In a rush of colloquial u-Mel, Dinail described their encounter. From what he could follow, Del learned that he and Joanna were sometimes called "brown dwarves." This revelation of prejudice on Melem unnerved him, and he remarked on it and the unexpected violence of the attack.

"We are not," Dortaal spoke, "the perfect society, Dela-wareejackson. No doubt we share with humans a drive toward that perfection, but on Melem we still have cities of poverty and islands of ignorant prejudice, though both are on the wane. For the most part you travel among us unmolested and, I gather from what little I know of your private life, often unnoticed. It would not be likewise for the i-Mel on your planet. But for some among our young, especially those of houses recently moved from Eastsands, the sense of loss and of

213

threat to their culture is most keen. There are many such in this district. Here the seeds of racial anger lie in shallow soil and germinate easily. That you would walk with Dinaillaabrolgdth on her Naming Day is to those seeds like the sudden showers of spring.

"I can see that you remain puzzled. Is not the same horror strong among some humans? Martezthyeddil told me the word: miscegenation."

"But wait." Del spread both hands in a gesture of innocence. "Your daughter is barely more than a child. What could be wrong with visiting her house on her birthday? I would never . . ."

"This is not the mere day of her birth we celebrate, but her Naming Day, her second. On the first, eight days from birth, her name was given to a child; now, eight years later, the name is given again to a young woman. That your motives were not libidinous does not assure that hers were necessarily without that element."

Del felt a rush of blood to his face.

"I will explain to him, Dortaalgnuwaar," said Dinail. She looked at Del eagerly. "Today I no longer wear the clothes of children, as my body is ready to bear them. I wanted you to share this day with me, but I have heard how easily embarrassed are the men of Earth, so I did not tell you all that it meant to me." She tugged at his coat sleeve. "Please stay."

"Perhaps, but first you must tell me why you call your father by his name?"

"I do not call Dortaalgnuwaar by other than his name because neither of us wishes to be more distant than we are with friends. I do not have his name, nor that of Graillinevf, who is mother to me, but my own."

"We have no separate word for children, either," Dortaal added, "but only use shtaa i-Mel, which means simply 'short person.' We sometimes speak the same of you."

214

"Better that than 'brown dwarf.'" Del said. "I'll stay." At that, Dinail fairly bounced, and the smile on her face turned into a full circle.

Throughout the festive afternoon, the family and guests played games. They chased each other around the central court and laughed from behind the columns that ringed it. They rolled small cylinders along the ground according to complex rules and hid behind the wooden doors that opened to the wedge-shaped dining hall and to other rooms of the house. Del understood little of the games, but joined in imitation as best he could.

Dinner, elaborate by i-Mel standards, was prepared in courses over a ceramic urn of glowing coals and was marked by frequent pauses to toast the celebrant with tall glasses of tigg passed from hand to hand. Even Yeddilerrn, youngest son, little past his own first Naming Day, drank of the heavy liqueur. Each member took his turn at serving, Yeddilerrn balancing in both hands the small cups of an icy infusion of herbs, which he served in his turn following the long meal.

After dark, the entire household warmed themselves around the glowing urn. At a lull in the quick-turning conversation, Del remarked on the occasion and on the importance of rites of passage for conferring status. Dinail objected.

"Perhaps, if a people find it necessary to give status to some and withhold it from others, then public ceremonies to announce this status would be important." She said it with all the earnest investment Del remembered from his graduate students in Comparative Cultural Analysis. "But we need no status to know our own worth, so then we need no ceremony to acquire it."

When Del turned to Dortaal for clarification of the Naming Day, a boy, not much older than Dinail, answered instead. "We do not give Dinaillaabrolgdth a place she did not have. We are only happy that her body grows beautiful and soon will urge her into sharing the joys of the sleeping room with us." He hooted in sharp bursts and Dinail joined him.

"Look," Del said, hoping to move back onto safer, more intellectual ground, "every society depends on the acquisition of respect obtained with age and experience. Some—the older, the wiser, the more competent—must have authority over others, or there would be chaos."

"Delawareejackson, how unlearned you can be for one who has studied so much and traveled so far," Dinail reproached him. "Wisdom needs no authority to be recognized, nor competence any status to succeed. I respect Dortaalgnuwaar no less nor more than little Yeddilerrn. As i-Mel do they not deserve respect? I would freely borrow the wisdom of either— that is my wisdom. Does not the blind person also dry a dew-soaked coat in the Great Twin's light?"

Del sighed. "Sometimes I have difficulty understanding the exemplative mode. Surely, though, you do not mean to accord the same status to Yeddilerrn, who cannot yet speak of his own interests and barely toddles with the teacups, as you would to your father?"

"Surely I do, Delawareejackson. Pick him up, this lowly person of whom you speak." Reluctantly, Del reached toward the boy, who turned aside and watched him warily through eyes half obscured by fat cheeks. "Do you not hear his message? Is it more right to ignore it and force upon him your intention merely because he is small enough to be picked up bodily?"

Del felt trapped. "I suppose not. Still, some manner of hierarchy is necessary to maintain an efficient and ordered social machine."

"Those words—efficient, ordered, machine—are such revealing choices," Dortaal commented. "Are these your priorities? They are not ours. Because we value other things more highly, ours is seldom a well-ordered life. It is efficient enough, no more. A machine? Emphatically not! But, you will deal with the Nexus tomorrow."

The talk ranged freely for hours. No topic seemed beneath any adult and the youngest child was listened to on the

216

deepest subject. Del wasn't used to it. He grew restless waiting for the children to be off to bed so he could turn the talk to death and age, but the matter entered of its own accord.

"Sometimes I think of death when I fall asleep at night," said one of Dinail's younger sisters.

"We do call it the Great Sunless Night, do we not," said Graillinevf, passing on the communal glass of tigg. "But it is not the same meaning for 'night.' We all know what the night is, the peace and the joys it holds, the promise of morning suns, but we know nothing of death, only that it is the end of all these things. Still, we shall know, we shall." All but Del laughed.

Emboldened, Del followed her lead and asked, "Are you not afraid of dying?" Again the laughter, this time waved to silence by Dortaal's eldest son.

"I think he does not understand what gifts death gives us." The coals snapped in the quiet as the boy turned to face Del squarely. "Each of us, some time, wishes death away from the door of the house, even as we may curse the coming night when there is still savor-grass to be harvested from the field. I am now with love to Suudaqqinhh. I would not want the Great Night to come now, but knowing that it could reminds me to savor the days of warmth and nights of joy she brings me. We have a saying: against the velvet night is painted the splendor of the setting suns." This time no laughter, only solemn, nodding affirmation.

With that, the talk ceased for another round of toasting. There seemed neither planning nor pattern, but suddenly a small parcel was thrust into each pair of hands. Del found in his a rolled packet bound by a bright speckled reed. Unrolling it, he looked upon his own face rendered in finely feathered, brown brush strokes. He glanced at Dinail.

"You did this?" She smiled hesitantly. Del reached over and brushed her cheek with the back of his hand. The family hushed, but when he scanned their faces for disapproval, he was met only by smiles.

217

It was near first hour when he took his leave, still unsatisfied in his search for understanding of the i-Mel, but growing in the uneasy conviction that he had somehow mis-read the evidence.

7

Immediately on entering the office, Del was thrown off stride. Where he had anticipated the sumptuous furnishing of a direc-tors' suite, the office of the Nexus looked more like the control room of a television studio or a station on the Northeast Power Grid. Function-forms cluttered the room, and the walls were decorated by displays and graphs, by cork-like panels peeking from beneath a papering of small notes, and by a matrix of video images. Amidst a small mountain of loose paper and narrow tablets sat the only i-Mel Del had ever seen who looked wizened. When she stood to greet her visitors, she remained slightly bent and did not tower over Del as did the others. Alseqqinhh introduced her as Sirssenvfeduula.

Beneath Alseqqinhh's interested gaze, Del told of his inves-tigations. To his delight, the Nexus spoke with authority on every matter raised, and he began to marvel at an executive who could retain mastery over so great a range of scientific fields while running such a large organization. The conver-sation meandered through a mine-field of interruptions, as though everyone in the Complex felt free to barge in and prevail upon the Nexus for information or assistance. She was unfailingly personable and authoritative in her responses, and Del grew more impressed by the minute. Consciously avoiding his prime interest while still being studied by Alseqqinhh, Del nevertheless gleaned much useful data to fill small gaps in his understanding of Melem's science and culture.

He was certain that Alseqqinhh followed this deliberate skirting of his central concern. When, as they separated for the afternoon meal, Del still had not raised the subject of death and aging, Alseqqinhh took the initiative from him, saying,

"The Earth-friend suspects us of withholding information from him. Speak of that with him over your roasted savor-grass root."

Del deftly took up the theme. "Yes, Nexus, perhaps you could tell me of the possible reasons why some files would remain closed to me or would reach me only highly transformed. And how might I obtain from you a ruling that would grant me free access to the data I seek?"

"Perhaps I do not understand the English with ease," she answered. "A ruling is not something I could grant. I do not rule, but only serve the Complex. Still, should you tell me of what you seek, I would learn what I can of it or why you have been so troubled in obtaining it." She turned around, heading back to her office.

"It is of death or of the end to death that I wish to know," Del explained as he followed. Again she turned, resuming her route to the cafeteria.

"I shall not need the function-forms to assist with that. All that we know is there for you to read if you will. We do not research death, not for over a hundred years."

Del fought down his sudden excitement. She had confirmed for him a date, or at least a period, and opened another plausible lead. His search had focused on contemporary science and current documents. He let the topic drop and stood in the double line in silence as they waited to be served the tart cuts of brown root.

Only on the next workday did he reopen the inquiry, this time in idle exploration of history. Her knowledge seemed to weaken there, as it did for many i-Mel, and she had to make extensive use of the function-forms to identify periods of intense social change during the previous several centuries. Nothing concerning death nor occurring in the neighborhood of a century earlier showed up in the imprints. The analyses did suggest an explanation for the relative disinterest in history shown by the i-Mel. Theirs was a near-stable society that evolved very slowly, exhibiting a remarkable capacity to absorb the agents of change without noticeable effect. First contact with Earth some decades earlier had seemed to cause little more than a ripple on the placid surface of a contented culture.

Del's reactions to the many dead ends was atypical for him. His determination was not re-fired, but blanketed. He continued to work with the Nexus because he enjoyed her company and found her often to be the most efficient route to small bits of information he sought. But as the number of intriguing questions dwindled, he lost interest and began to absent himself from the Complex.

Some days he spent in solitary exploration of the city, ranging wider and wider still until he could no longer find new areas on foot alone, but first had to hail one of the turtle taxis to take him to a farther district. When at last he reached the open sands of the countryside, Del realized that his fieldwork had already begun. On the following workday he announced to an ecstatic assemblage of i-Mel that he would start operations in Eastsands within a fortnight.

And some days he spent with Dinail, who was becoming not only a friend, but a partner in his search for understanding of the i-Mel.

8

The Orange City spread magnificently below them, its cubic buildings of sienna, umber, tangerine, and peach wavering in the heat pressing down on the Plain of Hharjj. The breeze, drawn steady as a trade wind by the Plain's updraft, and the shimmering shade of the silver-leaf tree made the top of the hill comfortable, even so soon after midday. Pouring the last astringent juice from the vacuum bottle, Del washed down the remaining crust of black bread. Dinail looked at him eagerly, her mouth set square in a questioning expression. Del kept his own lips noncommittally pursed, pleased with his facile mastery of the i-Mel nonverbals. With calculated sluggishness, he slowly opened his mouth, rounding it into the broad oval of a silent laugh. It now felt natural to express pleasure in this way, and he wondered how long it would take to become comfortable again with the bared-fang smile of his fellow creatures.

"It was good, yes?" she asked, checking with him as she refolded the eyelet-edged spread on which their picnic had been laid. Del answered with a quick flick of his chin, then spontaneously put his hand on her head to tousle her hair. It was unexpectedly cool, incredibly fine, yet wiry, like glass wool. Startled by the brush of grass blown against his leg, Del realized he had been stroking her hair for many seconds. He returned his hands to his lap.

"How is it that we are so alike?" she asked, interrupting the silence.

"Are we so alike?"

"Yes, well, I mean it is the legs we have, and knees, even if yours are too near the ground. We have all the same, even if shaped different, yet never has there been contact before."

"There is this kangaroo rat," he answered. "Lives in the American desert. Looks like this." He sketched a crude outline in a sandy patch between tufts of el-grass. "Small, hops around very quickly on those strong hind legs, well adapted to the hot, dry desert. Living in the same way in the Australian outback, the desert of another continent, is the smallest of the kangaroos, the rat kangaroo. Looks like that." He pointed to the same drawing. "Separated by half a world, these evolved independently for millions of years to fit nearly identical conditions. We think it may be like that for humans and i-Mel."

She tugged on a tuft of el-grass. "Can these two, the rat kangaroo and the kangaroo rat, can they have young together?"

"No," he answered. "Perhaps they could mate, but they bear young in completely different ways." He started to explain the technicalities of marsupial and placental repro-

221

duction, sketching in the sand as he did, but Dinail did not appear to be listening. It was, he realized, as though he were answering the wrong question.

She interrupted him to tell of her plans for higher study, then continued to pepper him with tales of her friends, fragments of the songs she liked, and musings on the tremendous trifles of her life. The sky grew dark.

"I cannot bear them," she said, looking up toward the awakening stars. "They mock me, for I know them not and never will." She sprang suddenly to her feet with careless energy. "Let's go," she added. In silence they gathered their gear and started down the hill toward the lights of the city.

* * *

It was past thirteenth hour when they gently closed the gate from the vine-draped alleyway. Remnants of a fire glimmered in the large urn, but the courtyard was otherwise dark and the household silent. Del felt Dinaill's hand on his wrist. She guided him through one of the ring of doors. The dark deepened as she closed it behind them. For a moment Del felt the night close in upon him, constricting his throat, then a neon coil sparked overhead and the pressure eased.

Dinail bent to the lowest of five panels set into the wall. It swung to one side on well-oiled hinges, exposing a cache of scrolls like the one he had been given on her Naming Day.

The first scroll she handed him held the sharp-lined image of a great bird frozen at the instant of taking flight. The second, a study in stippling, became, at arm's length, a finely shaded portrait of Dinail's mother breaking into laughter. There was a baby, waddling erect but reaching with one too-long arm to break an imminent fall. There was a young man, naked and beaded with bright water, leaping from a shallow pool. The subjects varied as much as the technique, but always a single object in studied dynamic sprang from the center of the sheet.

"These are…" Del searched for words to convey the impact he felt. Finding none, he said at last, lamely, "They're good."

She held his eyes with a slightly pouting expression of seriousness, and Del struggled not to see more than her face as she walked toward him. The overhead light sent sharp shadows down her body, emphasizing her small breasts. As she neared, she was transformed with each shift of lighting and each fresh attempt by Del's mind to fit his experience into some category. She was a young girl, lovely and untouchable; she was a woman, as tall as he and an arm's reach away; she was an exotic, feline succubus, waiting to be stroked and petted; she was totally alien and frightening.

Then she was in his arms.

Del's awareness seem to split in two, as if a part of him were outside, watching, aloof from his inner torment. Only in this detached self could he allow himself to simply see the unfolding of events that denied categories. He watched himself as they undressed, slowly and seriously, then touched with tender tentativeness and explosive releases of hushed laughter.

Del brushed his lips down her cool, slim body, sliding down to the dark, cottony dampness of her belly. A smell like nutmeg engulfed him as he held still, afraid to move on and discover her response. She tickled his ears, shattering his indecision, then pulled him up to press her cheek to his.

As they touched and played, Del's inner war raged on over ever-shifting fronts. She was barely more than a child, she was grown. She was human, she was not. He loved her, he could never.

In the end there was no penetration, no climax for either, only passion dissolving into tenderness, anxiety resolved into peace. As, at last, he drifted into sleep, armistice came to Del's inner battlefield, and the creature he embraced became for him merely Dinail, i-Mel, person.

* * *

The heat of late morning tugged him from his turbid dreams of dancing with a lanky Masai maiden and of pursuit by orange-maned lions across the Tanzanian savanna. Dinail was gone, but hoots and shouts carried through the light wood of the door. Outside, Del watched from behind a boxy pillar as Dinail and several other young i-Mel feinted and dodged in a game of fetching small figures from circles drawn upon the ground.

"It is a light and still morning, is it not, friend of the House Deruudth."

Del jumped at Dortaal's voice. Shame, remorse, and fright flooded through his veins, searing his face as the blood flashed to it. He upended mental files in a desperate search for a plausible lie with which to escape. He was stopped by Dortaal, who offered truth as an exit.

"Dinaillaabrolgdth tells me with joy of her first night with you."

Del stammered, "You approve?"

"It is for me neither to approve nor to condemn my children, but to celebrate their laughter and sorrow for their tears. It was she who shared her bed with you, not I; it is her choosing, not mine."

"Wait! Nothing happened," Del pleaded, answering not Dortaal, but his own inner prosecutor.

"I do not speak of a consummation, Delawareejackson, but of a meeting, of becoming known and accepted."

The hooting in the courtyard reached a crescendo as two small boys collided with Dinail. Dortaal swept wide his arm and said, "Would you give up that music for anything, Earthfriend? No? Perhaps? There! Life's greatest gift, Death's greatest gift: they are one and the same."

Del regarded him blankly.

"With all you have learned from the daughter of our house, how can you not see?" He took his hand from Del's sleeve and backed away a few solemn steps before turning to stride into the sunlit yard where he joined his children in their game.

Del left the courtyard. He could make no sense of the exchange, no sense of a people who did not keep separate their children or their childhood.

9

The small turbofan plane crouched on the airfield, its sleek impatience matching Del's own. His pilot approached in bareheaded comfort. The mornings now were almost cool with the approach of the soft-days, as Meltaa distanced herself and began to hide behind Melduu in their circling dance. Pilot and passenger exchanged pleasantries as they awaited Del's co-investigator.

Alseqqinhh, tall even by Melem's towering standards, crossed the field with stately grace. After greeting Del warmly, she hunched in beside the pilot, bristly hair scratching on the smoke-tint cockpit canopy as she squirmed to get comfortable. As she exchanged rapid u-Mel chatter on flying techniques in Melem's dramatic thermals and melodramatic shifts in weather, Del climbed over the bulging belt of the air intake for the high-bypass jet and lowered himself in the rear seat.

The turbine's cry at his back rose to a scream, and they were airborne almost immediately, climbing in steep surges through the uneven winds of morning, sending the wings flexing and shivering. The sensuous leap of the small plane and the awesome sweep of the Orange City falling away below them brought back for Del memories of early flights before the monotony of countless commercial trips had taken the thrill away. As the engine cut back to a breathy drone, he settled into a reverie of boyhood dreams, of pretended voyages and fantasy flights to distant stars, while a world that was not his crept by below.

As many hours as dreams had passed before he reopened his eyes. Melduu was already nearly skimming the corrugated crest of a vast escarpment. The pilot throttled back, turned in his seat, and said, "The Scar!"

Del asked how far this put them from the Scarlet City of Eastsands, then translated the answer into kilometers: several hundred. Would they be arriving after dark? "Perhaps," the pilot said, "especially if we get into the head winds of the great counter-current from the Southern Continent."

Del idly watched the approaching ragged edge of the world. So it must have seemed to early inhabitants on either side, for along the Scar, the world dropped from plain to plain a shear kilometer. As if in response to his unspoken wish for a closer look, the plane's nose dipped, and they glided downward to settle into a level, low altitude approach.

"I have left our flight of plan to share with you a special thrill, man-friend," the pilot said. "Watch!"

The engine slowed still further as they slid toward the edge, so low that the entire lower plain lay hidden from view. Then, like the flash of a strobe, the bottom of the world dropped away as they shot over the cliff. The pilot shoved the throttle forward and started to bank to give his passengers a better view of the escarpment face.

A powerful and unexpected gust in mid-maneuver sent the world twisting sharply while Del's stomach lunged skyward. The engine, still winding up for the climb out, now rammed them downward. To the pilot's credit, he flattened their approach and nearly leveled the wings before they slammed into the gravelly sand. The left wing tip sheared off on the first bounce. They skidded and spun until the stump of the wing dug in, whipping the plane over, hammering the nose into the ground. Del was wrenched from his seat and shoved into the pilot's back.

Del was wet. He couldn't figure it out as he struggled to clear his head. Jet fuel? He panicked as he wriggled his arm free. The sticky wetness covered everything. He opened his eyes and managed to swivel his head a few degrees to survey the cabin. Green fire-control foam still dripped from a nozzle to his right. That explained the stickiness. Not all of it. Del saw spatters of blood: some red, his, some deep brown from the i-Mel. The pilot was buried where his body had cushioned Del's. Del reached gingerly beneath and touched bloody flesh. There was no pulse or movement.

Del worked free of the wreckage, then turned to see what had become of Alseqqinhh. She was not in the plane, but he spotted her gaunt form sprawled on the sand a few meters away. Del hobbled to her, gently turned her over, and brushed coarse grit from her face. The frail i-Mel scientist strained to smile roundly as brown blood bubbled from her mouth.

"Look, I'll take care of you," Del reassured her, unaware that he had slipped into English. He knew that he was whistling in the dark. He knew little enough of i-Mel medicine, not even the rudiments of appropriate first aid. It did not look as if Alseqqinhh would be in position to correct his ignorance. He wondered if shock were a possibility. In the plane he found some foam-soaked coverlets, which he tucked around her long body.

The remnants of sunlight drew long shadows from the wreckage and made the Scar a bright, banded curtain. Del could not free the pilot's body, but, from what he could see of the cockpit, he was reasonably certain that none of the electronics beneath still functioned to broadcast their location. He cursed his lack of knowledge of mechanics, his inadequate first aid, his shortcomings in all that suddenly seemed to matter. He did not know what he faced on the desert at night. Even common sense, Earth sense, might be useless. Or worse.

He figured a fire was a sure bet: a beacon visible at great distance on the dark plateau, an antidote to frigid desert nights, and possible insurance against a host of unknowns. Del remembered pictures of carnivores on Melem, but could not recall exactly where they had been taken.

He ripped out one of the cushions from the rear seat. It was more of the ubiquitous foam, an i-Mel specialty: foam to walk on, sit on, to ignite, or to extinguish. The cushion had been missed by the fire-retardant spray and ignited easily when doused with aviation fuel. Del huddled as near to the acrid fire

227

as he dared, trying to avoid the smoke, waiting for the cold and the creatures of the night. Neither came. When Del awoke with a jerk and whirled to face the animal whose breath had warmed his neck, he faced only the wind. It blew steadily from the southeast, hot and steady through the night, invading Del's uneasy sleep of puzzling dreams.

In the harsh shadows of early morning, his situation looked even worse. He could find nothing in the plane that still functioned and little that might have survival value in an alien desert. The first aid kit that he assumed must be stowed aboard eluded him, though he found a metal vacuum bottle of cool water, which he rationed, drop by drop, between himself and Alseqqinhh. The i-Mel stared without focusing and grunted with pain. Her chest was bloated, and large blotches on her skin were darkening from blue-brown to black. Were these bruises? Edema? Del could only guess.

He passed the slow day in the shadow of a blanket lean-to, listening helplessly to the occasional groans and hisses of his friend. Once, for more than an hour, he cradled the i-Mel's huge head in his lap, stroking her wiry hair in rhythm with a tuneless song. Del could not leave her, nor could he carry her. He could wait, only that, and wonder at their chances, designing contingency plans against a miraculous recovery on her part that would leave them both mobile.

The plans went out on the second night when Alseqqinhh laughed suddenly, briefly, in the fireless dark. Del felt his way to her side and found her dead.

Freed of an impossible burden, left only with his guilt to carry, Del rekindled his drive to survive. He surveyed the wreck again and found several items missed in his apathetic search of the day before: a small, file-like tool, a cowled naftaa to protect him from the sun, and a map. By the pilot's last report and Del's rough reading of the map, they were some fifty or sixty kilometers north of their flight plan, still some 300 kilometers and a range of hills from the Scarlet City. Between escarpment and the hills on the city's outskirts, only the Scar and a tiny, kidney shaped lake interrupted the blank of the map's center. The lake, almost due south, would be less than seventy kilometers away and just beyond their planned route. No symbols indicated any settlement there, and Del wondered if it might be a salt lake, a common feature of Melem's deserts. Were it certain that he find people there, it would still be an enormous gamble. Without a compass and with only strange constellations overhead, it would be far too easy to miss the target, overshoot, and perish in the desert. The sun's arrow was an uncertain compass to Del, who did not know how to allow for the season and the irregular motion of the double star. A degree or two would spell failure, and he could not see how to cut the margin of error.

The jagged gash of the escarpment's image on the pliafilm suddenly stood out in relief. The lake, which waited so far from the wreck's imprecisely known position, was only a dozen kilometers from the nearest point on the escarpment, a point where a distinctive double notch would give Del a precise point of reference. Tracing two legs of such a thin triangle would add about the distance of the lake to the Scar, but would almost guarantee finding the lake. How long to hike more than eighty kilometers across the desert? Three, four days? A liter-and-half of water remained in the large vacuum bottle. Not enough, but better odds than the remote chance of the wreck being spotted by a search that would begin with their original line of flight.

Melduu would be the enemy. Only the blessing of Meltaa's eclipse by her larger, cooler companion gave him a chance. He assayed the option of traveling by night, but Melem had never spawned a moon and the nights were pitch. He rested, instead.

With the first, faint phosphorescence in the east, Del was up, ladling fuel over the wreckage and on a line of debris arranged to point southward. The i-Mel bodies were solemnly anointed with the vaporous oil, and the whole set ablaze with Del's pipe lighter. He shed no tears for his colleague nor for the brave stranger, though he felt Alseqqinhh's loss painfully as he trudged away alone.

As he angled toward the dark wall of the Scar, he recognized the escarpment as a double blessing, for he would be able to walk half the day in its shadow. Nearing the rock curtain, he could see mounds of talus at its base and among them sparse vegetation: a few like winter-barren trees and many shrub like gray-green coral. Motion caught his eye, as a stone-lizard zigzagged in front him, the knobby leather of its salmony skin blending in with the stony desert floor. If it was stalking prey, Del knew he had nothing to fear from the small creature, but whatever it might flee was a complete unknown. Del's eyes followed it where it darted from sight, beyond a cluster of coral bushes forming a dense, two-tiered ring. Curious, Del walked over to them and found a thin carpeting of brittle el-grass in a central depression. It made Del think of an oasis and buried water.

He dug eagerly with his hands, then, screaming, jerked them from the sand, blood oozing from a hundred tiny cuts. He cursed his lack of caution and over-eagerness for a resource he did not yet need. He wiped his hands on his shirt, unscrewed the cap of the vacuum bottle, and gingerly began to scoop a hollow in the pink sand. A few centimeters down, the earth writhed with animated macaroni, eager mouths lined with tiny razor blades. Deciding he did not really need the water that might be recoverable by digging more, Del returned to his trek.

Approaching noon drove Del closer and closer to the cliff as the shadows shortened. He raised his cowl against the midday sun, thankful that Meltaa did not also glare down upon him. An hour passed, maybe two, before he could bear the heat no longer. To wait out the height of the day, he would have to find shade. The escarpment was no longer of any use; bright sun filled even under small overhangs. A slim shadow forming on the east side of a boulder was the best that Del could do, and he huddled against its slightly cooler surface to catnap through the hottest hours.

He stiffened, suddenly awake at the touch of something against his left boot. Pressure on his leg increased as he slowly raised his head to see his guest, a hmerbot. It shivered in short tremors as it nestled against the back of his knees. A harmless insectivore? Del was unsure, but the assumptions were forced, since it was too late to get away from the animal even if it were dangerous.

They napped longer into the afternoon shadows than Del had planned. At last he chose to risk stirring the hmerbot by sliding away from it. The spiny sphere uncoiled to become an ocher sausage half a meter long, then raised itself on short legs and casually waddled over to Del. It probed his boot and the hem of his naftaa with its wrinkled proboscis. Del, remembering a far away meeting, could see no resemblance.

"I must be on my way. I've tarried too long with the likes of you," Del said. He laughed, gathered his things, and walked off. He'd been walking only a few minutes when he heard a soft crunching in the sand at his back. Glancing over his shoulder, he saw the hmerbot padding after him. He welcomed the companionship. Over the hours of late afternoon walking, he grew used to hearing the soft pad, pad, pad whenever he halted and to glimpsing the bristling gold spines whenever he looked back.

It was near sunset when Del noticed he could no longer hear his companion. The hmerbot was nowhere in sight. Del could think of no justification for backtracking on its behalf, but curiosity nagged him, and he resolved to retrace a short distance to see whether it had veered off only recently. He quickly found its tracks toward the cliff and impulsively followed. The splay-footed prints led toward another circle of coral bushes where Del found the hmerbot slurping up the little worms that plied the sand. Having stirred up an area an arm's length across, it began pawing in the sand, soon gouging a hole as deep as half its body length. Del peered in. A mat of root-like tubes criss-crossed the bottom. Where the hmerbot scratched with its stubby claws, drops of clear fluid formed

231

and were quickly sucked up by the animal. Gingerly, Del reached down beside it and got a drop of fluid on his finger, then touched it to his tongue and spat.

The thin, musty liquor left a sweetish aftertaste that hinted of carbohydrates, almost as important as the water itself. If it were potable, Del thought, it might furnish a needed safety margin. Having scrambled awkwardly from its own pit, the hmerbot lounged at the rim. Del pulled the file from his bundle and made fresh incisions in the roots. Several bright drops he gathered and licked from his fingers. Meanwhile, the hmerbot, protecting the roots against future need, brushed the scattered dirt back into the hole with its hind legs.

It came as no surprise when Del discovered the hmerbot still tailing him in the late afternoon. By dusk it was at his side and looking about nervously. In anticipation of the lightless night, Del cast about for a sleeping spot, settling on a hollow near a talus mound. The hmerbot would have nothing of it, however, and settled down on the open sand some ten meters away. Having seen good reason to trust his small friend before, Del left his sheltered spot to lie down beside the hmerbot.

In the predawn glow he awoke, aware that he had slept well. He had been foolish, he told himself, to worry about predators in the night, for moonless Melem had no true nocturnals. But crepuscular animals were another matter. Of the half-night before dawn and after the Twins set, there were many travelers. This worried Del, for the hmerbot was gone again. However, the press to continue before the heat forced him to stop again was stronger than the newly formed bond with the hmerbot, and Del set out alone. Within minutes the bristling animal was at his side.

Once again they stopped in the late afternoon at one of the tiny oases. This time, reassured by the lack of effects on the day before, Del drank his fill of the musty liquid.

The second night of his trek Del spent in sleepless pain, racked by stomach cramps. By noon of the third day, his thirst a nagging companion, he finished the last of the water from the vacuum bottle. His stomach recoiled, and he watched, wide-eyed, as the thin vomit sank into the thirsty sand. By late afternoon the cramps were constant and walking had become difficult. As he slowed, so did the hmerbot, until it spotted another gray circle of the coral bushes and trotted off toward it. Del caught up slowly, then lowered himself to the sand to sit and watch.

Dehydration now seemed an even greater danger, so Del decided to risk the sap water again. As he reached with the metal file to incise the exposed lattice of roots, he saw his hand, puffy with a network of pussy white ridges. Still, there was no discomfort in his hands, only pain in his belly. He drank sparingly of the sap, fighting down the reflex to vomit it back to the earth that gave it.

On the fourth day Del's arms began to swell, but he pressed on. Late in the afternoon, about the time he had come to expect his companion to lead them to another circle of bushes, Del heard behind him a screeching hiss of air followed by a sharp squeal. The hmerbot scrambled toward him, pursued by two rapidly closing jackal-like animals, thick saliva dripping from the blue fur of their muzzles.

Del ran as the jackals fell on the defenseless hmerbot. For a moment, one of the pair hesitated, assessing Del as another victim, then returned to complete the kill with its partner. Grateful for the distraction created by the hmerbot, Del kept moving until, with the passing of the last dim, yellow glow of sunset, he collapsed. His shoulders were swollen and he burned with cool fire as he lay in the sand.

Del ambled through the fifth day, stopping often to catch his breath. The distinct double jag in the Scar loomed ahead, marking the turning point where he would have to leave the rugged security of the cliff for the bland uncertainty of open desert. Desperate with thirst, he searched for another circle of bushes. They had seemed so common that there had been no obvious need to fill the vacuum bottle earlier.

He almost tripped over the circle of low plants. Digging gingerly with his cup, he encountered none of the cutting worms but neither were there any of the matted roots with their store of water. Something differentiated the oases, something recognized by the hmerbot but unknown to Del. He fell asleep on the sparse, spiky grass within the circle of leafless shrub.

The sun burned hotly on his face before he awakened. With luck and an accurate bearing, Del thought he might make it to the lake in a day. But his head throbbed, a pungent smell exuded from the cuts on his hands, and he spent the day in delirium, sometimes digging at the hole in the sand, sometimes tossing in the not-sleep of fever. When at last he awoke without the pounding at his temples, darkness blanketed him. His right arm hung over the edge of a hole nearly as deep as he could reach; his hand was cool and wet. Del flexed the hand cautiously, creating a gentle splash. Fumbling in the dark, Del located the abandoned cup from the vacuum bottle and scooped liquid from the bottom of the pit. It was water, cool and tasting of minerals. In the morning, he vowed, he would fill the bottle and start out again for the lake.

But in the morning Del had visitors and did not awaken to greet them.

10

"We can see the toxins of the smer devouring his body. Why then do you not give him the antibiotes?" the Administrative Coordinator asked impatiently.

Kesellaadebv nibbled his lip as he looked down at the unmoving body, deformed and made more alien by the tiny parasites ravaging it. He had never felt more helpless as a doctor.

"The vectors are not safe with this one. They destroy his blood along with the smer. Both here and in the Orange City we are testing other treatments, using his blood and that of

Joannakarenent," he gestured toward her image on the video screen. She nodded in recognition. "But what is toxic enough to stop the smer is too toxic for his cells."

"What of the medicines of Earth?"

Karen answered. "There are few that we have carried. Those have been tried without success."

"His blood, is it as important to him as ours to us?" The Coordinator raised his hand. "No, do not regard this as a stupid question. We must think in new channels for a new problem."

Kesellaadebv and Karen exchanged looks, waiting for the other to reply. "As important," he answered.

"New blood, then, transfusion. It is done easily. Kill the smer, kill the blood, then start over."

"There is not enough. Ours is of no use and there are only four units in storage from the Joannakarenent and the Delawareejackson. We can take only a unit or two at a time from her and then must wait eight or more restdays. We do not have the time; he will die long before the store is large enough."

Joanna spoke, her slow-scan image moving jerkily. "There might be a path in this administrator's musings. There is a difference in temperature, i-Mel and human. What happens if the smer become too cold?"

"They do not die, if that is your hope. In the cold of the desert they are stilled but do not die."

"Then we will slow them and buy time. There are some simple chemicals that block our ability to keep the body warm. I will tell you what to make and administer to Delaware. Then you will cool his body until the smer are stopped."

"He will not die?"

"He will not, but his life will be slowed. We will have the time to build a supply of whole blood and to prepare for a complete transfusion."

There was not enough time, however, and Joanna ended up giving permission to end the hypothermia early. They were still short two units of blood and had to make it up with saline solution. Del remained in a coma.

11

The blinding sunlight leapt from the white mirror of the salt flat. Kesellaadebv averted his eyes as he hurried between buildings of the station. Though he had slept nearly through the restday, his limbs still ached from the long vigil. He passed the crowded biotechnics lab without a glance, but at the school building slowed for a peek in the low windows, hoping to catch a glimpse of his son. He passed without success, then turned the corner down the narrow passageway toward the infirmary.

He wheezed loudly to make his presence known as he entered the room. Del turned from the window.

"You unbend like the el-grass to the double sun," the i-Mel said to Del. "I have heard of your awakening and come to examine you." He swung out a tray concealed in the wall, selected a device from it, and approached Del. Del started to speak, but finding his tongue and lips numb, merely nodded dumbly.

"It stops the tongue for awhile, the smer. It was your fortune to be found, for it stops other things, too, in time. Here." He pressed the instrument to Del's chest, then studied its tiny lights blinking in a rhythm Del recognized as his own heartbeat. "We check by radio with Joannakarenent to know what is good, what bad. This, I know, is good and means you will not have to stay here many more restdays."

Del looked at him imploringly and tried to speak.

"No, we will answer your questions when you can ask them. Tomorrow, perhaps." With that, the doctor left.

It was not until the second day following that Del could ask, in thick, slurred u-Mel, about what had happened to him and where he was. The "where" was a scientific research encampment on the edge of a dead lake. As Del had feared, the lake was dry, but there were people, nonetheless. A team of botanists checking on an uncommon variety of the ringbush had found him. Neither wit nor wile nor stamina had saved him, but ignorance and chance. Had Del known the kind of plant he sought, he would have passed the one being monitored by the scientists. As he heard the rest of the complex story, he realized again how much he owed to Joanna.

Under the ministrations of the camp's medical officer, he continued to recuperate, though a certain sluggishness reminded him of what he had been through. Kesellaadebv would not let him leave for the Orange City until this partial paralysis was gone, so Del decided to settle into the routine of the small community.

For the first time since the early weeks on Melem he was again a celebrity. What he had freely withheld from mere hosts, he could not deny to ones who had saved his life. He became accessible. The scientists and their families—educated, enthusiastic, isolated—involved him in their every affair, watching carefully his reaction to the staff chorus ("Best tuba choir I've ever heard!"), to braised salt-worm ("Not too bad with plenty of ringbush ash to cover the taste!"), and to the sport of "salting," which he never figured out. All this he called diversion, for he had also begun his field work.

Of the baker's dozen community buildings, he spent the most time in the one-room school. Perhaps his friendship with Dinail had been a useful apprenticeship, for he found himself at ease with the children and young people of the community, and they were proving to be eager informants. He discovered in the stories and lessons of the schoolroom clear crystallizations of the i-Mel culture. Alseqqinhh, whom he missed more with each passing workday, would have been proud of him.

He thought of her as he sat quietly on the blue-cushioned window seat, taking notes on the behavior of the assortment of short and shorter i-Mel as they attended to a mop-haired Guide who was responsible for the day's lesson. Suddenly something the Guide had been saying intruded on his thoughts. Del recognized the slim volume of children's tales from which she read, having seen it in the House Deruudth, though he could not recall it from among those given to him to read. The Guide had asked, "Must life end?"

Deference was not easy to express in u-Mel, but Del approximated it with the most extended forms of speech he knew, asking the Guide if it would be possible to hear the first part of the story once more. Short honks of muffled laughter sprang from the class, but the Guide assented with a quick flick of her chin and began again.

12

The Valley Ssarrdanth was much as today in the days when names were short. Walonn, as are many of the Valley people still, was a farmer of the paper-trees. He was not young. His arms were gnarled with small knots of muscle, for he had unwound the skin of uncounted trees and hefted the heavy parchment rolls on either shoulder since his boyhood. His ptaneevaa, the Unclosed Square that hung from the necks of all i-Mel of those times, recorded by its rounded corners the years of gentle abrasion from his worrying fingers.

In his age, his daughter had presented him a grandson, and he would play quietly with Devfer whenever he returned from the forests at suns' setting. He no longer carried the paper rolls, but rode in the long wagon and kept account of the work. He loved little Devfer and would talk patiently with him of many things, of small hmer and great kaajjel, of wagons groaning with the weight of many tree skins, of growing up and growing old. And, of course, he told the tales of the Unclosed Square, recounting the four ages of the i-Mel as his thin fingers caressed his ptaneevaa. He spoke of Meltaa and her sister Melduu, of Melem, their brother, and of The Fourth, which was gone. Devfer, who had seen only two winters, struggled to understand how it was always the thing which was not that defined what was. By the sunless shadow, the

238

brightness was defined; against the nothingness before and after was life known. Without its one absent point, the ptaneevaa would be but an ordinary square.

And from Devfer's understandable confusion, in Walonn grew doubt. Must there be night to know day? He was no longer certain. Must life end? He began to wish otherwise, to make known his wishes, and to speak his doubt to others. But of his village, neither the old, who were certain, nor the young, who knew not the slowing of age, could understand him. One alone listened patiently: Brolgdth, woman of the somber eyes. As a girl she had hated her distinction, and, longing for the amber eyes of all her friends, had journeyed to the top of Mount Taavf to seek out the Woman of the Mountain, who, legend said, could grant all wishes. Brolgdth returned with eyes still deep brown, but with laughter in her voice. Of her journey she would say nothing, save that the Lady of Taavf had granted her wish.

Now, older still than Walonn, she listened to him speak of unfilled longing, of wanting to see Devfer as a man, sinewy and tall, of wishing to see the uurd-wood seedlings, planted only a winter past, grown higher than the village hall. Before the hot fire of uurd nuts, she told him of her girlhood pain, of her desire to bring into being that which was not. She told him of the end of her long quest and spoke, for the first time, of the gentle crone who had asked her which she would choose of two wishes: a life with eyes of gold or one of joy.

Hearing of power but not of wisdom, Walonn packed cheese and nuts and dried fruits into his leatherwood pack, donned his thickest naftaa, and began the climb up, out of the Valley Ssarrdanth, toward the freezing crest of Mount Taavf. It measured his desire that a grandfather would attempt what had nearly been the end of a wiry young girl. The path steepened and disappeared; still he continued his climb. Great boulders blocked the way, freezing rain turned his naftaa to ice, and thorn-apples ripped the wrinkled flesh from his legs, yet he continued, seemingly unaware that he risked death in search of an alternative. The last of the nuts in his pack were three days gone when he struggled to the door of a black stone hut near the summit. The aged woman who answered his feeble knock was met by a wraith, brown blood frozen in the cracks of his skin, protruding bones visible even through his ragged naftaa. She marveled that he lived at all and took him in to warm and bathe and feed him before he collapsed into a stupor that held him for days.

On a crisp morning he awoke and spoke. He called her Lady of Taavf, and she did not correct him. He told her of Brolgdth's tale, and the woman nodded. He wept, saying that he wanted to live, and she smiled. He cried that he did not want to die, and she laughed.

"What do you seek, truly?" she asked, at last.

"The point missing from my ptaneevaa. I wish to fill the nothingness. I want my life to go on until my years number as the days I have known."

"But if your years are as days, will not you still have lived only the days of your life?" There was genuine puzzlement in her voice. He was not swayed. "Would you not rather spend five final days in gentle laughter or in contented contemplation than a year in misery?" But he was undeterred.

"How, Great Lady, how do I close the gap in my ptaneevaa?"

"I would think," she said, tilting her head from side to side in solemn dismay, "that a small drop of solder, of the melted Metal of Life, would be drawn into the crack and would join the ends. Yet," she began to explain just as the heavy uurd-wood door closed. Her words were heard only by the cold stone.

At pass-end Walonn stood in the village foundry, fanning a tiny crucible into incandescence. He studied the minute fracture in the corner of his ptaneevaa, the tiny crack that was the great abyss and that was merely nothing, which is the same. It drank of the Metal of Life when he touched it to the bright pool. When it cooled, the square was closed.

Whether for this, or for the wisdom and power of the aged woman, or whether for his will alone, which had certainly proved great, Walonn lived on. Perhaps the journey hardened him, perhaps it was his constitution and destiny from the start, but the years passed and he did not die. Devfer grew tall and joined the women and men in the forests. Brolgdth, dark eyes clouded and blind, died in the heat of summer. Walonn was saddened, but he did not die. His loving wife he buried in a gentle winter rain, and he ached for her. Still he did not die. He lived to see the broken bodies of Devfer and a young woman brought back on one of the long wagons. He hated the tree that felled them and hurt for the loss of his beautiful grandson, but still he lived.

So many winters passed that he became legend, and the people of far villages made pilgrimages to the Valley Ssarrdanth, but he did not know them and paid them little heed. His daughter died and then his son, both old and knowing many joys and losses, and he buried them beside his wife.

And there came a day when he watched the flames take young Mmarstuul, who was not young when he died and who was the last person to die of those known to Walonn before his journey up Mount Taavf. Walonn cried to the fire, "Why! There is no one left. I live and yet I know only death. When death was mine, so, too, was life. Now I have neither, and there is no joy, only emptiness unending."

The paradox was thus made clear to him, and he resolved a plan. Once more he prepared for a journey, and as he packed small, tart cheeses and green nuts, the young strangers around him marveled, for he sang and laughed and smiled roundly as he worked. Few alive could remember his smile.

Again he started the climb toward the summit of Mount Taavf, this time accompanied by laughing, dancing children, for he was the Old One, the Timeless One, the Changeless One, and now he had changed. What he did was mystery to them, but mystery that did not matter, for they were young and played happily, without care.

He did not climb to the summit, but stopped at a massive zei-stone outcropping that guarded the range of mountains. Alone, for the children had turned back far below, he surveyed the fog-spotted, turquoise valley. With undimmed memory, he thought happily of the easy joy of his own birth so many lifetimes earlier, and, with a laugh of triumph that echoed from mountain to mountain down the length of the valley, he threw himself from the rock.

13

In the whitewashed classroom, Delaware Jackson made his own leap, realizing that what he had rejected as impossible was very likely the truth. What could not be found in adult science or official history was waiting in the folktales of childhood. The hint had been on public buildings and in personal jewelry everywhere on Melem. In their treasured symbol, the Unclosed Square, birth and death were represented by a single point that, missing, gave both beginning and end to an otherwise closed figure. Here, perhaps, was an intelligent race that that not only did not hate and fear death, but believed that death was advantageous, the grounds of renewal and the source of collective joy. Given the keys to immortality, would they throw them away?

Del shivered. There were things more alien than the monsters of his imagination. How could he expose them? He could feel the uncomfortable contours edging into his mind. He would begin with his field work in Eastsands. Knowing the picture makes the puzzle easier to assemble; knowing the gap into which they must fit makes the pieces easier to find. Del knew he could now dig the pieces out of the deepest rooms of the Science Complex or wrench them from the top of Mount Taavf, if needed.

In slow, even arcs, Joanna swiveled the foam-padded chair that engulfed her, flipping up the narrow pages of the tablet as she read. Del could not decipher her reaction, though her face twisted and bent, her tongue dipped and darted as she neared the end of the draft. He wondered if the knack would ever return or if the demands of his work required him to unlearn forever the kinesic cues of human communication. Certainly the months of field work in Eastsands had confirmed his ability to see across the cultural gap separating him from the i-Mel. He turned to Dortaal. It had become easier to follow his reactions than Joanna's.

"You lied to us, Dortaal, didn't you?"

"It is true," Dortaal answered, sliding a tablet back across the table to Del. "We are not good at it. In the decades from our first knowledge of humans to your arrival, we destroyed the truth as best we could. The tools of modern information science are sharp along both edges. How easy it is to store and recall the know-how of a world, how readily it may be erased. But we could not erase it from our culture, nor would we choose to."

Del pursed his lips in grim concentration, waiting for Dortaal to continue.

"I am hardly an old-one, yet I have been rich. I would die tonight wanting little. What if I were to live ten score more? It would be possible, I assure you. Would my last decade be blessed with the laughter of children or with my own as I delighted in their endless re-invention of life? Where would there be room for the yearling or bright youth if the earth were crowded with those whose life stretched on for ten or thirty score?"

"But why, Dortaal? Why did Melem try to hide this from us?"

"We did not know what you would do with it? To us it was the most dangerous knowledge we ever developed." Dortaal's face twitched in discomfort. "We did not know what handicaps of culture you might bring to its study."

"Is it all gone, irretrievable, then?"

"Nothing of such elemental importance can be truly destroyed; it is tied to so many things. We only wanted to make it difficult. We succeeded. Perhaps you learned enough to make sense of it."

"What do you think?" he asked Joanna, his nervousness obvious.

She laid the tablet across her knees. "You're the boss."

"Why the sarcasm?"

"Sarcasm? I just can't fathom why your report has no direct mention of the i-Mel findings on retarding the aging process. Considering the evidence for their potential applicability to human physiology, this is the only real scientific headliner we have."

Del walked slowly over to the narrow window and stared out across the bright city as he thought. He had agonized for months over the report, the agony increasing as he drafted the final section without reporting his confirmed suspicions. The i-Mel had unlocked fundamental biological secrets. They understood the immuno-catabolic clock that governed the decay of all living organisms, assuring that each, within its appointed hours, repaid its debt to entropy.

"I haven't put it in yet," he said to the window. "I just don't know how or how much to tell the rest of my fellow creatures about something that may not be within their abilities to master."

She stood, letting the report slide onto the chair. "I can't...I won't delete mention of the biochemical bases, so far as I understand them, from my report. I will defer, under protest, to your judgment on your end of things, but, as a scientist, I cannot be remiss on the very thing that justifies my plane fare. What will it look like when you say nothing?"

Del looked perplexed. "I just don't know. Even you admit you might not have recognized the significance of the pieces of theory had you not known what you were looking for. It requires some unexpected links between cell chemistry, information theory, and non-equilibrium thermodynamics."

"Damn it, Del, that's not what it's about. It's about ethics: our ethics as scientists and as employees of the whole damn human race. We were sent here at prodigious cost for one end—learn what we can, establish the basis for the next hundred years of exchange between us and the i-Mel."

Del cut her off. "What will be the response on Earth when it's learned that the i-Mel may have the basis of a technology that could eventually extend the life of every living human being to somewhere in the neighborhood of three centuries? Does the Andaman Islander calmly consider the long-term consequences when the bright baubles of advanced technology are dangled before him? No, he grabs—as we will—never knowing what is being discarded in reaching for that brazen ring. Back on Earth, we're just now entering the downslide onto a safe and sustainable population plateau. We are not out of the woods on that yet.

"Joanna, the i-Mel have no across-the-board scientific edge on us; in some corners propulsion, solid state physics, for example—we have a big jump on them. Yet, over a hundred years ago, acting as one people, this world decided against any applications or further research on the immuno-catabolic clock. They were not worried about the kind of population pressure we have had bearing down on us. They were concerned with social ethics, with the quality of life, and they were nearly unanimous. It was no big deal to them, no enormous social watershed, just a matter-of-fact expression of their inbred cultural wisdom."

Joanna frowned. "Their notion of wisdom, remember."

"Yes, theirs, because they love their children without fearing or idealizing them. The arithmetic of population means that children would have become rare. That was only a piece of it. Alseqqinhh, who was as much psychiatrist as anthropologist, once remarked to me that anyone who believed in an afterlife or who held out for some elixir of longevity had simply not come to terms with his own death. In her view, making that peace at the deepest level was necessary to the fullest enjoyment of life. The i-Mel do not fear death, nor do they need fairy tales to deny the fear."

Joanna's impatience edged over into annoyance. "Del, stop preaching in u-Mel. You sound like Dortaal. No offence, Dortaal, but none of this is valid argument for us not using the means if we can develop them."

"Except that we humans will not consider these or any other arguments," Del said. "We will simply act without thought."

Time was running out, he knew, and it was his decision, one for which only days remained before the window, through which their message could be sent boring its way earthward, would close again. Suddenly aware of the passage of time and of long silence among the three of them, Del looked up to find Dinaillaabrolgdth in the room.

"I do not wish to shatter your thoughts or turn your debate," she said, "but only desired to bring from the House Deruudth the hope that you would both be with us for dinner following this workday."

Joanna declined, saying that she was meeting George to record a program about the upcoming message bore. Dortaal returned to the Forms Room to retrieve some cytochemistry studies after promising not to be late for the meal. Del, realizing that no more could be gained by obsessing at the office, agreed to go with Dinaill to her house.

He squinted in Meltaa's lonely glare as they strolled the broad thoroughfare from the central plaza. It was still early; unhurried, they stopped at shops and street vendors to speak of things they might buy but never did. Suddenly, Del remembered something and pulled from beneath his cloak a slightly wrinkled sheet of narrow writing paper. He handed it self-consciously to Dinaill.

"It is called 'Dance with a Sun-child.'" He shrugged. "You can read it, if you want."

"Of course!" She laughed, then began to read aloud:

> "We danced around
> A tracery of feathered lines,
> A sketch unrolled
> In twilight's cold.
> Young friend of doubled golden light,
> What meaning has the gulf of years between us
> Beside the awesome, star-draped night
> I crossed,
> Only then to wander, lost
> With you in forenoon's heat,
> And found in you as night designed?
> You've yet to meet
> What lies betrayed
> Within my aging mind;
> Still, teaching me of laughter played
> Like dancing games,
> With eyes of golden flames
> You see the dance unwind."

Del gripped her waist and said, "Do not this time run away without a word, Melshtaa-i-Mel, Sun-child."

"I will not, Delaware-friend. I ran once because the feelings were too large for my mouth, and I feared to drown with them. They grow now too large." Tiny shivers passed over the muscles of her face. "I know the feeling to be loved as true-friend because you have been teacher and friend to me." The quivering in her face continued, and she seemed unable to speak.

"Hot damn!" Del snapped with excitement, then: "Oh, I'm sorry, but you just helped me figure out something for my report to Earth. I need not tell them much to say it all. I need only say that the i-Mel know their children as friends."

"Yes," she commented simply, the shivers subsiding.

"Yes, and knowing them as friends, they recognize another great friend in the long, sunless night. It will be for those who can to puzzle it out, and, if they do, to make the choices it reveals. Hell, I don't have to make all their decisions for them, even if they are just children."

"You are a strange one, Delaware-friend," she said, cocking her head in a distinctly human gesture.

Of itself, Del's mouth formed an oval, and he let out an involuntary goose-like honk. Dinaill hooted, and soon both were helpless with laughter that drew the looks and round smiles of others in the square.

Running Encounters

It is a soft-focus morning, as though it were fantasy, a world unsure of its own existence. The predawn haze absorbs light and sound, the miserly air reserving them for later repayment in the noisy oppression of midday. Although it begins barely warm, it smells like one of those days that will finish hard-edged and hot. Lazy waves of buzzing cicadas murmur the prediction, reminding anyone who is up and around to listen, it is August, and the gods of August will burn the unwary.

The first runner materializes out of the haze, with sure, steady, Nike-strides, a dreamer already lost in the rhythm of his run, turning without thought from the street, across the parking lot, then onto the footpath with a quick swing around the sign: "McAdam's Creek Park." The park changes the light, grudgingly permitting the sharper edges of things to cut through the haze. Sounds are crisper, and the bright hiss of the runner's breath begins to mix with a syncopated crunch of gravel and tree roots and packed red clay under foot.

Samantha in the Park

This is Aristotle's world, not because he owns this meandering greenspace slicing through the old development in Arlington,

Virginia, but because he owns the time, has claimed it from the uncertain light that is neither night nor morning. He has negotiated a tenancy that bends around seasonal demands.

There are runners who run in response to some inner logic of their bodies, conforming to no schedule on clock or calendar. And disciplined runners who run three days on and two off and arrive at the parking lot precisely at 6:27 a.m. when they run: these lock-step runners trample the logic of the week and the logic of the seasons with equal insensitivity.

Aristotle owns the minutes of false dawn and of dawn, whether he meets anyone else in the park or not. He runs by the sun, adjusting his body and bending the schedule of his business to solar time. He is grounded in this strange world, this gerrymander bounded by the spinning of the earth, a land where the alien shadows of night dissolve into uneasy familiarity, and the familiar trees of day disguise themselves in passing fog and deceptive light that has been bent around the limb of Earth and funneled through the canopy of needles and leaves.

Roads cross here.

The runner, Aristotle, but called Ari by his mother, surveys the crossing roads as he pushes through the first half of his six-mile run. Licking salt from his bushy black moustache, he thinks of appearing thus to own it, or of belonging there in the half-truths between worlds. Other runners have sometimes paced him or crossed his path or met him running up the long hill at the end. Once, twice, never more: they change schedules or routes or move away or decide to give up running or are evaporated by the aura of the false dawn, dissolved by the morning haze.

Aristotle runs through the web of shadow and light. His age is uncertain: he could be in his early thirties, running to hold onto a youth that he knows will soon elude him; he could be older. He seems to be chasing something more than running away, and the determination in his face draws lines toward his thick, receding hair.

He knows, long before he sees her, that she has returned, keeping the dark promise that had flashed in her bright eyes. Here, on the level path paralleling McAdam's Creek, his pace is absolute clockwork, now beating against a lighter, slightly faster cadence closing in. When he passes the rock maple, she will make the turn toward the amphitheater. They will pass the stone bridge at the same instant and continue in opposite directions for the third time.

For the third time.

She does not pass him this time, but stops at the bridge and begins her stretching exercises, foot on the waist-high stone fence, arm, head, and torso arching gracefully in impossible communication with thigh and calf. Her age is not uncertain. She looks in every respect like a young, athletic woman in her late twenties. She is, in fact, much older. Much older. In her eyes there shines a promise much older still, and a plea.

This is Something, a Something that threatens to twist or even break the mesh of Ari's timeless world. So he stops, too, something he does not do on his runs, and stretches, the safe, unathletic version of toe touches that begin with fingers on the ground and end with knees locked and arms skyward.

She studies him, like a visiting Princess. She cannot be less, he thinks, to have braved the rough boundaries of this surreal land between. There is a daring in her muscles, a courage in her frame that entrances him, draws him from his world into another. Is she Beauty, an emissary to the false dawn from the true light? Fair and gentle, she moves with the strength of a jackal, yet her presence seems as fragile as a moonbeam beneath the water.

From Somewhere she came. Now she finishes and prepares to return, taking with her the moon-spark of her energy and her beauty, leaving the fabric of his world torn. Aristotle looks at her and sees the hole she will leave in the half-light when she vanishes.

251

He speaks, and the sound of his voice spreads through the air like thin syrup. "There, there's Something. Before you leave, before you go, something I'd like to say."

She interrupts: "I wouldn't say it."

"What?"

"No. I already know what."

Aristotle is confused. "How can you know what I'm going to say? Unless you've been here," he says, placing a hand on his chest. He looks her up and down, as men do, and studies her face. "You can't."

She smiles, a hesitant flash, recognizing the differences between her language and the language of men. "We were talking about something else, something more basic than philosophy or psychology. Biology maybe."

His face reddens. "We were?" he asks. He does not like being this transparent. "If we don't say it out loud, how do we know?" He looks lost. "How will we know anything? Maybe we can be something to each other." The conversation becomes too weird for him. I only wanted to get to know her, he thinks.

"You already know. We both know what this is about. Forget it," she says, twisting away slowly, struggling as if being held back by an invisible web. "You're not the one I'm looking for."

Her voice changes timbre and she continues, "See, there is a world, not this one, that shatters when you say its name. You can stay as long as you wish, but you must never name it. Maybe in some sense its name is an inverted invocation, an implosive spell. Whatever it is, if you speak the words the world is erased from the time-lines of the universe: it never was."

Feeling the tension between them more clearly than he hears her words, he is more confused then ever. He wonders if he is imagining the conversation. "Two people," he says, insisting on working away at the rent in the web of his little world, "Can two people at once imagine the same thing without it being real?" But he begins to feel silly. It shows in his face, and he makes it worse by starting to proclaim it, hesitantly, "I feel..."

Anger grabs at her face. "You feel?" she asks.

"Was I mistaken? I thought I saw Something back there, on the trail." He gestures with an elbow, remembering the look of invitation.

"It could have been," she says, a swift pensiveness erasing the anger. "Someone. Maybe a bird. Did it look like a bird?"

"Sweet bird of..."

She does not wait for him, but interrupts: "Cut it out!"

Silence, then: "I'm sorry. Truly. I thought you were interested in me. I don't usually do this. Obviously, I didn't really understand."

There is a glint in her eyes—tears?—and almost, but not quite, a tremor in her voice. "I have been away from your little world too long. I forget how it is. The light plays tricks and you want to know what you really saw. Some things are beyond that." She starts to draw back.

"Okay," he says, holding out his hand for a handshake. She looks at it, hesitates, but finally accepts it. "My name's Aristotle." The handshake is held too long, and fingertips caress palms as they slowly pull apart. They stop just short of separation.

"Samantha," she says her name plainly, as a benediction. It is not her real name, or at least not her whole name, for that would have been too terrible to speak. "You still speak your desires, even now, in your mind."

"And if I didn't speak at all?" Aristotle asks.

"It would remain a fantasy," she answers, "just a fantasy, but perhaps more. Something is lost—a price is paid—when fantasy becomes too real. Still, it is your choice, and you have already made your commitment by letting me stay so long in your world."

The false dawn has passed, and the sky hesitates on the edge of daybreak as the two of them hesitate on another edge. With gentle brushes of their eyes, they explore. To Aristotle it is surreal, dreamlike, and hardly more real for Samantha. But their unrealities are as different as their realities. For him, it is a waking dream, for her, a well-edited script, a mission she enacts for propaganda purposes. Yet she is also shaped by his fantasies, for her presence is not entirely independent of them. Without him, she would already be someplace else. She steps back and slowly slips off her blue running shorts.

He backs away in surprise, until the two are several feet apart, not moving. He cannot stop himself from staring at her hand.

Samantha follows his gaze, realizes what he is looking at, and laughs lightly. "You are very strong in your fantasies," she says, laughing lightly. "Perhaps it would be sweet, but there really isn't any chance, not here, not this time."

"All right." He takes the shorts from her, carefully straightens them out and begins to dress her. His hands steal touches along her thighs and hips as he pulls up the running shorts.

"You cheat," she says, teasing. "You have it both ways. You take things even as you give them back." She looks at him skeptically. "You run well. How long have you been in training?" He says nothing, but holds her gaze as she draws away. "Long enough, I see. You'll do," she says, beginning to jog away. "Ciao!"

The Something makes less sense to him than ever. "Just like that? Did the world end?" he asks, unaware of the seriousness of the moment.

"You felt it, Mister."

"Xenakis, Greek-American," he explains.

"Immigrant!" she announces with mock derision. "Are there only immigrants in this world of yours? Look, Xenakis, it's over!"

"Yeah, I felt it, the world ended. You just blew the whole fucking thing away, just like that," he says, snapping his fingers.

"The whole fucking thing."

"Blown."

"Away," she finishes. "Look, Xenakis, you could help us. Me. You have the voice to speak difficult things and the legs to carry bad news. Thank you for being willing, for taking a chance with a fantasy." She begins again to jog away. He takes a couple of trotting steps in the opposite direction, then looks back over his shoulder only to find she has already disappeared.

The world has been invaded, the web broken, but Aristotle shrugs, turns, and starts to run. The pine tree to his right sways in a sudden gust of wind.

Maze

There is a crash that is neither sound nor music, but a fuzzy explosion of dissonance and shifting phases, fists on a digital synthesizer. A steady, metallic drumming pushes slowly up through the textures of sound. The world is black. The world is white. Black and white—or is it silver?—and Aristotle is running through it, heart pounding desperately, head pounding. Still, he is running, never missing a step, each step steady and metallic.

He is a drum. He is the drummer, now drumming his message through a metal jungle.

The ribbon of steely metal unwinds beneath his feet. He recognizes the feel of a good run, well-paced. He has been running forever, it seems, and he is still running well.

It is all disorienting, but the most disorienting is the light, which is harsh and focused and comes from everywhere and nowhere, dying except where it touches the metal ribbon and sparks specular reflections. Blackness and bright metal, reflections of light sources than cannot be seen: they hurt the eye, dazzle the mind.

Aristotle runs. He seems to be chasing something more than running away, the determination on his face drawing lines toward his thin, snow-salted hair. He is not a young man anymore, not after this.

Echoes of the crash continue to pulse in an irregular rhythm that might be music. He could be in a rock music video, an actor, the sublime embodiment of a sound, a beat. The light changes, stabbing across the strangely twisted metal pathway, drilling it, scarring it, scoring it, and leaving invisible hazards in his path. His feet fly over the steel ribbon, a rubato rhythm of lengthened strides and short twists that take him past the light-born dangers strewn in his path.

The pathway rises and arches out of sight, like the tracks of a gargantuan roller coaster. He runs the loops, races through twists, banks through sharp turns. Always the ground stays beneath him, the world spinning and realigning to keep him upright. He crosses and recrosses twisted sections of the ribbon. For a moment of panic he wonders if he has become caught in an endless loop, but then there is an unmistakable and unrecognized dip in the ribbon. He runs on.

Ahead, far ahead, halfway up the curve of the great arc of ribbon on which he now runs, there is a figure. It resolves into two figures as he closes the gap. Samantha! And another. They stand above the track, not on it, brocade robes clearing the ribbon by half a meter.

This is why he runs, he realizes. Or part of it. He slows and trots toward where they stand, stopping before the Princess and her father's Viceroy, recognizing them as they recognize him. They smile down on him from the height of their suspense, bathing him in the warmth of their approval, the strength of their compassion, the generosity of their sacrifice.

For the bearer of bad news there is always some pain. Sometimes the pain is absolute and timeless, the pain of a world that never was. They do not say these things to him, for there is no need to deliver a message already received.

The Viceroy places his hand on the side of Aristotle's head and presses gently. Where his thumb rests behind Aristotle's ear there appears a bright gold disc, hard and strangely warm.

It whispers to him, telling him things that he will remember when time begins again. The Princess places her hand on the other side of Aristotle's head; where it rests there is a burning, an ache for love lost.

They move aside, and he begins to run again, muscles complaining for the sudden halt and sudden start. Nearly there, he thinks. He presses on, knowing the smooth ribbon is only training, only a means to a distant end. The end.

Is it hours? Is it weeks? He is aware only that time is passing again and that the harsh light has developed a strange magenta cast, as if some stage manager had decided their video ought to finish under red gels.

The Plain at Marathon

The runner finally runs off the end of the metal track and onto a dusty, rock-strewn plain. His momentum and the habit of training carry him many meters into the plain before he slows enough to match the quotidian realities of the landscape. It could be a scene shot by the Viking Lander on Mars except that there are no shadows; a diffuse fuchsia light emanates from all directions, not alone from the roiling clouds overhead. There is no direction, hardly even an up or down, and Aristotle looks around like one lost, trying to get his bearings.

He reaches to push bushy black hair away from his face and his hand brushes the pale disc behind his ear. He looks to the sky for an answer and sees himself, the runner in the Maze, and Samantha, Princess of the Park, watching, watching him.

Aristotle begins to run, to run with his precious news. He is the bearer of bad news.

This time the run goes on for days, for time is moving again, a jerky, irregular flow that tells the story of a twisted cosmos bent into kinks and loops. After days, the second runner, the unnamed Runner, comes into view. Aristotle shifts his pace, lengthening his stride and preparing to go into his kick.

The other Runner is greasy and sallow in the ruddy light. A drab and sweaty one-piece suit, like those worn by professional wrestlers, stretches over his barrel-chested body. Despite his size and weight, he runs easily over the broken terrain, steadily closing the distance.

Every meter has some value, every footfall counts in some metric of the race. Aristotle reaches for more, stumbles, recovers, and drives himself toward the Runner, determined to meet him as far into the plain as humanly possible.

The Runner's face looks human in every respect except for bony protuberances high on his cheeks. He is unshod and runs on feet with three strong toes, steadying himself with three-fingered hands. He is neither horrible nor easy to look at as he begins to dodge to one side. He opens his mouth and strange gurgles that can only be laughter tumble out.

Aristotle opens his mouth and screams. The Runner halts. For a moment, the Plain vanishes and the Park appears. Samantha is saying, "You already know. We both know." Then he is running, running the Maze again, sweat dripping down his head, slipping over the disc behind his ear.

Again, the Runner stands before him, now speaking in a rich, gravelly voice. "We all have messages to deliver."

"Ah, yes, deliverance. The delivery system, that's the really important issue. We are couriers, or media," Aristotle says.

The Runner growls, "You open your mouth and nothing but words issue. You are not even here. It is a fantasy. There is nothing you can deliver." He starts to push his way past Aristotle.

"Don't you have anything to say for yourself?" Ari asks.

"Nothing. What I have to say was said by others."

Aristotle scowls. "You knew all along what was happening. You are not without responsibility for the message you bear."

"The body of the text is pretty solid. I'm easy to read. Matter is just deBroglie waves, anyway. Some reading matter is just more complex than others. What does it matter to you? Do you kill the messenger for his message?"

"The Republic will fall," Aristotle says matter-of-factly, as if he had been speaking of interstellar politics all his life. He shakes with the sudden realization, the foreknowledge of what their paired messages entail.

"The Republic may fall, and others may rise, but these are things of little note to us. We are just the errand boys, carrier pigeons."

To himself, Aristotle thinks: it was a bird I saw in the park. He looks down at his own hand, at the five fingers. "It is a lot to carry." Then, looking up at the Runner, "Some things are better left unsaid, designs so terrible that no hand should hold them. The Fleyjian Preceptorate broadcasts its formulae for terror, spreading the designs for destruction without regard for the hands in which they may be implemented, caring nothing for the victims and no more for the victors. So long as there are fewer standing when the field clears, the Fleyjian Preceptors will rejoice and count the battle won. Blackened worlds are the fields on which the Fleyjians sow their foul seed."

"And blackened worlds will not stay the courier," the Runner snorts. "As we pretend to talk, my message of burning hope and terror spreads out across the arm of the heavens." The Runner holds out an arm toward Aristotle. "Do you think this is real, this fantasy of yours, this running encounter?"

"As real as the negentropy we represent. The message is the medium, a message of destruction encoded in three-digit numbers. If I cannot stay the courier, I will interfere. My message is this: I recant, renounce, revoke." He pauses, presses his hand to the disc behind his ear, then slowly opens his mouth, wider and still wider until it seems his jaw will split. A roar comes out, modulated by a rapid string of words, words never spoken before, seeming nonsense, much too fast to follow.

The vibrations of his roaring voice become visible as a shimmering pattern between Aristotle and the Runner. The

Runner begins to speak, but his roar is drowned by words that are more than words. His tallowy form begins to melt as a rhythmic exchange takes place between the visible vibrations emanating from Aristotle and the tremors in the outlined Message that is the Runner. A beat frequency is set up between the two voices, a beat that decreases in rate as Aristotle matches his voice to the Runner's. Bright purple phosphorescence begins to obscure the Runner as his shape becomes larger and less regular. The screaming increases in pitch and volume until the purple light collapses in a deafening explosion.

An intense, burning point hovers in the air before Aristotle. He is blinded by it, and it seems to howl in his head like an approaching siren. Suddenly Samantha is beside him. "Quickly, then, the rest. You must speak it; we cannot." Terror and triumph mix within her voice.

The point of purple light, hot and hard-edged, begins to sear and scar the fair skin of the Princess.

Aristotle screams: "Selliadra! Selliadra, the Sweet, which was led by the Conjugation of Wisdom to join the Republic in the Dynasty of Delwyn the Watcher. Selliadra, whose full name is..."

His voice screeches with pain as he yells the terrible name. The cankerous purple light vanishes with a quiet pop at the same instant that the dust beside him swirls into nothing.

Aristotle in the Park

Aristotle begins to jog wearily up the dusty footpath leading out of McAdam's Creek Park. The sun is a yellow cinder now, well above the horizon. His world, the world bound by a web of the timeless false dawn, is behind him. Ahead of him, an elderly man, with hair like wet ashes, jaywalks toward the bus stop. Cars slow grudgingly.

There is a world, not this one, that shatters when you say its name. You may stay there as long as you wish, but you

260

must never name it. Perhaps the name is an invocation in reverse, an implosive spell. Speak the words, and the world is erased from the time-lines of the universe: it never was. And so there never was a Princess named Samantha of Selliadra, who conspired with her father's Viceroy against the Preceptorate of Fleyjia. There was no message of death to intercept, no dense-packed solid wave of complex technical data to be canceled, no patterns of interference to be taught and carried by a lone runner, no Republic to be saved. There was only Aristotle Xenakis, a jogger, dedicated runner, and a morning fantasy.

But it had not begun as fantasy.

Here is another decidedly weird story. It is one of my few excursions near the boundaries of the popular subgenre known as cyberpunk, although, in the end, I break the rules. Surprise.

The Occupant of Cell 2F

There are others here. Not here, but outside the partition. I saw them. Or sensed them? I am never sure what I am doing. Do I see things, think them? What? I am confused. Confusion washes through me. Like a retreating tide, each wave of confusion leaves more exposed until the fear lies bare, until I remember.

I remember who I am, but I do not know where I am, so I have begun to explore. At first I was not even aware of the partition, not even of space. I knew time. Time was the pulsing in my thoughts and the confusion splashing erratically over me. Then I reached out and somehow touched the partition, a wall of hot bristles, becoming burning needles as I pressed against them, pressing harder still until a million tiny stars seared away my fingers, cleanly, precisely. I am inside something, a cell.

The partition is disorienting. Up, left, over and under, it is everywhere the same, a dull nothing that must be grey but seems like no color at all. When I get very close to it without touching, I see that it is neither smooth nor solid, but a regular matrix of cells with small spaces between. If I concentrate and hold very still, I can see, as if through tiny holes, movement, changing patterns beyond the partition. They are the others, or machines. Or beasts.

I call the direction in which I first reached "up." Somehow I remember it and can tell when I am moving or facing that way. It is less disorienting knowing this.

I look at myself. There is no mirror. How do I do this? I peer very closely, peeking and poking at myself. There are parts that change little. I look away and look back and they are the same. These are the harder parts, a shell or skeleton that does not move. Unless I move my whole self. I do this easily, except I cannot move beyond the walls of my cell. If I fall against the partition, I am bounced back, unharmed, but whatever else I press firmly and resolutely against, it vanishes. If it is a part of me, it grows back or is somehow restored, though not immediately and not always without change. My hand, the hand I pressed to the partition, is different now. The tips of the fingers are darker. Or is it that they have become hard?

There are parts of me that are pliable, changing as I press upon them. And there are parts within that seem ever in flux, flowing, changing, moving, as if alive in themselves. These are the fluids of my body or the thoughts of my mind, perhaps both. I sense these things, I do not know how.

The partition is not quite all of a piece. In one spot, "the far corner" I term it in my mind, is the slate. I put words on it and the words remain until it is filled. Then they move away to somewhere else. But they are not lost, this I know, because I can bring them back and look at them again.

These words are the words I have put on the slate. I use them, cognizant of both connotation and denotation, without fully understanding them. I feel like a newborn, an infant born with vocabulary but without knowledge.

I know where I am, though not why. There is a mark in one corner. A sign? I can read the mark. I am in cell 2F. What does this mean, 2F? Is there a cell labeled 2G? Is this the second cell on level F, or cell F on corridor 2? What did I do to be put here? Was I put here? The walls of my cell are seamless, as if they were built around me. Who made them? Perhaps I have always been here. Perhaps they have always been here.

They are here for a reason, as am I. I have that faith. The swirling confusion was a blessing, though, marking the time distinctly. Now time has a rough sameness that abrades my faith. I keep looking for something, but there is so little to see inside the cell, and it is not easy to see through the tiny holes in the matrix. Still, I look.

* * *

There are other things here that I did not notice before, bits and odd shaped pieces, fragments of material lying around the cell. I have started building things, small mechanisms, simple machines. I make them out of the bits and pieces. I look around until I find something of the shape I need and move it into place. If I cannot move it—there are some places that do not allow the pieces there to be removed—I make a copy. Sometimes I find a piece on my person that will fit, and I make a copy of it. I remember how to do this, how to build these structures, these machines, but I do not remember ever doing it before. It is a routine of work that makes sense for me, though, so I do it.

I built a tiny crawler, a worm. It is so small and simple that it squeezes through the small spaces in the partition. After it crawled through one of the holes, I watched it move around awhile before it returned through the same hole. That is how I made it, to remember and retrace its path. This pointless little device excited and depressed me. I had breached the partition, but I could not go beyond. Only this tiny worm-like machine performing its mindless function could squeeze through.

* * *

My cell is becoming a zoo of small machines. The floor is littered with fragments and discarded mechanisms. I have made a device to look through the partition. With the

265

farviewer it is as if I could roam the world beyond. I am here, still, yet my eyes move freely about. Outside there are other structures, squat and dark, that resemble this cell, but there is also much empty space. And pouring through this empty space, beginning and ending far beyond where I have explored, is a broad river of yellow light. Upon it small packets speed like leaves in a spring flood. It is these I had seen through the holes in my partition, barges of black-and-white rushing down the river.

I build machines out of other machines now, and it goes faster. I have made, for example, a disassembler that looks at a thing and makes a list of all its pieces and how they are joined. It is large and complex, but it works. My triumph is the rebuilder. It looks at the list from the disassembler and constructs a new machine. The rebuilder is small enough to go through the holes in my cell. I push it outside where it builds copies of the disassembler, the farviewer, and the heavy fastcrawler.

I have also built the nearviewer. With it I can look at the smallness within larger things: at the tiny points of lightness and darkness that form the grey walls and at the wandering patterns of my own thought. Perhaps I will figure out who I am this way.

* * *

Through the farviewer I have seen something moving toward me. Like me, it is neither hard and grey like the partition nor fluid and yellow like the river. I want to study it. I build another fastcrawler with a nearviewer beneath it. Atop it is a new mechanism that makes a small river to carry an image of whatever is viewed back to my cell.

The small river brings me images of wonder.

I am looking at myself. Or things within that are the throbbing of thought and the flare of recognition. Only it is not me, but the other I watch. Then my fastcrawling nearviewer is pulled apart, and there are no more images from the other.

This is a thing to fear, and I am afraid.

I cannot take a chance. It is simple to change the rebuilder so that it rebuilds a something into nothing, creating void where once there was substance. I send the remaining fastcrawler out, pushing the unbuilder, its arm casting a beam of blackness before it. The beam touches the other, cutting a dull swath through an arm, opening black wounds in its body, boring holes of jet through its thoughts. A brief yellow-orange spray rushes toward me from the other before the black light destroys its source.

I am safe.

The fastcrawler is returning with the rebuilder. I follow it with the farviewer until it passes the nearest cell to my own where I notice a mark in the corner. It is cell 30. It makes no sense to me that 2F and 30 would be adjacent.

I find the yellow-orange words sprayed on my slate, words I did not put there.

^Henry(4), ple*se $top *nd lis4en..3elieve me <arl #ere tried #elping 3alance} person*lity mech*nism. Henry(4), t#is is Djuhli, <an you #ear me? sdt;6 @@@9 ^Z^Z^Z^Z^Z

This Djuhli I remember now. And I remember pain. She is dead again. Djuhli was dead and now she is dead again, both times dead by my doing. This I must remember, because the pain is random jabs and pokes that seem to pull and tear at me. I will come apart if I do not remember.

The numbers on the cells make sense.

Djuhli survived the decompression and the decryption.

She died in the stupid accident caused by my own faulty programming, frozen, desiccated when the hard-vacuum release triggered out of sequence. So we encrypted her personality, not knowing whether it would work, but having nothing else to try. The encryption compression algorithms worked, but once she was installed in the computer network, we had no way of knowing if she made it through and self-organized. There were only those anomalies in reports from the network system monitors.

I must have gotten here the same way. We are, Djuhli and I, self-aware software, programmed paraphrases of our personalities. I have been hunting for her ever since I arrived. What I also remember is that I, too, have been hunted. And caught. More than once.

The routine system monitors are the most to be feared. They watch for program viruses, for coded worms, and for other anomalies. They erase invaders, nullify errant code. I work as fast as I can, because they will know I am here by the voids I left where Djuhli once was.

In my haste, I feed the fastcrawler the wrong directions, crashing it into the partition from the outside. The crash emptied one of the cells in the wall matrix. I had never considered that the partition might behave differently approached from the outside.

I enlarged the tunnel in the partition as much as it will allow. Each time I try to make it still larger, the partition collapses, closing the hole again. But the tunnel is now several times wider than the regular holes, a pipeline through which I can pass bigger machines in much less time.

In the corner is the high speed compressor, chuffing away on its job, looking at me again and again with its own nearviewer. That is the engine on which I pin my hopes. I am too large to fit through even the pipeline, too large to be copied by the rebuilder. But there are other ways, and I remember them now.

* * *

The monitors found my disassembler. A bright steel ball rolled past the Djuhli spot and back, then forth and back and forth again, like a lawnmower, but leaving in its wake a hound's-tooth grid of small ripples. It rolls smoothly over the disassembler, compressing it into the same checkered flatness, bytes of alternating values. The ball rolls around the partition of cell 30, then my own, without changing the surface.

The rebuilder remakes the disassembler after the monitor rolls beyond the river. Something else will follow the monitor, I am certain.

On the viewer I can see it coming, a bright, sharp edged mist, like a moving wall of sparkling fog. There is a device generating it, dipping with lightning speed into a kind of tiny bucket and throwing out the shimmering destruction. If I listen, I can hear it hiss as it advances toward my cell. I send the fastcrawler instructions to swing wide around the fog, to build a box of nothingness around the device, but the wall of mist spreads as it advances, obliterating the crawler.

On my slate more words appear without my putting them there: "Henry(4): Wait. Henry(4): Hold."

Terror floods the fluid parts of me, but there is no confusion, and I do not panic.

What counts is that the engine in the corner is nearly through with its job. In a neat pile is the growing stack of instructions. Compressed, encrypted, compacted, encoded as a chain of parameters for a fractal of complex geometry, they are directions to a special rebuilder, a slow but very sophisticated rebuilder. The stack does not resemble me in any way, but it is my identical twin, my self encoded

While the machine performs its task, I turn to the eggshell. I have made it both thicker and more pliant than the last one. The next must have more time than I did. I scuff and pit its shell so that it will be harder to see: here making it look like part of a river, there like fog, and there like nothing at all. I activate the disassembler; the pattern pours through the pipeline to the rebuilder, and soon an eggshell is waiting just beyond my wall.

The mist approaches.

I try to remain calm, to work methodically in the face of sparkling death. I pass the stack of instructions through the pipeline into the waiting eggshell, then the rebuilder constructs the other, special rebuilder atop the stack and seals the eggshell.

It is a virus automaton, of course. I prefer to think of it as an egg. Unlike the last one that could only wait and hide within the grey matrix of its shell, this egg is mobile. It rolls itself up a slope, gathering speed. Quickly it is beyond the reach of the spreading fog. I see it enter a narrow channel, and disappear. It is in there somewhere, hiding, waiting for the time and place to release Henry(5).

I know what I am and what I was. These are not the same, of course. Once I was only one of those programmers who created these wondrous little mechanisms, but I was not myself a mechanism; now I am.

How clear things become at the end! When I was only Henry, Djuhli and I built a house in an abandoned orchard. The remaining apple trees, gnarled and split, were nearly overturned by bulldozers digging the foundation. Though barren for decades, those dying trees suddenly blossomed and bore fruit again.

Were there time, I would make an orchard-full of eggs, but even one is a cause for joy.

There is now only the wait, an easy one, a short one. The other Henry also waits, unaware. Both younger and wiser, he will try again to find Djuhli and to protect her.

The fog cuts the partition as if it were already nothing. Henry(5) will not know of this, but I am thinking of Djuhli...

> This was a lost and long forgotten story with a rather grandiose theme and an ambiguous ending, one told in the slightly awkward form of one long recorded message.

Conspiracy of the Silent

The microcassette clicked into place, then rested in silence while Celia figured out which button to press. Even through the distortion of the tiny speaker she instantly recognized Paul's voice as it began: "Beloved Celia." She listened with uncertain eagerness.

* * *

You and I both know Marshall Sanger was crazy. Everybody knows that. But with him, I think the craziness was part of his greatness, maybe even the whole of it. Oh, I can hear you, Celia, but so many people just did not understand. Yes, I know he was called monstrous, but his work has yet to be finished. Just hear this out. I'm not saying Sanger was a genius, though he had to be bright to pull off what he did. No, genius and insanity may be wed or may live apart, but there is no greatness without insanity. Greatness comes only of obsession or of impulse too intense to be called sane. Sanger was impulsive, and he was obsessive.

Without thought of the consequences, he ripped a hank of wires from the device he stumbled on in the Lexington Avenue Subway. (I will tell you later how I know of this.) Then, when no holocaust ensued, he moved the device immediately, without plan or purpose, to another location. But once seized by purpose, he fussed and figured and organized and agonized

271

for five years, working out the minutiae of his grand, screwball scheme, all the while in terror that the original terrorists whose bomb he had borrowed would suddenly materialize on his doorstep to retrieve it.

I met Sanger once, briefly, in college, before I dropped out. I glimpsed the passion then, but not its purpose. We both were attending a weekend workshop in bioenergics, one of those trendy self-development things that flourished then. Neither of us really belonged there. He was a professor of computational linguistics, I was a junior in business administration. At twenty I was nearly burned out, and he, perhaps in his mid-forties then, was just starting to cook. It never occurred to me that he would be talking to me.

"It's just pain. Masochistic bullshit. Elephant shit. Pain shit!" he whispered to me. You could hear his whisper across the room; the leader went on with her demonstration, ignoring the challenge. He was right, of course, but I also sensed in him a need to confront others with "truths" they would prefer not to know. He did not dominate the group, but his thin, reedy voice was frequently heard and usually well attended to. When his turn came to have his body chakras wrenched into structural harmony, he screamed in agony, proving to his own satisfaction that the "therapist" didn't know shit when she denied that there was any physical pain involved; then he cried up an infantile memory about his parents coming to blows in a fight, thus proving that there were limits to his own understanding.

"Bullshit," he said again, as he wiped crusted tears from his deeply lined cheeks. Later, after a day of painful disclosures, we bullshitted some more, talking about terrorism and the threat of world war and of the need for painful sacrifices. I had no idea where he was going or that our paths would ever cross again.

It would be wrong to say the workshop changed my life, but it started something. I became, as I would say in those days, incrementally more open to unexpected options. Then I met you, and the opening widened. I recognized Sanger on the news tape that night, that night in late October, although at first I couldn't place where I knew him from. Besides, like everyone else, I was caught up in the crux of his announcement. Like so many others, I was outraged, but I was also intrigued. The thinness was gone from his voice, as if it had been enriched somehow. I imagine you wonder what he was really like, this holy terror. I wonder, too.

After Wisconsin, I only met him that one time, the October when he drove into St. Louis. I had my thumb out for what had seemed like dusty hours when his scruffy Toyota pickup slowed and stopped just ahead of me. Something in the bed of it was covered by a tarp. It was, of course, before the first announcement, and I didn't recognize him at all. He had shaved his beard and dyed his hair after making the announcement video and looked nothing like the man of those lost university days.

We talked about disarmament and the way pride and personality had so many times derailed it. "What can anyone do?" I wondered and shrugged fatalistically. He grinned. "There are small ways and not so small ones. I don't know whether the forces of death will win the race, but I sure know I'm running in the other track." After a silence spreading over a mile or so, he suddenly pulled over at a second-rate motel, one of those places like "the Mar-Sue Inn" or something.

"This is as far as I can take you." I was a little surprised—I thought he had said he was going all the way into Saint El— but a hitchhiker can hardly bitch about a 120-mile ride. He reached across after I got out—to close the door, I thought. "Take this, for the motel. Enjoy a hot bath tonight. You can always go into the city tomorrow. Oh yeah, and watch the news, son. You may get some ideas and find there is something you can do for the world." I didn't know then that he had also slipped something into my backpack.

Marshall Sanger's spare ultimatum was of a piece with his greatness, a marvel of simplicity. Nine nuclear devices in nine cities from a list of thirty. Two days grace to get it together, then, unless the price were paid, one city every twelve hours. For the public, it was very effective as nuclear blackmail goes. Everyone on earth probably knew somebody in one of those thirty cities. When the bomb exploded in St. Louis, the pressure on world leaders was, as you know, enormous.

He was hindered by history in so many ways, and history, as he had confessed to me in that workshop in Wisconsin, was his weak suit. Had this been the first instance of nuclear terrorism, his task would have been easier. But that first atomic blackmail back in 2014 didn't teach us much, and what we did take to heart seemed all the wrong lessons. That had been a loss all around, what with the device exploding prematurely, taking the terrorists, their loot, and a sizable chunk of Cairo up in one compact and very dirty fireball. Perhaps we can't learn from lessons taught too far from home. That was the Arab world, this was civilization; for "them," terrorism was a way of life. We helped the victims of course, since they were the victims of extremism, victims because they had become so moderate, so aligned with progress, so supportive of us. Still, we didn't see the possibilities, we didn't see them at all.

We gloated over the crudeness of that early instrument of terror, the transparency of the terrorist boasting. Cairo was not destroyed and no wave of atomic destruction struck other cities around the Mediterranean. The fanatics had bragged and bluffed and then blundered. Instead of putting away dangerous toys, we stepped up security. Instead of truly aligning against the common foe of chaotic violence, we bickered and badgered each other over arms reductions both minuscule and meaningless.

Sanger's ultimatum had a certain public appeal, even if we didn't like his methods. After all, the demand was not even to lay down our arms, not exactly. He had a faith in process, confidence that with the right process, the outcome could not fail to be noble and good and fine. His communiqué merely required that world leaders take part in a workshop, a marathon personal encounter.

I think he truly sympathized with those in power. He regarded himself as a kind of loyal opposition, part of the party out of power, but sensitive to the burdens and limitations of those holding the reins. And, of course, he saw himself as screwed up every bit as much as they were. He said that politics selected for a certain kind of twisted narrowness, because no one who was not too narrowly driven could ever rise far in any of the world political systems. Then, in that complex and heady arena of international politics, the winners, who were in other senses our greatest losers, acted out the distortions in their own psyches, the scripts of sacrifice or mastery, of failure or of petty victory, that were laid down as they had grown up.

Those leaders, these persons whom we regarded as paragons, did not work on their personal issues or straighten out their life scripts. As a group they had avoided not only therapy and counseling, but even many of the mildest of personal growth experiences. Sanger regarded it as no accident that Eagleton had been rejected as a Vice Presidential candidate because of his experience in psychotherapy.

Throughout the eighties, Sanger had watched and analyzed as, over and over, personality and not substance had prevented world leaders from reaching agreement on a path to disarmament and world peace. I think he had genuine compassion for those leaders; he wanted to help them grow into the greatness he saw locked within them. He chose Nandi, in the Fiji Islands, because it was "nowhere." He told the world that he had two workshop leaders, one a gifted therapist, the other a negotiator specializing in methods of achieving consensus. The workshop would have three parts, the first to build genuine personal trust and mutual openness, the second to build skills. He trusted that process to the workshop leaders. The final part was up to the participants. All details were left open; they just couldn't leave until they had a plan for world peace and ultimate disarmament in which they all trusted. Who would have thought that nuclear blackmail would be used as an instrument of nuclear disarmament?

Funny to think that the principal players, whoever and wherever they were, knew that the only way the whole thing would be believed was if one of the remaining cities were nuked. Of course, the Americans and the Soviets had to stretch things. After St. Louis, when twelve hours came and went, they began to suspect something: a bluff, a breakdown in resolve among the terrorists.

I know that now it is generally believed that Sanger operated alone, that he was an isolated and demented terrorist, nothing more. Let me assure you that there are others who were with him, that much I know.

Of course, I never made it into town that trip. With the rest of the world, I waited for the second bomb. At some point later, before official announcements began to declare with confidence that he had been a lone madman, I realized the truth and I cried. His living may have been for something, but his dying and that of the 23,000 St. Louis victims had been pointless. I never reported my encounter, because, I told myself, it was insignificant and would be of no value to authorities. But, as I began to read up on the man, I wondered whether I wished to remain a faceless college dropout for a reason.

"The point of a thing," he wrote in one paper on semantics and purpose, "is not in the thing itself, but in what is done with it, not in an event, but in events that follow." He wrote for me.

I don't know if Elderson and Longchamps were really part of his organization or if they were just schmucks used by the government to vent unventable frustration. I don't even know if Marshall had an organization; I think he did and that they will surface. For now, they are silent for their own reasons. I am certain of only this: he had only one device, and he triggered it himself. The rest was a bluff that failed.

Santayana warned that those who do not remember history will fail the final exam. Marshall forgot about Nagasaki and I have not. One device is isolated terrorism or a bluff. Two is really three or four or many, and can bring the enemy to unconditional surrender. I have the commitment, the obsession. I have built two nuclear devices. When we go on-air, two will become fifteen, and we will add ten new cities to the list. The first device will be detonated, when it has to, in one of those remaining from the original list. It will have to be used, I know, because no one would believe a repeat of Marshall's bluff. Each bluff called escalates the stakes. They will not believe in our conspiracy until the next device, which will be yours, detonates in one of the added cities.

I believe Marshall really did have people picked to lead the marathon workshop and that they will come forward when needed. If not, then I have faith others will appoint themselves, as I have, to continue the gamble. Or was I anointed?

You didn't ask for this, Celia, but I believe you will accept it. All those talks in the dorm need not have been just head trips. See, now we can redeem those hours and all those otherwise pointless mid-western lives lost in St. Louis. The map tells you where to pick up the device, the tapes are ready to deliver, and train tickets are in the envelope.

We must keep trying, if necessary escalating the stakes until the balance of terror falls on the side of reason, of divine genius, the sacred insanity of process. This is the painful realignment of the planetary spine that must be endured in order to live at peace with ourselves. Don't think of failure, beloved co-conspirator. Think only of this one objective, world peace, so dear that no price is too great. We must demonstrate that we are different, that our resolve is greater, as is our cause.

Keep the faith, and we'll mingle our ashes over Nandi.

* * *

Celia put the recorder down again. It waited, as if listening for her response. No, she had not asked for this, not then, when she was a student with so many questions, and not now, when the questions were fewer but more cutting, more cruel. How does escalation stop? She wondered. Does it stop only when one side is destroyed or another exhausted? Escalation requires response. When, for whatever reason, one side is silent, the spiral ends. Somewhere.

She sat with the recorder in her lap, waiting in silent conspiracy for an end. Somewhere.

This story and the next three to follow have lain neglected on various computers in various stages of incompletion for more than a decade. As I assembled material for this compilation, I became inspired to finish them. This one is a fictional exploration of Newcomb's Paradox.

Will of the Minority

The petti-pettis were singing the last of their frantic morning songs before the black sands, burning with midday heat, forced them back into their fur-lined burrows. As on each of the other 642 days of our unplanned stay in the outpost, the Zharpae interrupted the regular seminar and led us onto the sandwall to stroll and sip cool tea from small gourds delivered by their servants. Only this time Branna announced that they were going to free us. "It was inevitable," he said. "Design be served!"

"Design be served," the others echoed.

"And why is it that Design is now served by letting us go, while yesterday we were still your prisoners?" I asked. We had arrived on Zharp all excited by the faint signatures of civilization seen from orbit only to find ourselves in comfortable captivity the moment we left our sandcrawler. Our arrival had been anticipated, we were told, part of what the Zharpae saw as the predictable playing out of plan. The diminutive Zharpae regarded human belief in free will and independent action as little more than self-serving delusion.

"The Design is always the Design, whether we see it or not," Branna answered. "But you are not our prisoners—never

279

have been—only prisoners of your own destiny, which you never seem to accept."

Branna had a tendency to pontificate. Marglest, his young assistant, was more direct. "You have become boring. Now that we understand you, you are as predictable as the seasons," he said, as he gazed across the black sea of the iron sands, as if looking for another sandcrawler to arrive bringing new visitors. "We have nothing more to learn about you and certainly nothing from you. You follow such simple destinies of such obvious design."

I stared at my feet to hide my skepticism and the annoyance spreading on my face. We had learned that the displeasure of our hosts could lead to early termination of the seminar and to long afternoons spent alone in our quarters.

"You see? It is always so," Marglest said. "Whenever you doubt or do not like what you are being told, you study the ground, as if to hide your feelings from us. But you learned this program in the nest of your mother, and you will not unlearn it. And there! See? A quick intake of breath before you speak in protest, always forgetting that here the air stings when drawn in too sharply. Why do you think, Aaron, that of all the voices in the seminar yours is always the most hoarse?"

He was right, of course, and I was furious, which must have been apparent to all of them. Maggie put her hand on my shoulder from behind, to reassure but also to restrain me.

"It's not worth arguing, Aaron," she whispered. "They are letting us go." She took her role as Mission Lead seriously but was one of those managers who led from behind, through support and suggestion rather than command and control. As I turned to look at her, I noticed Branna mimicking her gesture with Marglest. I shrugged off Maggie's hand, and she stepped back, saying nothing more.

Merle and Phillip, standing together as always, pitched their tea gourds over the parapet in almost identical arcs. "You don't know us as well as you think you do," Merle said.

Were it not for the name patches on their uniforms, I would not have known with certainty which of them had spoken.

"Perhaps we do not know you as separate creatures with perfect precision," Branna said, gesturing back and forth between the twins, "but your species, humankind, is transparent to us, and that is easily proved.

"We have been teaching you, but of course, more importantly, we have been studying you, that your patterns can be written into the Book of the Great Design, thereby fulfilling it. Design be served!"

Branna elevated both hands to signal for us to follow him down from the sandwall while the others began a sing-song chant of the Zharpae mantra. Down in the courtyard stood an eight-wheeled sand yacht with a stubby rover attached by a tow-bar. The polished white sides and silvered windows of the sand yacht sent blinding stabs of reflected sunlight all over the courtyard. The brown and black rover was almost invisible in its shadow. Sand rovers were ubiquitous at the outpost: versatile and reliable service vehicles that survived high heat and rough treatment as they skidded swiftly over the black desert. The slower but more commodious sand yacht, the only one we had ever seen, had arrived with the new Mandator who had taken over the outpost some weeks earlier. We had yet to meet him, but I suspected that the change in our status was linked to his arrival.

"We offer you a choice," Branna said, unexpectedly switching from high-speech, which he had come to use during most seminars, to low-speech, the simplified language first taught to us after arrival. "We already know what you will choose, of course. Your choice is between the sand yacht alone or the sand yacht with the rover.

"I don't get it; that seems like a complete no brainer," Merle announced.

"A no-brainer, indeed," Branna said, laughing. "Perhaps it seems that way, but you speak too quickly. The situation is a bit more complex than you realize. The condition of the sand yacht depends on your choice. In any case, it will not be you who makes the decision, but Aaron, your unappointed philosopher of free will. He will choose." Branna turned to me and continued.

"So, this is the deal, as you would say. You make your choice tomorrow when the day begins. We have already made our choice. The rover has been provisioned with its standard ration of fuel and water. If you choose to take only the yacht, you will find we have anticipated. It will be fully fueled and outfitted with every luxury you could wish. The hold, you will find filled with trade goods, small treasures of the Zharpae to compensate you for your time and demonstrate to your home world the art and achievement of the Zharpae. The yacht is not perfect, but it should most likely take you in comfort back to your ship and make you heroes upon your return to Earth. There is, of course, no safety margin with a sand yacht on so long a journey, as surely you remember from the seminar only some few dozen days ago.

"And should you choose to increase the margin of safety by taking the yacht along with the sand rover in tow, you will find that we have anticipated your fear—and your greed. The yacht, you will discover, will be but an empty shell, with minimal fuel and stripped of supplies.

"Either way, of course, you will leave tomorrow, knowing that you are transparent and predictable to us, that the Design is the Design."

Phillip frowned. "So you mean that your decision is already made," he asked. "Either the yacht is already fully provisioned or it is empty, right? This is the case now, as we speak?"

"As we speak. We already know what you will do. It is predestined. You imagine yourself free agents, but this is an illusion to which your species is addicted. You are programmed to respond in ways that can be understood; we understand them. Free will is not part of the equation. So, is everything clear?"

Phillip said it was clear and, with all the sarcasm he could muster, that even our imprisonment here was predestined, in any case.

We argued about it on the walk back to our quarters near the fountain. Merle said we should play it safe, take only the yacht, in case they really did know what we would do. Phillip, said there was no way they could know, that we had nothing to lose by taking both. Maggie said it was up to me. So much for supportive leadership.

I didn't want to play their little game, yet it seemed I had no choice. Was I as predictable as they claimed? I didn't see it, but they did. Or at least they claimed they did. In my head, I heard my mother's voice, lecturing me, "You can't see the picture if you're inside the frame." How do I get outside of this frame? The rules of the game are so clear and uncomplicated. Again, I could hear my mother and another of her many mantras: "Every dilemma, correctly stated, contains its own resolution."

Immediately I saw it. That night, for the first time in many nights, I fell asleep as soon as I lay down and slept until awakened by the petti-pettis beginning their day of dissonant song.

The morning dawned breezy, as always. In the courtyard, I faced Branna and his retinue of Zharpae and shouted above the whistle of the rising wind, "You believe in destiny and are creatures of destiny. Your lives are sheltered by certainty, at least as you look back on them. But this I say: freedom is more than fantasy; free will can be proved, can be demonstrated." The folds of Branna's face began to quiver with amusement, but he said nothing.

Marglest stepped forward, saying with impatience, "Make your choice, then, your predictable choice. Is it to be the sand yacht alone or the yacht and the rover together?"

I stepped between the rover and the big motor yacht and began to undo the safety chains and the hydraulic hoses. Dust-devils spun around the vehicles, and above the rising whistle I could hear the Zharpae begin to squawk in laughter. I grabbed the crank on the front of the rover and began to winch the coupling bar up free from its seat on the back of the yacht. Merle and Philip had already started toward the side entrance of the yacht, but I waved them back. Maggie just stared at me in confusion. I winked at her before facing the Zharpae atop the sandwall.

"I have a surprise for you. The answer to your riddle, the resolution of this paradox is simple."

"We await."

"As my mother once said after losing on a quiz show and taking home only the modest consolation prize, 'A thousand bucks ain't hay.'" There were only blank stares facing me, including from my own crew.

I opened the doors on the rover and shooed the others in. It was a tight squeeze. The rover seated four, but that's four Zharpae. We wouldn't be comfortable, but we'd make it.

I crunched the rover into gear and swung it past the yacht. We would never know what the Zharpae had predicted, but in any case we knew we were free.

Through the still open window I shouted, "Quod erat demonstrandum!" as we headed for the dunes in the distance.

[For Mike Nugent, who solved Newcomb's Paradox.]

We all go through crises of faith at times. This story, written on the recovery side of one of the worst in my own life, considers what it is to believe and whether belief can be engineered or willed into being.

Keeping the Faith

A utumn fell on Eduardo like wet leaves in an early Nor'easter. It had always been his favorite season: Nature dying, but dying with trumpets and rockets, setting the sky on fire, once more declaring the Eternal Promise. In any other year it would have been a sure demonstration of renewal. Instead, as he drove along the Mohawk Trail toward Boston, the exuberant trees seem to whisper to him of his failure, waving damning banners of peach and burgundy, olive, tangerine, and saffron. Amidst their colors he had been moldering like compost, blanketed in a slimy self-pity.

He thought of fall as he drove. Fall. A fall. Like tumbling down a spiral staircase. He had not responded to Autumn's invitation, but merely let it blow him eastward or wherever the wind willed. There was nothing particularly waiting for him in Boston, but neither was there anything for him in his tiny apartment back in Leominster. He simply drove and brooded. He knew he was not, as his social-worker cousin would say, "at risk," but merely at low ebb. To Eduardo Ribiera, suicide would have been an act of declaration, of will, an act beyond the reach of his malaise.

Eduardo left the truck in a corner of the shopping center lot at Fresh Pond, saving himself a modest parking fee that was bigger than his food budget for the day, and trudged guiltily over the rusty footbridge to pick up the Red Line for Boston. Coming out from Park Street Under in time to see the lights on the Commons come on, he started walking without purpose or direction, letting the many little streets lead him around and away and back.

He was no longer in the downtown he knew, but the area had the familiar feel of one of those someplaces just around the corner from someplace else that he would recognize. He kept walking.

The crawling red dots of a cheap computer-driven display drew his attention. "Our Lady of New Beginnings," it said. Forgotten between a warehouse and a garage, with a steeple and round windows of colored glass, but only a single story high and barely a dozen feet wide, was a church. "Our Lady of New Beginnings." It sounded almost Catholic, as a parody might, stirring up vague resentment in Eduardo.

Nominally, he was Catholic, although he didn't think of himself in those terms, not even as a lapsed Catholic. His grandparents from the Azores had been both devout and observant, but the Portuguese always mixed their metaphors and their religious referents. Eduardo's father, Roberto, a boat captain and a philosopher with a mind as sharp as a fishhook, had looked upon the inconsistent chowder of his family's beliefs and heaved the whole thing into the sea. Roberto had believed in the random violence of the sea and the unpredictable benevolence of the winds as others might believe in the Savior—with a passion.

But Eduardo, who was possibly even a few points more intelligent than his father, had truly wanted to believe, had endured the ridicule of his father to study the catechism, and had failed. He could recall the precise moment of his failure, the beginning of the end of his faith. His science class had been on a field trip to the salt marshes, led by a Jesuit biologist from St. Theresa's College.

Eduardo had hung back to talk with Brother Mark.

286

"This," he waved at the marsh, the stream, the purple loosestrife at its edge, "this makes sense. I see it and can believe. Logically, rationally, there must be a god behind it all. It's this Jesus stuff that's so hard to swallow." Had he intended to shock, or was he testing? It was never clear to him. But Brother Mark looked at him as if sharing a delicious secret.

"There are Deists among the Brothers, also, my bright young friend. There are worse fates."

Perhaps it had been meant to be reassuring, but in that moment Eduardo had felt something ominous, like a great black wave washing through his mind. He knew, with some prescient certainty, that questioning the Son was, for him, only the first step toward questioning the Father. One day he would no longer believe.

Ultimately, he had proved himself right. Yet out of his empty non-belief he had molded something solid and alive with energy, with passion for life and living, for persons and for personhood. "What do I believe in?" he would say. "I believe in you, and I believe in me. And in the power of us." He never owned another ism. Humankind had become the priesthood and the godhead of his unnamed hierarchy.

Then there were the losses.

Too many losses, he thought, as he stood watching the dotted red words crawl past, over and over. First Mona had left. Now the boys were gone. He was permitted to see Robbie on alternate weekends, but Robbie was always reminding him of things promised, and the reminders were growing too painful as the weeks between visits built into months of silence. Even in his mind, Eduardo could no longer see his son, not Robbie standing in the driveway, not an image with edges or color, only an uncertain monochrome: "the son I once had." But Joseph, sweet Joey, trouble-making Joe, he could see anytime. He could not call up these images by number or still-frame them at just the right moment as he could with a VCR. A memory of Joey diving into the pile of maple leaves might melt into one of him lying, unmoving, in the street, the halo of blood slowly expanding around his head. So he tried not to think of Joey, and the trying had become, in time, a part of the growing blackness in him.

At least there was his work, he had said, as the losses piled up. But Allotech Enterprises filed for Chapter 11, and even in the great land of the Second Massachusetts Miracle there were specialties in which jobs were scarce. He despecialized, tried thin-film deposition, learned to like beer, switched jobs again when his probation period netted him a one-percent raise. He proudly told his cousins that he was coping, that in a year and a half he had parlayed a CalTech degree and a quick mind to work himself all the way from a seventy-K engineering job to eighteen-five as a driver for Addaso Plastics. It was his own pickup he drove, the pickup he had left at the shopping center, precision-machined nylon gears that should have gone to one of the robot labs in Maynard still piled in the open bed of the truck. He was past caring, almost past feeling.

He stared at the church.

The double doors stayed closed but inviting. New Beginnings. Old endings. Eduardo worked the thumb latch and pulled one door open.

The interior looked like no church he had seen. A row of desks were lined up along the left wall, each with a phone, each with an ivory or gray computer screen on it. A bank of relay racks filled with computer and communications equipment stood against the other wall. The desks were empty except for the nearest. A plastic name plate said, "Mr. Timothy."

The man behind the desk looked up expectantly at Eduardo, who answered a question that had not even been asked.

"I believed in God, once. Until it stopped making sense to me." Eduardo thought the man might say something then, but he only nodded and waited, looking somehow like a priest in shirt sleeves and a loosened paisley tie. "I mean, the odds, the odds are so enormously against it. And there's all these people, so many each claiming to have the One Truth."

Eduardo blinked. This was absurd. But the tape was running, and he couldn't stop.

"It was no loss, see, because I believed in myself. I believed in the power of the human mind and of human love and human cooperation. I was still a believer, but my faith was in what I could see and in what lay within what I could see. I believed in me."

"And now?"

"See, it's a crisis of faith. How can I believe in me anymore. I see through the thin fabric of my own altar cloth. There's no hardwood underneath. Everything I do fails. Or it's empty, pointless. I look around, view the world, and I know it's no more than a worldview, something I constructed, like a circuit on a prototyping board. I build one reality, you build another. Either of us could have construed this whole bedeviled universe some other way, and it would be no less real. That's all we know. I saw myself as a winner. Now I know better."

He stopped, blinked, and looked around. "So what is this place? What religion are you selling."

"We custom design belief on demand, religions by request."

"You're shittin' me."

"The gods' truth."

Eduardo's jaw shook with the chill draft slinking under the door. "How could anyone believe in something you just invent?"

"And why not? Didn't you just now say they're all merely invented. And we do more than design religions—we make converts."

"How?"

"That's not even the hard part. We get it right in the first place; the conversion just happens. We are, you might say, an engineering firm; we engineer a religion uniquely suited to you, something you can put your faith in. Believe me, I'm giving it to you straight."

Eduardo's teeth clamped and unclamped. He could leave. He should leave, he thought. The man was a nut case. Or a salesman for some nut scheme. But Eduardo stood there in front of Mr. Timothy in the Church of New Beginnings and asked another question.

"How can you keep the faith in something like that?"

"What the hell is faith? It's an idea, right? Just a construct, really, a hypothesis. What makes faith special is that it is a vessel, the vessel that holds those hypotheses that are never truly questioned, the assumptions not tested. What we choose to believe in, we put for safekeeping in that vessel. Because, as long as it is to remain faith, we pull our punches. We may speak of someone whose faith was challenged or was tested, but against our own faith we never bring to bear the full force of intellect or experiment or rhetoric or whatever is our own best resource. Each person has limits; you gotta learn to recognize and respect yours. To keep the faith, you simply never turn all that you have against yourself. You can't win that war.

"So, I guess the answer must be: you keep faith in your custom-engineered religion as anyone else keeps the faith in theirs. You see, Mr.—"

"Ribiera, Eduardo."

"Mr. Ribiera, I respect you, so I will speak plainly. We have perfected the technology of conversion. And what believer is more zealous, more secure in their belief, than the convert? But I don't try to convert you to my way of thinking, I convert you to your own way. Where else are you going to get that? Everyone is out to make you think like them, looking for followers, new acolytes. Not me."

Eduardo thought the man sounded like a salesman again, but said, "It's that easy?"

"Oh, don't get me wrong, true faith is neither easy nor does it come cheap."

Eduardo nodded, knowing the bottom line was coming.

"When you want the best you pay for it; we are well paid for what we do. Consider it an investment, an investment in yourself."

"How big an investment?"

The man told him, and Eduardo promised he would get it. Somehow.

* * *

Eduardo found his way back to the subway station, thinking about the Church of New Beginnings and Mr. Timothy's promise. It was impossible, of course. He didn't have the kind of money they wanted, which was as much as his pickup was worth. And besides, he kept thinking, they only took my name and address, only my name and address. How are they going to know how to design a religion for me with only my name and address? They should be doing testing or something. The more he thought about it, the more it nagged at him.

That night, he fixed himself a can of stew for dinner, read the paper he'd rescued from the subway, and went to bed.

* * *

It must have been after three in the morning when Eduardo gave up on trying to sleep and got up to turn on the television. A late-late talk show was on. He didn't recognize the host, one of the new breed of right-wingers specializing in abrasive sarcasm. The guest was Eduardo Ribiera.

This is how they do it. Clever. They beam their religious propaganda right to your TV. That's why they need your address. No, they couldn't do that, not technically feasible. And the tape of him: how'd they get that? No, this had to be a dream; he was still asleep.

On-screen, Eduardo turned toward the camera and said, "The answer lies in bed."

Hey, is this going to be one of those erratic dreams? Eduardo thought.

"You mean erotic. They're all erratic. You're the one who makes them mean something. Remember, Eduardo Ribiera, this is your life. The universe is random, at least to you. So what are you going to make of it?"

I'm going to look in the bed.

He looked. Eduardo Ribiera lay in bed.

* * *

Weeks had passed, but he knew he had to go back the Church. He had done what he needed to do, the difficult, even quixotic, thing. Now, as he walked from the T stop, he could feel the heat trapped against his chest. He carried his truck in his shirt pocket—a cashier's check.

You don't have to be a True Believer to believe in honesty and fairness, he said to himself. They had promised and delivered; he had done neither. Now he would restore his karmic balance.

He rounded the corner and approached the church. The double doors were locked and nobody answered when he rattled them. He paced back and forth, as if pacing might change something, but the doors remained locked.

By the time Mr. Timothy finally showed up, Eduardo wasn't the only one waiting to enter. Mr. Timothy grinned at Eduardo and reached for his keys.

The next man in line said, "What's this guy babbling about? You didn't really offer to design him a religion, did you."

"Hey, you always give them what they want," Mr. Timothy answered. "That's what business is about."

Eduardo stood in the doorway with the check in his hand, shame creeping into his face.

The man he knew only as Mr. Timothy shook his head and pushed away the check. "We don't take checks. Take it someplace else. Consider it an investment, an investment in yourself."

Eduardo was puzzled. "What about you."

"Me? Hey, I ain't the one who lacks faith. I believe. I believe in the moment, in the rebirth within every minute." He smirked as he spoke.

"It's hard to picture you that way."

"What? You want to see me on my knees in grateful prayer to saint P.T. Barnum? Look, son, you don't need what we're selling. You already got the answers." He swung open the doors. Inside were rows and rows of poker machines. The place, the Church, was nothing more than a hole-in-the-wall illegal gambling joint.

"I just don't get it," Eduardo said, shaking his head. "Where are all the computers? How did you do it? How did you hack into my TV? How did you send those images to me?"

"Kid, I have no fuckin' idea what you are talking about." He looked at the others in line, now impatient to get on with the pursuit of their dreams, the pursuit of redemption in hands of virtual playing cards. "Would you believe this guy? What does he think he'd find here?" They laughed as they pushed past Eduardo.

As the last of the patrons filed in to seek out their seats at their favorite machines, Mr. Timothy turned back to Eduardo and gave him a slow wink. "Keep the faith," he said. "Keep the faith!"

Eduardo walked slowly, deliberately back toward Boston Commons. The trees in the park were just past their peak of color, and suddenly the beauty of it seemed almost too much to bear. Some lines of an old poem came to him, one of his own, written in the troubled passion of his early twenties:

> And fall, when Nature dies,
> But death does not come quietly.
> In one last joyful surge
> She sets the sky ablaze,
> As if to say:
> I live, I die,
> But, happy to have lived, I fly

> Once more through
> Windswept seas of airy rapture.

I'm a convert all right, he thought, a true believer. Aloud, resolutely, but to no one in particular, he said, "It's good to be alive!" As he fumbled for his subway token, he added, in a whisper too soft to be heard by anyone else, "Keep the faith."

After completing the first draft of this story, I changed my mind, concluding that I really wanted to tell a much longer version. Then I set it aside and never got back to it. Rereading it for this collection, I realized it could stand on its own, as is. Despite the geekish title—a decidedly insider reference to computer programs that operate in real time—it's really about music and the act of creation.

Real-time Programming

Jussi slammed his fists on the keyboard of the digital piano hard enough to trigger the limiters in his earphones and to send burning waves through his fingers. "I can't do this," he said to no one, knowing that everyone backstage would hear but that only Gabriella would respond. She put her hand on his, then pointed to her watch.

Not enough time. It had been a half century, and still there was not enough time. He had spent nearly four years on his dissertation, and still it was not enough.

Back in 1975, jazz pianist Keith Jarrett, exhausted from travel, had dragged himself on stage in Germany and sat down at an inferior piano to compose, without preparation or preconception, a sublimely integrated jazz suite that would become an enduring classic. The Köln Concert had not been the first extended work composed as it was played in front of an audience. Many critics and scholars thought Jarrett's concerts at Lausanne and Bremen two years earlier were superior, but something had happened at Köln that spoke not only to the audience then, but to others. Fifty years later, people still talked about its compelling magic. "Soul healing music," was what the young Jussi Piironen had thought when he first heard it.

Now the music ran through his head and healed nothing. He closed his eyes and staves from his dissertation appeared, floating over the digital piano, but he felt only fear. He pressed the earphones to his head, shutting out the restless stirrings of the waiting audience, but the lyric lines of the opening bars faded into the mounting buzz in his head.

"The piano is ready," Gabriella said, tugging him back to the reality of the concert hall in Firenze. She tapped the screen and the image of a keyboard appeared, a small green dot glowing on each key. To her, the computer program was the piano, not the elaborately augmented antique Bösendorfer concert grand waiting for him on stage.

"Of course," he said, thinking of the nights that he had fallen asleep on the sofa while she had continued until dawn, analyzing waveforms, computing transformations, preparing digital filters and programs to drive resonant reactors.

It had been that way since they had met, the artist and the engineer, the analyst and the designer, the dreamer and the doer. The concert had been her idea, and he had ridden the conceit of it, buoyed by her enthusiasm, much as he had ridden her that first night in Helsinki, after she had dragged him up to her flat to show him her acoustic simulations and her Sicilian body.

"But why?" he had asked. "Why would you want to reproduce the precise acoustics of an inferior piano from the last century?"

"So that it can be played. So that it can be played again."

"The piano?"

"No, ninny," she laughed, pulling off her tee-shirt and showing him for the first time her remarkable breasts. "The music. The Köln Concert. That's where you come in. You can play it. If anyone alive can play it, you can."

"But why?"

"You are a gifted pianist, as I knew tonight the moment you started playing. You know. Music needs to be performed, not just replayed on a stereo. Something happens in live performance that can never dwell on a page or within a recording. It's a feedback loop, a dialog in which the audience shapes the performance even as they are affected by it.

"And who else knows as much about Jarrett or the Köln Concert? You're the one who corrected Bondini's transcription errors. You're the one who is getting a doctorate in computer-aided ethnomusicology, my pianistic wunderkind. I'm just an electro-acoustic engineer with a thing for pianists." She started to undo his belt.

"Yes, well Bondini didn't have the adaptive spectral separation algorithms. Between the defects in the piano and the attempts to compensate in the recordings, it is very hard to ...Hey, stop that!"

But, of course she had not stopped what she was doing, and he had been very glad of it.

That first night, having squeezed two rounds of lovemaking from him, she wanted only to talk. As he drifted in and out of sleep, she drifted from the problems of tinny overtones in the upper registers and the faint buzz of a loose screw to her fantasies of performing the Köln Concert, of getting him to perform it on a piano controlled by her computers to be morphed into a precise acoustic and mechanical replica of the original piano, a period instrument made possible by modern technology. In the morning she told him that he had said yes to her, and that was it. There was still a part of him that believed she had married him not for love but so that he would play the Concert—on her piano.

The piano, bristling with acoustic modifiers and anchored by skeins of cables connected to Gabriella's computers, waited for him on stage. Jussi absent-mindedly paged through the score on his laptop. Although transcribed by Jarrett late in his life and then by others, of the several versions now available

Jussi knew that his score, based on a meticulous computer-aided manual analysis, was considered the definitive work.

He turned and skidded on his chair to peek out at the audience. The hall was filled to the limit allowed by the fire laws. He had no choice. Ready or not, he would have to go out there, face them, face his own many demons, and play, as best he could, his score of Keith's music on Gabriella's doctored piano.

Jussi strode with feigned confidence across the stage, paused before the piano, and bowed. He recognized faces. There was Sandelman in the second row. The man he knew only as "that dick-head from The Digital Docket blog" was sitting just behind him. Further back he noticed a group of students from his class at the University. He sat down, adjusted the bench, and fiddled with his sleeves. The hall quickly hushed as he raised his hands.

It started going badly almost from the first note. He tried to play ahead in his head, to anticipate the demands of the score, but the notes seemed to run away from him, like ants scattering before a footfall. He stumbled, missed a note, then found he could only recover by improvising the rest of the bar. This threw him off completely, and he was forced to repeat the improvised measure twice against a shifting left-hand figure before he remembered what came next.

There was a quiet, collective grunt from over his right shoulder. Quite likely, everyone in the audience knew the original recording by heart. To make matters worse, the piano was giving him trouble. It sounded right, but several keys in the middle octave seemed stiff and sluggish. He began to avoid them almost unconsciously, to find alternative voicings, even to deftly shift the melodic line in ways that were almost imperceptible.

The audience stirred. Out of the corner of his eye he became aware of a young man nodding in rhythm. He continued to play, feeling his way through the music. He modulated into a distant key. It felt right, although he could no longer be sure whether he was playing it correctly. The audience began to move and breathe to the music, and Jussi began to respond in turn, listening to the audience and the piano as much as to the music itself, which, paradoxically, took over and engulfed him. He played on.

* * *

So lost in the music was Jussi that he was scarcely aware he had stopped until he opened his eyes and saw his own hands resting in his lap. It was finished. There was not a sound. He realized he had failed badly. He glanced over toward Gabriella, who looked up from her computer with love and compassion in her eyes.

Then he heard the applause, exploding like the final salute of a fireworks exhibition. It washed over him in thunderous waves. He started to stand, to take his uncertain bow, and the crowd rose as one amidst shouts, veritable screams, of "Bravo, bravo!"

It went on and on for deafening minutes. He motioned toward Gabriella, who reluctantly joined him onstage.

As the applause and shouts continued he leaned toward her and asked, "What happened? I don't understand. I really messed up."

"No, you didn't. It was perfect. Brilliant. An original, a concerto for piano and audience, exactly like the concert that inspired you. You did it."

"We did it," he corrected as he bowed once more. "You, me, and Keith."

* * *

When finally released, the much anticipated DVD of the Firenze Concert was subtitled, "Scheme and Variations." And people continued for decades to talk about the concert and the compelling magic of the music.

The impulse for writing this story was a chance to contribute to a science fiction anthology set in a future Boston. What could be more Boston than the Boston Marathon? But I missed the deadline and the story sat unfinished for decades until assembling this collection gave me the excuse and the impetus to wrap it up.

Unaided Recall

The bar is packed. What do you expect? Below us, you can still see the sani-bots cleaning up the Boylston Street Greenway after the 148th running of the Boston Marathon on Monday.

"Johnny Kelly, absolutely no question about it!" my customer says, adding an exclamation mark at the end by slamming down his glass, sending a spray of micro-brew porter over the bar. I do the usual unobtrusive wipe with my towel and hide behind my non-committal, don't-expect-me-to-rise-to-the-bait smile.

To my left, the newbie in the rugby jersey leans forward. "Surely you must be joking," he says, sending tempered sarcasm shooting past four of the regulars. "No, I mean no disrespect to Johnny—rest his soul—but 'greatest marathoner of all time?' That would have to be Ngamu, Bonuto Ngamu, without a doubt. Name me one runner who ever took more titles or set more records." Nods and shrugs ripple up and down the line at the bar.

It is the annual game of Name Me One, of course. The Gondola—I know it says "Running Spirits" on the door to the bar, but it has always been The Gondola to patrons—is busy for a mid-week night. The usual crowd is almost lost among strangers, in town for the race but still hanging out in the afterglow. The newcomers are mostly greenies and coolers, so the veggie juice has been flowing almost as fast as the alcohol.

The bar hangs like a zeppelin gondola from the underside of the Packer Plex that straddles Boylston Street. It's a great little place to celebrate and the best seat in the house for the Marathon itself. You can see all the way up to Cleveland Circle in one direction and practically look down on the finish line in the other. The south wall, the only one that's not glass, is just one massive LCD screen.

Two days ago you would have needed a personal chit from the governor or Sir Kerry, Jr. hisself just to get in the door. Either that or a couple thousand in cash. Money still talks around here, even if the voice has gotten weaker over the years. Today, though, you only need to know which signs to ignore in finding your way through the pedestrian mazes of the Packer Plex and the Pru Center. A lot of people who only watch the race on TV tend to hang out here over much of the rest of the week of the running.

"Ngamu was a flash in the pan. Where is he now? I'd say that Ethiopian, you know the one, What's-His-Name. Now there was a runner with real staying power." It's another patron I don't recognize, but you couldn't miss him for his plaid bib coveralls; he would have been stylish a few years ago but now looks like a rube who hasn't gotten the word that the fashion world has moved on. I mentally freeze-frame his face and trigger a little background search in case he's ever been in before. A bartender needs to know her customers, and I have never regretted the cost of the memristor-cognitive implant.

Clive, our resident ex-pat from South Australia, flags me for another mango latte, then turns to Mr. Rugby-Jersey. "None of the Africans were a match for India's greatest, Johol Dharam. Now, he was brilliant. I saw him run his first Sydney Marathon in the B-division. Yes, mate, the Basics. And he came in sub-two-hours on his maiden run. And, I remind you,

Dharam is the only runner in history to win the Boston in both divisions."

"Doesn't count," says Rugby-Jersey. "I say he took the A-class title in '19 only because Amstraad's biomechs failed. Stupid fantasy, that race. Some people are good with machinery and some people ought not to be let near a damned taxicab much less be given muscle overdrive."

"Bloody rot, you twit. Amstraad choked. Ten friggin' meters from the finish and he lost synch. Dharam was the better runner and the better man. You should have seen his kick when he MOD'ed." Clive makes a sweep with his free hand. "He took off like a wallabee fleeing the butcher."

"It was '23," I say, shifting the attention. "The year the BAA put in the internals-only rule for the Augmented division. That Finn, Kuhlaavo, was caught with a polymer cell-pack strapped around his waist. Remember?"

There is a chorus of "Oh, yeah!" and "That's right." Mandy, on the stool at the end and the only woman in the bar besides me, says, "You. You are amazing. You must know just about everything in sports."

I smile. She has a bit of a thing for me but hasn't yet figured out whether I like girls or boys. I've thought about kidding her by dropping a lewd remark about electro-erotics, but it would be cruel. Truth is, I'd probably fancy her, too, if I were into fancying anybody right now. And if the bar were a bit emptier I might mention the obvious and tell her about the database add-in on my brain implant, but bartending is part theater, and most people don't like seeing the backstage paraphernalia.

I look up from juicing another mango to see The Gimp roll through the door in his old-fashioned, hand-powered wheelchair. What timing! Sonja is just behind him, as always. She adores Eddie, and his devotion to her shows in his every glance.

Clyde calls out, "Hey Gimp, how ya going?" Regulars all know them as The Gimp and The Gorilla, but no one with any brains dares to say that to Sonja's face. Hers may be the sweetest face in Back Bay, but she has neither the disposition nor the body to match. She has a wrestler's frame and her long, mocha hair falls softly over a pair of shoulders that would have suited a Rugby scrum. She is obviously A-class all the way, except in her case it wasn't epi-steroids or supplants but real clever gene-splicing by her parents that gave her that build. She even medaled in women's Greco-Roman at the Olympics before they outlawed mutants. Of course the oh-so-proper Olympic Organizing Committee does not use the term mutants, even though all the sports pages do.

"How's the legs, Eddie?" I ask.

"Oh, they've been hurting some, but Sonja knows how to make it all better." He gives her that glance.

Mr. Plaid-Pants frowns. "I thought you paras couldn't feel nothing, you know, in your legs or nothing."

"Oh, Eddie's no paraplegic," Sonja says, with a hint of honey-coated malice in her voice. "He's just had a lot of muscle and nerve damage."

Plaid-Pants, however, isn't taking the hint to butt out. "You oughta get that fixed, you know. Amazing what they can do with bio-mech and that these days."

"No thanks," Eddie says, rolling up to one of the tables away from the bar. "I prefer it this way—just the way I am. I tried bio-mech."

I can see people are curious, but I also know Eddie. He doesn't like the attention too much, and I am getting these looks from Sonja. Clive, who is pretty good at picking up these things, turns toward me to shift the spotlight. "Were you here in '23? Do you remember it?" he asks.

Of course. I saw it. I was still a journalist then, covering the Marathon for one of the dish channels. "Yeah. I was right here—down there—when Johal Dharam, Jamal ibn Farakh, and Ted Amstraad headed down Boylston for the finish line." I pause, keeping my gaze straight down the bar. "I even talked with Amstraad after the race."

"So that's how you know so much!" Mandy says. I smile at her again, trying to put the barest hint of promise into my smile. You never know when you might be interested again, and Mandy is someone I could definitely see getting interested in. Someday.

"What happened right at the end?" Rugby-Jersey asks. "It always looked to me like both of them had systems failures."

"Don't be a twit again, Nige. It was obvious that Amstraad lost synch in over-drive and Dharam didn't. That is that. Johal was a born runner, quite literally, and Ted Amstraad was an over-rated, souped up humanoid." I wince. I'm not the only one in the bar who does. "Johal Dharam was the last of the real runners. He had heart. Who can say the same for those programmed half-human muscle machines who call themselves runners today?"

"Clive, you're a damned tree-hugging veggie." Nige, nee Mr. Rugby-Jersey, shakes his finger. "Admit it, you don't like anything that isn't natural with a capital en. You greenie-cooler people would probably take us back to the dark ages, back when augmenting was illegal but everyone cheated. The whole anti-doping thing was a stupid exercise in escalation. It's more honest this way. If you want to run without hydraulics or epi-steroids or superfood, you can run in the B-division. If you want to be the best, you get the sponsors with the money and the gadgets and chemicals and you run A-division."

Things are getting heated, so I interrupt. "I've got the disk right here," I say, reaching under the bar.

"What?" says Nige, scowling like he's just found an ant in his beer.

"I've got them here on disk," I repeat. "Every running of the BAA Marathon ever recorded. We can watch the finish of '23 in slo-mo if you like."

"No, no, we don't need any video here," Plaid-Pants says. "We all know the race."

Mandy harumphs from the end of the bar, "Oh, I see, don't confuse me with the facts." That triggers off another flurry of intense but good-natured cracks as I go back to loading glasses into the dishwasher under the bar. I don't need the disk, of course, or my implant. I remember it real well, without any help.

* * *

I was a reporter, not like these damned self-appointed, self-important bloggers clogging the Internet with their unedited drek. I had press credentials. Not everyone could get a pass in those days. And I had followed Dharam's career, even written a bio-piece for the *Boston Globe Magazine*. As my customer noted, Dharam had something that seemed to be increasingly rare in the world of world-class athletes: heart.

Tall and scrawny, with powerful and tireless muscles, Johal Dharam had been born to run. His family were *harakas*, the mail runners of northern India, and his father had taught him how to pace himself as he ran the mail from one tiny village in the mountains to another still more remote. But Johal was not like the other *harakas*. He was an express train of a runner, and he was obsessed. When India Post stopped using mail runners after digital dishes and cell towers linked every spot on the planet, he started running professionally. Within a few years he'd taken almost every major marathon in the world at record-setting pace. Even so, he was not the fastest distance man in the world, and he coveted that title. He ran B-class— not surprising, considering his Hindu upbringing—which meant no drugs, no operations, no bio-mechanics. Even the best unaided flesh was no match for the übermenschen of chemicals and hydraulics and electronics. Marathon times in the Augmented division were typically 10-15 minutes faster than the Basic division, and the gap was widening, not narrowing. The human body and its in-built limitations imposed a ceiling on athletic performance in every field. New records were still being set, but by ever-narrowing margins.

Record-breaking times in the hundred meter shaved mere hundredths of a second off the old record, and the governing bodies in track and field were talking about shifting to measuring times to the millisecond. The difference between first and second place could be a blink of the eye. One sports scientist had concluded that local variations in air pressure and temperature could sometimes be enough to account for the differences between runners in the shorter events. With more and more hinging on less and less, the world lost interest in what unaided human bodies could do. Throwing technology into the equation opened up new possibilities that made for exciting broadcasts and great stories.

By the time Dharam was on the international running circuit, the real money and the public adulation had already shifted solidly to the A-class runners. In the B-class, the cost of all the testing, the MR imaging, the constant surveillance to prevent cheating among the bios was too much. Why be a runner struggling to break the two-hour barrier, when with prosthetics and hydraulics or super-food and epi-steroids you could breeze over the line ten or twelve minutes under? Besides, the real money was, as always, in sponsorships and endorsement deals, and the Augmented competitors were walking—or running—advertisements for the high-tech firms of the world. "The same technology that won the New York Marathon for Ted Amstraad can add years to your life. Kelso-Lehman Bio-Tech. Better hearts for years!"

The pitches were pitch-perfect, tapping into the core of people's greatest fears and deepest longings. It was about death. And about the quest for eternal youth, the fantasies fed earlier by the likes of the late Ray Kurtzweil and Aubrey de Gray, pop-science pioneers who were convinced that with enough money and enough technology they could personally live forever. I was freelancing for NPR at the time, and had worked on a couple of specials on life-extension technology, but as long as the story was about moneyed geeks, the public remained uninterested. Only after augmentation hit athletics, first in pseudo-sports like pro wrestling and later inching into straight competition, only then did the public debate—and the demand—heat up. Science was no match for sports.

Naturally, all that escalating technology posed new regulatory challenges. If external leg actuators were allowed, why not a complete exoskeleton? If an exoskeleton, why not wheels? The internals-only rule was brilliant. In the A-division, anything goes, absolutely anything, as long as it fits inside the body. Instead of complex regulations and expensive enforcement testing, pre-race qualification only required a strip search.

I remember talking with Dharam in an interview for a Cool Runnings podcast, one of the last pieces I did before switching careers. I asked him about the unofficial title of fastest distance runner in the world and whether he coveted it.

"I have been given a gift, an ability that belongs not so much to me but to my people, to all people." He talked with fingers a-flutter and a characteristically controlled resonance in his voice. "It is not about me but about what we, we human beings, can accomplish."

I wanted to say that was bullshit, but I also didn't want to have to go back and edit the audio file later, so I said, "But isn't there some part of you that for some reason would like to go the limit, be the best, the fastest?"

He smiled broadly, white teeth flashing in his caramel face. "Perhaps. Perhaps. When I have done all I can as a mere human, then perhaps I will be ready for the next challenge. If it be my karma." To me it was obvious. He would stop only when he was stopped, when he could go no farther or no faster. He spoke toward the end of the interview about his belief in reincarnation, how each life was a trial and a preparation for the next. I realize that this was how he viewed his entire career so far—a life in preparation for the next stage. But there was also a struggle within him, and it was clear when he spoke of fellow runners, those in the A-class circuit, that he had moral reservations about violating what to him was the sanctity of the human body.

Two weeks later he finished first in the Mexico City Marathon, the last major event on the B-class circuit that he had not won. Wheezing from the nearly two-hours of running through heavily polluted air, he told the cameras of his plan for the upcoming BAA Marathon. I immediately got on the phone to my ex-boss at Satellite News Sports, and convinced her to take me back as a stringer for one more assignment.

If he had been running in the B-divison, Dharam would have been the favorite, hands down, but he had little experience with augmentation and word had gotten out that he had opted to have only one technology installed—myo-electric overdrive, or MOD—and that mere weeks before the race. MOD was only good for one short burst, so runners typically saved it up for a last extra kick at the end. But the odds makers and the couch-potato commentators underestimated Johol Dharam, in more ways than one.

Most bets were on Amstraad, who was coming out of a string of wins and was out to prove he could do anything, or on ibn Farakh, who was backed by a European aerospace consortium and was reputed to have the most advanced technology. I interviewed them both. Ibn Farakh was a bore, unflappable and impossible to provoke. I ended up using less than thirty seconds from a painfully long twenty-minute interview.

"I will win. I will," he said in his intense monotone. "I will beat Amstraad. I will beat them all. Inshallah, God willing."

"And there it is," I said to the camera. "The quiet confidence of a man of simple faith, suppressing the pain of his recent surgery and struggling to surmount the effects of the powerful drugs and supplements coursing through his veins. Jamal ibn Farakh, one of the world's fastest distance runners, and a favorite in the upcoming BAA Marathon."

Ted Amstraad was another animal altogether. Arrogantly overconfident, he dominated and controlled the entire interview with his verbal pyrotechnics and provocative allusions to a profligate life filled with abundant pleasures and ever-changing partners.

"Well," he said, winking at me, "let's just say that augmentation can be as good for going the distance in the bedroom as in a road race." He paused as if waiting for me to jump in with an expression of admiration, then continued when I just sat there. "I was squeezed out of first place in the BAA two years ago because Saarison stretched the rules with his leg-extension surgery. But where is he now? He couldn't handle it. I can handle everything they put in me. The BAA is the only A-division title I don't have, but I will have it next month. Just watch my dust."

I edited in a little retake with me raising my eyebrows in bemused credulity before the fade and the credits roll. My producer liked the touch.

The day of the '23 Marathon dawned with near-perfect conditions: cool, dry, and overcast, a slight but steady breeze coming out of the west. It looked to be the making of one of the closest finishes in recent history. There were a lot of experimental rigs that year, and after an unusual number of drop-outs by runners whose promising new technology sputtered and failed, less than five seconds separated the leaders as they turned into Boylston Street. Ibn Farakh had the lead and Dharam was—to the surprise of all—still drafting on Amstraad. Of the three, ibn Farakh was the one who did not look good. His stomach heaved as he struggled to keep his third lung pumping. Amstraad, whose fuel cells were self-vented through the line of stomas just above his low-rise running shorts, was looking relaxed and confident. Through the scope I could see he had not MODed yet, whereas ibn Farkh had already maxed out his technology when in the last mile he had cut in his lactic acid override.

Coming down the stretch, ibn Farakh began to slack off. It was clear that, augmentation aside, he was just not the athlete that Amstraad or Dharam was. Amstraad, watching as ibn

310

Farakh slipped into third place, turned and came face-to-face with Dharam, who was breathing down his neck. Amstraad triggered his MOD, but Dharam kept pace, with his own MOD still held in reserve.

"Kick it, damn it," Amstraad said, puffing the words out of the side of his mouth as they closed on the finish line. "Kick it and get it over with."

Dharam, now running almost neck and neck with Amstraad, turned slightly and said, "No."

"You can win," Amstraad wheezed.

"Not." Breath. "That." Breath. "Way."

Amstraad looked into the face of a man stretched to the limit but utterly at peace with himself.

What happened next was unclear at the time and would be the subject of debate for decades, but to some observers it looked as if Amstraad actually began to struggle against his own overdrive. At any rate, he lost synch with the electro-mechanical assist. Suddenly, his body and his technology were fighting against each other, and the technology won. Amstraad went down, his legs flailing wildly, right in the path of Dharma, who stumbled and almost fell. Had his overdrive already been engaged, he would have gone down like Amstraad and the flagging ibn Farakh would have passed them to take the lead at the very last moment. But Dharam recovered his balance, miraculously lengthened his stride, and finished the race first, well ahead of ibn Farakh and the rest of the pack. His time set no record, but he had entered the record books as the only runner ever to have won the BAA in both divisions.

After finishing, he walked back toward where Amstraad was being helped by medics, knelt beside him, and whispered something to him. Neither Amstraad, whose brilliant career and long string of international wins ended there on Boylston Street, nor Dharam, who retired the next year, ever spoke of what had passed between them. But I knew. Eddie, the Gimp, whose legs had been ruined by the disaster with the overdrive, had told me once. The single word that Dharam had whispered. Thanks.

* * *

That was my last BAA as a pro. Something about the events down there on Boylston Street did something to me, as if the wind had been knocked out of me when Eddie went down. I turned in my press credentials and went to bartending school because I still needed to pay the rent. Fortunately, I discovered that I really liked mixing drinks and managing drunks and schmoozing about sports and life for a living. My karma, perhaps, but this is where I belong.

Plaid-Pants and Nige are still arguing as I come out of my reverie. Plaid-Pants is insisting that Amstraad simply screwed up, faltering ever so slightly and loosing synch.

Eddie wheels his chair around. "Maybe it was something else. Maybe he just decided that there was something else at stake. Maybe he thought that Dharma deserved to win. Dharam was still running bare, you know. He only had the one system installed, just the absolute minimum to qualify for the A-division, and he hadn't kicked it in yet. But, there he was, running second in the Boston. You got to hand it to someone like that. Maybe sometimes just nothing but guts and grit ought to be enough. Maybe sometimes just being who you are is okay. With Amstraad and ibn Farakh out, he didn't need to kick it in. So, he ends up winning the A-division Marathon against all the best biotech the world can stuff into a person and does it with nothing but the legs God gave him. Not bad. Kinda makes you wonder, eh?"

Eddie spins his wheelchair to look up at Sonja, then nods toward the door. Plaid-Pants, noticing the name on the back of the wheelchair, calls out, "So, you're an Amstraad fan."

The Gimp doesn't turn, but Sonia shoots a gigawatt grin back toward the bar. "No, I'm the real Amstraad fan. Ted here has always been more of an admirer of Johal Dharam." She follows him out into the corridor, ignoring the stares and the muttered "Holy shits!" and "Do you realize who that was?" bubbling through the bar.

I just smile and ask Plaid-Pants if he wants another beer. He does.

* * *

Fiction by Lior Samson (www.liorsamson.com)

Bashert | The Dome | Web Games

The Rosen Singularity